NEAR PERFECT

NEAR PERFECT

SHARON MITCHELL

DUTTON

DUTTON
Published by the Penguin Group
Penguin Putnam Inc., 375 Hudson Street, New York, New York 10014, U.S.A.
Penguin Books Ltd, 80 Strand, London WC2R 0RL, England
Penguin Books Australia Ltd, Ringwood, Victoria, Australia
Penguin Books Canada Ltd, 10 Alcorn Avenue, Toronto, Ontario, Canada M4V 3B2
Penguin Books (N.Z.) Ltd, 182–190 Wairau Road, Auckland 10, New Zealand

Penguin Books Ltd, Registered Offices: Harmondsworth, Middlesex, England

Published by Dutton, a member of Penguin Putnam Inc.

Grateful acknowledgment is made for permission to reprint an excerpt from "Gone Too Soon," lyric by Alan Buz Kohan. Copyright 1991 by Fiddleback Music Pub., New Start Music Inc., Smith-Hemion Music, Hemion-Smith Music, and One Zee Music. Used by permission of Alan Buz Kohan.

 REGISTERED TRADEMARK—MARCA REGISTRADA

ISBN 0-525-94621-7 (alk. paper)

Printed in the United States of America
Set in Sabon
Designed by Eve L. Kirch

PUBLISHER'S NOTE

For my parents, Bertha and Curtis Mitchell.
The apple doesn't fall far from the tree.

Acknowledgments

To my parents: Thanks for supporting my goals and interests, for tolerating my independent ways, and for accepting that one of your kids really did prefer to curl up with a good book and a sleepy kitten instead of playing outside.

To my nieces and nephews: I truly believe that children are our future. Though some of you can't even read yet, just know that you have served as the inspiration for many of the children in my books. Angela Clark, Dante Mitchell, Jaron Hines, Darius Mitchell, Dakotah Love, Ta'Quanna Mitchell, Zaire Abbott, and A'Yahana Mitchell, your Auntie Sharon is wishing you nothing but love, happiness, and success in the future.

To my friends: You are there whenever and however I need you. Thanks for being so supportive and understanding. I especially want to thank Emily Carter and Mary Anne Lacour for listening to me, laughing with me (and sometimes at me), and generally helping me deal with the day-to-day stuff. I also want to thank Dr. Robin Dennings for being my medical consultant. Erica, thanks for letting me borrow him for a few minutes. With two little ones, you all have your hands full. Anne King, your needlepoint expertise was a big help with the last book. Forgive me for taking a while to acknowledge that.

To my fellow writers: I've been fortunate to meet many writers whom I have admired from afar. You have been more gracious and giving than I ever imagined or hoped for. The following people have been particularly helpful and nice to be around: Eric Dickey, E. Lynn Harris, Nicole Bailey Williams, Tim McCann, Franklin White, Yolanda Joe, and Patricia Haley Brown.

To my readers: I do listen to what you have to say whether it is in person or via e-mail. Your feedback influenced my decision to write this sequel to *Nothing But the Rent*. As always, I can't wait to hear what you think and feel.

NEAR PERFECT

Chapter

1

Roxanne tried to match her skittish heartbeat to the steady, even rise and fall of her husband's chest. Though she welcomed the weight of Jamal's spent, sweat-slicked body, which was still joined with hers, her thoughts were consumed yet again with the real reason for this late-morning coupling. *Please, God, let there be a baby. Give us a baby*, Roxanne silently prayed. Making a baby should have been as natural as the rhythm of Jamal's breathing, the only whisper of sound that filled the spacious master bedroom on this warm late-summer morning.

Roxanne sighed. After months of being poked and prodded, the doctors had finally figured out why they couldn't conceive. Who knew that a sluggish thyroid gland could cause so much trouble? Dr. Samuels put her on thyroid supplements. They were supposed to regulate everything so that her estrogen production would be normal and she could get pregnant. So far the darn things weren't working. A tightness gripped her stomach as she considered the possibility that something other than her thyroid was the problem and that she might never have kids. Both Jamal and the doctors kept telling her they'd only been trying to get pregnant for a little over a year. Roxanne was patient about most things, but a year felt like forever when you'd been waiting all of your life to have kids. Jamal was dealing with this infertility thing a lot better than she was. But then again, he wasn't the one with the problem.

Why couldn't she be like her sisters? A man just looked at them funny, and next thing you know, out pops a baby. Neither LaToya nor Denise had ever been overjoyed at the prospect of pregnancy. They were good mothers but had no illusions about raising kids. It was work. In Roxanne's opinion, both of them focused too much on the sacrifice and inconvenience of parenting. Still, she could partially understand why they felt that way. Their mother, Dot, though funny and sweet-natured, just hadn't been mature enough to handle raising three kids pretty much on her own. When she wasn't bone-tired from working dead-end jobs, hunting up a card game or a night out with her female cronies, she was enthralled with her latest man.

Roxanne sighed. It didn't have to be that way. When she had her kids, it wouldn't be that way.

She tried to shift into a more comfortable position, but the king-size mattress had very little give. Jamal's back had been roughed up so many times during his thirteen-year career as a professional football player that he had to sleep on an extra-firm mattress. Not exactly Roxanne's preference, but the other choice was to sleep in separate beds. Being with Jamal as much as possible was what she wanted. The least she could do was put up with a rock-hard mattress.

Overwhelming fears and lifelong messages about what it meant to be whole kept bombarding her. *When are y'all gonna have a baby? What are you waiting for? You're not getting any younger, Roxanne. A child completes a marriage. You're not a real woman until you bring a child in this world.*

What had happened to her? She used to feel such peace after making love with her husband. Roxanne squeezed her eyes shut, hoping to block the thoughts and the narrow strip of morning sunlight that entered where the bedroom curtains did not quite meet.

She listened to the sound of Jamal's breathing and tried to remind herself of all she had to be grateful for, baby or no baby. First of all, she had her health, as did most of her family. She had more emotional and material wealth than she'd ever dreamed of. To please her, Jamal had bought this five-bedroom house in the historic section of Towson. The house was smaller, and in a real neighborhood instead of that fortress out in Anne Arundel County that he had been eyeing. It was almost a hundred years old and needed a lot of work. Seeing the glint of challenge in her eye and listening to her ideas about how to revamp the place, Jamal forgot the other house even existed.

When she tried to discuss a budget for the renovations, Jamal told her the sky was the limit. Yet some things didn't change with wealth. Roxanne had been pinching pennies all her life, so now, even though she finally had some loot, the bargain shopper in her wasn't dead. And though he was no Mr. Fix-It, Jamal had given his best shot at helping out. But for the most part he left turning this old house into their home up to her. She was also blessed with Jamal's encouragement and support when she had decided to quit her job as a high-school teacher and to start Hope Springs. Although she had been involved in community service most of her life, Hope Springs was the most satisfying thing she'd ever been a part of.

The community center had been open for eighteen months. It served people of all ages, but the main focus was on kids, which for Roxanne was a dream come true. As a child, she had known love and been encouraged to blossom. Grandma Reynolds' belief in her potential to be whatever she dreamed was bottomless and unshakable. Roxanne knew it was both important and possible to help kids tap into their potential and to create opportunities for them to realize their dreams now and in the future.

Sighing, Roxanne longed to fulfill another dream that both she and Jamal had, to fill the rooms of this house with the sound of children's laughter, running feet, and scuffed knees and elbows.

A few years back, she and her closest friends, Monique, Cynthia, and Gayle were all approaching thirty without much hope of finding a husband, let alone having a family. They used to joke about adopting a child or going to a sperm bank. What her friends didn't know is that Roxanne had only been half joking. If she hadn't married by age thirty-five, she would seriously consider adopting a child. Just goes to show that she didn't know herself as well as she had thought. Back then Roxanne had believed herself beyond this kind of ego-tripping. But like most women when push came to shove, she wanted to do the family thing the old-fashioned way.

What was that song I used to sing as a kid? "First comes love, then comes marriage, then comes the baby in the baby carriage,"

Roxanne softly hummed. After she had married, the seed of desire for children blossomed into a full-blown longing. Being around other people's children when she wanted a child of her own had become increasingly bittersweet.

Had it really been almost six years ago that Linc, her oldest friend, had thrown her a surprise thirtieth birthday party and given her the most precious gift ever—an introduction to Jamal? Linc had been in Boston for a game against the Brahmins and, with Gayle, Cynthia, and Monique's help, had rounded up some of her local friends. Her sister, LaToya, had even flown in from St. Louis. She had thought she was meeting Linc at his hotel for dinner, and she ended up meeting her husband-to-be. Jamal had been the star wide receiver to Linc's quarterback when they played at Penn State. They only played together for a year, since Linc was a senior to Jamal's freshman status. But a bond had been forged nonetheless. When she first met him, Jamal had been playing for Boston, and Linc was the quarterback for Baltimore.

Life was funny. The way her luck with men had been running at the time, she started assuming any date she got would probably be her first and her last. Then she decided that God had put her through dating hell so that she'd really appreciate it when she found a good man. And God was right, because Jamal was definitely worth the wait.

The only thing missing was children to fill up these empty rooms and unleash the love she knew she had to give. She really wanted them to make this baby together. Roxanne Miller Steele was not a quitter. But there are kids out there right now who need love, a little voice whispered. Roxanne squeezed her eyes shut. Was she being selfish? Was it wrong to want her own flesh and blood? Maybe. But she wasn't ready to give up yet. Adoption would be conceding defeat.

Roxanne placed a soft kiss on the collarbone closest to her lips, then ran her hands down the length of Jamal's well-toned back. She was practically buried under him. Still, she held him to her. He really was too heavy to be using her as his personal pillow, but she liked him just where he was. It was like this between them, neither one wanted to be the first to part. The fusion, the oneness, whether the result of a slow burn or a raging fire, just felt right. From the moment they met, from the first time they held each other to the last, it was always like this. Near perfect. She smiled tiredly, absently running her fingertips down the ridges of his spine. She cupped his taut behind, and warm flesh quivered beneath her touch.

Again, Roxanne pressed her lips to a collarbone that seemed too delicate for such an otherwise masculine body.

Jamal lifted a bit, taking the weight of his upper torso off of her. "Sorry, hon. I guess I drifted off," he murmured, then let his head fall again. It came to rest lightly against her bare breasts.

"I forgive you. This baby-making stuff is hard work," Roxanne whispered and then wrapped her thighs around him to deepen the embrace. "Ouch," she said as her aching body finally protested. The spirit was willing but the flesh was another matter.

Locking his elbows, he pushed himself up, thereby slipping out of her. Before Roxanne could feel the loss, he reached his arm across her chest and snuggled until they were face-to-face. Strong fingers with a familiar touch moved from the nape of her neck to midway down her back, occasionally catching then escaping from the tangle of her dreadlocks. "You should have told me to get off you."

"Never." She said before her lips made contact with the tip of his chin. She nuzzled her face against his. She loved his new beard now that it had started to fill in and wasn't so scruffy. Jamal had never had a beard before, but he'd gotten two touchdown receptions in the first game of the preseason. He hadn't shaved that day, so he was convinced that his stubbled chin was the key. He hadn't shaved since then because it might jinx him.

As a professional athlete's wife, Roxanne had quickly become acquainted with jocks and their superstitions. Lucky shoulder pads, using the same route to get to the stadium, touching the gold cross she had given him before each play. Usually, she tolerated it for what it was, nonsense. Jamal scored touchdowns because he worked hard and was gifted. However, this particular superstition is working for me, Roxanne thought as she rubbed up against him like a cat.

The phone rang. With reluctance, Roxanne rolled over and picked up the Caller ID box. Another reminder of how life had changed A. J.—After Jamal. They changed their number frequently because some love-starved fan or shady character offering a "guaranteed" investment occasionally got hold of it. And even then

Jamal insisted that she not pick up the phone unless the person's name popped up or she recognized the number on the other end. He refused to listen when she told him he was asking the impossible. Between family, friends, and business associates, they knew hundreds of people who had legitimate reasons for calling. And folks changed their numbers all the time or called from cell phones. When he was around, Roxanne did as instructed because it really seemed to bother him. But when she was home alone, she picked up. If it was someone she didn't want to talk to, the five seconds it took to figure that out and then hang up was no biggie.

In her haste to jump Jamal's bones, she didn't know where she had put her glasses. Roxanne tilted her head back to fling her long dreads out of her face. Her nearsightedness forced her to bring the Caller ID box practically up to her nose. It was a number she recognized. By the time she put the box back on the nightstand, Jamal had eased out of bed, leaving only the lingering warmth of his body and the musky smell of satisfying sex to keep her company. She missed him immediately and couldn't help smiling and fantasizing as Jamal bent over to pick up the clothes she'd practically stripped off of him when the basal thermometer told her it was time to get busy. Eleven o'clock in the morning was as good a time as any.

Jamal draped the clothes on a nearby chaise lounge. He was the neat freak of the house. Not her. But those buns of steel of his were making her want to be a freak of another kind. She leaned back against the body pillow.

He really was beautiful, almost six foot tall, nut-brown skin stretched over nothing but muscle. Even the scar from some long-ago knee surgery looked good to her. *The scar was cute?* Roxanne, girl, you need to quit! Could it be that she was turning into a dirty old woman? Naw, she'd been a dirty young woman, too. But not twenty-four-seven, the way she was with her husband.

When Jamal straightened, she pushed away the lecherous thoughts and said, "That was Monique. She's probably calling me back with information about some grants that Hope Springs might be eligible for."

"Well, tell her I said hi. But don't go telling Monique I rolled over and fell asleep after sex."

"Now, why would I tell her something like that?"

One corner of his mouth lifted, as did an eyebrow. " 'Cause you tell her everything else," he explained.

When Roxanne tried to look offended, he continued, "Don't even try to front. I've heard y'all and I've seen y'all. 'Ooh, girl, I mean it was good to the last drop. Child, I had him screaming for Jesus, Allah, *and* Buddha,' " Jamal mimicked in a high-pitched voice that was supposed to be hers.

"Now, I don't ev-en sound like that," Roxanne denied. "But I did have you screaming for Allah one time," she said with a certain amount of pride and satisfaction. "And you're not even Muslim."

Jamal shook his head at her bragging tone. "You know you wrong. Only a woman would be paying attention to what a man is saying when he's at his most vulnerable. And I don't care what you claim, I don't remember calling for Allah."

"Of course you don't. You were too busy getting all up in it," she said matter-of-factly.

He shook his head, still denying. "Yeah right. I'm out of here before you start telling even bigger lies. I'm supposed to meet Linc to shoot some hoops."

Roxanne tried to keep a straight face. Linc and Jamal still thought they could run with the teenagers, who elbowed and shoved their way through pickup games at one of the local courts. He always grumbled about the dirty play but then went right back out there the next week.

"Well, don't break anything. I need you both in one piece for the fund-raiser tonight."

Roxanne wedged pillows behind her back and swung her legs up in the air. Doctor's orders. "Have fun. I'll have the Ben Gay on hand just in case," she said.

About to reply to that crack, Jamal, who was heading to the adjoining bathroom, stopped dead in his tracks. He was transfixed by the sight of long, dark twisty dreads spread over sunshine yellow pillows. His wife was so small, only around five feet tall, but she was all woman: a dramatically shapely frame, plump perky breasts, a small waist, and a high rounded behind that caused his mouth to water every time he saw it. Now she was looking at him through half-closed eyes, her smile blatantly teasing.

"Woman, if you didn't want me to leave, all you had to do was say so!" he growled before lunging for her.

Roxanne giggled, then swiveled her legs out of reach. She slapped his hands away from her thighs, laughing. "Jamal, keep your hands to yourself."

Despite her protest, he joined her on the bed. He dutifully positioned his hands behind his back and smiled down at her. Roxanne's pulse quickened as his eyes roamed over her naked body. She had seen that look before.

"Look, Ma, no hands," Jamal announced before slowly taking one of her nipples into his mouth."

She moaned deep in her throat. "Jamal," she said, her voice melting, instantly liquefying just like the rest of her. "We can't. The doctor says I'm supposed to keep my knees together."

His mouth slowly blazed a wet trail of kisses from her breast to her stomach. When he reached the flesh just below her belly button, he said, "How am I ever gonna get you pregnant, if you keep your knees together?"

"But . . . we got to give your little soldiers time to regroup," Roxanne reminded him. "The doctor said sex every other day."

She was wasting her breath. Jamal's next words confirmed what Roxanne already knew. If it were up to Jamal, they would be going at it like rabbits. Too bad they weren't breeding like them, too.

"Not to worry. My boys are strong swimmers," he boasted. "Besides, I've been taking my vitamins, eating my spinach, and downing Wheaties by the boxful." He placed her hand over his arousal. "See, we're good to go."

Roxanne didn't know whether to sigh or laugh at his self-serving line of thinking. Then her body decided for her as her legs came down and parted their surrender.

Chapter

2

The hotel's chandelier had nothing on the glitter of excitement in Roxanne's eyes. They could have lit up nearby Camden Yards stadium. She had put her heart and soul into planning this fundraiser for months, and three-quarters of the way through the night, she felt it safe to declare it an unqualified success. Consequently, the smile captured by the *Baltimore Sun* photographer was as real as the diamond solitaire on her left hand.

Every time she looked up, the female shutterbug seemed to be right on her heels, snapping away. Not that she minded. She would take all the free publicity she could get. This time, the woman had popped up as Roxanne vigorously pumped the hand of and sincerely thanked Yvette Richardson. The white-haired society matron had just presented Hope Springs with a ten-thousand-dollar check, which put the amount raised over the hundred-twenty-five-thousand-dollar mark. That would go a long way to hiring new after-school tutors and recreation aides for the center's Midnight Madness basketball program. Jamal was convinced that if kids could keep busy on a safe and well-supervised basketball court, a lot less of them would see the inside of a juvenile court.

Though Roxanne agreed, most of the money raised tonight was earmarked for parenting classes. Trying to improve the life of a child would only go so far without parental or family involvement. And that was proving to be the toughest row to hoe. A lot of parents were too tired from trying to make ends meet to spend a whole lot of time finding out what was going on in their kids' heads and hearts. So it was a matter of maximizing what time they did have, a case of developing quality time because quantity time was out of the question. Then there were some parents who just couldn't be bothered, job or no job. Those were the folks that Roxanne was determined to get through to. That's why everyone affiliated with Hope Springs had been invited tonight. Nothing like a party with free food held at a bus-accessible location to attract a crowd.

Roxanne nodded in agreement when Yvette Richardson remarked that the fund-raiser had brought together a diverse group of people. That was an understatement and a half. She had been worried about how folks from welfare mothers to descents from the *Mayflower* would get along. Of course, a lot of Jamal's fellow football players and their wives were coming, and she had worried they would be hounded by kids and adults alike. Jamal kept telling her that his friends were used to the attention, but Roxanne didn't want the evening to feel like a burden to them. She wanted everybody to have a good time. The presence of athletes was a big draw for not only the people in the East Side community, where Hope Springs was located, but also for the moneyed people. She had seen firsthand how starstruck folks could be. She didn't want any groupies crashing, which was why this event was by invitation only. And it had sparked the most interest she'd seen thus far from the community members. But since she couldn't feed the entire neighborhood, a lottery was held to determine who would get tickets to attend.

Roxanne had thought about having the fund-raiser at Hope Springs so the community members could feel more comfortable and the patrons could see for themselves what they were supporting. But then her friends, Cynthia and Monique, had both advised her that wealthy or not, most people liked to feel they got a little something, whether it be fun, booze, or entertainment, before reaching into their pockets and handing over loot. And those two would know, Cynthia from her public relations experience and Monique from her bougie upbringing. As the guest list started to take shape, Roxanne realized she didn't have much of a choice: Hope Springs just wasn't big enough for a gathering of this size.

She picked the Hilton because it was fancy enough for potential patrons and right on the Inner Harbor, so it wouldn't feel foreign or intimidating to the regular folks. And despite being married to a high-profile football player, she included herself in the latter group.

Everyone was decked out in what he or she considered to be their Sunday best, from designer gowns to FUBU sweat suits. Roxanne's ropes of hair were piled high on her head to give her five-foot-one frame the illusion of height. It was either that or spiked heels. And that wasn't happening, since she knew she'd be on her feet all night. Her one attempt at glamour was the silk Ghanaian print dress. The rich brown and gold earth tones suited her complexion. She also liked the way the dress clung to the curves of her breasts and hips. What little makeup she'd applied had long since rubbed off as she hugged and kissed countless people throughout the evening. Her only jewelry was a pair of large gold hoops and her wedding and engagement rings. Not exactly *Vogue* material, but then again neither was she.

The knot in the pit of her stomach began to loosen over the course of the evening. At first, not a whole lot of mixing was going on, but everyone started interacting after a group of the kids kicked off the evening with a selection of songs, including a rap about the Center. Their artwork was on display, as was a collection of essays about what parents, children, and volunteers liked best about Hope Springs. Then Jamal emceed the appreciation ceremony for the Board of Directors and patrons who had already pledged their support. Telling stories about Hope Springs with a dash of humor, Jamal had smoothly kept his audience entertained. But the bachelor and bachelorette auction had been the biggest hit of the night.

Roxanne had called in favors from every single friend she'd made in the three years that she had lived in Baltimore, from the florist delivery guy to Jamal's recently divorced lawyer to the principal at the school where she used to teach. The look on Linc's face had been priceless when after a round of cutthroat bidding, her friend, Cynthia, had emerged the winner. She'd have to tease him about that—if she could find him. Linc had mysteriously disappeared shortly after the auction. Probably hiding from Cyn.

But first, Roxanne had to rescue Jamal.

Judge Barrett literally had him cornered over by the buffet

table. The room temperature felt comfortable to her, but the judge used a handkerchief to mop his balding forehead like he was melting beneath a Louisiana summer sun instead of in a climate-controlled hotel ballroom. He grasped Jamal's forearm with this other hand. Did the judge, like Roxanne, suspect that Jamal would be out of there like a shot, if given half a chance? Roxanne didn't know what he was talking about so excitedly that he was breaking out in a sweat, and it really didn't matter. Judge Barrett was a nice man, but he had halitosis that was out of this world. And if Jamal strained his body away any farther, he'd be sitting in the gigantic bowl of pasta salad on the table behind him. Her husband, in his Armani tux and gold stud earring in his ear, the beard adding a dash of urban cool to his face, was by far the best-looking man in the room. She thanked Ms. Richardson for the umpteenth time before making a beeline for the buffet table.

She was interrupted several times by people congratulating her on the success of the event. As she passed the podium where Brandon, the DJ, was set up, she signaled him with a two-finger waggle of her hand. Despite the headphones and the disc in his hand, Brandon noticed and gave her a head nod in return. He was doing a good job mixing it up. She was glad she'd gone with a DJ and not a band for this diverse gathering of people. A DJ could be more flexible than a band with the kind of music he played. And she wanted everybody to be happy.

She came alongside Jamal, and he immediately put an arm around her waist, pulling her closer to him. Damn, he smelled good. She had this thing for men's cologne. When they had first started dating, Jamal never wore cologne. But she soon fixed that. She got him some for his birthday, and when he saw how it turned her on, he became a convert.

"Judge Barrett, it's so nice to see you again," Roxanne said. "And thank you so much for your generosity."

The jowly man smiled at her like a kindly bulldog. "Not at all, young lady. Anything I can do to help. It's very important work that you are doing."

"We think so. Thanks for supporting Hope Springs. With your money. And your time," Roxanne added. She pressed the side of her face against the smooth fabric of Jamal's jacket. "There is one little thing you could do for me, though."

"I am always happy to help if I can. What is it?"

"Well, I was wondering if I could steal my husband away from you. We've both been running around all night, and haven't taken advantage of the music. Now that that things have settled down, I want to dance with my sweetie."

Brandon had understood her signal and almost on cue, Jamal and Roxanne's "song," *Always and Forever,* the original Heatwave version, started to play.

"Why, of course, Roxanne. You all deserve a little fun." The little squeeze of gratitude Jamal gave her was almost comical.

Roxanne held her breath when Judge Barrett leaned forward to give her a parting peck on the cheek. She didn't exhale until she was several feet away. Poor Judge Barrett, somebody really ought to let him know his breath was kicking it. Maybe she could send him an anonymous note. He really was a sweet man.

"Thank you. Thank you. Thank you, gorgeous," Jamal said as soon as they were out of earshot. "Can you believe he was eating an onion roll on top of that breath?"

Roxanne laughed. "Shut up, Jamal. Somebody might hear you talking about him." She led him on the dance floor and promptly forgot all about Judge Barrett.

"Did I tell you that you're workin' that dress?" Jamal murmured. His hands roamed freely up and down her back.

"Yeah, about a thousand times," Roxanne said, her face somewhere near the middle of his chest and her arms clasped loosely around his waist as they swayed to the music. Jamal was a great dancer. Right on time with each beat and pause. Clearly in charge but bringing her along every step of the way.

When the song ended, they stayed on the dance floor for another, not speaking and caught up in their own little world. This feels good, Roxanne thought. With the new football season starting next week, Jamal would be at practice during the week or traveling with the team for away games. He was very focused on improving his game. Jamal was determined to make it to his first Championship Bowl before retiring, having only a few more playing years left.

Roxanne sighed. She got spoiled having him around in the off-season. After next Sunday, there wouldn't be a lot of moments like this. She relaxed into him, savoring it, knowing it might be a while before another opportunity to have him so totally focused on her, on them, came along.

"Ahem . . . May I cut in?"

Roxanne opened her eyes at the sound of Linc's voice. Its inflection was so similar to her own, a typical Midwestern flatness with a twist of Southern drawl thrown in. The arc of his smile fanned out beneath his broad nose and even teeth that had been replaced many times thanks to some hard knocks Linc had taken on the field. What would his football friends think if they knew she had actually beat the star quarterback in a footrace once? Now, granted, they were both in third grade and his twelve-inch growth spurt hadn't happened yet. At six-four, he was a few inches taller than Jamal and outweighed him by a good forty pounds.

Jamal shrugged off the finger that had tapped him on the shoulder and didn't stop moving to the music.

"Hey, man, I said, may I cut in?" Linc repeated.

"Nope. Go get your own woman."

"So it's like that?" Linc said, following them as they moved aside for other dancers. "You wouldn't even have known Roxy if it weren't for me."

Roxy. Roxanne smiled at the nickname. Linc had known Roxanne since grade school, so he was the only one besides family that she let get away with calling her that.

"Besides, I knew her first," Linc continued.

"Yeah, good point." Jamal said, finally stepping aside. "Just remember to bring her back. And no grinding," he warned.

Roxanne rolled her eyes at the two of them. *No grinding? Like that was even a possibility?* She and Linc were like brother and sister. No one could have been happier when his best girl and his best guy friend had hooked up. The back and forth squabbling over her was a constant. Best friend or not, Jamal was still a man, and like any brother, Linc liked to remind him to treat her right. And Jamal liked to remind Linc what an idiot he was for passing up what was, in his opinion, the perfect woman.

"Excuse me, but you two are not Rottweilers and I am not a bone. So, though I am fantastic, gorgeous, intelligent, and all that good stuff, I ain't got all night to stand here talking about it. Eventually I'll have to get back to playing hostess. So, Lincoln, are you gonna dance with me or what?"

Jamal cracked a smile and gave her a little wink before leaving them. He liked when she got sassy with him.

She noticed that Coach Lacour's wife waylaid Jamal just as he got off the dance floor. Vivian Lacour's red-tipped talons closed around the fabric of his tuxedo sleeve. The leggy redhead was almost as tall as Jamal's five-eleven. Roxanne's eyes narrowed as Vivian planted a kiss on Jamal's mouth then pulled away with a smile on her shiny, forty-something face that was almost cartoonish. Traces of what used to be a beautiful woman still lingered on her face, but Vivian had been under construction more times than a superhighway. And Roxanne could tell that Vivian was lit by the way she plastered herself all over Jamal. It was a well-known fact that Vivian had a drinking problem and pathetically flirted with just about every player on the team. It was her way of handling a husband who would screw anything with a pulse. She watched, curious, as Jamal grasped Vivian's elbow and began walking, half carrying her toward the exit.

With all the people milling around, Roxanne soon lost sight of them. Maybe Jamal was gonna put her in a cab before she did something to embarrass herself. She clucked her tongue in sympathy. Jamal just wasn't having any luck with his companions tonight. Roxanne gave a little shrug. Later, she would find out what that little encounter was all about.

Roxanne grabbed Linc by the hand to pull him toward the middle of the dancing crowd. Brandon put on a club version of a Dru Hill song. No grinding to that one to be sure. Besides, she didn't want to slow dance with Linc anyhow. He was even taller than Jamal, and her face would be somewhere around his belt buckle. And her toes were less likely to get stepped on if they were dancing apart. She knew from past experience that Linc's heavy feet were just as prone to land on her as they were on the floor.

Roxanne vowed to keep out of their way. She half closed her eyes and soon found the beat and snapped her fingers in tune to it. As the tempo picked up, she raised her arms and let them flow along to the music, her shoulders rolled in invitation and her hips pumped back and forth.

The zone she had slipped into came to an abrupt end as pain shot up her leg.

Right after a quick apology for crushing her foot, Linc said,

"I'm surprised you still got energy to dance, Roxy. You been workin' this crowd like a street-corner hoochie."

She glared at him and gave his chest a playful shove. "Lincoln, I know you did not just call me a hoochie!"

He moved closer to be heard over the music. "I meant it only in the nicest way," he said.

"And what way could that be?" she asked, her voice dripping with mock sarcasm. Roxanne skittered away from feet that were looming too close to hers.

"I mean you ain't letting nobody escape without giving up something. Time, money, their body."

Her eyes widened in surprise. "Their body?"

"Yeah, that bachelor auction you forced me to be in. It was humiliating."

"Why? You had half the women in here pulling out their check-books and a couple of the men, too. Turns out your rusty butt is worth a cool two grand. Besides, all you have to do is take the person out to dinner and a movie or something."

"That's what you say. You know who the highest bidder was? Your girl, Cynthia. The blue-eyed man-eater."

Now Roxanne's smile broadened. As a favor to her, Cyn had helped plan this whole thing and had flown in from Tampa to see how it turned out. Now Roxanne had to wonder if maybe her girl-friend had an ulterior motive. And though she was paid well, two thousand dollars was a lot of money to be dishing out. Cyn had always made it clear that she thought Linc was fine. But then again, Cyn thought just about any man that walked upright and had a job was fine. Her friend had gotten caught up with a married man a few years back, so Roxanne was grateful that nowadays Cyn was limiting her sights to men who weren't already taken.

"I didn't sic Cynthia on you," Roxanne replied. "And you need to make up your mind, am I a madam or a ten-dollar hooker. Which is it?"

"Neither, but just tell your girl that I'm a weekend rental, not a lease-to-own type of guy."

The music changed. A slow song. Linc held his arms wide in invitation. Roxanne eyed him dubiously and then gave a little laugh. How could someone who danced as badly as he did enjoy it so much? And how could she refuse that pleading look in his eyes?

As Roxanne stepped into his arms, she thought, I'll never walk again after this.

Once she was able to angle her face away—from his waist—so she could breathe and talk, she said, "Linc, why aren't you rent-to-own? What's wrong with a little commitment? It's the best thing that ever happened to me, and I think I can speak for Jamal, too, on that one."

She felt his sigh, then he stepped on her foot. Again.

"There's just too much of me to love to keep it all for one woman," he said. "If I'm stuck with one woman for life, I'll miss out on the buffet of life."

Roxanne took it for the joke that it was. *What "buffet of life" was he talking about?* The only thing a man in a committed relationship gave up was *the illusion* that he could spend the rest of his life having sex with ever increasingly beautiful, young, and freaky women. And the biggest flaw in that fantasy was that sex in and of itself would make him happy.

Though Linc might have been a player as a hormone-driven teenager and maybe even early in his college and pro career, he had slowed down a lot. Practically coming to a standstill, come to think of it. She could count on one hand the number of dates he'd had in the last year, and she knew about them all, too, because contrary to popular belief, men gossiped just like women did, and Jamal told her everything. And what he didn't volunteer, she pumped out of him. Literally.

She just wanted everybody to find the happiness she had in a relationship. Especially the people she cared about like Linc.

"Bringing Jamal into my life was the greatest gift anyone has given me. I just want to do the same for you."

"It wasn't intentional," he said. "Who knew that he'd fall under the spell of a gap-tooth, five-foot-nothing, baby-crazy, sex machine?"

She thumped against his back with a small fist.

Linc continued. "You don't have to pay me back, Roxy."

"But I want to," she insisted.

"But you can't. What you and Jamal have is a once in a lifetime kind of thing. I'm sure I'll settle down eventually with some pretty young thing to help me change my adult diapers and take me for a stroll in my wheelchair," he cracked.

Why was he joking when she was trying to be serious? A ton of attractive, eligible women were in this very room. "You know, I could hook you up"—she paused to snap her fingers—"just like that, my friend. All you gotta do is say the word." She pulled away to look at him, expecting to see a dismissive smile.

Instead, his eyes were distant, as if lost in his own thoughts. When he finally replied, the teasing in his voice had vanished. "Maybe, the woman I'm looking for doesn't exist or . . . is already taken. Someone like you, for example," he added.

Puzzled by his sudden change of mood, Roxanne was prevented from asking what he meant when Jamal's voice interrupted.

"That's right, my man. Roxanne is one of a kind *and* already taken. So get your big mitts off my woman and hand her over."

Linc's expression relaxed again. Instead of releasing Roxanne, he coolly informed Jamal, "I'm still getting my swerve on." He smiled as he said it.

Ignoring him, Jamal pulled Roxanne in his direction. "What you've been doing is killing my wife's toes. I saw her wincing from across the room. Besides, you asked for 'a dance.' That was two dances."

Before they could start up again, Roxanne interjected. "Stop talking about me like I'm not in the room. Anyway, the dance portion of the program is over, and it's back to business." She looped an arm through each man's. Flanked by a member of her Dynamic Duo on each side, she said, "C'mon. We still have a couple more hours to squeeze more volunteer hours and money out of these folks."

Linc and Jamal shared a smile over the head of the woman between them. Roxanne was impossible to refuse when she started giving orders. Not that either of them wanted to do anything but please her.

Chapter

3

J ust pull into the driveway behind the blue Camry," Roxanne told the cabdriver. She frowned when she saw lights shining from the first-floor windows of the two-family home that Jamal had given her as a wedding present. Why hadn't anyone come to pick her up at the airport? She'd told her mother and her sister that her plane would be getting in around six o'clock. She was pretty sure she'd told them which airline, too. When no one had met her at the gate at St. Louis International, she thought they might be waiting for her at baggage claim. Her luggage arrived and the rest of the passengers on her flight disappeared, so she finally accepted that no one was coming. She didn't bother to call, opting to take a cab instead. In the time it would take LaToya or her mother to belatedly drive to the airport, she could be at home. Or at her family's home at any rate. She had deeded them the house.

Holding two shopping bags that overflowed with gifts, Roxanne stood on the concrete path between the driveway and the house. The clean, uniformly manicured homes in this suburban development were a far cry from the housing project she'd grown up in, she noted with quiet satisfaction. She was thankful that she and Jamal had been able to do this for her family. LaToya and her husband and three kids lived on the bottom floor with Grandma Reynolds; and Roxanne's other sister, Denise, and her kids lived on the top floor with Dot, Roxanne's mother.

Despite the miscommunication about the airport, she couldn't wait to see everyone, especially Grandma Reynolds and the kids. She quickly peeled off two twenties and handed them to the driver, telling her to keep the change. "Thank God for suitcases on wheels," Roxanne said as she hefted the overnight bag on one shoulder and dragged her suitcase behind her. Once at the door, she managed to free a finger so that she could jab the doorbell. She had a key, but finding it would mean rooting through her purse and putting all of her stuff down.

Roxanne had to press the buzzer several times before LaToya finally opened the door. Her youngest, Zaire, clung to one hip, howling up a storm. Roxanne could see clear to the back of her niece's throat where that little pink thingy hung down. Hip-hop music blared from somewhere in the house. LaToya was dressed in beige leggings and a brown tunic that was littered with white patches. What was that? Flour? A thick red rubber band held her hair in a stubby, split ends–filled ponytail. LaToya had a cordless phone up to one ear. Annoyance at whoever was ringing the doorbell creased her forehead. There were faint circles beneath her eyes. She took a minute to register that it was her sister at the door.

"Roxy?" LaToya said as if surprised to see her.

"In the flesh," Roxanne said with a laugh as she stepped over the threshold. In one smooth movement, she gave her niece and her sister a peck on their cheeks. Zaire was still screaming like a banshee, so Roxanne dropped her bags and reached for her.

Still looking a little stunned, LaToya gladly handed her over. Covering the mouthpiece of the phone, she said, "Thanks." She turned her back and went into the living room, where presumably she could hear the person on the other end and vice versa.

Bouncing Zaire on her hip, Roxanne tried to calm her, "And what's bothering you, Suga Boo? What's making you cry, Sweetie Pie?" Normally Zaire was a beautiful child with light brown skin, adorable dimples, and fat Tweetie Bird cheeks, who constantly babbled in baby language. She wasn't looking so pretty now. Not with the angry flush in those plump cheeks and the racket she was making. It was all Roxanne could do to hold on to her as she thrashed around in her arms calling for her mama. Roxanne walked past the living room, then made a left when she got to the family room. It was littered with toys and overturned plastic cups, some empty and some not, if the still-damp stains on the carpet were anything to go by. She located the source of the loud music, an abandoned TV that had been cranked up and left on a music video channel. She picked up the remote and hit the mute button.

After settling with Zaire on the green-and-beige-plaid sofa that faced the television, Roxanne tried again to quiet the child. Her crying wasn't as painful to the ears now that she wasn't competing with the TV. "So what's wrong, Zai? Has one of your big brothers been mean to you? Tell Auntie which one, and she'll make 'em treat you right." Actually, her six-year-old nephew, Jaron, was too into video games to be bothered with his little sister, and twelve-year-old Dante was the classic protective older brother. It was cute how he was always keeping a watchful eye on Zaire. To have such short legs, she was awfully quick and was constantly putting stuff in her mouth. Like Roxanne's finger at this very moment. The little girl was rubbing the knuckle of one of Roxanne's fingers back and forth across her lower gums. That's when Roxanne noticed the soaking wet bib around her neck and the drool that she thought had been a by-product of all the crying.

She kissed the top of Zaire's head and stroked the colored beads at the end of her cornrowed braids. They matched the red-and-white outfit she was wearing. "Poor baby," she murmured. "Are you getting a new tooth? Is that what this fuss is all about?" Zaire continued to massage her gums with Roxanne's finger. It seemed to have quieted her down. Roxanne let her go on like that for a while—until she remembered where her fingers had been. All over a germ-infested airplane, airport, and cab.

"Come on, Suga Boo, let's go find you something to ease the pain that won't result in a communicable disease or worse." First she stopped by the bathroom and grabbed a clean face towel, then proceeded to the kitchen. Now she knew where the flour stains on LaToya's clothes had come from. A brown paper bag filled with flour sat next to a platter of uncooked pork chops on the kitchen table. More flour trailed from the bag to the uncovered plastic flour canister. LaToya had also set out a collection of spices: garlic salt, paprika, black pepper. Roxanne noticed that one of the burners was lit under a frying pan. When the phone rang, LaToya must have forgotten all about it. Roxanne sniffed the air appreciatively. Something with onions as a central ingredient was baking in the oven. She couldn't wait to find out what it was. She hadn't eaten since breakfast, and that was East Coast time. The pretzels and can of soda on the plane hadn't done a thing to satisfy her hunger.

Fearing that the hot oil from the skillet might splatter, Roxanne sat Zaire on the floor before going to turn off the burner. Zaire started to whimper. "Shush, sweetie. Auntie's not leaving you. I'll be right back. And then I'm gonna wrap a nice ice cube in this towel and hook you right up."

She did just that and was bending over to scoop up Zaire when the sweet Tennessee drawl that her grandma had never lost, despite living in the Midwest for fifty years, reached her ears.

"Roxy, is that you?" her grandma called. "You know I don't see so good no more. But I thought I heard your voice. I was taking a little nap, and I thought I was dreamin'."

Roxanne was smiling when she straightened and turned to face the woman she'd probably look like in forty years or so. Grandma Reynolds was even shorter than Roxanne. They both were curvy. They had the same medium brown complexion and even had the same little space between their two front teeth. At seventy-five, Grandma Reynolds' face was not webbed with wrinkles. She had only a few deep grooves to mark wisdom acquired over time. Her eyes were still bright, welcoming, and full of love.

"Dreamin'? Now, you know I wouldn't miss your birthday, Grandma," Roxanne teased. Not even when she was a broke student or living halfway across the country and earning so-so wages. "And before you ask, Jamal with his fine self"—her grandma always ended her sentences about Jamal with "his fine self"— "will be here later tonight. He's traveling with the team." They were playing the Steamrollers on Sunday, and there were tickets for the entire family and Linc's.

As her grandmother leaned on her walker and slowly moved over to the kitchen table, Roxanne had to acknowledge some changes. Her grandmother was a primary candidate for losing a leg to diabetes because she refused to give up fried fish and fried chicken and all the other wonderful but unhealthy foods she'd taught Roxanne to cook. And a certain sadness lingered in her eyes and in the way she held herself, a sadness that had taken root when Grandpa George had passed away. It would be ten years this December.

Balancing Zaire on one hip, Roxanne hurried over to help her grandmother get comfortably settled in a chair at the table. Then she squatted down to give her the hug and get the hug that she'd been longing for in the three months since she'd last been home.

"You're a sight for these tired old eyes, Sugar Plum," Grandma Reynolds said, squeezing her in a surprisingly strong way for someone who looked so frail.

"I missed you so much, Grandma," Roxanne said, breathing in the smells of her childhood. Cocoa butter lotion, the scent of peppermint on her grandma's breath, and the aroma of good food cooking. It gave her such peace.

Roxanne sat smiling, drinking in the comforting sight of Grandma and letting Zaire suck on the cloth-covered ice. One hand rested against Grandma Reynolds' smaller, more weathered one. It was warm, soft with a covering of papery thin skin. "I'm surprised you were able to sleep with all the commotion going on around here," she said.

Grandma Reynolds chuckled, "Child, living in this house, you learn to sleep through anything. It's never quiet."

Roxanne eyed her hopefully. "You could always come live with me and Jamal."

Grandma Reynolds slowly shook her head. They'd had this conversation many times. "You know I can't leave my church. Who would lead Sunday prayers? Surely not Mother Watson, she'd have folks praying for two hours straight."

Roxanne smiled. The "mothers" of the church took turns leading the prayers, and the morning service was at least a half hour longer than usual when it was Mother Watson's Sunday.

"We got churches in Baltimore, you know."

"But you ain't got my friends. And yo' mama still needs me to remind her she ain't no spring chicken no more. Wait till you meet her new boyfriend. And I do mean 'boy' . . ."

Roxanne could only imagine. Her mother would date anyone from eight to eighty, blind, crippled, or crazy. No one could accuse her of favoring a particular type.

". . . I try to give LaToya a hand with the kids, especially now that Jimmy's been laid low."

Her brother-in-law had been recently diagnosed with prostate cancer. Roxanne couldn't fathom it. Jimmy was so young, not even forty yet. She thought prostate cancer was a disease that plagued old men. Her brother-in-law had just undergone his first round of radiation treatment.

"How is Jimmy?" Roxanne asked. "LaToya was on the phone when I came in. I barely had time to say hi. And where are the boys?"

"Dante is at basketball practice. He made the junior varsity team," Grandma Reynolds told her, clearly proud of her great-grandson's achievement. Removing her hand from beneath Roxanne's, she reached for the gold locket watch that she wore on a chain around her neck. She brought it close to her eyes then held it away from her until the numbers on the dial came into proper focus. "He should be home any minute now." She dropped the locket, and it rested against her small bosom. "That rascal, Jaron, is around here somewhere. Probably down in the basement playing Pac-Man. That's all he ever does."

Roxanne rolled her eyes. "Grandma, don't nobody play Pac-Man anymore. *I* used to play Pac-Man so you know how ancient that game has gotta be. He's probably got some bloody, kill-the-alien-invader kind of videos for his Gameboy."

"Still a waste of time to me. Whatever happened to reading a book or playing outside with your friends? Kids today ain't gonna develop no social skills."

Roxanne could not agree more but decided to put the brakes on before Grandma Reynolds really got fired up about "the problem with kids today." "And Jimmy?" she asked.

Grandma Reynolds' eyes and voice softened. After a small sigh she replied, "Jimmy's resting, poor thing. The radiation treatment just knocks him right out. But he should be back at work by next week."

Roxanne didn't know anything about cancer, but that seemed kind of soon to her. "How's LaToya holding up? She seemed kind of frazzled when she answered the door."

She shrugged her slight shoulders. "You know your sister. She's just like you. Tries to handle everything on her own. Won't accept no help from anybody."

Roxanne drummed her short, neatly trimmed fingernails against the table. She had no idea what her grandma was talking about. She hadn't really ever needed help. Most of her adult life she had been short on cash, but then again so was everyone else in her family. So what would have been the point in asking them for something that they could not give? Besides, her problems were piddling compared to having a sick husband and three kids to raise.

Grandma Reynolds must have read something in her eyes. "Don't be looking at me like I've finally gone senile. You don't ask for help and won't accept it when it's given," she admonished.

"Like when?"

"How much time you got? It's a long list."

Roxanne laughed at her grandmother's bluntness. "When was the most recent time I refused to accept help?"

"I know you're upset about not being able to get pregnant. I can hear it in your voice, girl. And every time I try to talk to you about it for more than a New York minute, you change the subject."

" 'Cause there's nothing you can do about it. Not unless you can find a way to fix my thyroid or whatever is wrong with me," Roxanne said.

"Maybe I can help by being an ear to listen, a shoulder to cry on."

Maybe, but that still wasn't going to get her pregnant. Besides, she'd been leaning on her grandma all her life. It was time to reverse roles.

Her grandmother's eyes were calm and assessing. Most of all, they were knowing. She'd always been able to read her mind, her feelings.

"So you think your old granny can't help, huh?"

When Roxanne started to protest, Grandma Reynolds reached over and patted her check. "That's exactly what you think. That's OK, you ain't hurtin' my feelings." Her smile was quiet, her eyes full of time-earned wisdom. "You young folks think you invented problems. So naturally, you expect to find all the solutions."

Roxanne leaned into the caress. "Aw, Grandma, I don't mean to put down what you know about life. 'Cause there's a lot you can and have taught me. I just don't think there's much you can do to fix this particular problem."

Her grandma removed her hand, and Roxanne missed her touch immediately. "The doctors don't know everything. You should let my friend Drusilla mix you up a fertility potion. Her family is Geechee, you know."

Geechee? That was her grandmother's term for people who

came from the islands off the coast of Georgia and the Carolinas. Roxanne had to hold back a laugh. The country girl in her grandma still believed in people getting "fixed" or having "roots" put on them. "Grandma, if I don't get pregnant soon, I might just give Drusilla a call." She couldn't be any less effective than modern medicine had been thus far.

Water dripped from the towel where the ice had melted. Zaire had fallen asleep in her arms. The ice must have helped. Roxanne shifted the little girl's neck to a more comfortable angle. She'd take her to her room in a minute.

"I wonder who LaToya could be talking to. She's been on the phone a long time," Roxanne remarked. "Maybe I'll go ahead and fry up these pork chops." She pointed at her grandmother. "And don't even think you're getting one. I'm going to find something that fits the diet your doctor put you on." Her grandmother opened her mouth to complain, and Roxanne said, "Uh-huh. Didn't think I knew what you're *supposed* to be eating? You gonna eat right, old lady, because I want you around to spoil my kids— maybe even my grandkids."

"You do look right holding a child in your arms," her grand-mother said.

Roxanne locked eyes with her grandmother. She felt emotion well up in her throat. Would she ever hold her own child? Rock it to sleep at night, comfort it when it was sick?

As if reading her mind, her grandma said, "It'll happen, baby, you just mark my words. You're too good with children for it not to happen."

Roxanne hugged Zaire closer to her, inhaling her precious baby smell, and prayed her grandmother was right. She usually was.

After arguing with Grandma Reynolds about whether or not she was strong enough to hold a sleeping toddler while Roxanne finished cooking dinner, Roxanne finally gave up and handed Zaire over. Her grandma might be old, but she still ruled the roost. With unnecessary cooking tips from Grandma Reynolds, she sea-soned and fried the pork chops for the family. She took the veg-etable casserole out of the oven and baked a chicken breast for her grandmother, who was not happy. Linc and Jamal had shown up just in time for the food to be served and brought their massive appetites with them. They more than made up for Jimmy, who only managed a heated-up can of chicken broth and some crackers before he excused himself to go lie down.

"I'm sorry the house is in such a mess," LaToya said as she wiped off the tray of Zaire's high chair. Roxanne was using a damp dishcloth to do the same to the kitchen table. "I swear that girl left as much food on the floor as she put in her mouth," LaToya exclaimed. She rinsed the cloth out at the sink and snagged the broom that leaned against the fridge. As she swept away the debris that her daughter had littered the floor with, she fretted. "Did we clear all the dishes from the dining room table?" The adults had eaten in the dining room, but the kids, under Grandma Reynolds' supervision, had eaten in the kitchen.

"Yes, we did," Roxanne said. "I loaded the dishwasher. So you can go ahead and turn it on. The only things left are the bowls that Linc and Jamal are using for their ice cream." Linc, Jamal, the kids, and, if she was honest herself, she had made a huge dent in a gallon of Grandma Reynolds' homemade peach ice cream. "They can wash those by hand when they're finished." Neither one of the bums had done anything useful since walking through the door. Unless acting goofy with the kids and eating like food was going out of style were achievements.

"Oh, I can't have them cleaning up," LaToya said. "I've already shown what a lousy hostess I am by leaving you stranded at the airport."

Roxanne expelled a little laugh. LaToya took everything so seriously. "Lambert is not exactly the desert, Sis. I took a cab."

LaToya hurriedly pushed the day's grit and food crumbs onto the dustpan, then spun around to see what else needed to be done. "And what did I do? I left you standing at the front door. And if you wanted a meal, you had to cook it yourself."

The phone call that had LaToya so distracted had been from Jaron's teacher. Apparently, he had "an attitude problem," and after she got off the phone LaToya had sought him out to give him "an attitude adjustment." Roxanne and Grandma Reynolds had exchanged a startled look when they heard LaToya's raised voice followed by the sound of Jaron crying. All the howling woke up Zaire. But her gums must have been feeling better, because she wasn't fussy with Grandma Reynolds. Or maybe her grandma just had the magic touch with children.

"I just don't know what's gotten into that boy," LaToya said. "His teacher said he's constantly talking and messing with the other kids, so they can't concentrate, either. But what really ticked me off is that she says he talks back when she tries to discipline him. I don't know where he's getting *that* behavior from. Certainly not from around here."

Jimmy and LaToya were loving with their kids, but they were also firm. Clearly, the parents had the final say in their household. "Well, I don't know if whupping his butt is gonna change anything," Roxanne said. "Did you try to find out if something is bothering him?"

Suddenly LaToya's lip quivered as if she was about to cry. She stood stock-still in the center of the floor, holding on tightly to the broom a moment before she walked stiffly over to the trash can. "No . . . No . . . I just marched down to the basement. Gave him a piece of my mind and a few whacks." She blinked back a tear as she put the broom and dustpan away. "I guess I won't be winning mother of the year anytime soon," she said.

Roxanne draped an arm around her sister's waist and leaned her head against her shoulder. She could feel a tremor running through LaToya's body. "Maybe not today, but there are a lot of days in a year. Stop being so hard on yourself. You've got a lot to deal with right now. There's Jimmy and Grandma Reynolds and the kids." LaToya had taken two weeks off from her job as a bookkeeper at a local bakery to be with Jimmy, since he was just starting treatment.

"I know. I know," LaToya said, squeezing her back. "I just didn't expect it to be this hard. I didn't think Jimmy and I would be dealing with health problems while our kids are still so young. Roxy, I fall into bed exhausted every night, and though it seems like I've just shut my eyes, a new day is on me before I know it."

Roxanne stepped away from her to get a closer look. Given all her responsibilities, Roxanne was surprised that LaToya had only a few dark circles and tatty hair to show for it. Her sister was a few inches taller than her, a little thicker around the middle. Her complexion was a lighter brown and more even. She never had to battle acne the way Roxanne had. She gave a tired smile in response to Roxanne's blatant scrutiny.

Growing up, the kitchen had been a place for many serious conversations, confessions, and fights. Now, even though a different kitchen, the same principle held. Roxanne guided her sister over to the table and gently pushed her down in a chair. She took a seat across from her. "What about Mama and Denise?" she asked. "They can help out with Grandma Reynolds."

LaToya threw back her head and scoffed. "Girl, please. Those two are cut from the same cloth. If ain't nothing fun in it for them, they could care less. And you know it. Even though they live right upstairs, you think I've seen either one of them this week except in passing?"

She couldn't argue with her on that point. Though she had told her mother when her plane got in, she hadn't really expected *her* to pick her up from the airport, even though she had a car. At the very least, she thought she'd keep an eye out on the kids and the house so that LaToya could do it. She hadn't even bothered to ask Denise, not wanting to hear the excuses for why she couldn't do it.

"Look, if you need some extra help around here, we can hire someone."

LaToya shook her head and pursed her lips before speaking. "Now, you know Grandma won't like that. She doesn't like people touching her stuff, and she refuses to accept that she can't do as much as she used to."

Roxanne's answering look said that she would handle Grandma Reynolds. If LaToya didn't soon get some help running this household, there would be three sick folks around here instead of just two. She planned to talk to her mother ASAP. She looked at her wristwatch. It was after nine, and she hadn't heard any signs of life from upstairs. *Well, they have to come home eventually,* Roxanne figured. And when they do, she would want to know why Dot couldn't act like the mother for once instead of like a teenager. Well, maybe she wouldn't put it exactly like that, but it was her daughter and mother in need of a little help, not some stranger off the street.

"Why don't you go lie down, LaToya? I can finish straightening up, and I'll take care of the kids. Let's also talk about hiring a cleaning lady or cook or whoever it is you need, when you're feeling a little more rested."

With a tired but grateful smile, LaToya arose from her chair and smoothed her hair with her hand. "I'm overdue for my touch-up," she noted as she fingered the splintered ends of her ponytail.

"Go get your hair done tomorrow," Roxanne said.

"But what about Grandma's birthday party?"

"LaToya, you've got to stop running around like a chicken with its head cut off," she told her. Roxanne's tone softened as she added, "Don't worry, Big Sis is on the J-O-B."

Unable to stifle a yawn, LaToya murmured, "Thanks, Roxy."

"Take a long, relaxing bubble bath before you get in bed," Roxanne ordered as she watched her sister's flour-covered behind disappear down the hallway.

She made herself a cup of herbal tea and listened to the hypnotic drone of the dishwasher. This was the first quiet moment she had had all day. Her morning was filled with last-minute instructions to her assistant, Marita. Then the mad dash to the airport. And she'd been pitching in ever since she set foot in the house.

Roxanne sighed deeply, wishing she could wave a magic wand and make all of her family's problems disappear. Or maybe stumble across a genie in a bottle who would grant her three wishes. The first of which, of course, would be to make all of her family's problems disappear. Her second wish would be for a long and happy life with Jamal, and without question the third would be to have a healthy baby who would grow to adulthood and have a happy and productive life. Hopefully, the last wish would be granted before she was too old and decrepit. Laughter and good-natured arguing between Linc and Jamal intruded on her daydreaming.

"Throw her to me," Jamal shouted.

Linc held a squealing Zaire in both hands like she was a football. He checked first to left and then to the right, as if deciding which way to throw her. "Wait, wait. I think I see another play," Linc countered. "There's a receiver downfield," he said, zeroing in on Roxanne, where she sat at the table sipping her tea. "She's a little short. There's a scowl on her face, but she is wide open." He reared his arm back as if to throw her to Roxanne, but side-armed her to Jamal instead.

Zaire giggled hysterically. "Weee!" she cried. She had on a

food-stained bib and T-shirt and a pair of Pull-ups. She was drooling all over his hand.

"Jamal! Linc! Stop tossing her around like that before you drop her. She is not a football."

Jamal huffed and tucked Zaire under one arm and made some duck-and-run moves. "You're looking at the surest hands in professional football, woman. Besides, she likes it."

"She likes playing with the water in the toilet, too," Roxanne said.

Jamal held Zaire over his head and wiggled her around. He flinched in disgust as a long string of drool dripped onto his face. Linc roared as Jamal tried to bat it away with the back of his hand.

Served him right, Roxanne thought. He's lucky that all he got was a face full of drool. It could have been spit up from all that ice cream she'd just finished eating. Roxanne got up from the table and held out her hands. "Give her to me. She might like it, but you're giving her aunt a heart attack."

Zaire looked at Roxanne's open arms and then at Jamal, who winked at her. She turned away from her aunt and pressed her bowstring lips against her uncle's cheek. "Fine, be that way," Roxanne said, pretending to be hurt by the rejection.

"Told you she loves her Uncle Jamal." Still, he reached for a kitchen towel and wiped his face and hands, then playfully did the same to Zaire.

Roxanne said, "Right. But when her gums start hurting again, you'll be begging me to take her off your hands."

Linc took a seat at the table and stretched his long legs out in front, crossing them at the ankles. "That was a good meal, Roxy." His eyes had that droopy look they always got after he'd stuffed himself. Been like that all of his life.

"Thanks. How's your mom?" The team had rolled into town this morning, and Jamal had hung out with Linc as he made the rounds to his family and friends.

"Still bossy. Told me I should change out of the red sweater I was wearing 'cause it wasn't my color." That sounded just like Mrs. Weaver. And she noticed Linc was wearing a blue long-sleeved polo shirt. So, obviously, he listened to his mama. She was about the only woman he paid any attention to.

"She also told him it was time for him to get married and give her some grandchildren," Jamal informed her. "You should have seen how he was squirming. Like a fish on a hook."

"Hey, I changed my shirt, but a man has his limits as to what he is willing to do to please his mama."

Roxanne didn't see why. What was Linc waiting for? Perfection?

"My mama's trippin' anyhow. Between my brother and sister, she's already got seven grandchildren. How many does the woman need?" Linc whined, throwing his hands up in the air.

Zaire pointed to the fridge. "Want bottle!" she demanded.

Roxanne rolled her eyes. "Anybody who can ask for a bottle, doesn't need one," she said.

"Auntie is soooo mean," Jamal whispered to Zaire, who reached up to rub her hands against his rough beard. "I'll fix you a bottle." He opened a cupboard behind him to search for a bottle.

"Good, 'bout time you did something useful." Jamal handed Roxanne a bottle and nipple. She was only able to fill it halfway before she drained what was left in the half-gallon carton of whole milk. Roxanne handed Zaire the bottle and hoped it would be enough to last her through the night. Zaire noisily slurped it down.

Seeing that the baby was satisfied for the moment, Roxanne said, "Linc, what are you sitting there doing nothing for? You can go get those bowls and spoons you left in the other room. Ain't no maids around here."

Linc exchanged an amused, yet helpless, look with Jamal. "Damn, I got bossy women every which way I turn." As he pushed off from the table, there was a knock at the back door. Linc pulled back the curtain of the small window on the door then unlocked it.

Roxanne's mother flitted in followed by her sister, Denise, and some fine-looking brother in his early twenties that Roxanne had never laid eyes on before.

Dot squealed and ran over to her daughter. "Roxy, baby girl, you looking so good." She engulfed her with a huge hug, rocking from side to side. Roxanne hugged her back, but before she could get too comfortable in the embrace, Dot raced over to Linc.

"Linc!" she said before throwing herself at him.

Her mother was a bundle of energy. Snow melting on the sidewalk could excite her. Roxanne smiled and wondered how a five-foot-ten-inch-tall, rail-thin woman with light olive skin could give birth to a runt like herself. But then, none of the sisters really favored each other either, or their mother. They all had the same father, but Roxanne didn't remember him, since he was long gone by the time she was four or five years old. The few pictures she had seen of him were old and grainy so she had no idea what he really looked like. He always seemed to be at a party or a bar, and even those pictures had disappeared over the years.

Denise was the pretty one. Tall like their mother but lush where Dot was lean. Full ripe lips, more voluptuous hips, and as the guys said, plenty of junk in her trunk.

She flashed Roxanne a small wave, didn't acknowledge Linc at all, but sauntered over to Jamal and said, "So, don't I get a kiss hello, brother dear?"

Jamal was about to kiss her on the cheek when Denise gripped his free arm to pull him closer and turned her face at the last minute, so his lips landed on hers. Roxanne watched the display in amazement. Denise wasn't just flirtatious. She was downright sexually aggressive when it came to men. Though she usually didn't mean anything by it, Roxanne would be compelled to slap her silly if she tried to slip her tongue in Jamal's mouth. She wasn't jealous, just annoyed. And why was Denise carrying on like that anyhow? Was she trying to make her new boyfriend jealous? Maybe if she stopped all this game playing, she could keep a man.

Denise stepped back from him with a big grin. "I like the beard. It's a nice addition."

"Uh, thanks," Jamal said, taking several steps away from her. He quickly sought Roxanne's eyes, worried about how she might be reacting to Denise's brazenness. His wife merely shook her head from side to side and rolled her eyes at her sister. Jamal nearly sighed his relief that she wasn't blaming him for her crazy sister's behavior.

Caught off guard by her sister's antics, Roxanne almost forgot the man who'd come in with them. Upon closer inspection, she realized he was even younger than she had thought. He had a strong masculine jawline, a little mustache rested above his lip, but there was something not quite grown-up about his wide-set eyes. And he was dressed like a teenager; all casual clothes with the logo of some overpriced designer's name stitched into every piece from head to toe. At thirty-three had Denise finally resorted to robbing the cradle? This young'un looked like he would be carded if he tried to buy cigarettes at the neighborhood 7-Eleven.

Realizing that she was staring, Roxanne said, "So, Denise, aren't you going to introduce us to your friend?"

"Not my friend," Denise replied. "Mama's."

Mama's? Roxanne tried not to let her shock show. Grandma Reynolds had said something earlier about Mama's new man being a boy, but Roxanne was only half listening. Looking at the boy again, she finally introduced herself. "Oh, hi, I'm Roxanne." Was her mama going through some type of midlife crisis? Even if he was of legal age that would make her mama more than thirty-five years his senior.

He extended his hand. The smile he gave her was blinding. And Roxanne began to see why her mother was taken with him. Then he spoke.

"Pleased to meet you, ma'am. I am Etienne." He pronounced it "Ey-tee-n." His skin was flawless, the color of creamy coffee. His lilting voice was as smooth as silk, something all the women in the family appreciated. Hell, his accent was so cute, she could even forgive him for calling her ma'am.

"So, Etienne, what island are you from?" Roxanne asked.

Again, he flashed those impossibly white teeth. "Haiti, ma'am."

Her mother, who had moved over to hug Jamal, joined the conversation. "Yes, Etienne. This is my son-in-law, Jamal. And the big guy over there is Lincoln. Known him since he still had his baby teeth. He's like a member of the family. You already met Miss Zaire." She tweaked the toddler on the nose. "What are you still doing up, Zai? Don't want to miss anything, huh?"

Zaire gurgled a response that probably only her mother could decipher.

"Anyhow, Etienne works with me at the brewery. He's been there like, what, a year?"

"Almost ten months," he corrected.

"He's been good enough to be our escort and bag carrier all day."

Roxanne looked around for bags but didn't see any. "Where y'all been?"

"The Galleria. Dillards' is having a twenty-four-hour sale," Denise said. "We got some good stuff. Then we stopped by Harrah's for a little casino action—"

"I suppose you'd have money to do that," Linc said. "Seeing as you are living rent free."

"And I see you're still hanging around being a pain in the ass."

Linc and Denise had never gotten along. Roxanne never could figure out why. "Denise," Roxanne warned, "don't cuss in front of the baby. Next thing you know, she'll be repeating it." Probably somewhere embarrassing like in church. "Speaking of babies, where are yours?" Denise had twin six-year-olds, Ta'Quanna and A'Yahana. Her eldest, Jewel, was eight.

"They're at a sleepover. Thank God."

Roxanne laughed. "Dawg, you sound like you're happy to get rid of them."

"I am. If you could ever get yourself pregnant, you'd know how I feel. Having kids underfoot twenty-four-seven gets old real quick." Oblivious to the hurt in Roxanne's eyes, Denise kept going. "Geez, what is wrong with you people? How hard is it to get knocked up? You never see any poor, broke couples struggling to get pregnant. It's always the ones that can afford kids that make having them into a big production."

Linc snarled, "Thanks for that ignorant lecture on a subject you know absolutely nothing about, Denise. Do you think Roxy *wants* this to be a big production? Do you think this is fun for her?"

Denise arched an eyebrow at his tone. "Excuse me, if I hurt anybody's feelings. I was just stating an opinion. This is America, you know. Home of the brave, land of the free and all that."

"Well, feel free to keep your big trap shut sometimes," Linc suggested.

"Uh, maybe we should go now," Etienne said. He must have felt as uncomfortable as Roxanne did having her reproductive failures broadcast like it was today's headlines.

Jamal had come over to stand next to Roxanne, and he'd put a protective arm around her waist. "Well, it is late and we're still on eastern time. Linc and I have practice tomorrow and then Grandma Reynolds' big party. I guess we'll see you there," he said, leaving no doubt that he wanted them to leave.

"Definitely. Definitely," Dot said, willing to join the conversation now that the verbal exchanges had ceased. She avoided conflict like the plague.

"Wait," Denise said, when her mother and Etienne moved over to the back door. "We were so busy shopping, we didn't have time to eat. What y'all got to eat?"

"Oh, Denise," Roxanne moaned, "I already put everything away and cleaned up for the night. And I need to put Zaire to bed, it's after ten."

"You ain't gotta do nothing. Mama and Etienne can unload our packages. We left them in the car, and I'll just fix us a doggie bag and take it upstairs."

Etienne and Dot both eagerly agreed to that as if they couldn't wait to get away. When the door shut behind them, Roxanne felt a little guilty. She hadn't meant to be unwelcoming. But she really was dead on her feet.

"Roxy, why don't you and Jamal go ahead and get Zaire ready for bed? I'll see to it that Denise is kicked out . . . er . . . I mean I'll let her out. And I'll lock up after she's gone, and let myself out."

"Thanks, man," Jamal said, slapping Linc on the back as he passed by with Zaire, who was starting to droop in his arms.

"Could you wash her up, Jamal? I laid some PJs out on the bed." They always slept on the full-size bed in Zaire's room when they visited. Zaire slept on the twin bed.

Jamal nodded his agreement.

"I'll be there in a minute, hon," she told Jamal. Denise stared stony-faced at Linc. He returned her glare. "Look, you two, quit the Evil Eye contest. Denise, the pork chops are wrapped in aluminum foil, the casserole is in an oblong Tupperware pan. Help yourself to some macaroni and cheese. And good night," Roxanne said into the silence that followed.

The minute she was out of earshot, the fighting resumed. Denise didn't bother to transfer the food to smaller packages. Instead, she grabbed a plastic grocery bag from beneath the sink and put everything in it. Linc remained leaning against the sink, his arms folded across his chest.

Cocking her head to one side, Denise told him, "Roxy's got a husband. It's his job to defend her. Not yours, in case you didn't know that."

"She wouldn't need *anyone* to defend her, if she didn't have such an ungrateful sister." He walked over to the back door and held it open for her. "You really do believe in biting the hand that feeds you. Roxy is nothing but supportive of her family. Why can't you show her the same consideration?" he asked.

"Speaking of family, Linc, don't you have a family of your own to bother while you're in St. Louis?"

"Don't let the door hit you on the way out," Linc said as he practically slammed it with her still in the threshold. He forcefully turned the upper and lower locks. Denise just didn't get it, he silently fumed. Roxy *was* family.

Chapter

4

Jamal's house keys clattered noisily on the kitchen table. The room was robbed of its normal cheer because Roxanne wasn't in it doing what she loved to do: belting out Patti LaBelle while throwing together a quick meal. Of course, this only happened on the days when they could get away from the Center at a reasonable hour or when the team wasn't on the road. His woman loved to cook, and Jamal was an appreciative and enthusiastic eater. Roxanne didn't like help in "her kitchen," so most times he would take a seat and watch as she traipsed barefoot between the stainless-steel refrigerator, the walk-in pantry, and beech wood cabinets, gathering what she needed and placing them on the table and countertops. Her small feet were always purposeful if not efficient as they crisscrossed the navy and white tiles of the floor that they had put in together. Jamal didn't quite understand it, but there was something restful about watching her stir a bubbling pot or check on a pie baking in the oven.

Sometimes he would come home to find her sipping a cup of herbal tea. She'd hold out a hand for him to join her as she took in the ever-changing view afforded by the French doors that looked out on the backyard. The perspiring glass of Roxanne's greenhouse was always a constant in the picture. In the spring and summer, bright colors from the flower garden were eye candy. In the fall, the burnt reds and yellows of turning leaves edged the yard. Baltimore winters were nothing compared to the harsh Boston winters, but they did inspire critters like rabbits, squirrels, or chipmunks to show up on the wraparound porch or in the yard, where they foraged for food. Not that they had to look too hard, because Roxanne was always feeding them.

But none of that was happening today. He could usually count on finding Roxanne in her favorite room in the house. But not tonight.

Damn it! Where was she? When Jamal had seen her car in the garage, his step had quickened with an energy he didn't know he had. The fatigue and irritation that started with football practice and remained with him during the stop-and-go traffic on I-695 had started to fade. Now the silence of the lovingly decorated but empty room was loud to his ears.

So what if the Range Rover was in the garage? He should have known that didn't mean anything. She was probably with Marita. He wasn't sure exactly what Marita's job title was, but when she wasn't working on her degree in urban affairs, she drove Roxanne around, took her to various meetings, and generally took care of scheduling details so that Roxanne could have more time to interact with the people who used the services at the Center, especially the kids.

Roxanne had already left the house when he got up this morning. So he didn't know what she had on tap for the day. Only God knew when she'd be home. Jamal didn't need a mirror to know he was frowning, or rather, pouting.

Without meaning to, Roxanne had spoiled him. And like any brat, he was not dealing well with not getting what he wanted, which was his wife. Here. Now. He didn't really expect Roxanne to be at home *every* night with dinner waiting. But this was an evening when he could have truly done with some pampering.

Practice had been lousy. He was tired and his bad knee was aching. Welch, their clutch tight end, had pulled a groin muscle. That meant more pressure on him this coming Sunday. San Diego's pass coverage was tops in the league. At his height and weighing less than two hundred pounds, Jamal relied on fast moves and finesse cuts to elude his opponents rather than brute strength. He could take hard hits if he had to. But he preferred not to. And without a doubt, the Blue Streaks would be gunning for him. It was no big secret who Linc would be throwing to downfield. He hoped Kent Welch would heal in time for the game, but he wasn't holding his breath. He knew from painful, personal experience that groin injuries tended to linger and were aggravated by the least little thing like running, jumping, or having a cornerback wrestle you to the ground.

Jamal peeled off his jacket and hung it up in the downstairs closet. He was disgusted with himself. *Since when had he started worrying about being hit? That came with the territory, didn't it?* But he could hear footsteps. It was the sound of time marching on. Thirty-three was old in football years. As a wide receiver, getting hit came with the territory, but it got harder and harder every year to take those licks from massive corn-fed, country boys or sinewy street warriors in stride. The competition was getting bigger and stronger every season. Chronic aches and pains were the markers of years of punishment. Then at training camp, he could no longer take for granted that he would be a starter at his position. He had to prove he could out-perform the lineup of hungry, young players who wavered between awe of him and a desire to steal his job. He knew this to be true. He used to *be* them. But before that happened, Jamal was determined to get to the Big Dance. He had easily achieved just about all his professional goals, but a Championship Bowl ring had eluded him. And he didn't want to retire from the game with that one regret.

Isn't that why he'd left the Brahmins? Isn't it the reason he'd asked Roxanne to leave her life and friends in Boston to start over here? He wanted to end his career in his hometown and play for a team that had a better chance of winning the Big One.

As Jamal trudged up the spiral staircase of the five-bedroom Cape Cod, he reminded himself that the season was going well. It was mid-November and they were tied for first place in the Central Division. They really had a shot this year.

At the top of the stairs, he came to a sudden halt. The sound of running water interrupted the competing thoughts and fears that swirled around in his head.

Roxanne *was* home! The house was so big, and he had been so focused on her absence from the kitchen that it hadn't occurred to him that she might be upstairs.

She came in from the adjoining bathroom just as Jamal entered the bedroom. She held a small silver canister of incense in her hands. A tiger-striped headband pulled her hair back, and she wore a brown knee-length silk robe, which was tied at the waist with a sash. Her butterfly-shaped tortoiseshell frames were slightly crooked. The smile she gave him propelled him across the room.

"Hi, sweetie," she said, then sat the canister on the solid cherry chest of drawers.

"You're home," he said, stating the obvious right before he planted a kiss on her irresistible lips. His hands cupped her bottom. Her kisses and skin were lush. Brown velvet.

When they reluctantly broke apart, he said, "That's just what I needed after the day I've had. It's been a killer."

"I know," she said.

Jamal lifted a brow in surprise.

"I already got a scouting report about your day," she added, then took his hand and slowly back-pedaled toward the bathroom. A secret smile played around her lips. At his confused look, she said, "A little birdie named Linc called me at the Center and told me all about how the B squad roughed you up today. And Welch got hurt. So"—she drawled as she pulled him deeper into the room. Her smile widened at his stunned expression when he saw the bubbles rising from the sunken tub that was the centerpiece of the bathroom, the bottle of wine chilling on the vanity, the lighting dimmed, and the spicy aroma of incense and candles burning—"I decided to make it all better."

This was why he loved this woman. She was so sexy, yet playful. Full of pleasant surprises. He pulled her close for another kiss. "Thanks, gorgeous," he murmured against her cheek. "When do we get this party started?" he asked before pulling his shirt over his head.

"This is your party, baby," she purred. "I already showered. I just want you to climb into that big, old tub and soak all your cares away. Then I'm going to give you a little wine, play a little jazz, and do whatever I have to to help you get ready to face another day."

She reached for the snap on his jeans and eased his zipper

down. Jamal sucked in his breath. "If you want me to get in that tub alone, you need to stop teasing Mr. Willy," he warned.

Roxanne laughed but stepped away. "S-O-R-R-Y," she said.

Jamal immediately wished he hadn't complained. He reluctantly finished undressing himself. Though she had put in some of her girlie-scented bath beads, he wasn't complaining. She was right. He did need a good soak. Roxanne was always teasing him about "Jamal on the field" versus "Jamal the day after the game or first thing in the morning." It was a mystery to him how he managed to control the pain, to make the leaping plays and one-handed grabs. The fans just saw "the Man of Steele," but Roxanne got to see and hear him first thing in the morning when his knees creaked louder than a staircase in a haunted house, when his back was stiff and he had to limp around until his legs began working properly.

Jamal shed his remaining clothes and gingerly stepped into the tub. Roxanne put a fluffy bath sheet down on the marble platform that surrounded the tub and then turned the jets on.

After he got used to the shock of the warm water on his flesh, Jamal murmured and closed his eyes, "Ah . . . that feels good."

She stuck her hand in the water and splashed his chest with it.

"So what happened at the Center today?" he asked.

Roxanne put a wet finger to the side of her cheek. "Let's see. The new social worker we hired, Regina Shelton, started today."

Jamal remembered Regina from her job interview. Big woman, in her mid-thirties, whose compassionate eyes belied her drill-sergeant looks. They hadn't planned on providing counseling at Hope Springs. But people had issues. And the least they could do was find referrals for no-cost or low-cost services. While they were waiting to get hooked up, folks wanted some kind of short-term hand-holding, which no one at Hope Springs was qualified to do. Hence, the need for a social worker.

"Regina barely had time to take her coat off and lock her purse in her desk before Carmelita comes dragging in, looking like she'd gone a couple of rounds with Oscar De La Hoya. Black eye, split lip, and left arm dangling. She and Le Trey got into it again last night. Anyway, Regina went to work. She convinced Carmelita to go to the Free Clinic to get her injuries checked out and gave her some referrals for marital counseling."

When she plunged her hand in the water again, he nabbed it and held it to his chest. "Marital counseling?" Jamal scoffed. "She needs to leave the bum. I don't know why women put up with men who beat on them."

"Well, I think it was a fight more than a beat down. Le Trey showed up before she left and he looked as bad, if not worse than she did. Regina shipped them both off to the clinic." When Jamal let go of her hand, she brought it up to his shoulder and began to massage the muscles there. "But I know what you mean about abusive relationships. If a woman does fight back, she's more likely to end up hurt than the man."

"Pretty crazy, huh?" Jamal said, returning to the subject of Carmelita and Le Trey. "Neither one of them should be laying hands on the other." Not unless it was like the hands Roxanne was laying on the tight muscles. A moan escaped him as she shifted position so she could tackle the other shoulder as well.

Jamal couldn't imagine the two of them duking it out. He was too afraid of Roxanne's friends for one, especially Monique. She was the type that would put a hit out on your ass if you crossed her. Not that he would ever give her cause. Roxanne meant too much to him.

Jamal tilted his head to one side, letting his wife's kneading hands work their magic. "So anything else exciting happen today?" he asked.

If he had eyes in the back of his head, he would have seen Roxanne biting her lip. "Do you want the good news or the bad news first?" she said.

"The good news."

"We got a letter from the Planter Foundation. It looks like our educational grant has been approved. That's another fifty-thousand over two years."

"That's wonderful, baby. Why don't you come on in here, so I can give you a congratulatory back rub."

Roxanne laughed and shook her head. "Uh-Uh. I'm already nice and dry."

"But I thought you liked it when I made you wet."

"Cute, Jamal. Dirty, but cute," she said.

Roxanne got up and went over to the vanity. She handed him a glass of the cheap wine he favored. The sweeter the better, Jamal always thought. He noticed that Roxanne didn't have a glass for herself. Though she might indulge him, she had once informed him his taste in wines reminded her of spiked Kool-Aid. "Ready for the bad news?"

When was anyone ever ready for bad news, Jamal wondered. "Go ahead, hit me with it."

"Diggy made an SOS call from downtown."

Jamal pictured fifteen-year-old Diggy, a beanpole man-boy, who might have been a poet under more humane circumstances. Instead, he spent most days as a lookout for the drug dealers in his neighborhood. This was the source of inspiration for most of his angry, fist-to-the-gut poems. The raw truth as Diggy saw and lived it had drawn Jamal to him during a freestyle poetry slam sponsored by Hope Springs. Jamal had encouraged the boy's writing. Had even hooked him up with a writing instructor at the University of Maryland, Baltimore County. Though Diggy had been jazzed—as much as his cool-pose would allow him to show—it was gonna take more than a few "guy talks" with some dude he hadn't known a few months ago to convince him that there were alternatives to street hustling. Diggy had his homies to thank for today's court appearance. He had been in the wrong car at the wrong time with some blunt. Diggy claimed he didn't use drugs, and Jamal had never seen any evidence to the contrary.

"So the judge didn't buy Diggy's story that he was bumming a ride from friends and didn't know what was in the car?"

"Actually, it's worse than that. He was running late for his court appearance and decided to hot-wire a car to get there on time. Once he got to the courthouse, he couldn't find a parking spot, so he parked in the sheriff's space. The sheriff pulls up, no doubt pissed that somebody's in his spot, and as he's walking around the car inspecting it, he notices that it's hot-wired. Believe it or not, the charges against Diggy had been dropped, but the minute he stepped up to the stolen car, he was surrounded by cops." Roxanne pressed her thumbs against the knot at the base of Jamal's neck that she could have sworn hadn't been there five minutes ago. "So, what do you think happens when an underage car thief does something that dumb?"

He gets his dumb ass arrested. Jamal brought a wet hand up to his face, but the gesture did nothing to wipe away his disappointment. By the standards of the societal majority, Diggy had behaved like an idiot. But he was using street logic, thug mentality. The only logic he knew. Running late, need a car, steal one.

Jamal sighed heavily. "So, what did he want? Bail money?"

"Of course."

Given the reality of the community they worked in, Hope Springs had a small fund earmarked for such things. But Diggy didn't exactly meet the criteria for getting any of it. And he did such a bonehead thing, Jamal would have a hard time persuading the legal aid committee to make an exception.

"I told Diggy to sit tight, then I called Richard Sharf and asked if he would handle this pro bono."

Jamal nodded. Dick Sharf was cool, one of the best defense lawyers in Maryland. The pro bono work probably eased his conscience about all the rich lowlifes he kept out of jail. "I'll holler at Diggy tomorrow," Jamal said. He was angry with the boy, so it would take all the restraint he had not to holler at him literally. "Where are they keeping him?"

"The Youth Residence Center over on Woodbourne."

"I'll stop by tomorrow before practice," he said.

From behind him, Roxanne put her arms around him. She leaned her face against his cheek, and he could smell the coconut Jojoba oil that she used on her dreads. "I'm sorry, sweetie, I know how much you like Diggy. But I have good news that might cheer you up."

"What is it?" Jamal asked.

"I'm late."

"For what?"

Roxanne rolled her eyes, and her lips smacked her exasperation. "I'm late, as in my Aunt Flo has not paid her monthly visit."

Aunt Flo, that was Roxanne's pet name for her period. Aunt Flo was late! The water splashed as Jamal tried to turn around to face her.

"For real?" he said.

She smiled into his eyes. "Yep, I could hardly believe it myself, that's why I didn't say anything. But now I'm a week late."

His woman never ceased to amaze him. She'd been sitting on this for a week? Excitement stirred within him, but he didn't want to give in to it. This could be a false alarm. But then again Roxanne had *never* come to him and said her period was late. You could set a clock by how regular it was. Every twenty-seven days. Jamal knew because getting her period was a source of distress now that they were trying to have a baby. Roxanne usually acted like it didn't bother her when her period started, but she couldn't fool him. He knew her. She'd become less talkative, her smiles more forced, her determination to focus on others more pronounced.

Proceed with caution, a little voice urged. "Have you been to the doctor yet?" he asked.

"No, but I did buy a home pregnancy test."

"And?" He held his breath and crossed his fingers beneath the bubbling water.

"And I haven't taken it yet. I was waiting for you to get home."

Jamal's breath came out in a whoosh. "Well, woman, I'm here. Let's go find out!" He gave her a hard kiss because he needed to do something with the bolt of excitement that coursed through him. He couldn't help himself. Roxanne seemed frozen into place. Her lips were smiling but uncertainty lurked in her eyes. Jamal rose from the water and said, "Go take the test. I'm right behind you."

Despite his presence at her side, Roxanne remained in a tight ball on the king-size bed, her back to him. Out of the darkness of an evening that had long since lost its light, Roxanne's voice came in a whisper. "I don't understand," she said. "I'm never late."

Jamal rubbed her silk-covered arm. "Roxanne, it will happen. It will happen."

"Will it?" she countered, the simple question loaded with doubt.

Jamal hesitated, not sure what she needed. Assurance? Commiseration? Lies? He decided on honesty. With a sigh he replied, "I don't know." He turned her to face him, wishing she could see into his eyes and witness the truth there. "Roxanne, I don't know. And you know something else, it doesn't matter to me how we get a child."

He felt her whole body tense and wondered what that meant. Jamal rubbed her back, hoping to comfort her in some way but feeling at a loss as to how to do it. "Roxanne, I called Dr. Samuels the other day. I think we should talk to her about adoption options. You know, it doesn't matter to me how we get a child."

He pressed a kiss along her jawbone. "It doesn't matter if the child is blood or not. Once it's here, we're gonna love it and raise it to be a decent human being, no matter what. And he or she will love you. How could the kid not? Everybody else does."

He felt a single, warm teardrop fall on his skin then as she kissed his hand. "You're sweet. Too good to me."

"Not nearly good enough," he countered.

"Why do you always say that?" she asked, her voice husky from held-back tears.

Jamal wished she would just go ahead and have a good cry. Disappointment pressed down on him, too, but he had to remain strong despite the weight. He was sad, upset for her but not crushed. Having their biological child meant more to Roxanne than it did to him. A child added to their happiness, but he pretty much had all he needed in her. A child was gravy. Dessert.

"Jamal, I know I need to get over this," she whispered so low, he had to lean forward to catch the words. "It's my problem."

"Our problem," he immediately contradicted.

He felt her head move back and forth across his arm. She was shaking her head in disagreement. "You always try to make things right for me. Just last year you bought me a Range Rover because you missed our pseudo-anniversary. And it wasn't your fault." The team had been stranded in Denver. "My birthday was that same week, and you had already gotten me extravagant gifts for that, too." Emerald earrings because green was her favorite color and a trip to Hawaii—after the season was over. "You always try to make things right for me. And I love you for it, but some things, you just can't fix. You do too much."

"None of that is enough, if you're still not happy," he said. "Baby, I hate to see you like this."

Seconds, minutes ticked by without a response from her. So Jamal just held her. Wondering what was going on in her head. In her heart. He could feel its furious beat under the hand that rested on her breast.

"Talk to me," he pleaded when he couldn't stand the silence anymore. He felt like his whole day had been filled with awkward pain and uncertainty. And he was sick of it.

"Jamal, I—"

The phone rang.

On the second ring, Roxanne said, "Please answer that. It could be important."

And this conversation wasn't? Her feelings weren't? "No way," Jamal replied through tight lips. Why did she always shut down rather than let him see a Roxanne who was less than full of joy and optimism? Did she think that was what he wanted?

The phone continued to blare. Who turned the damn answering machine off? he wondered.

"Jamal, would you please see who that is before I get a headache," Roxanne said, and then she rolled away from him. Again.

Jamal snatched the phone from the cradle, for once not stopping to check Caller ID. "What?" he barked.

His agent's voice came over the line. "Did I get you at a bad time?" Mark Krautheim asked.

"Yes," Jamal said.

"Fine. Just one question, then. Do you know a woman named Honey Brown?"

Jamal's free hand gripped the edge of the mattress. "Say that name again."

"Honey Brown. She's from Denver."

Jamal's eyes tried to find his wife in the darkness and the vast king-size bed. He saw only a small huddled lump. "Mark, hold on a minute." He tried to reach over for Roxanne, but she was as far from his side as the bed allowed. "Roxanne, I'm going to take this call in another room."

"That's fine. I feel a headache coming on."

That made two of them, Jamal thought as he got up from the bed. Once the door to the bedroom had closed behind him, he said, "OK, I'm back. You said her name was Honey Brown?"

Mark said, "Yeah, she called here asking for you. I tried to reach you before you left the clubhouse. Please, please tell me you don't know this woman."

A shiver went through Jamal, and it wasn't because he was standing in a drafty hallway wearing only boxer shorts. He leaned with his back against the wall and suddenly weak knees forced him to ease down the wall until he was sitting on the floor.

He wished to God he didn't know Honey Brown, but unfortunately he did.

Chapter

5

Jamal became tangled in his own thoughts as he listened to his agent explain why Honey Brown had made a sudden and unwelcome reappearance in his life. Just the mention of her name brought back memories and images and unanswered questions that he'd tried to block from his mind in the year since he'd seen her for the first and last time . . .

The pain in Jamal's left thigh had been a welcome distraction from the sight of the flapping breasts of the damn near naked woman who determinedly ground her pelvis into a much-abused metal pole that protruded from the raised dance platform. While his fellow teammates hooted, hollered, and begged for more, Jamal flexed and unflexed his leg, a move that didn't go unnoticed by Linc.

Linc raised an eyebrow, and over the wolf whistles, Jamal thought he mouthed, "Are you OK?" He couldn't be absolutely sure, because at that moment the stripper chose to demonstrate her flexibility by doing a standing leg split along the length of the pole. Jamal's lips twisted in amusement as the same men who had barely been able to drag themselves into the locker room after a beatdown by the Denver Stallions were now up on their feet, whooping and cheering with the enthusiasm of a flock of buzzards who had stumbled across a fresh carcass.

Jamal shook his head and reached for his glass of ginger ale.

The dancer sashayed her way over to the edge of the stage and dropped into an open leg squat right in front of the loudest of the bunch. Lingering, pinching, grasping hands filled the edge of her G-string with greenbacks, making Jamal thankful that he'd insisted they get a table as far away from the action as possible. God only knew why he let Linc convince him to come to this place. He would have been better off staying at the hotel. At least he could have been miserable in peace there.

Linc, one of the few men in the room who was still seated, grinned at Jamal. Linc had changed into a thick navy cable knit sweater and jeans for the three-block walk from the hotel to the club. Jamal's team parka was slung over the back of a nearby chair. Most of the small tables had a crowd of guys wedged around them, but there was only the two of them at this table. Earlier in the evening, Linc had complained that Jamal's sour disposition had scared off anybody who had tried to talk to him.

Jamal's foul mood had started when he had pulled up short after a twenty-yard dash into the end zone in the second quarter. Once he limped over to the sideline, the team trainer told him what he already knew, muscle spasms. Jamal's grip tightened around the three-dollar flat-tasting soda in his hand. The biggest game he'd had in five years, and he had come up gimpy. Muscle spasms were usually no big deal, but despite massages from the trainer both on the sidelines and in the locker room during halftime, his leg remained tight as a drawn bow. Denver had proceeded to crush them, and any hope for his first shot at a play-off game since he'd signed on in Baltimore.

"How's the leg?" Linc asked when the noise subsided to a low clamor.

"It hurts like hell," Jamal grumbled. "How's your butt?"

Their offensive line had pretty much rolled over and died at the sight of Denver's defense, and Linc's old record for being sacked was now a thing of the past. He had gone down six times, most of them hard. One hit had caused his mouthpiece to pop out, and Jamal swore the blow had reverberated all the way over to the sideline, where he was hobbling around.

Linc stared into his vodka tonic, then finally answered Jamal's question. "My ass is as sore as a new con's his first night in the joint."

Jamal grimaced at both the unpleasant image Linc's words brought to mind and at the ache in his thigh. Though he could walk on the leg, he kept getting these shooting sensations like someone was zapping him with a laser. "I get the picture," he said. "The Stallions ripped you a new one, huh?"

This hadn't been a great day for either of them. After a solid season, they'd been eliminated as a wild card berth from the play-offs, and then a blizzard had shut down the airport. There was no way any of them were gonna make it back to Baltimore tonight. So much for a "Happy Anniversary."

Linc waved a big hand in front of Jamal's face. "Ain't none of that allowed in here."

"None of what?" Jamal said, grabbing Linc by the wrist to shove his hand away.

"No moping around, feeling sorry for yourself. You thinking about Roxy, again?" It was more of a statement than a question.

"Is it that obvious?" Jamal said.

"Naw, not much," Linc said. "I mean just because you're the only guy in here who seems more interested in watching the ice in your glass melt than watching these fine honeys steam up the mirrors. Naw, it ain't obvious."

Jamal looked around the room. Muted lighting, clean tables. Gold bracelets and gold tassels edging the waitresses' butt-cheek-level costumes clinked and swayed as the women worked the room, taking drink orders. Golden asps circled the wrists of the topless woman etched on the damp napkin where his soda rested. Larger asps slithered among Egyptian hieroglyphics in expensive wallpaper. Cleopatra's Lair reminded him of Caesar's Palace minus the gambling. It seemed a decent place—for a strip club. Not that he'd had much experience with them. And nobody else but him seemed to be checking out the decor. All eyes and heads were straining toward the stage. Male mouths hung open like the beaks of hungry gigantic birds waiting for someone to drop a tasty worm in them.

Jamal gave a little laugh. "This is pathetic. Look at Jonesy over there," he said, referring to the three-hundred-pound offensive lineman, "Somebody ought to throw him a towel so he can wipe that drool off his chin, make that chins. He is acting like he ain't ever seen a woman before in his life. And we know that ain't true, 'cause he's got the three ex-wives to prove it."

As if he had heard Jamal talking about him, Jonesy did wipe at his face with a paw-like hand. Probably to stem the sweat that was pouring off him as one of the dancers eased into his lap. She positioned herself straddling one of Jonesy's knees and rubbed her crotch back and forth across his leg.

Linc laughed as Jonesy's eyes rolled back in his head. "What's wrong with a man enjoying himself?" Linc asked. "Jamal, you so whipped, it ain't even funny."

"My leg is killing me. We lost the big game. It's cold as a witch's you-know-what outside. And I want to be with my wife. Is there a law against a husband missing his wife? Especially on his anniversary?"

"Man, it ain't your anniversary," Linc scoffed. "Not your wedding anniversary, anyway. It's five years to the day that y'all met. That is not a legit day of celebration. I can't believe how Roxy has turned the Man of Steele into mush. If you ask me, I think Roxy was just looking for an excuse to get another present. Besides, her birthday was just two days ago."

How could he make Linc understand that Roxanne wasn't making him do anything for her? He *wanted* to. If a man hadn't been in love the way he was in love, he probably couldn't understand. "I just wish I had been able to see her . . . or at least talk to her today," Jamal said.

As usual, he'd been so hyped up before the game, he hadn't called, because seeing Roxanne or even hearing her voice made him soft. Messed with his concentration. Would have broken his focus. Cracked his game face. Then after the game, they kept missing each other's calls.

"Well, Roxy could have come, but she turned you down," Linc reminded him. "Apparently *she* can stand to be separated from you for seventy-two hours."

"Now, it wasn't like that and you know it." A major holiday party was being held for all the movers and shakers in the Baltimore area, and Roxanne needed to be there to drum up dollars for Hope Springs. When Roxanne had decided not to come out to Denver, it was because they thought they would have tonight. "If either of us had known this storm would keep me holed up here, I'm sure she would have been here. You know how sentimental Roxanne is . . ." Anyone who spent ten minutes with her soon learned what a hopeless romantic she was. Nothing but love, peace, and happiness for Roxanne. For her there were no clouds, just silver linings that needed a good washing to get rid of all that dark, gloomy stuff hovering around them.

Jamal had never been much of a romantic himself, but damn if Roxanne hadn't started to rub off on him. He nearly groaned his frustration, knowing that he was missing some good loving tonight, even though he wouldn't have been home until the middle of the night. She would have been waiting for him. And Roxanne went all out, sexually and otherwise, on special occasions. *Lucky me*. Just about every day was a special occasion according to Roxanne. Hell, one time she'd declared it "Jamal Came Home at 6:15 Day." And what a day *and* night it had been . . .

"Buddy, I'm losing you again." Linc's teasing voice pierced the sensual haze that caused Jamal's eyelids to grow heavy. He blinked and rubbed a hand over his closely shaven head. The pads of his thumbs brushed against the curve of his wire-rimmed glasses. Roxanne had helped him pick out the frames, said they made him look more like a college professor than a jock.

Leaning forward, elbows on the table, face above his knuckles, Jamal regarded Linc in silence. "How is it that a bunch of guys can show up in a strange town in the middle of the blizzard, yet still find the nearest titty bar?" Not really expecting an answer, he added, "Too bad we didn't have the same sense of direction when it came to finding the end zone this afternoon."

"You know, you're one ungrateful son of a gun. I brought you, no, dragged you here to cheer you up, and you're worse off than when we left the hotel."

"A brother can't help it."

"Maybe not, but do you think you're the only one who is disappointed? We stank to high heaven. Not even the thin air in Denver could disguise that."

"Yeah, well at least *you* finished the game."

"Just barely," Linc mumbled. "It ain't as easy as it used to be. There were a couple times today when I felt like playing possum. I was sorely tempted to lay on that ground until they whisked me away on a stretcher."

Jamal's eyes widened in surprise. Coming from Linc, this was a major confession. Linc was one tough competitor. The defense had to think twice when they came after him, because they were just as likely to get hurt as he was. But tough or not, Jamal knew exactly how Linc felt. At thirty-four, some people would say Linc was lucky to still be playing in the NFA at his "advanced" age.

For the first time all day, Jamal tried to put his own misery aside. The fast-ticking clock of an athlete's career was something they all lived with. And Linc, like Roxanne, was two years older than him. "It was brutal out there," he said. "How much longer do you think we got before they put us out to pasture?"

"Dunno, but one of the rookies keeps calling me sir."

Jamal laughed. "Sir? Damn, we're getting old. It's one thing to be called a veteran of the game, but sir? I'd say our days are numbered. So what are you gonna do when you hang up the old shoulder pads?"

Linc drained the last of his drink and slammed the glass on the table. "Man, don't start asking me questions I haven't begun to answer."

"Well, we better start thinking about it 'cause there ain't no Championship Bowl ring in our immediate future, and we won't have too many more opportunities to get one," Jamal warned.

Linc held up a hand signaling for a waitress. "I was supposed to be cheering you up. Now I'm depressed as hell. I need another drink, and this time I don't plan on drinking alone."

Jamal shrugged. What the hell, he might as well have a drink, too, he thought, as he gave the waitress his order. Maybe it would take his mind off the fact that he hadn't been able to reach Roxanne by phone to tell her the bad news. She had probably already left for that damn party. And what was the point in having a cell phone if she never turned the thing on? Jamal had been forced to leave a message on her voice mail.

Two dancers strutted onto the stage and did their stuff. They exited the stage with G-strings that were full of cash. Out of the blue, Linc said, "Man, Jamal, why did you have to mess with my mind?" Jamal gave him a puzzled look, which prompted him to add, "You know, talking about retirement and stuff when all I wanted to do was take our minds off the fact that we'll be watching the Cleveland Big Dawgs whup the Pittsburgh Panthers next week—in our living rooms and dens just like the rest of the country."

"Sorry," Jamal said, taking a gulp of his second bourbon and soda, or was it his third? His empty stomach churned from the punch of the alcohol. He was a lightweight when it came to drinking, and it didn't help that he had skipped dinner. Pain and disappointment had robbed him of his appetite. This would be his last drink of the night, or Linc would have to carry him out of here. And not because of his bum leg, either.

"At least you got Roxy and Hope Springs. What the hell am I gonna do? You, on the other hand, could go into the family business," Linc said.

The family business? Linc could forget that idea. Working with his father and older brother at one of the car dealerships his family owned was out of the question. Jamal didn't see himself as a salesman even if his degree had been in business. He also wasn't sure if full-time work at Hope Springs would satisfy him, either. But like Linc said, he did have Roxanne, and they'd figure something out together. He smiled at that thought.

A new song blared from a hidden speaker, and the strippers started doing some kind of ensemble number. One had on a leather mask, a dog chain around her neck, and was teasingly flicking a whip at the nicely rounded behind of a second woman. The singer was asking, "Do you think I'm a nasty girl?" If Jamal had to venture a guess, he'd say, "yes."

He blew out a long breath. *What am I doing here?* The women onstage could shake, shimmy, and simulate all the sexual positions in the book. But for him, it all came back to Roxanne. She was a sweet invasion that had spread through every nook and cranny of his life. In fact, looking at the insincere attempts at seduction going on in here made him think about how good it felt when Roxanne's arms would steal around him from behind. He closed his eyes and could almost feel her pulling him close, her face resting only a few inches above his waist because he was so much taller than she was. He could feel her warm breath against his skin and the little hitch of sound as she breathed him in.

"Hey, Chocolate Kiss, could I interest you in a private dance?"

He opened his eyes, and they fell upon a small, mysterious navel surrounded by a sea of smooth caramel-colored skin. A small triangle of gold metal connected to a chain that encircled her waist. His eyes traveled upward and were immediately mesmerized by the two slightly smaller triangles that by design did not cover her D-cup breasts. A slick covering of body glitter spread from her cleavage to her face.

Almond-shaped eyes smiled at him, as if they knew a secret he didn't.

"So how about it, Chocolate Kiss?" The words flowed from rich plum-tinted lips. She had a strong Southern accent.

"Huh?" Jamal said dumbly. The thin braids that stopped halfway down her back were fake—he found his gaze wandering over her again—but everything else seemed like the real deal.

"I said, are you interested in a private dance?"

Linc spoke for him. "Sorry, but you're looking at a married man."

"Happily married?" she asked, smiling. Her eyes were bold as they roamed over Jamal. They traveled up his jean-clad legs to the hunter-green turtleneck that stretched across a muscled chest and chiseled biceps, then finally rested on his face. There she studied the faint lines on his forehead, the alcohol-induced confusion in brown eyes with their thick sweep of lashes, and his strong jaw that was in need of a shave.

Noticing the predatory gleam in her eyes, Linc said, "Very happily married."

Jamal would have done it himself, but he seemed to have lost the power of speech. Hell, her stuff was right in his face. He tried to lean back in his chair, but it was already against the wall.

"Well, he don't look happy to me," she said. Her shapely figure came even closer, not stopping until she was knee to knee with Jamal. "I been watching you off and on all night. You look a little sad." She ran a hand over Jamal's scalp and said, "Tell you what, it's the end of the night and I'm feeling generous. This one's a freebie," she whispered as she took a seat on his lap.

Jamal made a choking noise when her warm, naked-except-for-a-G-string bottom made contact with his pant leg. It wasn't the muscle spasms that had him stumbling over his words. "Uh . . . that's very sweet of you but . . . I'm OK."

Ignoring him, she said, "My name is Honey. What's yours?" Her hands now began to stray over his chest. Sitting here thinking about Roxy, he'd already been getting kind of hard, but he didn't need the whole world to know. Dumping her off his lap wouldn't be right, either. Jamal looked past her to Linc for help. What the hell was he laughing at? Jamal wondered.

"Hey, sugar—" Linc began.

"Honey," she corrected him.

"Well, Honey, I'm feeling kind of blue myself, so if you're giving out free samples, I got a big old empty lap over here."

She tossed him a disbelieving smile. "You look perfectly fine to me."

"Honey, the same could be said about you," Linc drawled.

She laughed then. A knowing sound. Nothing girlish or innocent about it. Jamal was just about to politely ask her to get off him before those hands wandered any farther south, when Jonesy stumbled over to their table. The alcohol fumes leaking out of his pores reached them before he did.

"Hey, dudes," he said in a voice like the sound of crunching gravel, "the party's moving over to the hotel. My room."

"Is that right?" Honey said from her perch on Jamal's lap.

"Yeah, and y'all girls are the guests of honor."

"Well, all right then," Honey said, hopping up. "I'm there. We're closing early tonight anyhow. On account of the snow." Jonesy gave her the name of the hotel and his suite number.

Honey rewarded him by patting Jonesy's already red cheek. "It's closing time anyway. I'm gonna make myself more presentable, and I'll see y'all in a minute," she promised before sauntering away.

"Oh-oh, Jonesy, looks like you got yourself another admirer," Linc said.

A broad grin broke out over his homely face. "That's right. I gets more ass than a toilet." He gave them a cheeky salute, then stumbled his way over to the front door.

Linc said, "We better go after that fool. Did you notice that he didn't even have a coat on?"

Jamal hadn't noticed much of anything except feeling extremely relieved that Honey hadn't discovered his hard-on, and suddenly he was very sleepy. He stood up, surprised to find that he was not too steady on his feet. "Well, hurry up and get Jonesy's jacket. As soon as we get back to the hotel, I'm gonna crawl into my lonely bed and get some sleep."

"Didn't you hear what the man said, the party is moving to our hotel," Linc said.

"Well, I'm going to *my* room in *our* hotel, and taking my butt to bed. I'm beat."

"C'mon, Jamal, I'm wide awake. *And* depressed, thanks to you. Hang out with me and the fellows for a while." Before Jamal could say no again, Linc cut him off, "The cold air and the walk back to the hotel will wake you up. Just watch."

Jamal wasn't too sure about that. A couple more voices joined Linc's.

"Party won't be the same without ya."

"Yeah, Captain. You gotta stop by and help us drown our sorrows."

Jamal stared into the excited and persuasive faces of his teammates. *What the hell*? He was done arguing for the night. As one of the team captains, the least he could do was put in an appearance. He'd spend a few minutes with the fellows, then he was out. "Yo', Linc, remind me to call Roxanne when we get back to the hotel," he said, reaching for his parka.

Linc checked the watch on his wrist, "Man, it's two o'clock in the morning back East. You ain't getting me cussed out."

"But she's gonna be upset . . . I missed our anniversary."

"Listen, it's not your fault. You can't control the weather."

That was true, Jamal thought as he eased into his jacket.

"Besides," Linc added, "you know Roxy would forgive you for anything. Now zip your coat up. Roxy'll find some way to blame me if you come back home sick. Call her before we leave tomorrow."

A couple of the dancers were already huddled by the entrance when they got there. The one named Honey stepped up to him and linked arms with him. Jamal was grateful for the support because between his aching leg and the bourbon, he wouldn't be surprised if he fell flat on his face. As they walked arm and arm out into the snowy night, Jamal thought Linc was right. No point in waking up Roxanne. It was already tomorrow. He'd see her beautiful face in a few hours.

Chapter

6

Jamal should have seen it coming. Should have expected it. Now he didn't have time to duck. No time to brace himself. Linc's flying fist caught him square on the jaw and sent him staggering backward. His legs crashed into the end of Linc's coffee table, then the back of his knees buckled as they slammed into the ottoman in front of a leather armchair. He was airborne for a millisecond and then felt his body hit the chair itself.

Gratefully, Jamal let himself sink into it. He put a hand to his face then worked his jaw a couple of times to make sure it wasn't broken. All the while he kept a wary eye on Linc, who had apparently followed his path across the room and from the venom in his eyes, might not be through with him yet.

He had come here to get help. Not to get his ass kicked—even if he deserved it. "Linc," he said, hoping he didn't sound like a whiny punk, despite feeling like one. "You got to let me explain."

"Explain!" Linc roared. "You come in here. Tell me you knocked up some stripper. What's to explain? It doesn't get any clearer than that."

"I didn't knock her up . . ." Jamal stopped, and then shook his head. "I mean, I don't think I did . . . I don't even know what happened. I don't remember . . ."

"So what do you remember?" Linc asked, but it sounded like a dare, and he still towered over him with clenched fists. No doubt ready to clean his clock again, if he didn't like what he heard. The sad part was, he probably wouldn't try to defend himself. Still, Jamal felt scorched by the waves of anger coming from the man who up until five minutes ago had been his best friend in the world. He and Linc had never had any beef with each other. Not even about how things went down on the football field. The only time Linc had threatened Jamal in any way was when he first started dating Roxanne, and even then he'd been kidding. Or at least half kidding, when he warned Jamal not to hurt Roxanne. Now he was not kidding at all, if his still-balled fists were anything to go by.

Despite swallowing several times, Jamal found it impossible to clear his throat. He forced himself to tell Linc what he could. "So after we got back to the hotel, I had one more drink . . . nonalcoholic this time. I hung out in Jonesy's suite for, what, like, fifteen . . . twenty minutes. And Honey and a few other girls were there. She sat on my lap and all, but I wasn't touching her. In fact, I asked her to get up because my leg was hurting. Remember? That's when I decided to go to bed. I went back to my room and took a muscle relaxant. Next thing I know I wake up, it's the next morning and this woman Honey is in my bed . . . with . . . no clothes on."

"And you don't remember anything from the time you went to your room to the time you woke up?" Linc asked. The look Linc gave him was full of skepticism.

Jamal knew his memory loss claim sounded shady even to his own ears. How would it sound to Roxanne? "I swear, Linc, I took the muscle relaxant and I was out of it. You have to remember I had had a couple of drinks on top of that, and I hadn't eaten dinner and I was dead tired. I don't even remember letting anyone into the room." Jamal braved a glance in his friend's direction. "God, how could I have made such a series of bad choices? One after the other." He was surprised Linc had not reminded him of that himself.

Not interested in Jamal's pity party, Linc asked, "So what did you do when you woke up?"

Jamal was too embarrassed and too smart to admit that at first he had snuggled up to the warm feminine bundle tangled in his sheets. He didn't want Linc coming after him again. But he truly *had* thought it was Roxanne lying there beside him. Just for a moment. Then it had slowly dawned on his waking mind that the feel of the body, the smell of the skin, and the texture of the hair brushing his chest were all wrong. "I jumped out of bed. Put some clothes on. Got her up. Called for a cab and sent her on her way."

"Without talking to her?"

"I panicked. She was naked and I was naked." Not that that necessarily meant anything. He always slept in the nude. He couldn't speak for Honey. Of course, she didn't come to the hotel carrying an overnight bag. But that still did not explain why she had hopped into his bed without a stitch of clothing on. Not even panties and a bra for crying out loud.

Jamal couldn't meet Linc's eyes. Instead, he muttered, "I wasn't interested in getting a blow-by-blow—" He winced at his choice of words. Sure, Honey had tried to rehash, talking about how she had enjoyed the night before. But he hadn't wanted to hear it. Jamal could count on one hand the number of one-night stands he'd had, and that had been back in his college days. He'd never been proud of himself after the fact and had a hard time facing whoever it was. And this time in particular, he'd felt lower than low. On most road trips, he usually shared a room with one of the other guys. But this time Roxanne was supposed to have been his roommate. Instead, he'd ended up with a room to himself, a king-size bed, and a naked woman who was not his wife. Everything would have turned out so differently if Roxanne had been able to join him as planned or if they had been able to get the hell out of Denver before the snowstorm. "If only," famous last words.

"Linc, I just wanted her out my room before you or somebody else found her in there. I don't know for sure what happened. And to be honest, I didn't want to know. Whatever happened . . . it didn't mean anything. Or at least it hadn't until I got that phone call from Mark."

Linc leaned back against the couch, the back of his head cradled in his hands, elbows askew. He expelled a long breath. "Do you realize what this is going to do to Roxy?"

"Of course, I realize." He gave Linc his props. He and Roxanne went way back, but even Linc didn't know her like he did. Inside and out. Jamal noticed every smile that didn't ring true. He recalled the nights when she'd creep out of bed, thinking he was still asleep. He could hear her moving around in the adjoining room that was to be the nursery *when and if* they ever had a baby. Oh yeah, he knew better than anybody, including Linc and that close-knit group of sister-friends of hers, what this would do to Roxanne. "It would kill her," he told Linc with quiet certainty.

Linc looked stunned then confused and then said, "That's wack! What are you trying to say? That she'd get all suicidal? Have a nervous breakdown or something?" He scoffed at the idea, "No way. Don't flatter yourself. Roxy is a lot stronger than that."

Spoken as a matter of fact, but a question, a sliver of doubt lingered in the troubled and still angry eyes that bored into Jamal's.

"No, Roxanne would not kill herself, at least not in the way you're talking about. But this would break her. She'd paste on one of those fake smiles she wears so well when she is hurting, and she would seek out a person or project that she felt needed more attention than she did. And she'd give and give until it wore her out. Until it numbed her out. Before long every smile would be forced and every laugh would ring hollow. Because she'd be dead inside. And that's not Roxanne."

Behind Linc's eyes, Jamal could see him searching through the vast collection of memories that made up the long friendship he and Roxanne shared. And when their eyes met again, Jamal knew that Linc had remembered the cover-up behavior he was talking about. Roxanne's front. ". . . and she'd become quiet, into herself, and she would leave me quicker than a ice cube melts on hot cement."

"C'mon, Roxanne would never leave you. She loves you. And everybody knows that you worship the ground she walks on. She'll realize you had a slip. You weren't in your right mind—"

On this Linc was dead wrong. Jamal shook his head. "She will leave me, and this news will shake her to the core. I'm just not sure which would come first. If this Honey woman is on the up and up, everything, the entire story will come down to one fact for Roxanne: I have a child with another woman. I made a baby with another woman when we couldn't make one together." Jamal swung away from Linc's eyes to stare unseeing out the window, past the balcony. The magnificence of the yellow-orange orb melding into indigo blue waters of the Inner Harbor was completely lost on him. But he couldn't bear to focus too much on the contents of Linc's condo.

Roxanne's presence was everywhere. She had helped Linc locate and purchase the three-bedroom condominium in the first place. She picked out the leather furniture, the African sculptures, and original paintings on the wall. She was the one who loved being near large bodies of water, and therefore had insisted that Linc should live on the top floor of the luxury high-rise so that he would have the best view. So, he had turned to the view to blot everything else out, to find some peace. He was kidding himself. Nothing could take his mind off of Roxanne and the potential damage to his marriage.

Jamal wasn't sure how long he stared into nothingness. Eventually, he turned back to face his friend. "How am I supposed to tell a woman who has never had a reliable, trustworthy man in her entire life that I *might* have cheated on her?" Her last boyfriend, Marcus, had messed with her mind. He was inattentive, critical, and in the end opted for a white woman. Roxanne couldn't even remember her real father. He had walked out on his kids so long ago. And though her mother had paraded a variety of father substitutes through Roxanne's life, eventually all of them left. And their presence had done more harm than good. Roxanne had learned not to open her heart to men because they would only leave her.

Oh, she was friendly with men, with everyone really. But Linc was her only male friend. Jamal suspected she and Linc were still tight because she'd known him forever, long before men had started breaking her heart. It didn't hurt that Linc had been such a player in high school. Roxanne wouldn't have let her tender, romantic heart within miles of that. By the time Jamal met her, the door to her heart had been firmly closed from the inside out.

Even though she kept him at arm's length, there were little things about her that made Jamal refuse to believe she had thrown away the key to her heart. For one, romance novels lined the shelves in her tiny one-bedroom apartment. And he'd witnessed how she was a bright beacon that drew out secrets and soothed weary spirits with all her volunteer work. She was capable of being open—just not with him. She learned the game of football so she could understand what his job meant to him. She laughed at his corny jokes. Made love with him until he was delirious. But still, she held back. She dismissed his attempts to talk about love and forever, yet he was convinced that in her heart that's exactly what she wanted. She was just afraid to believe it could happen.

So he set out to woo her. He'd never had to woo a woman in his life. His friends thought he was crazy. But he didn't care. He had been on a mission to show Roxanne what true love was. He had been determined to wear her down, to win her trust. And he had. Now this. One major error in judgment could ruin everything.

He blew out a long sigh. "How am I supposed to tell my wife, a woman who has been agonizing over having a baby for two years, that I have a child with someone else? How can I tell her something like that when is she is just now considering the possibility of adoption and viewing *that* as a sign of personal failure?" Jamal could hear his voice cracking, hear the fear in every word he uttered. "It would break her heart. And probably doom our marriage. I can't do it." He dropped his head and stared helplessly at clasped hands that dangled between his legs.

He heard Linc move, then Jamal felt a hand on his shoulder. A strong squeeze between his shoulder blades, the first bit of comfort he'd felt since his conversation with his agent the day before.

"I know," Linc said. "I know." Linc's other hand reached down, grasping him, pulling Jamal out of his chair, reminding him of the many times they hauled each other off the turf when some defensive play had upended them.

Jamal stood before his closest friend outside of Roxanne and said, "You gotta help me, Linc."

"I will. I'll do everything I can to help you both," Linc promised, before enveloping him in a quick, masculine embrace that, despite its brevity, erased some of the burden that wore on Jamal.

They began to make a plan.

Jamal removed the ice pack from his jaw, which Linc silently passed to him at some point in the discussion. It was a peace offering of sorts. "Do you really think it's possible that nothing happened between me and . . . and Honey?" Jamal knew it was ridiculous, but even saying her name made him feel like they had shared some intimacy that he could not remember—and certainly did not feel.

Now that he felt he had someone on his side, he was starting to think more clearly. He only had Honey's word for it that something had happened. Regret pierced him. If only he had let her talk that morning, instead of allowing his guilt and confusion to make him hustle her out of the hotel and hopefully out of his life. She might have said something that clued him in.

Linc rubbed his chin. Thinking aloud he mused, "If you were as out of it as you say you were—"

"I swear, Linc, man, I was. You know my tolerance for booze is about zero."

Linc smiled. Jamal had taken a lot of flake about drinking like an old lady by some of his teammates. They called him a teetotaler. A lightweight.

"I believe you, Jamal. We're on the same side now. I was just wondering if you were in any condition to have sex if you were, as they say, 'tore up from the floor up.' "

Jamal hadn't even thought about that, and the possibility cheered him up considerably. "God, I hope that's what happened. I hope she's lying."

"Could very well be," Linc said. "And remember, my brother, this is America. Innocent until proven guilty."

Historically, that axiom had not meant much to a black man, but Jamal was willing to cling to any thread of hope, no matter how slender.

"So the first thing we got to do is get a paternity test," Linc said. "And you don't say anything to Roxanne until we get the results."

"Right," Jamal agreed. Then he told Linc how disappointed Roxanne had been the night before when she found out that she was not pregnant. "She's really shaky right now. Even without this paternity crap. I really want to wait before I say anything." Jamal knew that he might be postponing the inevitable, but prayed that he would never have to tell Roxanne anything about what happened in Denver. "Let's spare Roxanne any unnecessary upset. She doesn't need this kind of grief," he said. But it was the fear that his marriage could not survive an infidelity that most influenced his decision to keep his mouth shut. For now.

When Jamal got home that night, Roxanne was already in bed. She was reading one of those trashy historical romances she loved. It didn't surprise him that she was so engrossed she hadn't heard him come in. Besides, he'd been trying to be quiet just in case she was asleep. Jamal hesitated in the threshold of the bedroom, not sure what kind of reception he would get. They had barely spoken more than two words all day, including when he came over to the Center after practice. She had put him to work helping kids who had brought in homework, but always seemed to find something else for herself to do that took her away from him. He must have stood there for five minutes before she felt his presence. Rather than being surprised or startled, she put the book down and held her arms out to him. He crawled over the big bed until he could sink into her arms. The place where he felt most at home.

When he pulled back, she touched his cheek and said, "What happened to your face?"

"Linc decked me." He had put in a few hours at the Center, and then he told her he was meeting Linc for a basketball game.

Roxanne laughed softly. "I thought you two were supposed to be on the same team."

Jamal ruefully rubbed his cheek. "We are . . . now," he murmured. Before she could ask what he meant, Jamal leaned in for the kiss he knew was coming. Roxanne had this thing about kissing his various bumps and bruises to make them feel better. Her head came to rest on his chest, making him wish she would kiss him there. Perhaps she could kiss away the pain that was weighing down his heart.

Instead he gently rearranged the springy ropes of her hair. She whispered against his chest, "I'm sorry for acting like such a witch yesterday."

"You weren't a witch. It was only natural to feel disappointed, Roxanne."

"It's just . . . just . . . you know, how I am. I just want everything to be perfect."

He held her tighter to him, could feel tears burning the back of his eyes and a lump forming in his throat. His hand cupped the sides of her face. "Nothing is perfect, Roxanne," he told her, hoping she could see into his heart, to his very soul. Could she see how very sorry he was for any pain he might cause her down the line?

But instead, she shook her head. "That's not true," she refuted. "You're perfect."

The lie was uttered with such absolute conviction, Jamal had to close his eyes in the face of it.

Chapter

7

Jamal found it impossible to sit still. He paced the length of the small conference room where he was meeting with Mark, his agent and lawyer, the private detective Mark had hired, and a rep from the genetics firm that would be doing the paternity testing. Mark's office was in Manhattan, but he'd flown down to Baltimore as soon as he could rearrange his schedule. Linc was here, too. Jamal didn't have to look his way to know that Linc's eyes were on him.

He'd like to think that Linc was here to provide moral support, but he mostly wanted to know what was going down because he was looking out for Roxanne's best interest. Linc didn't seem to believe that Roxanne's welfare was his top priority, too. It stung that Linc didn't trust his judgment anymore. Though Linc was standing by him—sort of—it would be a long time before his best friend forgave him for messing up so badly.

"Jamal, do you think you could stop wearing a hole in the carpet and get over here," Mark said with a Jersey accent. In his late thirties and balding, Mark had the beginnings of a middle-age spread that was well hidden beneath his two-thousand-dollar suit and Hugo Boss tie. At six-five, tipping the scales at somewhere between two-thirty and two-forty, Mark had been a college football player himself. At Notre Dame. But he'd learned early on that his powers of persuasion and charm were a lot stronger and more lucrative than his physical strength. His slightly homely face carried an easy smile. Behind tortoiseshell frames, though, his brown eyes were alert and assessing. No doubt he had everybody in the room's number. Mark didn't acquire the roster of superstars and up-and-coming talent by being a fool.

His long legs were stretched out in front of him, his head cradled in the big mitt made by his two hands laced together. He was totally at ease. And why wouldn't he be? It was not his marriage and his reputation on the line. And this was not the first time he'd had to clean up after his clients' fun and games got out of hand.

It made Jamal sick to his stomach to be lumped in the same category as some of his fellow athletes and entertainers. *They* would hump anything that moved—and some things that didn't. He'd never been busted on drug charges or for soliciting a hooker or for having sex with a minor. No one had ever accused him of rape or had to bail him out of jail after a drunken bar brawl. He was an honest-to-goodness Boy Scout and had the merit badges to prove it. His face clouded over as reality set in. If his record was so clean, why was he holed up in a hotel suite with a private eye, his lawyer, a genetics lab employee, and a best friend who was looking at him like he was week-old dog shit?

Jamal swallowed the sour taste that had filled his mouth. With heavy feet and drooping shoulders, he took a seat next to the private detective.

"All right, folks, here's the bottom line," Mark said, taking charge of the meeting, "Miss Honey Brown claims Jamal fathered her child. Jamal claims he didn't, but because he was under the influence of alcohol and prescription medication"—Jamal winced. Described that way, his behavior was just plain irresponsible— "when he met the woman. For that same reason, he's not one hundred percent sure what took place during their encounter." He paused to push a manila folder in Jamal's direction.

Jamal's hand hesitated for a moment, and then he opened it up.

"Here's a dossier on Miss Brown," Mark said. "Charlie, why don't you take it from here," he said, turning to the private detective.

"Charlie" turned out to be a girl-next-door type in her early forties. With a natural blush on her cheeks, her rounded face, shining eyes, and short mop of curly brown hair, she would look more at home at a PTA bake sale rather than investigating greasy personal cases like his. But apparently she and Mark had worked together many times before. It wasn't that Jamal felt a woman couldn't do a good job, but Charlie just didn't fit with his TV-fed image of a private eye: middle-age white male, crumpled raincoat, slightly sleazy but shrewd and methodical in his pursuit of the truth. If Charlie possessed the last trait alone, he'd be satisfied.

Though most of the information was contained in the written report Mark had passed to him, Charlie summarized the key facts. "The subject is a twenty-six-year-old never-married black female. Some minor trouble with the law in her teens—shoplifting, truancy, a chronic runaway. Not that I can blame her for running away. From some reports filed by child protective services, sounds like her mom's boyfriend was molesting her, and there are a few reports of domestic violence on record as well." She paused to catch her breath, and then added, "No other children besides Jamal Steele Brown. Born August 14 of this year."

Jamal groaned aloud. This was bad. She'd named the kid after him? Linc's expression was grim as he absorbed this news.

Grasping for straws, Jamal asked, "What about the time frame? Does it fit? The game against the Stallions was back in December." He knew this because it was all he had been thinking about since he had gotten the call from Mark.

"I'm afraid it does, my friend," Mark said, shaking his head. "Little Jamal was born a few weeks early, but it's close enough."

Both hope and desperation drove Jamal to demand, "What do you mean close enough? Doesn't it take nine months to have baby? Either it was nine months or it wasn't." He leaned forward, and his fingers curled around the edge of the table as he waited for a response.

Charlie clarified for him. "Mr. Steele, it was around eight months, but Miss Brown allowed us access to her medical records and indeed the baby was a bit premature."

The hope that had begun to well within him fizzled just as quickly, leaving him as flat as day-old beer.

Seeing Jamal's deflated expression, Linc said, "That still doesn't mean it's Jamal's baby. Hell, the woman's a stripper, not a Sunday-school teacher. It was around Christmastime; maybe she was spreading a little Christmas cheer to a whole lot of other guys. Maybe one of them is the baby's daddy."

"We did a very thorough investigation, and the last relationship Miss Brown had been involved in had ended several months prior to her . . . her making Mr. Steele's acquaintance." Charlie replied calmly, determined to stick to the facts rather than speculation like the men around her.

Linc snorted in disgust. "Did I say anything about a relationship? I remember this woman, and she was not shy. If she had a one-night stand with Jamal, whose to say she didn't have a one-nighter with a thousand other guys."

Jamal looked down at where his fingers gripped the edge of the table and forced himself to loosen them. He didn't even want to think about who or how many men Honey might have slept with. A still-furious Linc had reminded him of that. And he was already scheduled for an HIV test with a doctor friend of his who was willing to do it anonymously. He ran a shaky hand from his forehead to the nape of his neck and felt the bones in his neck crack one by one as he moved it from side to side. First a baby to worry about, and now the possibility that he had exposed Roxanne to a sexually transmitted disease. In this day and age, penicillin couldn't fix everything. AIDS was a matter of life and death. And while herpes didn't kill you, it stopped by for a visit and took up permanent residence.

If only he'd gotten tested after he returned from Denver. But back then he'd convinced himself that nothing had happened. *But what if it had? What if that was the reason Roxanne couldn't conceive?*

Come on, Jamal, he said, trying to be his own voice of reason. Roxanne was having trouble conceiving long before last December. Still, there was the chance he could have passed something on to her. Expelling a long breath, he tried to hold on to hope. After all, they'd both had so many medical tests and exams over the past year, surely something would have turned up if STDs were a problem. He prayed that wasn't the case, because he would never forgive himself if he'd somehow put Roxanne's health at risk.

Jamal stared at the glossy eight by ten of Honey Brown. She

wore only a thong bikini and a mane of waist-length hair exten-
sions. It looked like an appropriate publicity shot for someone in
her line of work. Some kind of gold rope weaved throughout her
hair. Her skin was tight and flawless. No panty hose, just some
kind of shiny all-over body lotion. Finally, he allowed himself to
study her face. She wasn't what you'd call pretty. Her eyes and
smile were confident and knowing. The kind of smile that could
get a man to do things he normally wouldn't do.

Jamal found himself fixated on the picture. Even in a photo,
Honey Brown had an undeniable sexiness. God help him for even
thinking it, but she was fine. *There is no way in hell I could have
sex with a woman like her and not remember it. It couldn't have
happened. Could it?* A skeptical voice crept up out of nowhere.

"So because there's some doubt, it's prudent that we establish
paternity, and then we can proceed from there." Mark's voice
spared Jamal from more anxiety-provoking speculation. "That's
where Genetrack Labs comes in."

Up until this point he hadn't paid the fourth man in the room
much attention. Jamal focused on him now. He couldn't even
remember his full name. Ricardo Something-Or-Other. Despite the
Spanish-sounding name, he looked Asian. About Jamal's height
and age and a neutral expression on his cratered face.

"What's does the paternity testing involve? What do I need to
do?" Jamal said. "I can't go on living in limbo." If the child *were*
his, of course, he would do right by him. Financially to start. He
wasn't sure what kind of father-son relationship he was prepared
to offer. Roxanne would not hold his desire to be a father to his
son against him. It was having sex with the child's mother that she
might not be able to forgive.

Ricardo explained that since it was a "routine" paternity test—
not that Jamal saw anything routine about it—samples would be
collected from him, Honey, and the baby. Although a sample from
Honey was not really necessary, they wanted to establish maternity
as well. Ricardo suggested that blood samples rather than buccal
swabs from inside the mouth be used because the saliva in the
mouth didn't always yield a sufficient amount of DNA.

"Fine," Jamal said, rolling up his shirtsleeve. "You can draw
my blood right now."

At this point Ricardo looked from Jamal to Mark.

"Well," Mark said, "there's one little snag."

"What snag?" Linc demanded, his eyes narrowing. "The man agreed to take the test, what's the problem."

Mark took it from there. "I spoke with Miss Brown over the phone and gave her the name of a clinic in her area that provides specimen collection services for Genetrack. And she had a problem with that."

"What kind of problem?" Jamal asked. "You would think that she more than anyone would want to get this settled."

"Not if you ain't the father," Linc offered.

Jamal tried to tune that prospect out. He didn't want to get his hopes up. From here on out, he only intended to respond to cold, hard facts. Ever since hearing the news, his emotions had been on an out-of-control roller-coaster ride that showed no signs of stopping. So, he'd have to take steps to put the brakes on himself. "How exactly is that a problem? She has to know we'll pay all the expenses for the testing or any transportation costs."

"She thinks we're going to tamper with the results. Actually, she doesn't even believe that you'll be the one to provide the sample."

"What!" Even if he didn't want this child to be his, did the woman really think that he would deny his own son? Jamal wondered. He struggled to check his indignation. Once he calmed down, Jamal reminded himself of Honey's history with men from her mother's boyfriend to the lowlifes she undoubtedly met on the job. Of course, she didn't trust him. And he didn't trust her, either. This was a F-ed-up situation. "So what does she propose we do?"

"She wants you to come to Denver, so that all three of you can be tested together."

Jamal was already shaking his head. "No. Uh-huh, no way."

"Her request really isn't so unusual," Ricardo hastened to assure him. "In fact, my company usually recommends that the samples be collected at the same time and in the same place from all parties involved. We generally take a Polaroid and thumbprint of all the parties at the time of sample collection. That way there is less room for error and less room for anyone to accuse the other of fudging the results."

"That's all well and good," Jamal said, "but we're in the middle of the football season. How the hell am I supposed to just take off for a day or two? It's impossible."

"We could always fly Miss Brown and the baby here," Mark suggested.

Sweat broke out on his back and forehead at the mere thought of that. If Jamal had his way, he'd want to keep the width of the country between his wife and Honey Brown. And for all his internal conversations about taking care of his child, for some reason seeing the boy in the flesh scared him spitless. Made him real. Up until now he was just a hypothetical. "How the hell is that gonna work?" Jamal said, his voice sounding shrill to his own ears. "This is my hometown. People know me. I can't just go waltzing into a clinic with a woman who is not my wife and her child, and announce that we're there for a paternity test."

Linc grabbed him by the shoulders, as if he feared Jamal would bolt from the room. And with his speed, they'd never catch him. "Man, calm down," he advised. "You were just about to get tested in the privacy of this conference room not five minutes ago. I'm sure you won't have to go to a public place to do it."

Ricardo nodded his agreement.

Feeling relieved, Jamal allowed some of the tension to leave his body.

"Listen to your bud," Mark said, "He's right. We've given samples on the q.t., a thousand times. So relax. Ya got nothing to worry about."

Rather than be reassured, Jamal felt sick to his stomach. Mark might have sat in on a private paternity test or set one up a thousand times. But he didn't know what the hell he was talking about when he said there was nothing to worry about. Jamal was worried about his entire world—Roxanne, his marriage, his career—being turned upside down.

Jamal swatted Roxanne on the behind with a towel as she climbed aboard the elliptical trainer. Their home gym consisted mostly of weight-training equipment: free weights, a mini-circuit training set. He'd gotten the elliptical cross trainer because it was kinder to his knees than an old-fashioned stepper. The treadmill was good for interval training, but he hardly ever used it. Why run inside when he could enjoy the fresh air and watch the scenery passing by?

"Ouch, cut it out," she cried, pretending to be annoyed. "This is serious business." Then she scrunched up her face and stared in confusion at all the buttons on the panel before her. When she glanced his way, Jamal tried to hide a smile. "Roxanne, you really don't have to do this," he said. "I know you hate exercising."

She rolled her eyes and slowly began pressing buttons to set up her workout. "I do not *hate* exercising," she said. "I just don't have time for it." This time he was the one making faces. Responding to his disbelieving look, she added, "Besides, I usually get all the exercise I need chasing after kids, tracking down grant money, and roping volunteers for Hope Springs. I know you're the Man of Steele and all, but I ain't that out of shape. A little exercise won't kill me." She hoped. "I'm just trying to spend a little time with my man." She cocked her head to one side. "You got a problem with that?" The machine started to hum as she pressed down on the footholds.

Actually, he did have a problem with it. How was he supposed to concentrate when she was bobbing up and down in nothing but a sports bra and a pair of spandex drawers? She claimed they were shorts. If so, they were the shortest shorts he'd ever seen. But she did look damn fine in them. And that was just the problem. With Roxanne around, he could easily spend most of the workout drooling over her. Instead, he forced himself to move over to the closet and pull out his weight belt.

When he turned around, he noticed Roxanne had been staring at him, too. They both were crazy. "Can't take your eyes off of me, huh?"

"Nope," she freely admitted. "Actually, I've barely seen you all week. And the team will be out in San Francisco this weekend, so I figured I better get an eyeful while I could."

Jamal's fingers fumbled where he tried to cinch the belt around his waist. He looked down, pretending to look for the belt hole but in actuality he didn't want her to see the guilt in his eyes. "Yeah, it's been a hectic week," he mumbled. No busier than usual in terms of work, but he needed something to distract him from the stuff Honey Brown had thrown at him. He was spending more time than usual at the clubhouse. He had been a slightly unwelcome guest at Linc's every day this week. His wife knew him so well, he was afraid that she'd pick up on something, a troubled or distracted expression or lack of his usual energy. And he was feeling tired, this waiting to find out about his fate was downright exhausting. But Honey and the baby were flying in today. They'd all take the test tomorrow.

A part of him wished tomorrow would never come. That he could just turn back the clock. That he'd never gone to that strip club. He especially wished he'd never combined alcohol and medication. But wishing for things wouldn't make them so. Now he'd just have to deal with tomorrow. But not today. Maybe he'd take Roxanne out on the town tonight. She deserved it. He had done a disappearing act ever since this paternity stuff came up. If the paternity thing went down the wrong way, it might be the last pleasant memory his wife had of him.

He walked over to a row of barbell poles lined up against the wall, trying not to think the worst. He picked out a short curled one. He'd work on biceps today. After he loaded it up with weights, he stood in front of the mirror and began doing curls.

"What are you doing?" Roxanne asked.

"I would have thought that was obvious," he said, grunting from the exertion of lifting and talking at the same time.

"I mean, what are you doing over there? You're supposed to be over here talking to me."

"Am I not talking to you right now?" he said, pausing to hold the bar before slowly lowering it.

"Don't get smart, Jamal. I'm not working up a sweat for nothing. You better turn around and talk to me. Don't make me get off this machine," she warned.

Jamal gave a little laugh, and he did turn around. With the curl bar still in his hands, he walked over until he stood directly in front of her. Roxanne took her hands off the side rails long enough to push the hair off her face. There was a slight sheen to her skin, and her breathing was a little faster than normal.

He grinned. "You know you *want* to get off that machine. In fact, you're dying to get off that machine. So, don't go trying to blame it on me."

"Blame you?" she scoffed. "I was just trying to get your attention. That's all."

"You always have my attention."

Then all the teasing drained from her face. She shook her head. "Not lately."

He opened his mouth to deny it and then closed it. She continued to press the pedals and patiently wait for his response.

He looked at her and then sat the weights on the floor in front of him. He wasn't getting anything done anyhow. "Baby, I'm sorry. It's just that this season is so important to me. For the first time, everything I've ever dreamed of seems within reach." She thought he was talking about football. If she only knew. He rubbed a hand across his chin. "I guess it's just making me worried. I'm feeling a lot of pressure. I don't want to blow everything."

The machine came to an abrupt halt. Roxanne had hit the stop button. She gave her face a quick wipe and then stepped off. She circumvented the barbell until she stood too-to-toe with him. She had to crane her neck up to meet his eyes. "So talk to me," she invited. "That's what I'm here for. Your troubles are mine."

He put a hand to the back of her head and pulled her close for an embrace. He felt like crying. *Your troubles are mine.* She didn't know how close to the truth she was. His hands stroked her hair. He couldn't believe it, but his hands were shaking. Maybe if he kept them in motion, Roxanne wouldn't notice. Her arms came up around him, holding him close.

"So tell me. What's been keeping you up at night?" she urged.

"The future."

"The future? Say more," she encouraged.

"I just want to make the next few months as perfect as possible. I don't want to cheat the team. I don't want to shortchange you. I know I've been slacking at Hope Springs."

She pulled away, forcing him to meet her eyes. "Hope Springs? Sweetie, let that be the least of your worries. I understand how important these next few years of football are to you. We have the rest of our lives to develop Hope Springs. As for shortchanging me, I just want to know what's on your mind—"

"But what about the baby?" he said, abruptly switching gears.

"I'm still hopeful. I've been praying," she admitted. Her smile was sad as she added, "But I can't make a baby all by myself." There was a question in her eye. And he hated himself for putting it there. He hadn't attempted to touch her in the past week or so. At least not with sex on his mind. He'd kissed her, held her, but that was as far as it went. He hadn't had an appetite for anything, including food, sex, or laughter. Now she was thinking his physical and emotional distance was about her.

"I'm sorry," he said. "I know I haven't been a very good husband lately."

"It be like that sometimes," she quipped. She squeezed his hand. "I understand. I just wanted to make sure we're OK. I know you want me to start considering other options like fertility treatments and adoption. And I have."

"You have?" he said, unable to hide his surprise. They hadn't talked much about it since the false alarm with the pregnancy test.

"Yes," she said. "As much as I would like to have a baby the old-fashioned way. You. Me. Engaged in the horizontal tango. I've come to accept that there are other ways."

"And?"

"And I think I've been idealistic and stubborn. And that it needs to stop."

He kissed the top of her head. "But I like your idealism. The stubbornness can be kind of cute, too."

"Not this time. We need to move on. This fixation on getting pregnant has been taking up a lot of emotional energy. It's energy that neither of us has to spare." When he would have contradicted her, she put a finger to his lips. "No really, it's time. So I've been thinking adoption will be the way to go. We could undergo fertility treatments, but that's just being selfish. It can be time-consuming and expensive. And, frankly, I don't know if I could handle it if it didn't work."

"Roxanne, I don't care about the money," he hastened to reassure her.

"But I do. And it's not necessary. Not when there are plenty of kids already born who are in need of . . . love." She was smiling, but Jamal saw that she could not contain the tears that leaked from her eyes. He cupped her face with his hands and used the pads of his thumbs to wipe away the tears.

"Oh, Roxanne," he said softly. "You don't seem to sure about this. We can wait. You sound like you need more time."

She shook her head. "No. I've already thought it through. It's just that saying the words out loud made it more real. I'm just a little sad, though. But that's normal, don't you think?"

"Of course it is. I just don't want you to rush into anything."

"I'm not. I feel like we've been treading in rough seas for a while now, and I want to do my part to get us to calmer water. You've got an important goal. Hope Springs is a dream come true. That takes up a lot of my time. Fretting over a baby is unnecessary drama that neither of us needs."

How could this woman have called herself selfish? She was so attuned to him, to their marriage, she scared him sometimes. He leaned forward to kiss her. "Do you know how much I love you?" he murmured against her cheek.

Her voice came out in a whisper. "Yes. Yes, I do."

Roxanne hadn't wanted a night out on the town. They had had a quiet dinner. And now that she had made up her mind about the adoption thing, she had turned on her laptop to see what she could find out about it on the Internet. She was printing out pages when a call from Mark came in around ten o'clock.

"What do you mean, she never showed up at the hotel?" Jamal demanded. Roxanne was working in the office on the first floor, so he had taken the call upstairs. As aggravated as he was, he tried to speak in hushed tones not wanting to chance that Roxanne might overhear his conversation and question him about it.

"Just what I said, I called to see if she was settling in at the hotel, and they told me she hadn't checked in yet."

"Maybe her plane was delayed."

"I already checked. It wasn't and she wasn't on it. There was only one other flight coming in after that one, and she wasn't on that one, either."

Damn! Damn! Damn and double damn! Jamal had been psyching himself up to face the woman who could change his entire life, and here she was blowing him off. They were supposed to be getting the paternity test done first thing in the morning. "Where the hell is she, then?" he asked.

"I wish I could tell you. I have been trying to call her place, and I keep getting her voice mail."

Swell. This was just great. "Mark, something ain't right here.

You need to track her down. I want that test done, and I want it done now. Not knowing is messing with my mind." And that was putting it mildly. He hadn't been sleeping right. He had lost his appetite, a fact that hadn't gone unnoticed by Roxanne, because it was unheard of. Even when he was laid low with the flu or whatever, he still liked to eat. He was trying to stay in the zone, trying to stay focused on his game, and failing miserably. How could he be a good husband and an asset to the team when the mind, body, and spirit were all interconnected, and none were functioning all that well at the moment?

Chapter

8

"S he sprained her ankle?" Though it was phrased as a question, Linc's tone of voice and eyes screamed flat-out disbelief.

While Roxanne was taking a shower this morning, Jamal had slipped downstairs to call Mark. According to his agent, Honey had missed her plane because she twisted her ankle while "performing" earlier in the week. After getting the bad news, Jamal felt like the walls of his usually happy home were closing in on him. He had thought about visiting his parents or one of his brothers but decided that would only make him feel even lonelier. He loved his family, but he'd learned early that the Steeles bonded around success and achievements. Problems were to be avoided or, at the very least, handled without dragging other people into them. So, Jamal had driven around aimlessly for a while. He wandered as far south as Chevy Chase before he doubled back and found himself at Linc's condo. Linc was the only one besides Mark who knew what he was going through, but Jamal had hesitated before turning to him. That was something that had never happened before in their long friendship. Lately, he never knew what kind of reception he'd get from his friend. Linc fluctuated between wanting to help him out and being pissed at him because Roxanne would be hurt if all of this came out.

Avoiding his friend's eyes, Jamal used one fingernail to scrape dirt from underneath another. His hands were usually clean. The little black speck annoyed him, and he wasn't satisfied until he had removed it. He rubbed it off on the back of his pants leg.

Most of the chocolate brown leather couch was covered by Linc's six-foot-plus length. Linc reached for his Coors Light, which rested on a Rock and Roll Hall of Fame coaster on the end table next to the couch. Jamal perched on the very edge of a matching armchair that was to the right of the couch. He had declined Linc's offer of a beer. His head was muddled enough as it was.

"She's playing you, Jamal. I would bet my last dollar on it. She gets through nine long months of pregnancy without a single medical problem, and then boom, the minute she's supposed to bring her lying behind here to get a paternity test, she has a leg injury. I'm telling you, her leg ain't the only thing that's lame, so is her whole story."

"I'm starting to think so, too," Jamal said. He rubbed his hands wearily across tired eyes. He was praying with each breath he took that Honey was just a con artist whose game would be up the minute the results of the paternity test came back. In the meantime . . . "Well, if Honey is a liar, she's not alone. You should have heard all the excuses I was coming up with to get out of the house," Jamal said.

Linc paused in the act of bringing the beer can to his lips. His eyes narrowed. "Why you in such a rush to get out of the house? Does Roxy suspect something?"

Jamal quickly shook his head. "No and I don't want her to. That's why I had to leave. Roxanne was trying to show me all this stuff about adoption that she had downloaded from the Internet." Her change of heart about adopting a child had left him with mixed feelings. He was happy she wouldn't be moping around as much about not getting pregnant. Now the problem was that *he* couldn't get into all this baby talk. "Lord knows I tried to seem interested. I wanted to be, but I'm just not feeling it. My stomach turns every time I hear the word 'baby.' That's how my pathetic attempts to lie started." He wasn't going to be right until this mess with Honey got resolved one way or the other. So Jamal had to leave before Roxanne caught on to him.

"When I told Roxanne I was headed over to your place, she had wanted to come, too." Roxanne had reminded him that she hadn't spent much time with Linc lately, either, and he *was* her best friend, too. When Jamal tried to think up a good excuse as to why she couldn't tag along, nothing came to mind. The only thing that saved him was that Roxanne had remembered that *she* was supposed to meet someone named Candace for lunch. Jamal had never heard tell of the woman before, but this new friend was teaching Roxanne something called feng shui. It was supposed to help her decorate the house in tune with nature. And when the chairs and the rugs were properly aligned, it would bring harmony and happiness into your life.

Hell, if the mumbo jumbo worked, maybe he should take it up, too. He was running real short on harmonious living these days. This situation was getting out of hand. When he'd said he was headed over to Linc's, he had told Roxanne a bold-faced lie. Somehow lying to her face seemed worse than the lie of omission, the secret he'd been living with all these months. "I have to be the world's worst liar," Jamal muttered.

Linc laughed at Jamal's self-disgust with his inability to lie. "Yeah, well, that's why I like playing poker with you. I'm guaranteed to leave with not only my money but yours, too."

Normally, Jamal would have laughed along with him, but it was a rare lie that might be his downfall in the end. A lie of omission, but still a lie. Maybe he should have told Roxanne about finding Honey in his hotel room as soon as it had happened. Instead, ostrichlike, he'd buried his head in the sand, and pretended it never happened. Well, the sands were shifting. And if he wasn't careful, he was gonna end up with his ass in the air, a prime position for getting it kicked, and with the sting of tears in his eyes from the same sands of denial that he had once viewed as protection.

Jamal's palms moved restlessly across his kneecaps. A thumb-sized pain throbbed at the base of his neck. The team's massage therapist had worked on it, but the relief was only temporary. The knot was back within a matter of hours. "There's nothing funny about wishing I was a better liar," he told Linc.

Linc immediately sobered. "You're right, man. Now is not the time for jokes. Just tell me what I can do to help."

"I wish I knew. I don't even know how to help myself. I can't fly out to Denver, and I can't force her to come here. Yet, I have this threat hanging over me. I live, sleep, eat and piss with this fear . . ." Jamal stopped as he ran out of words to express how messed up this not knowing had him. "Maybe, I should just call Honey and ask her what she wants."

Linc moved from a sprawling position to an upright one. As denim rubbed against leather, the couch squeaked its protest. He loosely held the beer can in his big palms. "You know what she wants, Jamal. She wants money. I mean, has she asked for anything else? She hasn't once mentioned a desire to have you spend time with little Jamal."

Inwardly, Jamal cringed. Little Jamal? He did not like the sound of that. The thumb-sized neck pain pulsed and expanded its borders. With a heavy sigh, he replied, "I don't know what Honey is thinking, because I haven't spoken to the woman since I put her in a cab one snow-covered morning last December."

A silence followed that last pronouncement. Jamal closed his eyes to block out the penetrating look Linc was giving him. He stretched his arms over his head and rolled his neck around trying to undo the knot of pain that had put down roots in his neck and left shoulder. When that didn't work, he clamped a hand on his shoulder and tried self-massage. He felt a little relief as long as he kept working the bunched muscles by rubbing them and rotating his shoulders.

Honey was like the knot. A pain that wouldn't go away unless he addressed it head-on.

When he opened his eyes, Linc's gaze was still steady on him.

"What?" Jamal said, breaking the silence.

"I know what you're thinking, and I'd advise you to lose that thought."

Linc's claim that he could read his mind didn't surprise Jamal. After Roxanne, Linc could read him best, so he didn't even try to front. "What's wrong with me giving her a call?" Jamal challenged. "So far, I only have Mark and that detective's version of what Honey is all about. And Mark is cool and all, but he's also the master of spin. He thinks it's his job to protect me, even if it means sugarcoating the truth. And, Linc, I have a right to know just what I'm up against, and only Honey can tell me that."

Linc remained unconvinced. "I think it would be a mistake to talk to her. It would just draw you in; make it personal. Jamal, keep your distance. Don't deal directly with Honey until you absolutely have to."

Jamal didn't feel like arguing, so he didn't. But Linc didn't know what he was asking. How was he supposed to keep his distance when Honey was holding his life hostage? How was he supposed to face his trusting wife every day, when at any time, Honey might start trippin' and call Roxanne and tell her version of things before he had a chance to tell his. That fear activated the acid that churned away in his gut. "Maybe you're right," he said, while thinking Linc was anything but.

Jamal got up from the chair, and Linc stood as well. Jamal looked at his watch. It was after two. "I'd better get going. Roxanne told me to be home by three." Jamal cast his gaze about the room, not really seeing anything, as he tried to remember why he had to be home by a specific time. He was certain Roxanne had given a reason, but in his rush to get of the house, he hadn't really been listening.

Linc put a hand on his shoulder, gripping the same spot that ached, almost as if he knew it was in need of constant attention. "I'm sorry you're going through this. And even though I don't have any easy answers, I'm here to listen. You have a key, so feel free to come and go as you please when things get too intense at home."

Jamal expressed his gratitude with a small nod. Linc couldn't fix this, but Jamal intended to—as soon as humanly possible. Linc offered to walk him to his car, but in a complete turnaround from his earlier mood, Jamal suddenly wanted to be alone. "I'll see you tomorrow," he told his friend.

On the way home, Jamal used his cell phone to make a call to a local florist. Guilt about how he'd practically ran out of the house this morning had him ordering two dozen roses for Roxanne. He was a regular with this particular florist, and Mr. Boone had promised that the flowers would be delivered later this afternoon. Instead of making him feel better, Jamal felt even guiltier. No way was a bunch of flowers going to make up for the way he'd been acting lately.

He pounded a fist on the steering wheel. He couldn't take much more of this cloak-and-dagger stuff. It just wasn't his nature. He needed the suspense to be over.

Taking his eyes off the flow of Saturday traffic on 695, Jamal eyed his wallet, which he had tossed on the passenger seat before pulling out of the parking lot at Linc's. Despite his friend's advice, Jamal was itching to call Honey. The green-and-white exit sign for Loch Raven flashed by on his right. He switched from the left to a center lane.

If he was going to make this call, he better do it soon. The exits for Towson would be coming up in the next couple of miles. What the hell? He needed to know where things stood. Jamal snatched up his wallet and quickly sorted through a small pile of business cards until he found the one that he had scribbled Honey's phone number on. He picked up his cell and punched in the numbers before he lost the nerve.

The phone rang five times before someone picked up.

"Hello."

"Is this Honey . . . Honey Brown?"

"It had better be since she's the only one paying the bills up in this joint" came the saucy reply. "And who might this be?" The husky voice with its Southern twang sounded vaguely familiar. A sliver of unease settled in his stomach. He hadn't wanted anything about this woman to seem familiar. His palms started to sweat, making him wish he had had the presence of mind to put her on the speakerphone. He didn't dare do it now. As nervous as he was, he might end up hitting the wrong button and disconnecting them.

He finally found his voice and answered Honey's question. "This is Jamal. Jamal Steele."

"Well, all right now. The Man of Steele himself," Honey drawled, her voice suddenly taking on a more seductive flavor. "I was wondering when I was gonna hear from my baby's daddy."

Why did she have to call him that? He wasn't anybody's daddy until the tests said so. Suddenly cotton-mouthed, Jamal attempted to swallow. Using what little moisture he had managed to generate, he licked his lips to wet them. He still sounded like a frog when he spoke again. "That's why I'm calling. I want to get this thing settled. Why didn't you fly out here for the paternity test like you were supposed to?"

"Didn't your lawyer tell ya? I'm indisposed," she said airily.

He found her laid-back attitude aggravating. Through gritted teeth, he said, "It's just a sprained ankle. Nothing that should have kept you from getting on a plane."

"Says you," she fired back. "Have you ever tried schlepping anywhere with a baby? Let alone around an airport? And I'm talking about doing it *without* a messed-up ankle."

"Why didn't you contact us after you hurt your ankle? You had a couple of days before you were due in Baltimore. We could have arranged for someone to help you with the baby."

"His name is Jamal."

He didn't need to be reminded of the boy's name. He chose not to respond to her deliberate baiting. Jamal struggled to keep his tone civil. "There was no good reason why you couldn't have gotten on that plane. Honey, I just don't want you tryin' to run a game on me. Too much is at stake."

"Look, Jamal, I don't mean to cause problems between you and the wife, but I got problems of my own."

Jamal could only shake his head. If she really believed that, they wouldn't even be having this conversation.

"My ankle swelled up the size of an orange," she claimed. "What do you want from me? Pictures? A doctor's note?"

"Do you have one?" he asked.

She laughed. "I like you. You get straight to the point. But then I remember that from the last time I saw ya."

Jamal stopped her trip down memory lane. He didn't care if Honey liked him or not. He just wanted her to take the test and, hopefully, get out of his life. How had he ever gotten tangled up in this mess? "So when *do* you think you'll be able to make it to Baltimore?"

"I couldn't say."

He could picture her tossing the mane of weaved hair as she replied. Her indifference to the stress she was causing him couldn't have been plainer. "The doctor told me to stay off my feet for at least a week. And since I dance for a living, he warned me that that might reinjure it if I didn't let it properly heal first. So, I'm thinking two weeks."

Two weeks! Living like this for two more weeks would be torture.

"Speaking of which, since I'm gonna be unable to work for a couple of weeks, I was wondering if you could send your first child-support check now?"

Jamal blinked his surprise. She was bold. He had to give her that. "I don't think so. It's just a couple of weeks before you get back to work. You can't be that broke that you can't get by for a couple of weeks." Besides, what would she have done if he hadn't been stupid enough to place this call?

Half a country away, and he still heard her suck her teeth in anger. The eye and neck rolling couldn't be far behind judging from what she said next. "You don't know nothing about my financial situation, Jamal. For your information, stripping is not exactly a job that comes with health benefits. I make good money . . . when I'm working. When I was pregnant and started to show, I stopped working. Apparently, a pregnant stripper ain't every man's fantasy. Imagine that?" she said, dripping sarcasm that he could have done without. "I burned a lot of my savings then. I was thinking about a couple thousand. Something to pay the bills and tide us over until I can get back to work. Or don't you care? Maybe *you* think I should go on welfare?"

Jamal sighed. Did she really think he believed she didn't have *anyone* she could borrow a few dollars from? No friends, none of the other girls at the club who were also making good money or not even a customer who was sweet on her? He had a solid and pretty consistent upper-middle-class upbringing. He didn't know squat about how welfare worked, but he was pretty sure it wasn't something you could sign up for and get a check on the spot. Honey would probably be waiting a lot longer than two weeks for welfare to kick in. *Not that she let that fact stop her from trying to make him feel guilty enough to send her money*, Jamal thought.

She must think I am straight-up sucker, Jamal concluded. He was so tempted to tell her to go to hell and to take her scheming with her. But one little worry stopped him cold. He didn't know this woman. Didn't know what she was capable of.

He could see the headline now: FOOTBALL STAR'S LOVE CHILD ON PUBLIC ASSISTANCE. A horn honked as Jamal drifted into the next lane. He jumped, almost losing the phone in the process.

"Where is the baby right now?" he asked.

"He's staying with a friend, so I can get some rest."

What friend? A responsible one, he hoped. The juices in his stomach continued to boil. He had so many other questions. Who was keeping the baby while she strutted her stuff every night? He hoped it was someone grandmotherly and reliable. But in his mind's eye he saw a boozy ex-stripper. Maybe Honey took the boy to the club with her. Did her fellow strippers keep an eye on him between sets? He grimaced just thinking about it. It was not a pretty picture. A strip joint was not the kind of environment any child should grow up in.

Damn, he silently cursed. He should have listened to Linc and kept his distance. Now she had him worried. Had him concerned about this child. You would think that as a mother, she'd have something else to say about the child other than he was disrupting her rest and so had to be shipped off to a friend.

"Jamal? Jamal, are you still there?" Honey asked after the long pause.

Dulaney Valley Road, his exit, was coming up next. Jamal put on his blinker and switched to the far right lane. "Yeah, I'm here," he said.

"So you gonna send the money or what?"

An intense pounding pummeled his head. His vision in his left eye blurred for a moment. Unnerved, Jamal had to wait until he was able to see the cars in front of him with the same clarity as the right eye had. He expelled a breath when it finally did. It was time for him to get off the road before he hurt himself or someone else. He'd had two or three of these sudden, blinding headaches in the past week. Now this conversation with Honey had brought on another.

If he started giving her money before it was proven he was the father, she might keep stalling. If he didn't give her money, he'd worry about the safety of the little boy, and if the child did turn out to be his, he'd look like a deadbeat dad for not paying up sooner. And even if he did give her money, who was to say she'd really use it to look after the baby?

He never should have made this call. Now he didn't know what to do. Mark and Linc were going to kill him. "I'll have to get back to you," he said.

"Yeah, you do that," she said. Her voice was like a block of ice. All pretense at sweetness had disappeared. The phone went dead in his ear.

"I guess that means she didn't like my answer," Jamal fretted before putting the phone in its cradle to recharge. "Nice going, Jamal. Now you've made things worse."

Mall traffic had created a slight backup at the exit. This was the stop for all the folks headed to Towson Town Center. Jamal wished he could be like them. He wished he had nothing better to worry about than catching a good sale at Nordstrom's Rack. Instead, he opened the glove compartment and took out an opened roll of Tums. There were only three left; he popped all of them in his mouth. His conversation with Honey had left him spitless, so it was hard work chewing and swallowing the already pasty antacids—like eating a piece of minty chalk. As he inched his way toward the intersection, Jamal realized that whether he started dol-ing out cash to Honey or not, he needed to clue his wife in. Now that he had opened up this can of worms called Honey, there was no telling what the woman might do, especially since he'd pissed her off.

He had to tell Roxanne the truth.

The first thing Jamal noticed when he pulled into his driveway was the strange car parked at the front door. Rather than follow-ing the curve of the circular drive as the owner of the car had obvi-ously done, Jamal kept straight until he reached the outside of the three-car garage. He didn't hit the automatic garage-door opener. Instead he killed the engine and glanced over at the PT Cruiser again. It wasn't unusual to find an unknown car at his house, but he didn't know anyone who owned that Chrysler-built throwback to the early 1900s. He kept his seat belt fastened, not at all eager to leave the confines of the vehicle. He didn't want to talk to anyone right now except Roxanne. And wasn't looking forward to that, either.

Knowing he couldn't sit outside forever, Jamal reached over to open the door and was surprised by the numbness radiating down his left arm and into his hand. He pulled his arm back and used his hand to massage the life back into it. He flexed his hand and cracked his knuckles before trying again. His left arm still felt a lit-tle weak but was strong enough to open the door. Jamal stepped out of the car. He pocketed his keys and walked along the flagstone path to enter through the front of the house.

After hanging his jacket on a coatrack, he headed for the kitchen—the most logical place to find Roxanne. Eager to meet, greet, and retreat from whomever the visitor was, Jamal opted to the cut through the dining room rather than taking the long route past the home office, the dining room, and the utility room. Next to the living room, the dining room was the largest room in the house. They used it only for large-scale entertaining. Roxanne had tried to give it a casual elegance and warmth by adding rugs and baskets of plants and small trees from her greenhouse. Despite her efforts, it still wasn't a room either one of them hung out in.

He opened the two double doors leading to the kitchen. The contrast was immediate. Natural sunlight streamed in from the bay windows and French doors. The bright yellow accents surrounded him with a cheeriness that did not fit his mood. Past the butcher-block island in the center of the room, he spied a ceramic teapot sitting atop a trivet in the middle of the kitchen table. Sugar, honey, lemon, and a mesh tea ball infuser were close at hand. He was surprised Roxanne hadn't used her fancy steeper, which let her set the strength she wanted the tea to be, steeped it at the perfect temperature for the optimal amount of time, and came equipped with a glass carafe that rested on its own base, so she didn't need to put anything under it to keep it from ruining the table. Jamal knew these things because Roxanne flooded him with this kind of info every time she came home with some new kitchen gadget, which was often.

Both Roxanne and the woman she was sitting at the table with looked up when they heard his footfall on the marble tiles. Jamal acknowledged them both with a small smile and "hello." This must be the friend Roxanne had met for lunch. The brown-skinned woman was more hair than anything else. A cloud of thick, curly, jet-black hair framed her face. She had a small but square jaw and full lips that dominated her other features. She was kind of dressed up for a Saturday afternoon, Jamal thought. The woman wore a gold silk blouse under a tan wool suit. Dangerously high brown leather pumps covered her small feet. She was a short one. Her feet didn't even touch the floor.

Roxanne returned his smile and extended a child-size hand to him. "Hey, Jamal, come in and join us," she invited.

He closed the distance between them and took her outstretched hand in his. Only after planting a kiss on her warm lips did he straighten and greet their guest. "Hi, nice to meet you," he said.

"Nice to meet you too, Mr. Steele," she said, sticking her hand out, so that he could shake it.

Jamal obliged, but his eyes widened at her formality. "You can call me Jamal." He looked down into his wife's smiling eyes. "So how did your Kung Fu lesson go?" he asked, deliberately messing up the name.

She playfully poked him in the ribs. "It's feng shui and it was great. I learned a lot. I'll have to tell you about it later."

Not if he told her about Honey first, he thought, finally remembering his vow to come clean. Roxanne had a way of making him forget about anything negative. His troubles would evaporate in the warmth of her smile, the optimism shining in her eyes, or the comfort of her touch. That's what had happened when he laid eyes on her a minute ago. He'd forgotten himself. This was not just like old times. It hadn't been like old times for a while now. Roxanne just didn't know it. And he felt sick thinking about the revelation that was soon to come. The thought of small talk with a stranger when he was torn up inside seemed unbearable. He had to get out of here.

"Since Candace is still here, I won't interrupt your conversation. I'll head on downstairs to get in a quick workout," he said, and included the woman in his fake smile. Up close, she was younger than Jamal had first thought. Early twenties, maybe.

The other woman's mug clattered on the saucer when it slipped from her fingers. Jamal turned to leave, but Roxanne hadn't let go of his hand. So much for a quick escape. After righting the cup, the woman opened her mouth to speak but Roxanne beat her to it.

"Jamal, this isn't Candace," she explained in a voice that she used with the kids at Hope Springs when they were having problems following directions. "This is Michelle Reeves. She's here to do the interview."

He parroted her words. "The interview?"

"Yes," she said, making it a two-syllable word. "The one for *Baltimore Style*. Michelle is doing the interview, and when the photographer finishes with the exterior shots, he's going to take

pictures of us. I'm surprised you didn't run into him outside."
When he still didn't respond, Roxanne rolled her eyes at his for-
getfulness. She shared a look with Michelle as if to say, Men!
"Michelle is doing a story on Baltimore's hottest couples. Some
power-that-be decided that includes you and me, sweetie."

Jamal noticed for the first time the small notebook in Michelle
Reeves' lap and the microcassette recorder that was partially hidden by her coffee mug. So this was the reason he had to be back by
three. Jamal could have screamed his frustration. He didn't like
interviews on a good day. He usually got asked questions that he'd
answered a million times, or the interviewer already had a slant
in mind so he asked leading questions and ignored anything he
said that didn't fit with it. But this was a couples' thing, so there
was no way for him to get out of it. At least not without making
Roxanne wonder about why he was being so rude. Besides, it was
obviously something she wanted to do, and he wasn't about to
spoil it for her.

Michelle's eyes darted from husband to wife. Sensing Jamal's
reluctance, she began to plead her case. "Mr. Steele, I promise not
to take up much of your time. But I've only been working at the
magazine for two months, and this is my first byline. My first big
story, if you know what I mean."

"Don't worry," Roxanne assured her. "He's not going anywhere. I told him all about the interview earlier this week and
reminded him this morning. But he was too busy trying to get over
to Linc's to do whatever it is they do." She waved a hand. "It obviously went in one ear and out of the other."

Michelle moved the cassette player to the center of the table
and pushed the red record button. "By Linc, you mean Linc
Weaver, the team's quarterback?"

"The one and only," Roxanne replied. "If it weren't for Linc,
there would be no 'hot couple' to interview." Jamal pulled up a
chair next to Roxanne while she told the story of how Linc had
brought them together. Bless her romantic heart. She loved to tell
that story. And always ended with "and we lived happily ever
after." One could only hope she'd be able to say that a year from
now. Or maybe even a few hours from now.

"What about you, Mr. Steele?" the reporter asked. He stared at
her, not sure where Roxanne had left off in the fairy tale. "Did you

find it hard to give up the swinging bachelor lifestyle?" she prompted.

He shrugged. "I don't know that I was ever a swinging bachelor. And I had no problems giving it up . . ." He felt an overpowering needed to touch his wife. A need driven by the fear that someday soon she might no longer welcome his touch. So, he cupped the back of her head and lost his hand in the tangled and textured, yet all natural essence that was Roxanne. ". . . because I knew almost immediately that Roxanne was the woman for me."

"Almost?" Roxanne scoffed, pretending to be offended. "It was love at first sight, buster."

He didn't bother to deny it. Why should he? It was true.

"Was it love at first sight for you as well, Roxanne?" Michelle asked.

He could feel Roxanne relax into the palm of his hand as she gave him a somewhat apologetic smile. "No . . . I wouldn't say that," she replied. At Michelle's arched brow, she said with a laugh, "But that wasn't Jamal's fault. I was so anti-man when I first met him, he could have been Jesus Christ and I would have been questioning his motives."

"Sounds like you got burned by somebody, girlfriend." Michelle's reporter mask dropped while she offered sympathy as one woman to another. Obviously, she had been there and done that.

"His loss was my gain," Jamal said. He'd felt Roxanne's neck tense up at the mention of the disastrous relationship she'd been in before they met. What little information he'd gleaned about Marcus he'd gotten from Linc and her other friends. Roxanne had this remarkable ability to live only in the present. She always told him, "The day I realized I loved you, all other men ceased to exist for me past and future."

"Jamal is my soul mate in so many ways. We really support each other in our interests. Like I know this year is a big year for him, so I'm trying to make his home life as stress-free as possible. We also have shared interests, like Hope Springs—"

Jamal had to suppress a smile. Now he was starting to see the real reason Roxanne had granted this interview in the first place. Hope Springs. His wife was a smart woman. Jamal continued to play with the heavy ropes of her hair. He liked their weight and substance. Roxanne gave him something to hold on to. He slid his hand behind the curtain of hair and let his fingertips casually caress the back of her neck. It was a sensitive spot for her. And though the sound was faint, her heard her sharp intake of breath. After a heartbeat, Roxanne launched into her next sentence. But not before she grasped his hand to keep it from further distracting her.

Suddenly, an intense desire to cry bubbled up inside him. Here in the brightness of his kitchen with his wife innocently singing his praises and a stranger hanging on every word, he wanted to weep because he knew how to touch this woman in the right way. God willing, he'd be doing it until they both were so old and frail, the only thing they *could* do was stroke each other with shaky, arthritic but still loving hands.

"Wow, it really does sound like a storybook romance," Michelle said. "What's the hardest part about being married?"

"Being away from each other," they both said in unison, then laughed.

Michelle grinned. "You two are unbelievable. You've got to give me something that makes you mere mortals like the rest of us. Next you're going to try to have me believe you never fight."

"I wouldn't call it fighting. More like disagreements," Roxanne said. "It's over the usual stuff. What money will be spent on? He's more extravagant than I am. I see to it that we stay in the budget—" Her brown eyes danced with amusement. "Actually, I see to it that we have a budget." She prettily scrunched up her face. "Let's see. We sometimes *disagree*"—she stressed that last word—"about how chores around the house will get done. Believe it or not, Jamal is the neat freak. So he's always on my case. What else?" she said, half talking to herself. "We both come from large families, so from time to time, something is going on with family members that requires our attention and that takes away from us as a couple. You know how that is." She looked over at Jamal. "I'm doing all the talking here, sweetie. Let's hear your two cents."

"I couldn't have possibly put it any better than you did, Roxanne," he said, wishing this interview would be over. "In a nutshell, we are deeply in love with each other, we work at not letting our differences come between us, and we're committed to this marriage."

"Oh, sweetie," Roxanne said with a ragged sigh, "you're making me cry." Through teary eyes, she appealed to Michelle, "Have you ever seen a man be so open about his feelings?" she asked.

Jamal grabbed a paper dinner napkin out of its wooden holder and handed it to his wife. She was breaking his heart. Roxanne dabbed at her eyes, prompting him to pull her onto his lap for a bracing hug.

Watching the way they were with each other, Michelle murmured, "Not often," in response to Roxanne's earlier question. "You two are clearly all into each other. Very much in love. How do children fit into this picture? And if you have kids, are you worried that they might feel excluded?"

Jamal tensed. Why did the woman have to ask about babies? Where he came from, that was a very personal question. And right now, it was a painful one for both of them—though the source of his pain was now different from his wife's. He looked her way to see how she was taking it and gave her hand a supportive squeeze.

Roxanne reared back, so that she could more clearly capture his gaze. "Absolutely not," she said to Michelle with conviction. "Believe me, we got love to spare. Isn't that right, Jamal?"

She smiled into his eyes, and the impact of just how precious she was to him accelerated the beating of his heart. She was without a doubt the best thing that had ever happened to him.

Jamal had to swallow the emotion that clogged his throat before he could reply. "Yes, it is. Having children is definitely one of our top priorities."

"Well, that's just wonderful," Michelle said. "You two are making me want to go out and get hitched myself." As an afterthought, she added. "But first, I guess, I got to find a man who sticks around for longer than six months."

"Well, don't rush into anything on account of us," Roxanne advised her. "I waited a long time to find my knight in shining armor." She used a loosely balled fist to pretend to polish the armor on his chest. "And believe me, I thank the Lord every day that I did."

Jamal closed his eyes and held her close. His head rested against the firm skin of her upper arm. He was acutely aware of every place that her body touched his. He knew she was a strong person, but every time he saw her and touched her, all he wanted to do was protect her. He breathed in her unique scent, felt her warmth, and knew that there was no way that he was going to tell her about Honey. He just couldn't. Not today and hopefully not ever.

Chapter

9

The blue grass turf looked great except for a few churned-up places where the two teams had done battle over possession of the football. The sixty-nine-thousand-seat stadium was filled to capacity. The collective excitement in the air was a tangible thing. Jamal was playing one of the most important games of his life, and Roxanne was missing most of it. She was only catching snippets of the game because Sabina Carter sat next to her having a bona fide fit that was impossible to ignore.

"I swear to God, Roxanne, if that heifer looks my way one more time, I'm gonna go over there and slap the taste outta her mouth," Sabina hissed.

Without taking her eyes off the field, Roxanne put a restraining hand on Sabina Carter's shoulder to make sure she didn't rise from her seat and carry out her threat. It didn't stop the threats from coming, though, as Sabina continued to spew out all the ways she wanted to hurt her husband's girlfriend.

Linc threw the ball to Jamal. He managed only five or six yards before he was brought down by the Pittsburgh free safety. It had been third down and long, and Roxanne wasn't sure Jamal had gotten enough yardage on the play. After the play, a handful of players from both teams tried to assist the official in spotting the ball. He waved them off and placed the football at Pittsburgh's forty-five yard line. It was a Baltimore first down, and the crowd cheered. There was a pause in play while officials on the field scurried to reset the first-down markers. The two teams squared off against each other again.

"The skanky home wrecker," Sabina muttered.

As Sabina's voice grew louder, Roxanne realized that she wasn't going to be able to concentrate on the game. At least not until she calmed Sabina down.

How could Steve Carter be so stupid as to give *his woman* tickets in the players' section when *his wife* was gonna be there? Furthermore, why did the fleet-footed kick returner have a woman and a wife in the first place?

Sabina Carter just about lost her mind during the second quarter when she spotted Steve's girlfriend sitting only a few feet away, in the same row no less. Sabina had been spitting mad ever since. She hadn't furnished Roxanne with a name but simply called the girlfriend "that heifer." It didn't take a genius to figure out what was up, so pretty soon the other wives and players' guests had one eye on the game and the other on the potential fight that might break out right next to them. Roxanne had dragged Sabina down to the Southwest Plaza during halftime. She should have known a Coke and a pretzel wouldn't begin to extinguish Sabina's fire. But she figured it was worth a try, since eating always made her feel better.

"What the hell is *she* giving him that he can't get at home?" Sabina hissed as they returned to their seats.

Roxanne's heart panged at the anger and hurt that one sentence conveyed. Steve's girlfriend was openly staring at them, tossing her bottled blond hair over her shoulders. She was reed thin, almost boyish with keen facial features. What did Steve see in her? Roxanne wondered. She wasn't really even pretty. Maybe it was her age. She looked young, barely out of her teens. The weather was more like September than mid-December, so the girl had a lightweight nylon jacket tied around her waist, its arms dangled along the length of her jean-clad legs, and sure enough she had Steve's jersey number emblazoned across her chest.

Seeing that she had their attention, the girl—Roxanne couldn't really think of her as a woman given how ignorant she was acting—gave them a little wave. Then giggled along with the brunette next to her. Her friend was about the same height, five-foot-five give or take an inch, and had the same pointed features. They were probably related.

"That's it!" Sabina said, "I'm gonna go over there and wring that flat-chested, no-behind, stringy-haired bitch's neck." Like Roxanne, Sabina was petite, her black hair cut short in a pageboy. And her normally cheerful brown eyes were outraged. Half Puerto-Rican, half-Russian Jew, Sabina's Latin side was in full force at the moment.

Roxanne grabbed her by the arm and blocked her path. As much as she sympathized, she could not let her get into a brawl. It would only give her and the team the kind of publicity Sabina would regret later. "Sabina, let's go to the team's loge," Roxanne pleaded. It would mean sitting with the owners and other organizational bigwigs, but Roxanne had an open invitation, since Jamal was the team's star receiver. Plus, she was friendly with the owner's wife. Margo Leventhal was a frequent volunteer at Hope Springs.

"*I'm* not going anywhere!" Sabina declared, trying to twist free of Roxanne's grasp. "Why the hell should I leave? She's invading my territory, not the other way around." Her Bronx accent was more pronounced than usual. And Roxanne wouldn't have been surprised if Sabina had reached in her purse, whipped out some Vaseline, and smeared her face with it before the fight started to keep her opponent's scratches from sinking in.

Seeing the blaze in Sabina's eyes, Roxanne tried to reason with her. "Fine. You're right, but you know you can't throw down. Not now. Look," she said, glancing to a camera operator on the sidelines who had his camera facing the stands. "Do you want to be the lead story on *SportsCenter* tonight?"

Sabina's eyes slowly moved around the sold-out stadium. A sea of red and gold—the team's colors—shimmered. Surprise registered on her face. She seemed to notice for the first time the din of the crowd, the unconcealed excitement in the air. Their team had just scored again. A field goal. This game was for the Central Division championship. Win or lose, Baltimore was going to the playoffs for the first time in two years. This game was about home field advantage. *And* there were cameras everywhere.

As the fact that this was a nationally televised game sank in, Roxanne didn't hear Sabina's sigh of frustration but did feel the muscles where she clutched her arm slowly relax. When Roxanne eased her grip, Sabina gave "that heifer" one last glare and then took her seat. "I'm all right now," Sabina assured her and all the nosy folks who'd been all up in their conversation.

Vivian Lacour tapped Sabina on the shoulder from behind. She held out a small silver flask. Vivian always had a ready supply of Hennessey, if not on her, then nearby. "Here, honey, have a sip of this. It'll make you feel better," she said.

Looking at the skin stretched across Vivian's face like a death mask, the heavily applied makeup that cracked and caked in places, not to mention the sad look of commiseration in her eyes, Roxanne seriously doubted that. Vivian had been more subdued around her ever since Jamal had sent her home in a cab in the middle of the Hope Springs fund-raiser. She had been pissy drunk at the time. The last thing Sabina needed was for Vivian to be her role model for how to deal with an unfaithful husband.

How many times had Vivian endured this same situation? Roxanne wondered. Why did they put up with the blatant cheating? Roxanne knew *she* wouldn't. She didn't understand it. The doggish reputation of professional athletes was well-known, and Roxanne had told Jamal from the get-go that she wasn't having it. "Divorce me," she had told him. "If you meet some other woman, and you gotta have her that bad, divorce me. When I marry, I vow to forsake all other men, and I don't expect any less from my husband."

There were very few things that she was inflexible on and cheating within a marriage was one of them. What was the point of getting married if you still intended to pursue other people? Three was definitely a crowd. A marriage couldn't last with unnecessary drama going on. For Roxanne, it had to be "until death do us part." So she had held out, waiting until she found a man who could do what it took to keep a marriage together. Jamal swore up and down that he was up to the task. And as a joke, he had asked Linc to write him a character reference letter that claimed that Jamal was faithful to all his former girlfriends. Not that she was interested in hearing anything about his exes, but with both of them ganging up on her, she found herself believing Jamal was sincere.

Maybe Sabina should have laid down the law with Steve, too.

Roxanne's pity turned to disappointment when Sabina turned

the flask up for a long drink. She handed it back to Vivian and said, "Thanks, Viv. I'll take care of that skank later."

Twisting the ends of a handful of dreads around her fingers, Roxanne sat down next to Sabina. She hoped Sabina planned to "take care" of her cheating husband later as well. Thank God, she didn't have to worry about Jamal disrespecting her like that. Actually, she didn't have to worry about him disrespecting her at all, she silently added before turning her attention back to the game.

They were up by two touchdowns. Linc had been a machine today. He had connected with Jamal for two touchdowns in the first quarter and then for another with Cage just before the half. Though it was early in the fourth quarter, they were gonna win this one. Roxanne could feel it. She had never been a big sports fan before meeting Jamal, but when you were with someone who lived and breathed sports, you either got with the program or prepared for a lifetime of limited conversation. And Roxanne decided to get with the program. Now she was almost as bad as Jamal was. He had her watching everything from ski jumping to high school wrestling. Somebody just meeting her wouldn't know how relatively new all this sports fanaticism was.

But Roxanne was a passionate person and was easily drawn in by the passion of others. If you had something you absolutely loved and cared about, she was down for that. Her good friend Gayle always seemed amazed and fascinated by how easily Roxanne made friends. Gayle sometimes spoke as if Roxanne had some kind of magnetic . . . no magic personality. It wasn't magic that drew her to people and vice versa. It was mutual passion, combining and catching hold to create a closeness in no time at all.

Like right now. Roxanne felt at one with this red-and-gold-clad mass of humanity. She and these people, who she didn't even know, shared a common goal: to will their team to win this game. So Roxanne gasped and held her breath along with the rest of the crowd when one of Pittsburgh's running backs eluded several tackles. Number Thirty-two was a rookie trying to make a name for himself. Squat, powerful legs and near steamroller unstoppable, he ran for twenty yards before someone brought him down.

"Damn! They're getting close to the red zone," she exclaimed, referring to the area between the ten-yard line and the goal line.

The pace of her dreadlock twirling accelerated. Before the anxiety about this new development could solidify, Roxanne surged to her feet and cheered when the play was called back due to offensive holding. She checked the Smart Vision board above the cheap seats. Eight more minutes. They were going to win this one.

Roxanne reached down to pick up her purse, which had fallen when she jumped up so quickly. She leaned forward in her seat, her eyes searching the home team bench on the south sideline. Where was Jamal? He had to be beyond thrilled. This was it. If they won this game, they could sit out wild-card weekend and rest up for the divisional play-offs, where Baltimore would have home-field advantage. Two games away from the Championship Bowl. Or the "Big Dance," as he liked to call it.

The players' box was on the forty-yard line on the home-team side. Usually, she could find Jamal prowling around watching every play while the defense was on the field. She squinted against the glare of the sun, wishing she'd thought to bring her prescription sunglasses. Unfortunately, everybody milling around down there sported the same colors. But luckily, there was a body type for every position, which helped in the process of elimination. The kickers tended to be short. The linemen huge. The receivers streamlined, long-legged, narrow-hipped. Roxanne could usually pick Jamal out from the crowd by his confident, flat-footed stride. And that tight behind, she would recognize anywhere. She located Linc almost immediately. He held his helmet in one hand. His head was cocked to one side, where he listened via headphone as one of the offensive coaches barked new plays after viewing the action on the field from a perch in one of the skyboxes.

So where was her husband? Then she saw him, the double eight of his jersey, partially hidden from view by the center and Jonesy, one of the offensive linemen. Jamal was sitting on an overturned Gatorade bucket and had a clear plastic cup over his nose and was gulping in air from a nearby oxygen tank.

Poor baby, Roxanne thought. He'd had a rough day. They were winning, and although the last expansion draft and salary cap limitations had left the Panthers' defense sorely lacking in depth, they were not going down without a fight. Jamal had taken a couple of hard hits. One had sent him flying up over the shoulder of the safety, who stopped him, and then he landed on his tailbone. Roxanne had learned to control her outward reaction to plays like that, but inside, she still quaked every time.

She only had a side view of his face but could see the fatigue in the droop of his shoulders, his lowered head. Jamal wasn't wearing the long-sleeve turtleneck under his uniform that was typical gear for this time of year. The seventy-degree temperature after a week in the forties probably was hard on his body. Or maybe the hype of the game was getting to him. Roxanne nibbled on the end of one of her dreads as Jamal's chest heaved in and out, and then she glanced at the game clock. Four more minutes, babe. Then we'll spend the rest of the night celebrating. After a long hot soak in the hot tub, of course. Jamal had not looked her way, but she hoped the thought communicated itself past the din of the frenzied crowd, which was shouting, "De-fense! De-fense! De-fense!"

Roxanne looked downfield just in time to see Number Thirty-two finally tunnel his way through the mountain of linemen Baltimore had formed in a wasted attempt to prevent him from scoring. The point after was good. The Baltimore fans quieted down, became a little less cocky as they realized that Pittsburgh was now trailing by only a touchdown. Three minutes to go. That was a lot of time.

Roxanne closed her eyes and focused only on positive thoughts. This *was* going to be the year that Jamal got his Championship Bowl ring. She silently prayed the Panthers would go down like the *Titanic*, knowing that it was bad sportsmanship to root against the opposing team. You were supposed to root for your team. But she didn't care. She wanted her baby to get his Championship Bowl ring. Selfishly, she knew that would bring him one step closer to retirement and perhaps put an end to all this restlessness Jamal seemed to be experiencing lately.

He was quieter. Training like a fiend. Huddling with Linc, strategizing for every game, trying to come up with a response to each opponent, she supposed. Though he never talked much about it, Roxanne knew the possibility of not reaching the Championship Bowl was weighing on his mind. All the sports writers and bookies were hyping Baltimore as a sure bet. Everything, the offense, the defense, and fan spirit had come together this year.

Rather than being reassuring, all the high expectations seemed to have put more pressure on Jamal. Roxanne had noticed that though he went through the motions of eating, Jamal lacked his usual enthusiasm for food. And she often caught him deep in thought, zoned out. He stayed up late watching TV. Though he stared at the images flickering across the screen, Roxanne knew that he couldn't have told her what was on to save his life. He played pool in the game room by himself in the middle of the night. He hadn't slept well for several weeks. Last night was particularly bad for him. Finally, Jamal had gotten up and moved to one of the spare bedrooms, probably because he didn't want to keep her up. But it was too late for that. How could she sleep knowing that he was alone with his thoughts and doubts? After about five minutes, she followed him and curled up next to him. He hadn't uttered a word, just pulled her arms tight across his stomach. Sometime in the early hours of the morning, she heard his breathing deepen, felt his chest rise and fall as he slept in her arms.

When the commercial time-out was over, Jamal removed the oxygen mask and handed it to one of the trainers. Roxanne returned her attention to the game. She and the rest of the fans held their breaths to see what would happen on the kick return. Steve Carter and Cornelius Bell waited at the twenty-yard line. The kicker booted the ball, and Pittsburgh rushed down the field toward the kick returners. The kick was short, and Steve caught it at the thirty-yard line. He skimmed the sideline. Forty-yard line. Fifty-yard line. On her left, Sabina yelled, "Run, Stevie. Run." Her earlier anger gone in the excitement of the moment. Finally, he was knocked out of bounds at Pittsburgh's forty-two-yard line.

The stadium exploded with relief and jubilation. They were at the two-minute warning, and Steve Carter's run had made the Baltimore fans believers. If they could get a few more first downs and not make any mistakes, they would win. Jamal was one of the many players thumping Steve on the back over at the sideline. Before running out to the field, he looked toward the player's box, and Roxanne knew he was looking for her. It was sure sign that Jamal thought this game was over. He liked to know that Roxanne was there, but tried not to interact with her much until he felt the game was out of reach either way. She jumped to her feet and stretched her red-and-gold "Man of Steele" towel over her head. It was almost as long as she was in length. She swayed from side to side to get his attention.

Jamal saw her and gave the thumbs-up sign. Roxanne smiled and wished she were closer to the field. Jamal had to be mad happy about the way the game was going. Jamal turned and jogged out to the field to join his teams in the huddle, though he was probably done for the day. No way was Linc going to throw downfield in this situation. They just needed to get into field-goal range and not fumble the ball.

Roxanne sat back down hugging her towel to her. She was so happy for him. For Linc. For the team. She forgot about Sabina and "that heifer." Linc had twenty-five seconds to get the play off, and he took his sweet time. He kept shoveling the ball to his running backs, who held it tightly in both hands, protectively like a cherished possession. *That's what they better do, Roxanne silently coached. Now was not the time for a fumble.* If a player screwed up at this point in the game, he would never live it down. The media and fans would be cursing his name into the next football season.

Baltimore methodically marched down the field and, more importantly, ate time off the clock. The offense moved like snails when it came to picking themselves off the ground after a play. Pittsburgh used up their time-outs, but it didn't do any good. The first downs kept piling up. There was no need to bring the kicking team on. Baltimore was on a mission. With thirty-four seconds on the clock, they were on the nine-yard line. Half of the players seemed to be in the end zone. Roxanne didn't know why. At this point, Linc was not going to throw the ball. He didn't need to.

But when the play was set in motion, Roxanne saw Jamal moving to his right. Linc began backpeddling. Her eyes widened in amazement. The coach had not called this play. Of that, she was sure. Roxanne found herself grinning. The Dynamic Duo had come up with this all on their own. Linc's arm went up in the air, and then he jerked it across his body. Everything was in slow motion as the ball sailed over the heads and hands of defenders who, completely caught off guard, tried to take a last-minute swipe at it.

Roxanne was already on her feet by the time Jamal's hands went up and snatched the ball out of the air. Both his feet touched down in the back of the end zone, clearly in bounds. Roxanne couldn't see what happened next, because the noise in the stadium was deafening, people were on the chairs dancing around, hugging and kissing the folks next to them. It was crazy. And players on the field slowly began picking themselves up.

Roxanne hugged Sabina and then turned around to look for Jamal. This time, he'd probably have two thumbs-up. That's when she noticed that the players and coaches who had rushed to the field to join the celebration had pulled up short. She saw one of the trainers dashing back over to the sideline. A group of the players, including Linc, were standing around someone who was sprawled on the field. What was going on? Slowly, like in an eerie imitation of "The Wave," the excited spectators realized that something was wrong. An unnatural quiet settled over the stadium. It wasn't like TV where the announcer told you what had happened and who the injured player was. A big question mark of confusion hovered over the stadium.

The trainer returned with a stretcher. The crowd around the injured player parted for him. The stretcher was laid on the turf, and the other trainer assisted him and lifted the prone player onto it. Though she clearly saw double eight on the jersey, Roxanne found herself asking, "Where's Jamal?" Why was Linc holding Jamal's helmet?

"Where's Jamal?" she repeated. In the silence that followed, Roxanne began making her way out of the row. Why wasn't anyone answering her? Somebody grabbed her hand. She wrenched it free without looking back to see who. She only had eyes for the red-and-white ambulance that had pulled up to the side gate. She reached the end of the row and rushed to the railing that separated the player's box from a lower box. Her left leg was over the railing. Suddenly, she felt herself being pulled backward. She whirled around to find two stadium security officers who grabbed her by the waist and one arm. Her feet were not touching the ground.

"Let me go!" Roxanne screamed. As the ambulance began to pull away, she cried, "Jamal!"

One of the men said, "Please, Mrs. Steele, come this way."

Roxanne looked at the slowly emptying field. Then back at the sea of strangers surrounding her. "Jamal!" still she cried. Someone stepped up and put an arm around her shoulder, helping her down the walkway. Nearly seventy thousand people were on their feet, and she was the only one making any sound. The only one still shouting.

Chapter

10

Roxanne pinched the flesh between her thumb and forefinger, trying in vain to awaken some crumb of feeling in herself. From her seat in the front row of the church where she had been married, she stared at the spray of red roses partially hiding the shiny veneer of Jamal's casket. Jamal. He had wanted to get married in *his* church. In *his* hometown. He could have suggested they tie the knot on the planet Pluto, and Roxanne would have asked when the next space shuttle was due for takeoff. They were supposed to spend the rest of their lives together. Long, happy, lives. They were supposed to grow old together. They were going be the elderly couple holding hands as they walked around the mall or a local park.

At least that's what she had thought. On the day of their wedding, Roxanne had basked in the blessings and smiles of friends and family. Had heard nothing but well wishes, congratulations, and dirty jokes about what would happen on the honeymoon.

Roxanne pressed her back against the hard wood of the pew, hoping it would ground her. She still felt like she was floating. Not all there. This confusing, mind-numbing state had been going on for days now. Starting with the ride to John Hopkins Medical Center, then hearing the regret in the doctor's voice when she told Roxanne that she had been unable to revive Jamal. A confusion and disbelief so powerful had settled over her. She couldn't stop asking, *how?* She needed someone to explain to her how a man as young and fit as Jamal could die of a stroke?

But no answers made any sense, and an ever-widening dark pit inside consumed her. Blackness surrounded her. Black suits. Black dresses. Black coats worn to compete with the gray of winter. Even the faces of Jamal's white teammates were dark and overcast like the December sky outside. There was standing room only in a church that seated over seven hundred. Most folks had taken off their coats, but not Roxanne. Held by the icy hands of grief, she huddled in her fawn-colored trench coat, underneath which she wore an olive dress suit. She could not bring herself to wear black. Instead she donned the colors that Jamal liked to see her in. Staring at the bronze coffin, Roxanne wondered if Jamal could see her now? Did he approve of the funeral arrangement? Or was he feeling just as lost and confused? Maybe he was trying to recapture the joy and smiles of their wedding day, too.

There were no smiles today, just sobs that punctuated each sentence of Reverend Blake's eulogy, sobs that filled each pause for breath and lingered in the air. Someone was crying as if her heart was being fed through a paper shredder. Dried-eyed and straight-backed, Roxanne couldn't muster up enough energy to turn to see who it was. All she wanted to know was *Why can't I cry?* Given that Roxanne had been crying for a week, and the tears had only left her numb and exhausted, it seemed a crazy yearning. Still, she continued to hope they might bring her some relief. Help her accept that Jamal was gone.

On the coffin, a single rose disengaged from the rest. Roxanne's eyes followed as it first hung in midair and then in slow motion, silently fell to the carpeted floor. Suddenly, she was at Jamal's feet, her arms curled around his legs, her head resting on his thighs as she told him about her day. His strong hands touched her hair. Touched her face.

Roxanne closed her eyes reveling in the image. When she opened her eyes the rose lay motionless beneath the cold steel frames that supported Jamal's casket. She still couldn't believe it. In the back of her mind, she had always known the day would come when she had to attend her first funeral. She'd been sick with the flu the day Grandpa George had been buried. She'd felt sad.

She'd missed playing dominoes and checkers with him. But those feelings could not compare to the ache she felt now. Jamal's death wasn't right. It wasn't fair. He was too young. *They* were just starting to build their life together.

Supposedly, God had a plan. Had taken Jamal from her for a reason. At least, that's what everyone had been telling her in the past week. If it was supposed to make her feel better, make her miss him any less, make her understand how Death had stolen a young, supremely fit man, it wasn't working.

"Jamal Steele was a man who cared about community. A man dedicated to entertaining, thrilling, and most importantly, serving others—"

"Speak the truth, Rev," a voice Roxanne didn't recognize called out.

That was hardly surprising. The memorial service for family and a few close friends had been held at the funeral home the day before. Today's service was for the community Reverend Black had just referred to. Jamal was born and raised in Baltimore, so Roxanne had expected that a lot of people would turn out to show their respects, but still she was not prepared for the three-ring circus it had turned out to be. Reporters and cameras were everywhere. Jamal's death was sports news, local news, and even national news. And the mourners inside the church were nothing compared to the throng that lined both sides of Druid Hill Avenue from Lanvale Street down to McMechen. A police motorcade had escorted the limo carrying Roxanne, her mother, and Jamal's parents to the historic church, which had provided refuge and solace to the African-American community for six generations. Even though Roxanne didn't want her private pain to be on public display, it would have been selfish to deny folks the chance to say good-bye.

Roxanne flinched as the microphone screeched when Reverend Blake's voice rose in pitch. The minister's words had become background noise, indecipherable gibberish that could not compete with the memories crowding her mind. Despite the crush of people, Roxanne shivered, all the while knowing that the draft she felt was only in her mind like the images that swam before her eyes. She hadn't felt warm in over a week. She walked around the house wearing oversize sweaters and sweatshirts and sipping hot herbal tea to the point that her mother had produced an electric blanket from somewhere. A blanket that did nothing to warm the empty side of Roxanne's king-size bed.

The rustling sound of paper drew her attention to the fact that Reverend Blake had finished his eulogy. People were checking their program to see what was next on the agenda like they were at a Broadway show. Their guess was as good as hers. The program, with its color photo of Jamal, lay facedown and unopened on her lap.

Within hours of Jamal's death, everybody wanted her to make the funeral arrangements. At a time when she could barely think straight, couldn't comprehend that she would never hear his voice, never tease him about his creaky knees, she was expected to go from wondering what Jamal wanted for dinner to wondering what to bury him in. A suit? His football uniform? His mother had shoved a funeral-planning brochure under her nose. The coffin had to be selected. Not to mention the flowers and who would be on the guest list for the private ceremony?

Roxanne couldn't handle all the questions, all the decisions. Lord knows she had tried, but Jamal's family always treated her like she was a little off. They had stopped short of laughing in her face when she first described her plans for Hope Springs. All of them were business owners of some kind. Car dealerships. Fast-food franchises. Computer consultants. Dawson Steele, Jamal's father, would shake his salt-and-pepper head and ask why she was trying to save a world that was long past saving. Jamal's mother was just as skeptical. They didn't even acknowledge that Jamal was with her one hundred percent because, of course, no child of theirs could possibly be that stupid with his money. It was OK to donate *some* money to charity, but you didn't make it your life's work.

Bottom line, Roxanne suspected they were just worried that she was going to spend all Jamal's money. Jamal had always advised her to tune them out when they got on the subject of money. That's how he coped. But it bothered her that she couldn't like them more. Roxanne was not used to feeling that way about anyone. It wasn't right to feel so uncomfortable around family. But something about the whole bunch reminded her of Marcus, the guy she'd dated before Jamal. According to Marcus, nothing Roxanne ever did was good enough. Nothing she believed in made sense. If she had listened to him, sooner or later she would have forgotten who she was and would have become just as shallow and self-absorbed as he was. Then Jamal came along and proved that style *and* substance could exist hand in hand.

She glanced over at Ima and Dawson Steele. Her father-in-law was handsome even in his sorrow. Firm, medium brown skin, antique gold eyeglasses perched on a nose that was broad like Jamal's, and a thick mustache. His head was bent toward his wife who openly cried. His wide shoulders were unable to muffle the sound. Ima leaned into her husband. She looked nowhere near the six-foot height Roxanne knew her to be. Normally, she used that height and her supreme confidence to keep all her men in check. Streaks of mascara and puffy eyes marred her usually determined and proud face. Her son's death had temporarily felled a woman who took flying lessons to relax. Humanized her. Across the gap on the pew between her and her in-laws—a space big enough to fit another person—Roxanne noticed their tightly clasped hands. She was glad that they had each other to rely on. The space also reminded her that while they had each other, she could expect no support from the Steeles. She regretted but was not surprised that Jamal's death widened rather than closed the distance between them. They couldn't even agree on the funeral arrangements.

Ima, as she insisted Roxanne call her—not Mama, not Mom or even Mother—put up a fuss about the closed casket. Roxanne held her ground. That lifeless body cushioned on white velvet for all eternity was not her husband. She didn't want to see it. She especially didn't want to hear people talk about how good Jamal looked or gush over what a great job the embalmers had done to make him look natural. Her beloved, sweet, sweet husband was dead, and there was nothing natural about that. The closed casket and the request that donations be made to Hope Springs in lieu of flowers were the only things Roxanne had insisted on. She didn't have the strength or inclination to fight over anything else. Then Monique and Cynthia stepped in and knew just how to get Roxanne to think through what she really wanted. Even Ima didn't stand a chance against the combined power of her two friends.

She gladly let Cynthia and Monique handle the rest of the arrangements. The choir had sung two selections at the start, and

Linc had said his piece. The day before, Roxanne had managed a few words at the private memorial. And it had been hard. But there she'd been surrounded by love, which gave her the courage to speak. The first time in her life she *needed* to summon the courage to speak. To find the words. She got through it but knew instinctively that she couldn't face all the strangers at the public service. It was asking too much.

Thank God for her friends. She didn't even have to call. Messages from Cynthia and Monique had already been on her machine before she got the chance to phone. They had both arrived the day after Jamal died. Monique from Houston. And Cynthia from Tampa. Gayle was pregnant and unable to fly, but she and her husband, Reggie, drove down from Ohio as soon as they could. She had the room, so they were all staying at her house.

A flash of movement caught Roxanne's eye as Cynthia got out of the pew behind her and moved in front of the choir stand. Out of respect for the solemnness of the occasion, Cynthia, who was partial to pastels and bright colors, had worn a simple knee-length black dress. But Roxanne noticed that Cyn couldn't resist accenting it with a silky gold scarf. Her reddish-brown hair was pulled back into a knot and her makeup toned down. Only a dash of coral lipstick and some blush graced her extremely fair skin. Her blue eyes were devoid of their usual heavy dusting of shadow. A teenage member of the choir handed her a microphone. Cynthia thanked him then cleared her throat.

Her rich soprano soon filled the air:

"Like a comet blazing 'cross the evening sky, gone too soon. Like a rainbow fading in the twinkling of an eye, gone too soon . . ."

Sung a cappella, the words streaked into the safety of her dark pit, yanking on her. Suddenly, Roxanne sucked in a breath as if she had had the wind knocked out of her.

"Shiny and sparkly and splendidly bright. Here one day, gone one night . . ."

Roxanne's breath came faster. The haunting lyrics pulled at her, relentlessly dragging her away from the shielded harbor of numbness. Her hand went to her breast, blindly seeking the comfort of Jamal's wedding band, which now hung suspended from a gold chain around her neck. She kept it hidden under her clothes, close to her heart. She gently fingered the gold metal, searching for calm. She could only feel her furiously beating heart. It had come to life with a vengeance.

Roxanne's fingers gripped the ring even tighter when a warm hand came to rest on her shoulder. Even before she felt his warm breath near her ear, she recognized Linc's touch. The same hand had held hers when disbelief turned her to stone as she stood beside Jamal's still warm, yet unmoving body in the hospital emergency room. His arms had held her when reality sunk in and she broke down. And he had cried along with her.

"Roxy, are you all right?" Linc whispered.

The floral tribute on the coffin shimmered before her watery eyes. Where had all this emotion come from, she wondered? Twenty minutes ago, she'd been convinced that she was all cried out. Roxanne could only manage a brief nod, not trusting herself to speak.

A small squeeze of her shoulders then Linc's hand left her back. And the shivering started again. Roxanne pulled her coat lapels closer together and hugged herself. She bowed her head, straining for composure and silently willed Cynthia to finish the song before she completely lost control. She still had to get through the graveside ceremony.

She sensed rather than saw her mother get up from the pew. Probably going to get more Kleenex. Roxanne had been surprised how emotional her mother had been at Jamal's passing. It's not like they were that close. They only saw each other once or twice a year.

A muscled arm came around her, causing Roxanne to look up in surprise. Linc eased his big body in the spot where her mother had been. Wordless, she relaxed into the shelter of Linc's strong arms. Then gave way to what felt like a bottomless well of sorrow.

After the service was over, with Linc supporting her, his hand at her elbow practically holding her up, Roxanne managed to get through another round of condolences. She gave a big sigh. She was so tired, she could have fallen asleep standing up, and the funeral wasn't even over yet.

Linc peered into her face, then frowned as if he didn't like what he saw.

Self-consciously, Roxanne patted her cheek. It was hot to the touch, and no doubt her face was puffy. She was not one of those women who looked pretty when she cried. "I probably look like hell," she murmured.

"You look fine," he assured her.

Yeah right. "Spoken like a true friend," Roxanne replied, managing to muster up a faint smile. She looked around. The church was starting to clear out, but there had to be at least thirty people still milling around. Jamal's parents were talking to a group of people. Roxanne believed they'd been introduced as out-of-town relatives. Her mother had gone off somewhere with Monique, Gayle, and Cyn. Probably handling some last-minute detail. For which Roxanne was grateful. Though she was out of it most of the time, lost in her own thoughts and pain, she was very aware that somebody was handling her business.

Her girls. Not her sisters. Neither Denise nor LaToya had come for the funeral. Denise claimed she couldn't find anyone to keep her three kids. Which was a lie, because she quickly turned down Roxanne's offer to fly all of them to Baltimore. Roxanne could hear Denise's nervous cackle, "Girl, you ain't getting me up on no plane. If God had wanted me to fly, he would have given me wings." If ever there was a time to get over her fear of flying, this was it. That's what Roxanne had thought but didn't say. If Denise couldn't see that her big sister needed her, if she couldn't rise to the occasion just this once, then she wasn't going to beg her to come.

LaToya, on the other hand, wanted to come but Jimmy wasn't up to managing three kids on his own. He was still undergoing chemo and then there was Grandma Reynolds to tend to. Roxanne felt that the travel and funeral preparations would be too stressful for her grandma. Her grandma felt differently and after coming close to having their first argument, she had convinced Grandma Reynolds not to make the trip. Now she wished she hadn't. She needed her more than ever before. Tears began to tighten Roxanne's throat. She tried to shake off the cloak of self-pity. How dare she feel so alone when people who cared about her surrounded her?

Roxanne automatically accepted the bruising hugs of a couple of Jamal's teammates when they came over to her. Then her friend

Sabina, after searching her face, burst into tears. Roxanne's arms went around her slim waist, giving more comfort than she was getting.

She closed her eyes and saw Grandma Reynolds holding her to her soft bosom, her gray hair pulled back into a large plait that ended a couple of inches below her shoulders. Her apron was smeared with flour, and the hands that wiped away her tears smelled of chopped onions and seasoning salt. Her grandmother had both soothed and cried when Roxanne lost the race for student council secretary by seven votes.

Grandma Reynolds, that's who she needed right now. Someone who knew how to hold her just right. They had spoken on the phone every night since Jamal passed rather than the usual once or twice a week. Grandma Reynolds understood that the pain she was feeling was beyond words. So the wise old woman did most of the talking. Just hearing her voice over the line had been a salve to Roxanne's aching heart. Grandma Reynolds knew when she needed to talk or when to distract her with stories of her nieces and nephews. The last time they had spoken, as always she called her Sugar Plum and ordered her to take care of herself and trust in the Lord.

Roxanne blinked back tears; she wished Grandma Reynolds could be here now. But she didn't need to be around all this doom and gloom.

Unsure what she'd said in response to Sabina, who had just walked away from her, Roxanne was surprised when Linc announced, "Roxy, it's time . . ."

No need for him to finish his thought. It was time to go to the cemetery. Roxanne wiped away the tears in the corners of her eyes. Meanwhile, her stomach tightened then churned at the prospect of seeing Jamal's coffin lowered into the ground then covered with dirt.

Lord, give me the strength, she prayed silently.

"I need to stop by the ladies room before we leave," she said. She almost smiled when Linc took her hand in his, just like that day in second grade when the crossing guard hadn't shown up and they had to cross four lanes of traffic all by themselves to get to school.

When he pushed open the door of the ladies room with the palm of his hand, Roxanne did smile. She craned her neck up and then pointed to the sign beneath his hand. "I think this is where you and I part company, my brother."

Linc flashed her a sheepish smile. "I was just opening the door for you."

"Uh-huh. Thanks. I'll be out in a minute."

Roxanne was splashing water on her face when the bathroom door opened.

"Linc said I'd find you in here. Is everything OK?"

Roxanne turned at the sound of Monique's voice. Water dripped from her face as they boldly checked each other out as only old friends could do. Monique was, in a word, stunning. Model tall. Statuesque. Creamy complexion. Intelligent brown eyes. Her naturally wavy black hair was several inches shorter than usual, stopping just short of her shoulders. The black tailored pantsuit fit her to perfection. The greenish opal and diamond ring on her left hand was an antique and sparkled despite the dim light in the bathroom.

"What are you staring at?" Monique said with a bluntness that might have intimidated someone who didn't know her better. Instead, Monique's bitchiness was a sliver of normalcy in an otherwise unreal day.

When Roxanne simply smiled at her, Monique shook her head as if to say, Roxanne had finally lost her mind. Monique ripped a few brown paper towels from the holder and held them out to her. "Wipe your face, Roxanne, before you flood the floor."

Roxanne blotted her face with the towels, not wanting to further irritate her skin by rubbing it with the rough paper. It was already itchy from the deluge of salty tears. Not surprisingly, her acne was acting up. She had been avoiding mirrors all week. Sometimes you just didn't want to know what the damage was.

The bathroom door opened again. This time Cyn appeared. "The limo is outside, Roxanne. They are waiting for you," she said, while automatically walking over to the rectangular mirror above the row of sinks. Monique and Roxanne shared a smile when Cyn opened an oversize black leather bag and took out a brush, lipstick, blush, and an atomizer.

She caught their reflection in the mirror. "What?"

"Nothing," Roxanne said with a small laugh. It was good to have her friends here.

"I don't know why y'all laughing at me. Ain't nothing wrong with trying to look your best." She paused long enough to apply her lipstick. "Besides, I'm riding with that fine Lincoln. Maybe he can round up a few more football-playing hotties to ride with us. A girl's gotta work it when she can."

So Cyn was planning on "working it" at her husband's funeral. Roxanne should have been offended, but Cyn was being honest, so you had to love her for it.

"I thought you were riding with me and Gayle and Reggie," Monique said.

Cyn shrugged as she lined her lower lid. "Change of plans," she replied.

Monique rolled her eyes. "Why am I not surprised? Well, hurry up. And stop putting that gook on like you're using a shovel."

"Well, you gotta suffer for beauty."

"Whatever. I just hope you own some stock in cosmetic companies, because you're single-handedly keeping most of them in business."

Now, where was Gayle when Roxanne needed her? She was the one who usually broke up spats before they got out of hand. With a smile Roxanne reminded them, "Y'all are supposed to be here to support me, not sniping at each other."

"Who's sniping?" Cynthia said, tossing all her makeup and perfume bottle back in the bag. "Not me. Talk to the Yellow Rose of Texas over there—"

Despite the fact that Cyn was trying to get one last look in the mirror, Roxanne grabbed her by the arm and propelled her out the bathroom door.

A few minutes later everyone had gotten his or her coat, and Linc held open the heavy oak door of the church for Roxanne. The glare of the sun, which had decided to put in a belated appearance, blinded her as she stepped outside. At first she didn't see the reporters lined up on both sides of the gray slab steps.

A microphone was shoved in her face. "Mrs. Steele, would you care to comment on the rumors that your husband's death was brought on by drug use?"

"What?" Roxanne blinked, still trying to adjust to the sunlight.

"Is it true that your husband in his desperation to lead his team to the Championship Bowl was using steroids?"

"What? No!"

"What about allegations of illegal drug use? Crack cocaine?"

"Crack cocaine?" she numbly repeated, trying to edge away from the lights and microphones that seemed to be coming at her from all sides. What was happening here?

"Mrs. Steele, would you care to comment?"

"Hell, no, she wouldn't care to comment!" Monique had appeared. Stepping in front of Roxanne, she pushed the chest of the cameraman closest to her. "What the hell is wrong with you people?" she shouted. "My friend is trying to bury her husband today, and you're coming at her with this stupid bullshit! You insensitive pack of sensation-seeking assholes. Get that damn camera out of her face and get out of our way!"

Someone grabbed her around the waist. Startled, Roxanne jerked away then realized it was Linc. The expression on his face was fiercer than any he'd worn on the football field. He looked ready to do some damage to somebody, and unlike Monique, he didn't utter a word. Didn't have to. The reporters retreated. That didn't stop Monique from continuing to give them a piece of her mind. Linc seized the opportunity to rush Roxanne into the limo that waited for her at the curb. She was shaking uncontrollably but scooted over when he nudged her as he climbed in to join her, the Steeles, and her mother. Linc pulled her close and put his arm around her shoulder, trying to calm her.

As the limo pulled away, she belatedly realized that Cyn would have to hitch a ride to the cemetery with Monique after all.

Chapter

11

Once in the limo, Roxanne was unable to answer any of the questions Jamal's parents were firing at her. She was still reeling from the barrage of accusations and insinuations herself. So, it was Linc who tried to calm everyone down by assuring them that everything the reporters alleged was bull. But where would they have come up with a crazy idea like that in the first place is what Roxanne wanted to know.

She had been in such a daze that it never occurred to her that the news hounds would follow them to the cemetery, when they were unable to get answers at the church. Part of her was grateful for the distraction. It gave her something else to think about besides watching her husband's coffin being lowered into the cold ground. Knowing she had an audience lining the drive leading to the cemetery kept her from hurling herself into the dark hole alongside Jamal.

The reporters waited until the service was over—not that they got any points for that—before they hit her again with the same insane questions and insinuations. And this time none of the mourners were spared. Finally, Linc and some of Jamal's teammates shoved and pushed their way back to the cars, not giving a thought as to how the league brass might flip out when they saw pictures of that on the news and all the morning papers.

Again, Roxanne had been hurried into the waiting limo. It was not the kind of good-bye that Jamal deserved.

Sitting at her kitchen table, Roxanne inhaled and could easily recall the smell of the rich, slightly damp earth surrounding Jamal's grave. She could see the warm breaths of the crowd of thirty or so making contact with the frosty air and hear her own sobs echoing in her ears. She closed her eyes to focus on calming her stomach.

"Roxanne, are you sure I can't get you something to eat?" Gayle asked.

When Roxanne reluctantly opened her eyes, they honed in on the worry lines etched in her friend's forehead. "No. I'm not hungry," Roxanne replied, then pretended not to see the little looks her friends were throwing each other as they sat around her kitchen table. She knew what they were thinking. *Since when has Roxanne ever turned down food?* The big joke between them was that Roxanne was always hungry, Gayle always had to pee, Monique was always *pissed* about something, and Cynthia, well, Cyn never met a mirror or a man she could resist.

Roxanne longed to be her normal self—if only to put everyone's mind at ease. But in truth, she hadn't been eating. Couldn't. And she could tell by the way her clothes were fitting that she'd lost a few pounds in the last week. Jamal would hate that. He said he loved her curves, her hips, and her big behind and generous breasts. Every chance he could, his hands would seek out each spot, and he'd laughingly tell her that God had blessed her with fat in all the right places.

"And other local news . . . allegations of drug use have surfaced in connection with the untimely death of hometown hero Jamal Steele—"

They all turned to stare at the 13-inch color television that sat on the butcher block island in the center of the kitchen. A twentysomething blonde with an unnatural winter tan stood on the steps of New Jerusalem. The camera panned to show Roxanne emerging from the church with Linc and then being stopped as reporters swarmed her.

Roxanne barely recognized herself. Is that what she looked like these days? Swollen nose and tired-looking eyes that were the result of too little sleep and too much crying.

Monique quickly reached for the remote and changed the channel. The next station was running more of the same. "Roxanne Steele, widow of pro football star Jamal Steele and community activist in her own right, declined to comment—"

"Oh, hell," Monique exclaimed before turning the TV off altogether. "This trash is everywhere you look."

"You would think that they had some important *and* factual news to report," Gayle agreed.

"Ha!" Monique snorted. "Factual and news. Now, those are two words you don't often see in the same sentence."

Cynthia delicately cleared her throat. "Hey y'all don't forget that someone at this table has a degree in journalism," she reminded them. "Roxanne, maybe you should give a statement. It kind of leaves room for speculation if you don't say anything. I could come up with a brief press release if you like."

Roxanne pushed the hair off of her face and slowly shook her head. "What's the point? People are going to believe what they want." Besides, she was pretty sure the team would be siccing its own spin doctors on the story. She slapped her hand on the table in frustration. "It's all a big fat lie!" The look she gave them dared anyone to contradict her.

"Of course it is, sweetie," Gayle interjected into the brief silence that followed. "I just wish the press had shown a little respect and restraint on today of all days."

Roxanne could feel tears welling up in her eyes *again*. Her sigh was heavy. She was so sick of this. One minute she felt empty, dead inside. The next minute she was turning on a waterworks display that could rival Niagara Falls.

"Are you all right, Roxanne?" Gayle asked.

"I'm OK. I just don't want to talk about this anymore."

Gayle reached across the table and covered Roxanne's hand with her own slightly swollen one. Her simple gold wedding band seemed to cut into her flesh. It looked painful. But Roxanne knew that there was no way her friend would ever take the ring off. Just as until now she'd never seen Jamal without his ring, unless he was playing in a football game. Now the weight of his ring hung heavy around her neck.

Without realizing it, she had begun to finger the ring and

stopped only when she caught Gayle watching her, matching tears glistening in her eyes. At eight months pregnant, Gayle's body had enlarged and tightened, like a fruit at the height of its ripeness. Her protruding belly kept her from pulling her chair up close to the table.

To soothe the achy, hollow place in her heart, Roxanne made herself look at something else. Anything else but the obvious reminder of her own empty womb.

Gayle managed to keep her tears at bay but still begged, "Roxanne, please eat something."

Her pregnancy had stretched Gayle's dark chocolate skin even tighter across the high cheekbones that were the highlight of her face. She wasn't exactly glowing, but there was a balance to Gayle that hadn't been there before. She was always tending to other people: her family, her job, and, of course, her friends. Which was why she'd been waddling around the house the past few days following Roxanne like a shadow, handling phone calls, making sure everyone was comfortable. She always noticed the little things, like the laundry that needed doing and the condolence cards, telegrams, and faxes that needed organizing.

It went without saying that Gayle was going to make a great mother.

And waddling or not, pregnancy suited her. However, the concern in her brown eyes did not. It was out of sync with the rest of her obvious contentment. Roxanne blamed herself for that. She'd forgotten how sensitive to and affected by other people's feelings Gayle could be.

"I've been here three days, and I haven't seen you take more than a bite or two," Gayle said.

"Don't worry about me," Roxanne said. "It's just a lot to absorb all at once. I'm . . . I'll be fine." She felt like that last phrase was a mantra that she'd been repeating again and again until it had little real meaning. She wasn't fine. Her life had been turned inside out. But telling other people wasn't going to fix anything, so she kept it to herself. She didn't want people worrying about her.

"I know, Roxanne," Gayle said. "But you gotta eat something. You gotta keep your strength up."

Her eyes held compassion, but the hand touching hers increased its pressure for just an instant, long enough for Roxanne to know that Gayle wasn't going to let up until she ate something. In her own caring way, Gayle could be pushy.

"All right," Roxanne conceded with a sigh. But she didn't know how she was going to get any food past the lump in her throat. All around them, on the table and countertops were casseroles, cakes, and pies that people had brought by the house over the last few days. Now that all the other visitors had gone, they'd congregated in the kitchen to clear away some of the mess.

Roxanne had begged her assistant, Marita, to get rid of her mother for a while because she really needed some space from her constant attempts to cheer her up. Marita said something about going over to Hope Springs on the pretext of picking up some files and checking on the office and invited Dot to come along. Her mother was not one to sit in one place for very long, so she jumped at the chance to get out of the house. Linc was in the basement playing pool with Gayle's husband, Reggie. That was the farthest he'd been from her side all day, she realized. The men had offered to help, but Roxanne had insisted they could do it themselves. Which was only partially true.

To her surprise and shame, she was finding it hard to be around Reggie. More precisely, she was finding it hard to be around Gayle and Reggie. Try as she might, she could not shake herself of the jealousy she felt when she saw how it was between the two of them. Jealousy was a foreign emotion to her, one that made her feel small and petty. But she couldn't bear to see the way Reggie's eyes were drawn to Gayle. No matter what he was doing or what he was talking about, sooner or later his gaze sought out his wife. And when they caught each other's eye, it was like a blow to Roxanne's heart. She knew that look. She missed that look. Longed for it. She knew they weren't being goo-goo-eyed deliberately, weren't trying to rub their happiness in her face. Gayle would have been mortified if she'd known what effect it was having on Roxanne. She wasn't proud of herself, but one of them had to go, and Reggie was the obvious choice.

"Roxanne, what can I get you? Something filling is what you need. A little something in your stomach will make you feel better. You've got to be running on empty by now," Gayle said, not letting up on her mission to get Roxanne to eat.

When Roxanne noticed Gayle using her free hand to rub her stomach over the red-and-black maternity blouse she wore, she said, "I'll try to eat something, but Gayle you gotta stop worrying about me. I don't want you passing that anxiety on to my little godson or goddaughter."

Gayle's mouth curved into a satisfied smile as she lumbered out of her seat. She opened the door of the fridge and studied the contents of the overcrowded shelves. "Let's see what I can find. How about some vegetable soup? And maybe some cornbread to go with it?" Taking Roxanne's indifferent shrug as approval, she took out a large green Tupperware bowl.

As Gayle braced the bowl against her swollen belly to pry off the lid, Monique said, "Girl, you are as big as a house. When is your rugrat due to make an appearance?"

Gayle grimaced as, with a little grunt, the clear plastic top came off. She grabbed a small ceramic bowl from the cabinet and spooned some soup into it and then popped it in the microwave. "The doctor said four weeks. But from the way he or she has been doing flips lately, it feels like any day now. I think Roxanne's godbaby is gonna be a gymnast."

Cynthia paused in wrapping up what was left of a pound cake. They had all changed into more casual clothes, and Cynthia was back in her usual pastels, a pink-and-white nylon jogging suit. "Hold up a minute. Roxanne is not going to be Little Cindy's godmother. I am."

Monique scoffed. "Little Cindy? We don't even know if it's a boy or a girl, and you already got the kid named, and after you, no less."

"We're out of foil," Cynthia announced, clearly expecting someone to make that problem go away. "What?" she said when she caught Monique rolling her eyes.

"Nothing, little Miss Southern Belle," Monique replied. "Don't trouble yourself. One of us servants will get it for you."

Monique made a commotion as she rooted through the cabinet where Roxanne kept her supplies like paper towels, napkins, and plastic wrap. "Where the hell is the aluminum foil?" Finally, she triumphantly held up the shiny blue-and-silver box, and then slammed the drawer with such force, Roxanne was surprised she didn't smash her fingers. Patience was not Monique's strong suit.

She tossed the box to Cynthia, who made a halfhearted grab for it, probably afraid of chipping one of her store-bought nails. She missed it by a mile. It landed on the floor next to her chair.

Roxanne wasn't surprised. This was the same woman who almost didn't graduate from college because she kept putting off the physical education requirement until the last semester of her senior year. She smiled when she noticed that Cynthia gestured for Monique to pick the foil up off the floor and properly hand it to her. Monique did so with exaggerated care. Those two were a trip.

Setting aside the foil, Cynthia dipped a finger on the edge of a deep-dish peach pie that she was supposed to be covering and brought it to her mouth. She smacked her lips appreciatively. Roxanne was happy that someone still had an appetite. She was particularly happy it was Cyn, especially after what she went through a few years ago, practically starving herself to death because she got into her fool head the idea that men liked women who resembled stick figures.

After watching Cynthia go to town on the pie, Monique said, "They have invented this thing. It's called a fork. You should try using one sometime. Better yet, why don't you cut yourself a piece and stop digging around in it with your fingers."

"Uh-uh. It tastes better when you eat it straight from your fingers."

Now Roxanne smiled in earnest. Cynthia was the most mannered of them all. She even owned a copy of Emily Post's book on etiquette. This bantering back and forth between her friends was like old times. Pretty soon they'd be playing the dozens, and Gayle would have to break it up.

"You know your mama didn't raise you like that," Monique said with a mock frown. "And to think, you expect Gayle to make you her baby's godmother. And, besides, you got a lot of nerve declaring yourself the godmother anyhow."

Cynthia scooped up another finger full of pie, totally unconcerned with Monique's opinion of her. "Well, ain't nobody else here having a baby anytime soon. And there's no point in my holding my breath waiting on you and Tyson to produce a godchild," she told Monique.

Roxanne's hand flew to her heart. It couldn't have hurt any

more if Cyn had picked up one of the copper pots hanging on the rack above the sink and hit her with it.

Seeing Roxanne's stricken look, Gayle said, "Cyn!"

Cynthia put her pie-covered fingers to her mouth in dismay. When she took her hand away, filling and crust crumbs dotted her lips. "Oh, Roxanne, I'm so, so sorry. I didn't mean it like it sounded . . . I . . . wasn't even thinking about you and Jamal."

"Obviously," Monique said. "You weren't thinking at all."

Not taking her eyes off Roxanne, Cynthia said, "Seriously, honey. I didn't mean to cause you any pain. I was talking about Monique and Tyson—"

"Don't even go there," Monique warned, stopping Cynthia in mid-sentence.

Another look passed between the three of them. A look that Roxanne couldn't decipher.

They were keeping something from her.

Looking from one to the other, she said, "What?" Gayle averted her eyes, and Cynthia's cheeks had gone from blush pink to bright red under the fiery glare Monique gave her.

The microwave dinged. "Your soup is ready," Gayle cheerfully announced, and then busied herself with bringing the food over to Roxanne.

Ignoring her, Roxanne's eyes narrowed, taking in Cynthia's preoccupation with the aluminum foil box and the fact that Monique's face had turned stone-like, giving nothing away. "How about somebody telling me what's going on?" Roxanne said.

"Nothing," Monique muttered. "Cyn is just being her usual, open-mouth-insert-foot self."

Quickly, nodding her agreement, Cyn said, "She's right. Let's just forget about it."

Suddenly everybody was avoiding her eyes. They were all lying. "Y'all must think I'm an idiot. Just tell me what it is."

Monique reached for the pack of cigarettes and silver lighter that were always nearby. She lit one up and took a drag before speaking. Gayle moved over to the sink and out of range of the smoke. "I really didn't want to get into this . . ." Monique said, then paused to level another heated look at Cynthia, ". . . because it didn't seem like the right time."

"Get into what?"

"Me and Tyson."

"What about you and Tyson?"

"Tyson is about to get fired. We're separated."

"What? Since when?" Monique had told her that Tyson couldn't get away from the hospital. First those lying reporters and now this. Didn't anybody tell the truth anymore? she wondered.

"Since about a couple of weeks ago."

"Why didn't you tell me?" Roxanne demanded. They always told each other everything or knew each other so well, they could sense when something was wrong and drag it out of the other person. But she'd been so out of it, she hadn't caught a whiff of this one.

"I was going to but . . ." Monique shrugged, looking elegant even in a long-sleeve UT Austin T-shirt, ". . . before I got the chance . . ."

Before she got the chance, Jamal had died. Roxanne slumped back in her chair, restlessly twirling the ends of her dreads. Monique and Tyson had been engaged twice, once in college and then again years later. The last engagement had been short. Lasting only long enough to give Monique's socialite mother a chance to put together the kind of wedding she felt befitted her daughter. "Monique, you've got to get back to Texas. You and Tyson need to work this out."

Monique curled her lips. "Ain't nothing to work out."

"How can you say something like that?" Tyson, who was an OB/GYN, had been nothing but helpful and supportive, providing information about infertility and giving her the names of specialists when she and Jamal started to have problems conceiving. "Tyson is one of the good guys. A real sweetheart."

"He'd have to be to put up with the likes of her," Cynthia offered.

"Nobody asked you, Cyn," Monique retorted.

Gayle put a steaming bowl of soup and a saucer that was almost completely taken up by a hunk of cornbread down in front of Roxanne. "Do we really need to get into this now?" she asked. Her voice was soft, but the look she gave Cynthia and Monique was anything but. "It's been a long day, and I'm sure Roxanne doesn't need to hear this."

"Of course I need to hear it. Girlfriend is sitting up in my kitchen when she needs to be at home working things out with her husband," Roxanne said. "Besides, what did he do that was so bad that you can't imagine working things out with him? Did he commit a crime? Does he have a bimbo on the side?" Roxanne asked that last question knowing it was about as likely as Jamal having a girlfriend. She could not imagine the straight-laced Tyson cheating.

"No, Tyson is not creepin' on me. He is many things, but crazy is not one of them," Monique said with the utter confidence that Roxanne had come to expect from her.

"Then, what did he do?" Roxanne repeated her earlier question.

"He accepted a partnership with my father and my brother, Maurice. Can you believe he's joining their medical practice?" Monique cried, and followed up this revelation by viciously stubbing out the cigarette in a nearby saucer.

Roxanne cocked her head to one side. That was it? Monique made it sound like the end of the world or something. Slowly Roxanne inquired, "And that's a problem . . . how?"

Monique looked around the table at her friends. "You even have to ask? You know how I feel about my family. They're always up in my business. I never should have moved back to Texas in the first place," she muttered.

When Monique and Tyson had hooked up for the second time, she had been working as an assistant prosecutor in Cleveland. Tyson had been finishing up his residency at Texas Medical Center. After much debate and discussion, they had decided to live in Houston because it had the best job possibilities for them both. Roxanne thought Monique had gotten this aversion to her family out of her system. So what if they were bougie? Some people might call Roxanne's family ghetto. But nobody got to pick their relatives; you just learn to take the good with the bad, and work around the bad whenever you could.

"Monique, I still don't get it. So what if Tyson works with your brother and father. What's so precious about your 'business' that you can't have them knowing about it?" When Monique didn't bother to answer, Roxanne asked, "So what does your family have to say about this separation?"

Monique lowered her eyes and said something Roxanne couldn't quite catch. "Say that again."

"I haven't told them, yet."

"For heavens' sake, why not?"

"I just don't want to deal with them constantly butting into my business. The more involved we become with my family the worse it's going to get. My mother's already on my case about not having kids yet. You'd think she'd be satisfied with Maurice's two. If I let her, Gloria would take up all my free time with family functions and social events. She's relentless. 'Join this organization. Monique, it is essential that Tyson be seen at this party or that gala,' " Monique mimicked her mother's deep, cultured voice. "And she's still harassing me about my job not being good enough. At least now, when she's trying to drag me into something I want no part of, I can lie and say we have other plans. But with Tyson working alongside my father and brother, Gloria will have the 411 on my every waking moment."

The spoon that Roxanne had picked up clattered on the table. Her soup went untouched. "From what you've just said, I don't think Tyson is the one who has a hard time dealing with your interfering family," Roxanne told her. "It's you. Why should Tyson turn down a perfectly good job opportunity? From everything you've said, both your father and brother are top-notch physicians. You need to stop trippin' and just be glad you have a husband who loves you . . . and is a . . . a . . . alive and can be there with you whether it's in Houston . . . or any damn place. You're so, so, stupid . . ." Roxanne said, her voice breaking. "I would give anything. I mean anything to have Jamal back and to : . . and to have a family that wanted to be a part of my life. Think about it. I buried my husband today, and I have one family member here. Just one. A little family interference would feel real good about now . . ." Roxanne's outburst came to an end as the tears started to flow.

"I hope you're satisfied, Monique," Cynthia said. "You've gotten her all upset."

"I've gotten her upset?" came Monique's swift and indignant reply. "If you hadn't opened your big mouth, we wouldn't even be having this conversation."

Tears blurred Roxanne's vision. Steam no longer rose from the vegetable soup Gayle had given her. It had cooled off quickly, as microwaved food was prone to do. Looking at it was making her sick just like this conversation. She had to get out of here. Roxanne pushed away from the table and stood up.

Sensing her intentions, Gayle came over to her and laid a hand on her arm, "Roxanne, don't leave. You still haven't eaten anything."

Torn between sparing Gayle more worry and knocking Monique upside the head, Roxanne said softly, "I'm really not hungry. But I am tired, so I'm gonna go lie down."

As Monique reached for another cancer stick and her lighter, Roxanne slowly shook her head. "You don't know how lucky you are, Monique. You just don't know." Then she left the room.

Roxanne went into the bedroom and pretended to be asleep whenever anyone came in to check on her. Eventually, she heard the sounds of people settling down for the night: the shower running, bedroom doors opening and closing, in the room next to hers, Gayle telling Reggie to turn down the television so he wouldn't disturb her.

With a long sigh, Roxanne sat up and leaned back against the headboard. If Gayle only knew how "disturbed" she already was, she thought. The dial on the alarm clock told her it was after midnight. A new day found Roxanne shivering and so alone. When her teeth actually started to chatter, she got out of bed and took a throw blanket from the nearby settee. She wrapped it around her shoulders, and as quietly as she could, crept downstairs to make herself something warm to drink.

The track lighting that edged the walkway in the backyard always provided some illumination in the kitchen at night, so Roxanne skipped the main light switch and turned on only the fluorescent above the sink. Draping the blanket over the back of a chair, Roxanne took out a tin of Godiva mocha-flavored hot chocolate and found herself thinking about how much Jamal indulged her sweet tooth. She could always count on him to bring her a box of chocolates or maybe even a candy bar that he had gotten out of the vending machine at the clubhouse. And he had arranged a cake-of-the-month deal with a local gourmet bakery, so there was always something sweet in the house—besides him.

Roxanne sat two mugs on the counter. She poured milk into one and put it in the microwave and put several scoops of the chocolate in the other. As she waited for the milk to warm, she wrapped herself in the blanket again and surveyed her now immaculate kitchen. If you included the walk-in pantry, the kitchen was probably bigger than the entire one-bedroom apartment she had been living in when she first met Jamal. Roxanne wondered where her friends had put all the food, since the refrigerator had been pretty full already. When they left, she was going to take it all to a homeless shelter or food bank. She was a coward for not saying that in the first place, but it just would have made everyone worry that she wouldn't be eating enough.

The microwave dinged. She poured the hot milk over the powdered chocolate. After adding a dash of cinnamon and vanilla, Roxanne moved with drink in hand over to the table. She sat in one chair while propping her feet in another, idly stirring the contents of her cup while staring out into the barrenness of the winter landscape. Leafless tree branches stood out against a moonlight sky like skeletons. At this hour, it was hard to tell if it was a layer of ice or dew that covered the paved walk leading to the greenhouse near the back of the property. It was a sanctuary that Jamal had had built especially for her, so that she could garden year-round because he knew that besides cooking, gardening was one of the few activities that relaxed her.

Roxanne took a sip of the sweet liquid and cradled the cup in her hands to warm them. She winced as a flash of pain followed the image of Jamal's mother tossing a handful of dirt on his coffin. Roxanne wondered if she'd ever be able to relish the feel of dirt in her hands again. Right now, she couldn't imagine it.

Linc's deep voice suddenly interrupted the path her thoughts had taken. "Everything OK?"

Roxanne had to react quickly to keep the cup from slipping out of her hands at the unexpected sound of his voice. Openmouthed, she raised her eyes to stare at him. Linc wore a pair of gray sweatpants but was shirtless and barefoot. Once she found her voice again, she said, "What are you doing here? I thought you went home."

Shaking his head, Linc pulled a chair up right next to hers. His long legs joined her much shorter ones on the other chair. He grabbed a couple of paper napkins from the holder and extended them to her. When she didn't immediately take them, he pointed to her hand. Chocolate had sloshed over the rim of the mug and was running down her fingers. Linc took the cup from her, wiped it down, and did the same with her fingers. He playfully sniffed the mug. "What you got in here? Kahlúa? Bailey's?"

"I wish. There's just a drop of vanilla in it. You can have it if you want."

Linc sat the mug on the table instead. "What's the matter? Couldn't sleep?"

"I was cold. I thought a hot drink might warm me up."

"Did it?"

"Not really."

"You've been chilled all week. I think you should see a doctor. Maybe you're coming down with something."

Yes, she thought, a bad case of grief and loneliness. "I don't think so," she said, then changed the subject. "I thought you were going home."

He grinned, his teeth gleaming in the near darkness. "I was, until I heard you were on the warpath."

The warpath? The argument with Monique. Roxanne ducked her head. "Oh? You heard about that. I'll apologize to her in the morning. Who am I to tell her how to live her life?"

"I didn't get all the details, but I'm sure whatever you said to her was out of love and concern."

"You're giving me too much credit. The fact is, I was pissed. Some people just don't know how good they've got it until it's gone. I should know," she said, her mouth twisting into a tight, pained smile.

He shook his head and put an arm around her. "That's not true. You showed Jamal all the time how much you loved him. And I *know* he realized what a prize he had in you. In fact, I made it my job to remind him of that each and every day."

Roxanne laid her head on his shoulder. "I know you did and that is one of the many reasons I love you, my brother." Linc reached his other arm across her waist and pulled her closer. Roxanne sighed and relaxed into his big strong embrace. She could feel the steady rise and fall of his chest. Her hand gently touched the springy hair that covered that vast area. His skin was warm, and in turn it began to warm her. So far it was the only thing that had taken the chill off the least little bit.

They sat that way for several minutes. Finally Linc whispered, "Are you asleep, Roxy?"

"No, I was just thinking."

" 'Bout what?"

"About what the reporters are saying . . ." She couldn't even bring herself to ask the question.

"All lies. Roxy, you got to try not to take this personally. Whenever something happens to a professional athlete, the press makes more out of it than it is. They can allege all they want, but they're not going to find any dirt on Jamal. I would know if he was using steroids or anything else. And I swear to you he wasn't."

Roxanne burrowed her face against his shoulder. Breathing in soap, a hint of spice, and pure, familiar Linc. She relaxed a bit more. If Linc said Jamal was clean, then she believed him. Other than her, he knew Jamal better than anyone. "I feel stupid for even asking. But Jamal had started to work out more, had beefed up some—"

"Roxy, that's just because he was a man with a mission. He really wanted this to be his Championship Bowl year. Jamal was a warrior. He was just preparing for battle. And the way he did it was strictly legit. I was there with him from jump street."

He took her hand and placed it on the biceps of his left arm. "Here, feel this. Feel that cut. And it's all na-tu-ral, baby. Just like my boy, Jamal," he said. His cockiness was just for show.

As far as Roxanne could tell, his muscles had always looked and felt like this. But she had his word that Jamal's bulking up had nothing to do with drugs, and that was good enough for her. Still, there were other things that niggled at the back of her mind. "Jamal had been so moody these past few weeks. Sometimes he was so loving and attentive, it was almost suffocating, and other times it was like he was on another planet. Then there was me acting so stupid about having a baby. I just don't know if he was happy . . ." She paused, trying not to let her emotions get the best of her. "And it would break my heart to think that he died and wasn't one hundred percent happy."

Linc hugged her closer to him and rested his chin on the top of her head. "Roxy, don't do this. First of all, who *is* one hundred percent happy all of the time? Secondly, if Jamal was unhappy, and I'm not saying that he was, believe me it had nothing to do with you."

Roxanne levered herself away from him and tried to see his eyes. In the semidarkness, they were luminous but hard to read. "So there was something. I knew he wasn't quite himself."

"No . . . no, there was nothing wrong," he insisted. "Jamal was just preoccupied . . ." Responding to her questioning look, Linc hastily added, "With football. He wanted to excel this season, and he did. He broke his own reception and TD records. That distance you felt was just focus and commitment. Promise me that you will stop thinking it was something you did."

"OK."

"No, I want you to promise that you believe it had nothing to do with you."

"OK. I promise to stop blaming myself."

"Good girl."

She half expected him to pat her on the head the way he used to do to that mutt, Guido. They had found him abandoned under a bridge while they were out riding their bikes one summer. Linc had extracted a promise from her then, too. "Promise me, that you won't tell my mama that we found him and brought him home. We'll just say we found him in the backyard, right? She'll have to let me keep him if he is already living on the property."

Linc had been right about his mama. She let him keep the dog. She hoped he was right about Jamal, too. That he had been happy.

"You 'bout ready to go back to bed?"

"Not really. It's weird, but this is where I feel closest to Jamal. We designed this kitchen together. We picked out this old table. We put in the tiles. Jamal added shelves to the pantry."

Linc gave a little laugh. "That in and of itself should tell you how much he loved you, because Jamal may have had the surest hands in football, but he was pathetic with a hammer and nail. He probably pounded his thumb more than the nails."

Roxanne's lips curved at the memories of working on the kitchen. There had been a lot of cursing and muttering going on as they had laid the tiles, and they hadn't been coming from her. Jamal's clumsiness was worth it because then she got to kiss and make all his boo-boos better. "It's nice to talk about him like this. I feel like you're the only one who understands what Jamal meant to me."

"He meant a lot to me, too. He wasn't just my friend. He was more like an older brother."

"What do you mean older brother? You're two years older than him."

"But he was light-years more mature and focused than me. He pulled me along."

This had to be hard on him, too. Jamal had been his running buddy both on and off the field. "Linc, how are you doing?" Roxanne couldn't believe she was just getting around to checking in with him. Other than their mutual emotional meltdown at Jamal's bedside, she had no idea how Linc was feeling.

His arms tightened around her waist, crushing her a little. She felt his whole body heave with the sigh he expelled. "It's hard. Nothing is the same without him." She nodded her understanding against his bare chest. "The play-offs start this week," he added.

The play-offs! Roxanne had forgotten all about that. Her mind had been filled with only thoughts of Jamal. She'd forgotten that they had won the game against Pittsburgh. No wonder Linc and so many of Jamal's teammates had been there offering support all weekend. Having won their division outright, they had a week off while the wild cards duked it out.

When she didn't say anything after a while, Linc said, "Roxy, did you hear what I said?"

"Yes, the show must go on," she choked out. Hot tears leaked onto his chest.

"Sssh," he said, rocking her from side to side, the same motions used to quiet a fussing baby. "I didn't mean to make you cry, Roxy. But come tomorrow, I won't be around as much because we'll be in a lot of team meetings this week."

"I understand," she sniffed, trying to keep in the tears. She backed up a little and used the palms of her hands to wipe away the moisture she'd left on his skin. "It's just that it was Jamal's dream to go to the Championship Bowl . . . and now . . . now that dream is gone."

He took hold of her hands and brought her back into the circle of his embrace. "No, it's not. His dream lives on in me. I know how badly Jamal wanted to go all the way this year, and I'm going to do everything in my power to make his dream a reality. The team wouldn't have gotten this far without him."

Though Roxanne appreciated what he was saying, every word was a reminder that Jamal was not here. That Linc would have to go it alone. And so would she. "Lincoln, I want you to win. I wish the team the best. But I don't think I'm ready to sit through a foot-ball game."

"Don't you think I know that? I just wanted you to be prepared when all the play-off talk starts heating up. I know you *and* Jamal will be there in spirit."

He was such a good friend, even more so in this moment when she really needed him to understand. The tears fell anew. "I . . . I'll be glad when all this weepy stuff stops," Roxanne said, "I'm going to drown your poor chest hair if it doesn't."

"Do you see me complaining? My mama always said if you're crying, there must be a reason. So if there's a tear left in you, let it fall."

And because she couldn't help herself, she did.

When she was done, a thought occurred to her. All five bed-rooms were occupied. "Where are you sleeping?"

"On the fold out in the basement."

Ever the conscientious hostess, Roxanne groaned. No wonder he was up in the middle of the night. That sofa bed was not made for a six-foot-four giant like him. "Oh, Linc, you should have gone home. You're going to have all sorts of kinks in your back tomorrow."

"Yeah, but it was my choice. Besides, I had another offer. Cyn-thia said I could sleep with her."

Roxanne laughed. "I just bet she did. You should count your-self lucky. Cyn is prone to having X-rated dreams. Usually about

Danny Glover. I don't want you to get molested while you're under my roof." She stood up and grabbed his hand. "I'm going to sleep with my mom or Monique. So you can have my bed." He might as well have it, because memories of Jamal were too fresh for her to find any peace there.

Chapter

12

Gayle sat on one of the two bar stools at the island in the center of Roxanne's kitchen. Amused, she watched with her chin propped on her hand as two grown women played beauty salon. Though they had only met each other a handful of times and there was at least a twenty-year age difference, Cynthia and Roxanne's mother were definitely birds of a feather. They had gone shopping together and swapped beauty and fashion magazines when they both complained they couldn't find "anything good" to read around the house. Today they were giving each other makeovers. Cynthia had given Miss Miller a facial and "sculpted her eyebrows." Now Roxanne's mother was in the process of giving Cyn a manicure. Despite the sad reason for this trip, Cyn had come with a fully equipped makeup kit. She had no less than five nail polishes to choose from. And it had taken her forever to pick one.

Gayle had sat a safe distance away from the nail polish and other fumes. These days she never knew what smell would make her sick to her stomach. Monique was also at the kitchen table—hiding behind a newspaper. After insisting on making them breakfast, Roxanne, who looked like a participant in a sleep deprivation experiment, had announced she needed some time alone. Gayle had a feeling that Roxanne didn't know what she needed. She was lost without Jamal. But for once, all of them kept their opinions to themselves. Roxanne left them to clean up. Gayle didn't know where she'd disappeared to. It was a big house. Reggie and Linc were in the basement working out.

A frown wrinkled her brow as she tried to remember how long ago that had been. *Over an hour?* Her husband was an accountant, not a professional athlete like Linc. She didn't want him hurting himself by trying to keep up with someone whose physical fitness was a job requirement. Thoughts of Jamal threatened to overwhelm her. *He* had been in excellent shape, and that hadn't saved him. And if she couldn't believe someone as healthy as Jamal had passed on the way he did, what must Roxanne be going through? Her heart ached for her friend because she couldn't imagine what she'd do if Reggie were taken from her without warning like that. *That's it,* Gayle decided. *If Reggie doesn't show up in ten minutes, I'll go down there and drag him away from that weight bench myself.*

The sunburst yellow phone that was right at her fingertips chirped, which forced Gayle to deal with reality and not what-ifs. Without thinking, she picked it up. She'd been answering Roxanne's phone and doorbell ever since she got here.

There was a brief pause and then a computerized voice came on. "I have a collect call from . . ."

A male voice with a Caribbean accent said, "Etienne."

"Will you accept the charges?"

Who could be calling Roxanne collect? Gayle wondered, but only for a second. Feeling like she needed to make up her mind quickly, she went ahead and said, "Yes."

"Thank you very much," the man politely said. "This is Etienne. I wish to speak to Dot."

"Just a minute," Gayle replied, then pressed the mute button. "Miss Miller, the phone is for you," she said, holding the cordless phone out to Roxanne's mother. "It's long distance. It's somebody named Etienne."

Cynthia grinned and said, "Go on with your bad self, Miss Miller. You got a man tracking you down." Not waiting for a response from the woman she was teasing, she glanced down at her still drying nails and then blew on them to speed up the process.

Monique lowered her *Washington Post* long enough to shoot

Cynthia a disgusted look. She still hadn't quite forgiven her for blurting out her business yesterday. This was despite apologies from Cynthia and Roxanne.

From her comment, it was obvious that Cyn hadn't noticed Miss Miller's dismayed expression, but Gayle had. "Do you want me to tell him that you're not here?" she offered.

Dot shook her head and then hurriedly twisted the top back on the nail polish she'd been using. She stood up so fast, she nearly knocked the chair over.

Gayle hit the mute button again before handing her the phone. She couldn't help but be curious about the mysterious caller. And unlike Cyn, she didn't assume it was something to cheer about, especially when Miss Miller took the phone and kept walking with it until she was out in the hallway. Before she got out of earshot, Gayle heard her high-pitched girlish voice demand, "How did you get this number?"

Dot couldn't believe Etienne had tracked her down. She ducked into the first room she came to, the laundry room, and closed the door behind her.

"Denise gave me the number," Etienne told her.

Frustrated, Dot stamped her foot. This was her fault; she hadn't told her family *not* to give Etienne Roxanne's number. She had been in such a hurry to get to Baltimore—for more reasons than one—that it never occurred to her Etienne might come looking for her, especially after the way she had told him off the last time she saw him. Dot braced herself by placing both hands on the cool metal of the washing machine. She crooked her neck to one side to keep the phone pressed to her ear.

"I am sorry to hear about your son-in-law's death, Dot."

"I appreciate that Etienne, but please don't call me again," she said.

"Dot, don't hang up. Please," he begged, "I need your help. When are you coming back to St. Louis? The INS wants to interview us again."

She couldn't help but be moved by the desperation in his voice, but there was no way she was talking to those Immigration and Naturalization agents again. Those people had scared ten years off her life. And she was still mad at Etienne because he hadn't told her the *whole* truth before she married him. At least she would have known what she was getting into. *There's no fool like an old fool,* she reminded herself.

It wasn't so much that he married her only to get his green card. She knew that. Ever since she'd known him, Etienne told anyone at work that would listen the most pitiful stories about his life in Haiti. She had known that he was desperate to stay in the United States. And he never asked *her* to marry him. She'd done all the asking. Just trying to do a friend a favor, she'd told him. But then again, it wasn't like he had to think twice before taking her up on her offer. Her head realized that the only thing he felt for her was friendship and gratitude. But her heart had hoped that the sham marriage would turn into something more. His sweetness and politeness combined with mixed-race good looks did funny things to her battered old heart.

The simple justice-of-the-peace ceremony back in February had taken only a few minutes. Etienne had warned her that one day, the INS might come calling. They would want proof that the marriage was legit. He tried to coach her on the kinds of questions they'd ask. Dot had been only half listening most of the time. She hadn't been worried. She and Etienne were already good friends, so it wasn't like they didn't know each other. And she'd always heard that the INS had a backlog of cases. She hadn't expected to hear from them in years. By then she had thought she and Etienne would be married in every sense of the word. Living as man and wife for real.

The minute they'd arrived at the INS Service Center, they'd been separated. She knew they wouldn't be questioned together, but she hadn't been prepared for the questions the agent threw at her. She'd asked plenty of questions just like Etienne had said she would, but none of them were questions she knew the answers to.

Where did you go on your honeymoon? What honeymoon? She should have said they didn't take one, but she named the place she'd always wanted to go on a honeymoon. Hawaii.

What city in Haiti is your husband from? She couldn't have named a city in Haiti to save her life.

What color are the walls in your bedroom? Do you have wedding pictures or proof of joint assets and liabilities? Why haven't you changed your driver's license to reflect your married name?

Dot wished there was some place to sit down. Her knees had started shaking all over again just thinking about the grilling she had gone through. Now Etienne was asking her to go back for more? She didn't think she could do it.

"Dot. I could be in big trouble. If we don't do better at the next interview, I could be deported. I can't go back to Haiti," he said, sounding more desperate with each word he uttered. "I won't." He went on to remind her what would happen to him if he went back. He reminded her of the violence and poverty he'd come from.

Dot felt herself weakening. She felt sorry for him. *Well, snap out of it, girlfriend,* she advised herself. *You got to look out for yourself.* He was her friend, and she wanted to help him, but she didn't know what she could do. "Etienne, I already told you, I'm not going back for a second interview. They made me feel stupid and worse than that, they made me feel like a criminal. I'm too old and too pretty to go to jail," she said, attempting to joke herself into a lighter mood.

"Dot, I'm begging you to come back to St. Louis so that we can prepare for the next interview," he said. "If we don't get our stories straight this time, I could be arrested and immediately deported."

Like she didn't know that. In fact, given the things the INS had told her, they were lucky they *both* hadn't been arrested on the spot. What a time to find out that Etienne Duvall wasn't even his real name! It was Jean Claude Dubois. And that was just the beginning.

Did you know your husband entered the country illegally? Did you know he is using a false social security number? Are you aware that he has a common-law wife and a two-year-old son in Port-au-Prince?

That's when Dot realized she didn't know squat about her new husband except what he had chosen to tell her. The shaking knees gave way to hysterical crying and hyperventilating that she was not faking. For the first time since she had walked into the INS office, she was being completely honest; she didn't know nothing about nothing.

"I married my husband for love," she kept saying. So maybe it was "for like" or "for lust," but that was close enough. She had hoped it would turn into love. And she sure as hell didn't know he was an illegal alien. When the INS finally let them go, with a warning that the case was still under review, she had cursed Etienne out six ways from Sunday. That had been two weeks ago. She hadn't seen him since. She had been a wreck and was relieved when he hadn't shown up for work. And then Jamal had died, and she hadn't thought about him since. Until now.

"Etienne, as you found out at the interview, I am a lousy liar. And I am too old to go to jail," she repeated. This time she was not joking. "I'm getting an annulment as soon as I can. I felt like a criminal. I have never been so scared in my life. I can't help you this time, Etienne. I'm sorry," she said, before hanging up on him. And she truly was. He was a good kid. At least he was from what little she'd witnessed since he came to work at the brewery. He had treated her nice.

And now she was in a world of trouble because she'd lost her mind over a little kindness from a man. Keeping this mistake of a marriage from her kids and her mama had been the one smart thing she'd done. Dot hadn't wanted to hear what a bad idea it was before the fact, and she certainly didn't want to hear "I told you so" after the fact. She hoped Etienne had gotten the message and would leave her alone. She didn't need to bring her problems to Roxanne's doorstep. She never had been that way with her kids and didn't want to start now.

Not yet ready to face her daughter or her friends, Dot lingered. Noticing a pile of unfolded clothes on the long counter space on the right side of the room, Dot walked over and began folding. If a laundry room could be called beautiful, this one was just that. About forty square feet, it was obvious that a lot of thought had gone into its layout. The sink, with its pullout spray faucet, was next to the washer. A rod for drip-drying clothes was suspended over most of the countertop and had a drain board beneath it. Recessed lights were above the sink and counter space, which probably helped Roxanne see better when she had to treat stained clothes or match dark-colored socks. A tall cabinet housed a free-standing ironing board and ample cabinet space for storing detergent, bleach, and stuff like that. Bins for sorting clothes were next to the laundry chute. Another little extra that saved Roxanne from having to carry clothes from upstairs.

Dot used the flat of her hand to smooth the last of a stack of fluffy bath towels she had folded. A surge of pride went through her. For a kid who had to trudge down to the local Laundromat once a week and watch the family's clothes like a hawk to make sure no one stole them, her little Roxy had come up in the world. And she wasn't about to be the one to bring her down in any way, shape, or form. Etienne would have to deal with his problems on his own. She was staying out of it.

Gayle poured herself a second cup of decaf. "I'll be so glad when this baby gets here. It's been forever since I had a real cup of coffee," she said, coming about as close as she ever would to complaining. "I miss caffeine."

Cynthia looked at her friend's huge stomach and swollen ankles. "Caffeine? That's what you miss? I'd miss being able to see or touch my feet. I'd miss being able to wear clothes that didn't have rubber at the waistline."

"*You* would," Monique snorted.

Gayle interrupted before a fight broke out. "This has nothing to do with being pregnant. But I'll tell you what else I miss. I miss the time when all four of us could get together once or twice a year without having to consider husbands and boyfriends."

"Well, the way things are looking now, a return to the good old days may not be far off," Monique remarked. "You're the only one that's still got a husband."

Cynthia gasped. "I can't believe you said that. It's not Roxanne's fault her husband died." Unspoken was the implication that it was Monique's fault that she and her husband had split up. Cynthia, who could never quite find Mr. Right herself, always blamed the woman when something went wrong in a relationship. She was confident she would never "blow it" if given a chance to make a good man happy.

Her indignant attitude finally got Monique to stop reading the paper. She slammed it on the table and asked Cynthia, "Since when would you know anything about getting *or* keeping a man?"

Before Monique completely went off, Gayle pleaded, "Don't get started, y'all. Bickering about nothing is one way to pass the time, but what we really need to do is figure out how we're going to help Roxanne through this."

"You're right, as usual," Monique agreed. "I just wish other people could be smart enough to know what's important and what's not." She aimed a pointed look in Cynthia's direction as she said it.

"Look, Roxanne is not sleeping. She's not eating. And you know that's never happened before. She's not really telling us how she's feeling. We can't just leave her in this house by herself," Gayle declared. "I'm on maternity leave, and I'd be happy to stay here and look out for her, but being this close to my due date, I know Reggie won't hear of it and I probably need to be near my own doctor."

"I can stay maybe two or three more days," Cynthia said. "Then I have to get back to work."

"Same for me," Monique said. She picked up the ever-present pack of cigarettes, which had been on the table next to the salt and pepper shakers. She took one look at Gayle's enlarged belly before putting them back down again with a little sigh. "I told Roxanne that I'd stick around for the reading of the will."

Gayle's eyes widened in alarm. She hadn't even thought about stuff like that. "Does she expect any problems there?"

"Not a one," Monique assured her. "It's no big secret that he left just about everything to her. Roxanne is gonna have more money than she knows what to do with. Plus, there is the remainder of his football contract, and he did die on the job. Roxanne doesn't know a whole lot about Jamal's exact net worth, but she's gonna have a lot of money coming in from a variety of sources, including endorsements and bonuses. I can tell she doesn't really want to talk about it. I'm sure her mind is on other things. Fortunately, that's all stuff that can be sorted out later. But you never know how ignorant people can get when it comes to money. So just in case his family decides to act crazy 'cause they ain't happy with what he left them, I thought I should be there."

Seeing the hard look in Monique's eyes, Gayle pitied the Steeles if they did decide to cause trouble. Which brought her back to her original question. "It's going to be a long, long, time before Roxanne gets back to anything that resembles normal. She really should have someone here with her."

Monique sighed. "Even if I volunteered to stay, she's not going to let me. You heard her this morning. She thinks Tyson and I can work this out. If it were up to her, she would have had me on a plane back to Texas yesterday. Should I thank you again for opening your big mouth, Cyn?"

Cynthia leaned back in her chair and put her newly polished hands on her generous hips. She pursed her lipsticked lips and declared. "I am not taking responsibility for Roxanne's reaction to this. She would have felt the same way no matter when she was told or by whom. So stop blaming me. Thank you very much."

Monique chewed on that for a moment, and Gayle couldn't believe it when she actually agreed with Cyn—out loud.

"Well, I'm glad we can agree on something," Gayle said. "Now, what are we going to do about it? I know Linc is going to be here as much as he can, but the football season is not over yet. So he probably won't be around much for the next few weeks, if all goes well in the play-offs. And as for Roxanne's mother . . ."

Gayle didn't bother to finish that sentence, because they all knew what remained unspoken. Miss Miller was a sweetheart, but kind of ditzy. The woman always had a smile on her face and refused to deal with anything upsetting. She wouldn't be able to tolerate Roxanne's up-and-down moods. From what Roxanne had told them, she had acted more like a kid or another sister rather than a mother when Roxanne was growing up. And she hadn't exactly been of much practical help during the whole ordeal surrounding Jamal's death.

As if on cue, Dot stepped back into the kitchen. She placed the phone in its charger. The smile on her face evaporated in the presence of the suddenly solemn faces of her daughter's friends. "What's the problem, girls?" she asked, eager to focus on something other than her own troubles.

"Nothing," Gayle said. "Is everything OK?" She hoped she wasn't being too nosy when she added, "You didn't seem too happy to get that call."

Dot waved a dismissive hand. "No, it was just one of my co-workers, who sometimes thinks we're closer than we actually are. I straightened him out. So everything is fine."

"Good," Gayle said. "Good." She exchanged a glance with her two friends and said, "I guess I'll go rescue my husband before he hurts himself."

Dot cocked her head and smiled. "No so fast, missy. Not that you *could* move all that fast with that extra cargo," she said, then patted Gayle's round tummy. "You can't leave until you tell me what's got you all looking so serious."

Monique spoke before Gayle could come up with a nice way to deflect the question. "We're just trying to figure out who is going to look out for Roxanne. None of us can stay indefinitely."

"Well, that's simple," Dot said. "I'll stay with her."

"You?" Gayle said, and then ducked her head, embarrassed by her rudeness.

"Why not me?" Dot said, trying to pretend that she hadn't surprised herself. "After all, I am her mother." She silently added, *and I am in no hurry to get back to St. Louis.*

Torn between relief and disbelief, Gayle said, "Are you sure?"

Suddenly, Dot had never been surer of anything in her life. Her job was just that. A job. She could always get another. It would be nice to take a break from Denise's unruly kids. She definitely didn't want to deal with Etienne. And most of all, for the first time in her adult life, her daughter needed her.

"Absolutely sure," she told Gayle. Behind her back, she crossed her fingers, hoping that she'd finally be able to be the mother that Roxanne had always deserved.

Chapter

13

Linc scowled at the sight of the lone car occupying Hope Springs' parking lot. He pulled his black Blazer into the empty slot next to it and turned off the ignition. He sat for a minute, counting to ten in the wasted belief that it would calm him down before he went into talk to Roxanne. When he'd stopped by the house with a bottle of champagne to celebrate the team's playoff victory, he thought Dot had been joking when she told him Roxy was over at the Center. Linc had rushed off before he said something to Dot that he lived to regret. Even though Roxy was a grown woman, he felt Dot was doing a piss-poor job of looking after her. How could she let her daughter—her recently widowed daughter, her emotionally unpredictable daughter—go off by herself this late at night? The least she could have done was gone with her. Instead, he'd found her lounging around wearing some kind of face cream and eating Cheez-Its. No, Dot had settled in for the evening without a thought to Roxy's safety.

And Roxy, what was she thinking? She had no business being alone in that building, in this neighborhood at this time of the night. Just what time was it? Linc looked at the clock on his dashboard. So much had happened today, he'd long since lost track of time. It was a few minutes shy of ten o'clock. A cloud-covered moon emitted the faintest of illumination. Streetlights hit nearby apartment buildings and storefronts, casting gloomy shadows along the cracked and chipped sidewalks. With temperatures dropping to the low twenties, even the most dedicated loafers and hustlers had abandoned their street corners for the night. Even they had sense enough to come in out of the cold. That and the rarely empty, despite being locked, basketball courts were enough proof that Roxy should be somewhere other than here.

Linc leapt out of his Blazer. Long, worried strides took him across the asphalt and to the front door of Hope Springs in record time. He stopped only to search for his key to the front door. One of the lamps next to the entrance had burned out. Linc held up his key ring next to the one that was still functioning to find the right key. When he finally did, he stuck the key in the lock. The hair on the back of his neck pricked up. Linc looked down dumbly at the silver handicap-accessible handle in his hand. The door was already unlocked.

All kinds of frightening thoughts went through his head. Had someone followed Roxy in? Had he or they forced their way in? The East Side was notorious for its gangs. Everybody around here knew Roxanne was a wealthy woman. There was no telling what greed or desperation for that next hit of the crack pipe might motivate people to do. The heart-stopping image of her lying in a crumpled heap, somewhere just beyond the crack in the door, hurt or worse, made his mouth go dry. Fear had him rushing into the building. Linc began bellowing her name. "Roxy! Roxy, are you in here?"

The reception area was empty. Linc kept moving. The large meeting room to the right of the entrance, where the afternoon school program and social functions were held, was dark. He quickly hit the light switch by the door to make sure she wasn't lying in the dark on the floor lost among the tables and chairs. Short-lived relief surged through him when he found the place looked just as it should. The small stage at the front and center of the room was decorated with a manger scene left over from the Christmas play that had been cancelled due to Jamal's death. Nothing and no one was on the floor. Nothing looked disturbed. Without turning the lights off, he ran back to the central hall, then for the first time noticed lights on the left side of the building. He heard a rustling sound coming from the office Roxanne and Jamal had shared.

"Roxy," he cried, and then almost knocked her down in his haste to discover what was beyond the open door to the office.

Suddenly she was there.

"Whoa!" Roxanne said, bracing a hand against his chest to keep him from barreling into her. "I'm right here. Stop yelling before you wake up the whole neighborhood."

She wore a brown cable-knit sweater and a pair of olive khakis. There was not a mark on her. Not a scratch. No sign that she'd been hurt or molested in any way. In fact, she was smiling up at him. Breathing hard, Linc grasped both her elbows and resisted the urge to give her a hard shake. She had scared him half to death, and she was grinning.

"Why didn't you answer me?" he demanded. "I've been shouting your name for five minutes straight."

"I didn't hear you."

She hadn't heard him! "You didn't hear me?" he said, then let go of her arms before he shook her for real.

Noticing his wild-eyed look and the heaving of his chest beneath her palm for the first time, Roxanne took a step back. Linc had his drawers in a bunch about something. "What's wrong?" she said.

He blew out a long breath and gave a little shake of his head before answering. "What's wrong is that I stop by your house to tell you some good news. And I'm told you're working alone *at night* in one of the most drug-ridden, high crime neighborhoods in the city. I come looking for you and find the door to the Center wide open."

"It was open?" she said in soft surprise. "I thought I closed it."

She thought? She thought? And she was saying it so calmly, too. That's the part that had turned his fear to anger. Roxanne was too naive and trusting. There were a lot of good people in the Oliver and Broadway East community, but there were a lot of criminals, too. If she insisted on coming here at night, the place should be locked up tighter than Fort Knox. "Hell no, it wasn't closed," Linc growled. "The alarm wasn't on. And I couldn't find you anywhere for five long minutes. Can you imagine what kind of thoughts I was having in those five minutes? I thought maybe somebody had knocked you upside the head, raped you." Her eyes grew as round as brown marbles. Good, he hoped he was scaring some sense into her. "Or God knows what else."

Shocked by the intensity of his anger, Roxanne didn't know what to say. Even if she hadn't been so short by any standards, Linc was a big man and right now he seemed bigger, and broader than usual. His eyes flashed their displeasure with her, and though he had stopped talking, she could tell by the way the muscles worked in this jaw that he was struggling not to yell at her even more. She appreciated his effort to control himself. Linc hadn't been this mad at her in a long, long time. Not since she'd been dating Marcus and putting up with his lackluster attention—against Linc's advice. When she thought about it, Roxanne realized the only time Linc got mad at her was when he felt like she wasn't taking care of herself. He was protective like that. So his anger didn't scare her since it stemmed from concern about her. But she loved him dearly and didn't like upsetting him.

Determined to make peace, she reached out and pried his balled hand from around his keys. He was holding them so tightly they had to be boring a hole in his palm. At first there was no give, but then he surrendered them with a sigh. She looped a finger in the key ring and began straightening and smoothing his still rigid fingers with her other hand.

Linc sucked in a surprised breath. The soothing movements of her hand gliding over his were having the opposite of their intended effect. A jolt of something like electricity started at his fingertips, radiated up his arm, down his suddenly convulsing Adam's apple, and stopped smack dead at his groin. His first instinct was to snatch his hand away from hers. But then Roxy would *know* he was as crazy as he felt. He couldn't have moved if he wanted to. He just prayed Roxy wouldn't look down and notice the huge bulge in his pants. *What the hell is the matter with me?* How could he go from furious to hot and rock hard from the mere touch of a woman's hand? And not just any woman, Roxy! His best friend's widow.

I must have taken one too many whacks on the head today, he told himself, trying to find a rational explanation for why his best, *platonic* female friend could ignite a fire in him without even trying.

Unaware of Linc's private torment, Roxanne pushed her hair out of her line of vision and leaned over his stiff fingers. She had taken a palmistry class once at the Y. Not that she remembered much from it. So she faked it, hoping to change Linc's scowl to a smile. She traced a hand along one of the lines of his palm that was almost twice as large as hers. "This line is your head line," she informed him. "It's short and straight, which suggests that your thinking is clear, simple, and straight to the point."

Linc stood stock still. What the hell was Roxy talking about? He was in the middle of telling her off and trying get his libido to chill, and she decides to read his palm? Maybe he wasn't the only crazy one up in here.

Roxanne noted Linc's puzzled expression with satisfaction. He couldn't be angry and confused at the same time, could he? At least she was distracting him. She licked her lips and tasted the remnants of the tea she'd been drinking earlier. She gave his hand a little tug to get his attention. "And this one that extends from the edge of your hand below your little finger to between your first and second fingers . . . That is your heart line," she said.

Linc swallowed. He didn't want hear about his heart line because right now his heart was full of lust. And having her touch him with those small, soft hands and slim fingers was not helping the situation.

Roxanne waited for him to look at her again. There was a wariness in his eyes that she didn't understand. "Linc, you have a big heart, a loving heart, and most important, a forgiving one. I'm sorry I scared you by coming here tonight. You forgive me, don't you?"

Feeling like an idiot, Linc released a breath. Roxy knew him so well, for a minute he truly believed she had picked up on what he was feeling. He'd been convinced she'd say, "You have a raging sex drive that is on the brink of spiraling out of control." And all she wanted was for him to stop breathing fire of another kind. She wanted forgiveness.

Linc was taking his sweet time before answering but Roxanne wasn't worried. She knew Linc's anger would blow over sooner rather than later. He reminded her of one of those sparklers they used to play with on summer holidays. He lit up pretty easily, and though he gave off flecks of heat and fire, there was little chance of him burning you or exploding, say, like a firecracker. And like those sparklers, his temper fizzled out pretty quickly. She could feel the tension easing out of his fingers already.

Linc had never thought of himself as someone with an overactive sex drive. In fact, his buddies would be shocked to know that he hadn't had sex in over six months. There was no particular reason for it. He just hadn't met anyone who got his juices flowing. And getting some just because he was horny wasn't worth all the trouble he'd have to go through to get rid of any woman who thought what they'd shared was anything more than sex. *Maybe that's why I'm panting after Roxy right now.* I just need to get laid. He hoped that's what the problem was, because anything else would be just plain sick.

Hoping his body had gotten itself under control, Linc risked stepping into Roxanne's outstretched arms. She nestled her head just a few inches above his belly button. He had to hold back a groan. Of course, she would try to wrap herself around him. She squeezed his back on each side, since her arms weren't long enough to meet in the middle. Linc could feel himself stirring to life again and backed away, disgusted with himself. Roxanne had always been one of those touchy-feely types, and it had never bothered him before. *What has gotten into me?* He felt like a twelve-year-old who was just discovering the power of the beast and who would get hard if the wind changed directions. Thank God, he was still wearing his thick pea coat.

"OK, so I forgive you," he said, sounding gruffer than he had intended to. "No need to squeeze me like a melon in a supermarket."

She stepped back and rolled her eyes at him. She dangled his keys. He snagged them and pocketed them. Roxanne walked back over to the desk where her flying toasters screen saver suggested that it had been a while since she'd touched the keyboard. Crumbled papers and ring notebooks spilled over onto the floor, and a jumbo coffee thermos stood at the ready. A Mexican-style shawl was draped over the arm of the desk chair. Linc trailed behind her to get a closer look at what she'd been working on. Roxanne stopped to scoop up an armful of papers and books. She dumped them all on the desk.

"So what was so important it couldn't wait until tomorrow morning?" he asked.

She took a seat before answering him. "I'm trying to figure out what to do about the tutoring program. We have all these extremely busy people volunteering their time, and only a handful of kids show up. I decided to work on it tonight because I never have a moment to myself when the Center is actually open. I needed to be able to think." That was even more the case now that neither Linc nor Jamal were around in the evenings to help out. Roxanne closed her eyes. She would not cry. Not when she was trying so hard not to worry Linc. Nor would she make him feel guilty because he had a life that existed outside of her and Hope Springs.

Roxanne had closed her eyes. It could mean only one thing. There was something in them that she didn't want him to see. Linc touched her on the shoulder, and she lifted her eyes to meet his. "What's wrong?" he asked.

What was wrong? A lot of things, but only a few she was willing to share. "I'm just frustrated. I came here to do work, and next thing I know I'm fast asleep and don't wake up until I heard you calling my name."

He had been so relieved to find her still in one piece physically that he wasn't paying too much attention to what Roxy looked like. Now he noticed for the first time the little sleep indentations on her face and the slightly red, shell-shocked eyes of someone who had been awakened before she was done sleeping. "Of course you fell asleep." And he was glad. "Roxy, you haven't gotten a solid night's rest since . . . since Jamal passed away. That was bound to catch up with you eventually."

A shadow crossed her face at the mention of Jamal.

"Yeah, well, I didn't come here to sleep. I couldn't get anything done at home because Mama wouldn't leave me alone. I swear to God that woman never stops talking—even in her sleep. I would go to another room, and she would find a reason to come in there. If it wasn't 'Do you know where I put my purse?' it was 'Oh, honey, I just saw the funniest commercial on TV. Did you see it, too?' Of course I didn't see it. I was working in a room that didn't have a TV for a reason."

Linc laughed. Dot wasn't the most restful person to be around. She was in constant motion and would and could frequently talk your ear off. Maybe she'd be a good distraction and keep Roxy from withdrawing into herself. He'd noticed her doing that quite a bit since Jamal died.

Seeing his smile, Roxanne said, "It's not funny. I really need to get the program working before we have volunteers quitting on me."

"You mean on us. Don't you?"

She regarded him with uncertain eyes. "Us?"

Hurt pricked him. He shouldn't have to tell her this. Why was she excluding him? "Yes, you, me, and everyone else who is on the board of this organization. You don't have to do everything on your own, you know."

Then, why did she suddenly feel that way? Roxanne wondered. "Us" had always meant her and Jamal. Hope Springs had been their shared dream. Linc and others cared, but it was not the same.

"Roxanne, I know I haven't been around much this past week, but I do plan to be here for you."

She patted his hand. "I know, Linc . . . I don't expect you to drop everything for me. I really don't need or want you to do that. I understand that you have a job to do. I can take care of myself. Besides, I got Mama here."

The look he gave her was doubtful of Dot's abilities. "I know you can take care of yourself. I'm just saying you don't have to."

"Thanks."

Why did that sound like thanks but no thanks to him? Maybe because Roxy was just being Roxy: stubbornly independent. He'd always known that was an act. Roxy wanted nothing more than someone to take care of her. With the exception of her grandmother and later Jamal, she'd never had too many people she could rely on or even acknowledge she needed that. He didn't think she'd been interested in his attempts to analyze her, so he took another tack. "Is the media still hounding you with questions about how Jamal died?"

Pain flashed in her eyes. She slowly shook her head. "It's still in the papers and on the news, from what Mama tells me." She hadn't read the papers and tried not to watch the news. "At least it's not the lead story anymore. Apparently, they've found something even worse than the alleged drug use of an athlete to talk about."

He balled a fist. It was so unfair that she was going through this. As if losing Jamal wasn't traumatic enough. "Don't worry. It won't be a story at all once the toxicology reports come out. A whole lot of people are going to be making a retraction."

"Of course they will," she said. The report was supposed to come out in a week or so. Jamal's name would be cleared. She was certain of that, but nothing could take away the hurt the accusations had caused her. Was that journalistic practice these days? To tell lies first and apologize later? And how could they do that to Jamal, after all he'd done for this city? That alone should have earned him the benefit of the doubt.

Roxy was looking not at him but through him. He wanted to pull her into his arms and demand that she tell him what she was feeling so that he could share her pain. But Roxanne had made it clear that she could only tolerate so much concern, whether it was done via yelling or comforting hugs or coaxing her to share her feelings. Besides, he'd pushed her enough for one night.

Linc countered her silence with action. He began straightening the mess that was her desk. Random papers were collated but not sorted. Roxanne could do that later—tomorrow, to be specific. He neatly stacked the books and manuals. He righted an overturned pen and pencil holder. The screen saver was making his head spin, so he pressed the enter key just to get it to stop.

"Jamal used to do that," Roxanne said. Her lips curved into a small, sad smile.

"Do what?" he asked, genuinely confused by her comment.

"He used to clean up after me all the time. He said I was a slob."

"A lovable slob, though," Linc said, and wondered why it bothered him that she was comparing him to Jamal.

Roxanne relieved him of a batch of papers he'd collected. She stuck them in the nearest drawer. Linc was trying so hard to be a good friend. He was the best. Then she remembered what he'd said when he'd first burst into the office like Superman and Batman all rolled into one. "You came by to tell me something," she reminded him. "You had some good news?"

His high over winning had worn off a long time ago. So much so, it suddenly felt weird bringing it up now. What if it upset her? He never knew what would from moment to moment. "We won our game today," he told her, then braced himself for her reaction. It was a short wait.

She jumped up from the chair and gave him another one of those hard half hugs of hers. "Oh, Lincoln, that's wonderful. I'm so happy for you." She pulled his head down so she could kiss him on both cheeks. "You must be thrilled," she said.

"I am." He had been. He could barely wait to get through the obligatory post-game interviews and had skipped the team celebrations altogether. All he could think about was getting to Roxy and sharing the news with her. Now he wondered if that was such a good idea. If every little thing he did reminded her of Jamal, talking about football had to be painful for her.

She gave him a cockeyed look. "You could have fooled me. You ought to be jumping up and down. Dancing in the street."

"Well, that's why I stopped by to see you. You're my favorite dance partner," he couldn't stop himself from confessing.

Roxanne's smile was also a grimace. "I'm happy for you, bro, but you ain't crushing my toes."

He could keep up this lighthearted chitchat, but he and Roxy both deserved more than that. They meant too much to each other not to be real. "Roxy, I have to be honest. You and Jamal were on my mind all day. Part of my wanting to win is because Jamal wanted it so much. I know he would have been just as happy about what happened on that field today as I am. But . . . but I don't want to bring you more pain by talking about football."

Roxanne was touched, yet disturbed. Linc was treating her like she was something fragile, easily broken. He'd never been careful with her. He was blunt, uncensored. He could tell her anything and knew she could handle it. So much had changed in her life in the last few days. She couldn't take it if Linc changed, too. He'd been her constant since grade school. So she begged him, "Please. Please, don't feel like you have to protect me. Not if it means shutting me out of your life."

"But talking about football hurts you," Linc insisted. "I can see it in your eyes." And in the little hitch in your voice and the way you just wrapped your arms around yourself. She was hugging herself so tightly, as if afraid she'd unravel if she let go.

Unable to lie, she nodded at the truthfulness of what he was saying. "If you can stand a few tears every now and then, I really do want to know what's going on in your life . . . and that includes football." Hearing about his successes on the field was going to be bittersweet for a while. That's why she hadn't been able to watch the game today. *That's* why all of sudden the problems with the tutoring program needed to be resolved ASAP. But Linc's careful handling of her reminded her that football was Jamal's first true love, and he would want her to cheer Linc and the rest of the team on. She was going to try. "So the conference championships are next week," she said, issuing an invitation for him to share his world.

Linc wasn't convinced she was up for talking football, but it was her call. "Yeah, this one's a road game. We're headed to Denver. No more home field advantage."

"I'm sure you'll do fine. Denver has a weak secondary."

Linc laughed. "Listen to you. You sound like a commentator."

The sound of her answering laughter seemed foreign to her ears and a little rusty. There hadn't been much to laugh about lately. Bless Linc for being able to tease a laugh out of her. "Well, I do know football," she bragged. More than she'd ever imagined possible. She'd lived and breathed it for five years because of Jamal.

Not wanting to think too much about him, Roxanne focused on the stacks of paperwork on her desk. "I just wish I knew more about running a successful community tutoring program."

She was going to drown herself in work. Linc could see all the signs. Linc wanted her to go on the road trip with him to Denver. So that he could keep an eye on her. But he knew better than to suggest it. She wasn't ready to be around the team and would turn him down flat.

With a sigh, he pulled up a chair. She wasn't going to leave until she felt like she'd made some progress. "Two heads are better than one," he said. "Let's see what we can come up with."

Her look of gratitude did funny things to his insides. Linc grabbed a pen and clicked it against his lips before he leaned over and kissed her. Which was exactly what he longed to do. A yearning that made no sense at all.

"Linc, you are a genius," Roxanne announced after about a half hour of tossing out ideas. "Here I was thinking we might have to bring in a consultant. But I think we have two good ideas on the table." The best idea was Linc's suggestion that participation in some of the recreational and social activities be contingent on involvement in the tutoring program. Sort of an incentive program. The other was to do a more direct appeal to parents. Maybe a door-to-door campaign.

"I wouldn't exactly call myself a genius. I'm just versatile," he joked. "A football player can be a great thinker, too, you know."

"Of course," she said quickly. "You're a regular Einstein." *And you have an ego as big as the Grand Canyon,* she silently added.

He lifted an eyebrow. "Don't think I didn't hear the sarcasm in your voice. And that hurts. Especially when I have nothing but compliments for you. Just a little while ago, I told you that you could be a sports commentator. Didn't I? And that's high praise coming from me."

Roxanne favored him with a smile. "True. True. But," she added with a sigh, "I'm not ready to give up my day job just—" Her stomach growled, drowning out the end of her sentence.

Linc's eyes narrowed as he watched her put a hand to her stomach as if to quiet it. "So when was the last time you ate something?" he casually inquired.

Roxanne rubbed her stomach and avoided his eyes. "Linc, don't get mad. Even though my stomach is rumbling, every time I try to eat something, I have no appetite."

"Too bad. You need to make yourself eat anyhow."

"Even if doing that makes me feel like I'm gonna gag?"

"Yep."

That was easy for him to say. No matter how hungry she might be physically, the smell and sight of food made her ill. Linc wouldn't know anything about turning down food. She *used* to be the same way. She'd resigned herself to waiting out this loss of appetite thing.

When her stomach growled again, Linc said, "I would order pizza or Chinese, but it's Sunday. Plus, even if we found something open, I don't think we could tip them enough to deliver in this neighborhood at this time of night."

"My, Lincoln, listening to you talk, no one would know you grew up in a neighborhood just like this one."

"I ain't being snobby. It's *because* I grew up in a neighborhood like this that I know restaurants don't deliver. About the only person who made deliveries on our block was Cochise."

God, Roxanne had all but forgotten about the ponytailed

Indian who used to be the numbers runner in their housing project. "I wonder what old Cochise is doing now that gambling has been legalized." It wasn't just the state lottery but riverboats, too.

"Don't try to change the subject," Linc warned.

"I wasn't. You're the one that brought him up."

"Uh-huh. Let's get out of here. I'll trail you back to your place, and I'm not leaving until I see you eat something."

"Even if I throw it all up on your size fourteen shoes?"

"That's a chance I'm willing to take," Linc confirmed. "Now, get your stuff and let's get out of here."

She hesitated. It was hard to believe. Linc was bossing *her* around. When had they switched roles, and why did it give her such a warm glow inside to have him taking charge?

Linc held up her coat and purse. She took both and he ushered her out of the office before she could come up with the answers to the questions she was suddenly asking herself.

Chapter

14

The team's chartered bus stopped in front of the Westin Hotel in LoDo or Lower Downtown, as the Denver natives called it. Linc was weary from the game, the post game interviews, not to mention the nonstop testosterone-induced trash talking and excitement of his fellow teammates as they traveled from the stadium to the hotel. He tried to keep a low profile and focused on the passing scenery. Downtown Denver was a mixture of gleaming glass towers and renovated warehouses that had been turned into shops and galleries. All of these co-existed with preserved Victorian houses and the magnificent Rockies as a backdrop. Linc had never had spent much time out West, so he was awed by it every time. Nothing that man threw together in a few months could compare to what nature had created over thousands of years. He gave the mountains in the distance one last look before leaving his seat. How could winning a football game compare to that? he wondered. Linc scratched his head, confused by his lack of enthusiasm. He'd just won the biggest game of his career and now it was nothing? What was wrong with him? He needed to figure *that* out instead of getting all worked up over some snow-capped mountains.

As he nudged his way down the aisle past guys who were taking their sweet time getting up and out of their seats, a few people slapped him on the butt or gave him a high-five.

His answering smile was only slightly warmer than the January temperature they had played and won the game in. He ducked to avoid hitting his head on the door as he stepped off the bus. He sucked in cold, crisp air and felt a little light-headed. He'd been here most of the week and still hadn't adjusted to the altitude of the Mile High City. Looking around, he had to admit that Denver was beautiful. Nestled in the foothills of the Rocky Mountains, it was a lot cleaner than most East Coast cities. Sometimes when he'd been in New York, a strong wind would blow and the grit and grime of the city would literally hit him in the face.

Linc stuck his unprotected hands in his pockets. The brilliant sun, which shone from a clear blue sky, was deceptive. It was bitterly cold outside. He reached into the breast pocket of his jacket and took out his sunglasses. He didn't care what the travel brochures said, Denver did get cold and the snow didn't always melt soon after it fell. He felt like he'd been playing around in a slush cone for three hours. A thin layer of watery ice had covered the field. He'd changed uniforms during halftime, and they had heaters on the sideline, which was fine as long as you were standing right next to them.

For the millionth time today, Linc thought, Boy, do baseball players have it made. The minute it started to drizzle, the game is stopped and an army of grounds people come running out to cover the field with a tarp. When the rain stopped, they came running back out with towels, a squeegee, and some dry dirt for the infield. And if the rain didn't stop, the game was called off altogether. "Must be nice," he muttered to himself. Despite a locker room shower, he was still chilled to the bone.

Being so cold that it felt like he'd never warm up again made him think of Roxanne. Ever since Jamal's death, she hadn't been herself. He could understand that. He wasn't himself, either. But he had a job to do. People were depending on him to lead this team to its second ever Championship Bowl. He felt like Jamal was depending on him. And frankly, sometimes that was the only thing that kept him going. But what kept Roxy going? he wondered. What would warm her so she wouldn't have to bundle up in bulky sweaters and thick socks or shroud herself in a blanket or shawl. Hell, he'd never heard her complaining about being cold, not even when she'd gone off to college in Minnesota, of all places.

And why should she? Roxy generated a warmth all her own. And people were attracted to it the way they are drawn to any heat source during cold times.

He wondered if Roxy had watched the game. Or maybe it was still too soon. Would she be able to sit through the announcers' explanation of the black armbands that the team wore in honor of Jamal? And of course, they'd have to rehash how he died. And the story would not be complete without footage of him lying helpless on the ground and being taken away in an ambulance. Linc wondered if Roxy was feeling as heart-sore and confused as he was.

Jonesy locked his arm around Linc's neck. "Yo, dude, why so glum-looking? We won the game."

"I know that's right!" Steve Carter bragged. "We didn't just win. We rode the Stallions like rodeo cowboys. Yee-haw! Maybe they should start calling themselves the Nags."

"Yee-haw?" Linc repeated with a trace of a smile.

"When in Denver, do as the cowpokes do," Steve said. Steve was from Chicago, so any city that had less than a million people or only a small percentage of minorities was redneck country to him. He let out another "Yee-haw!" and swaggered toward the hotel entrance like a bowlegged cowboy.

Jonesy still had a choke hold on Linc's neck. Jonesy was about four inches taller than him and about a hundred pounds heavier. The boy didn't know his own strength. Linc placed an arm around Jonesy's waist so that their strides would match and the air to his windpipe wouldn't get blocked if he did something so stupid as to lag behind Jonesy's pace.

"I know you love me and all, Jonesy," Linc joked, "but is this really the picture of yourself you want to see on the ten o'clock news?" Linc pointed over at a local CBS news affiliate van, which was illegally parked in front of their hotel. The crew was hauling equipment out of the open double doors at the rear of the van.

Jonesy, who was as homophobic as they come, let go of Linc's neck like it was a hot coal. He quickly looked around to see if he'd been caught in the act and moved to a manlier distance.

Normally, the terrified look on his face would have cracked Linc up. He liked playing with Jonesy's head just to see how far he would go to prove how straight he was. Usually it resulted in some depraved tale about how many women he'd "done" in the last week. Maybe that was why Jonesy went through wives like some people went through clothes.

Out of the corner of his eye, Linc saw that Johnny James, a shellac-haired CBS sportscaster known for his weak chin and even weaker interviewing style, was stalking him. If he hadn't been wearing sunglasses, Johnny James would have seen just how unwelcome his presence was. Linc had given all the interviews he planned to give while he was still at the stadium. Yes, he was glad to have the easy 30–7 win, because it meant they wouldn't go into the Championship Bowl beaten up and bruised. Yes, Jamal had been on his mind today and no, he didn't want to talk about it. Not to millions of strangers who had no idea what Jamal meant to him and who could probably care less.

Seeing that James and his gang were gaining ground, Linc broke into a slow jog and resisted the impulse to look over his shoulder to see if the guy was running after him. He leapt into a half-full elevator just before the doors closed. The last thing he saw was the frustrated expression of Johnny James. Linc waggled a couple of fingers. Pitiful, he thought, the man actually had been chasing him down! Anything for an exclusive, he guessed.

The team had commandeered three floors of the Westin. The team owner had sprung for the extra night at the hotel. They'd been told that if they won, he would give them a day of rest. No one dared voice the other possibility; if they had lost, it would give them time to lick their wounds before facing disappointed fans back in Baltimore. Linc got off the elevator on the seventeenth floor with a couple of his rowdy teammates. It wasn't just the mile-high altitude of Denver that had them giddy. They were flying high on the sweet taste of victory. But the excitement that Linc had felt on the field had quickly dissipated, leaving him acutely unfulfilled. Just like everyone else, he'd tasted victory, but it didn't last long. It wasn't what he was hungry for. It was same way he felt when he settled for pasta when he had really wanted prime rib—restless and still unsatisfied.

Linc walked halfway down the hall from the elevator and used his key card to let himself into his empty hotel room. It was dinnertime, and a lot of the guys had brought along wives, girlfriends, and kids. Linc's family had been clamoring to come, but he was feeling strangely reluctant to have them around. So he made up some story about not wanting them at the game because he thought it would bring bad luck. His mother, brother, and sister hadn't been at any of the other games this season except the one in St. Louis, and the team had suffered an unexpected loss. He told them if they came to Denver, they might jinx him. There was a whole lot of grumbling and hurt feelings, but they didn't press— since jinx potential or not, none of them would tolerate being banned from the Championship Bowl and that was the one that counted.

Linc unzipped his leather jacket and tossed it onto a chair. The frantically blinking message light on his phone caught his eye. Figuring it was calls from well-wishers or well-meaning dinner invitations, he decided to ignore it. And it had better not be that none too bright reporter Johnny James. He hoped the guy would take a hint and go find someone else to pester.

The king-size mattress gave only a fraction as he stretched out on it, raising his arms above his head. It didn't take much for Linc to feel every bump and bruise that Denver had inflicted. Despite the heavy padding he'd worn for protection, his ribs felt like someone had kicked them with a steel-toed boot. He had some ibuprofen in his suitcase but was too lazy to look for it. What he really needed was a full-body massage, *and* he was feeling a little sorry for himself because he'd have to pay someone or use the team's masseur in order to get one.

Jamal used to tell him about the sensual massages Roxy gave him after a particularly tough workout or day on the field. Stories of warm oil and scented candles. Roxanne straddling his back, sitting on his butt like it was a saddle, or the feel of her heavy hair trailing across his chest as her hands worked over his pecs. Linc used to beg him to stop. It was like hearing one of your friends brag about the hottie he was with last night only to find out it was your mother or, in Roxy's case, your sister. He hadn't wanted to picture Roxy like that. And though Jamal had too much respect for Roxy to give explicit details about their sex life, he made it clear that he was one sexually satisfied guy. Linc wasn't down for hearing that, either. Jamal would laugh at his pained expression and tell him that married life was great and that he didn't know what he was missing.

Linc lowered his arms, bringing them to rest at his sides. He remembered how uncomfortable he got whenever Jamal assaulted his ears and mind's eye with descriptions of how Roxy's slightest touch affected him. Back then Linc had seen Roxanne as a sister to him. So he didn't want to know about stuff like that. Now he was starting to wonder if that had been the only reason. His feelings for Roxy hadn't seemed all that brotherly on Sunday. He flung an arm across his face and groaned. His shame, embarrassment, and fear that his body would betray him had kept him away from her most of the week. They had talked on the phone every day, but he couldn't bring himself to face her. He'd been relieved when the team flew out to Denver in mid-week. The grueling practices and strategy sessions gave him something else to think about. With the game over, however, the questions about Roxy came flooding back, so persistent and deep, he almost drowned in them.

What would Roxy have thought if she'd accidentally brushed up against the massive hard-on I was sporting last Sunday? She probably would have freaked. And to think, he was supposed to be rescuing her from other people who might take advantage of her. *Were my intentions any better than the thugs that might be after her for her money or a cheap thrill?* He hoped so but wasn't so sure. He had wanted her. Despite his concern for her safety and her complete lack of interest in him, he had wanted her. What a way to comfort a grieving widow, who also happened to be his closest friend! He was in the wild, wild, West. People had been strung up for less. Why not him, too?

Then half-asleep, he saw her face. She was wearing one of those tight sweaters that she loved and bestowing upon him a full gapped-tooth smile that told of bottomless optimism. Only then did the emptiness in the pit of his stomach warm and slowly fill.

He was satisfied.

Linc woke up to semidarkness. The curtains had been open when he came in, so now moonlight and the red light from the phone were his sole illumination. He rolled over on his left side to see the alarm clock. He ignored the stabs of pain that accompanied the movement. He was used to it. He'd been out for two hours. It was almost nine o'clock.

His growling stomach reminded him that he was overdue for his evening meal. Rather than lie there and stiffen up more, Linc decided to try one of the hotel's three restaurants. Before sitting up,

Linc braced himself for the throbbing he'd feel in his lower back, the sharp twinges where his rib cage would cry out in protest and the hinky knee that always felt like it had something floating around in it. He hobbled over to the bathroom, where he took a long piss that was also disrupted by the pain he was feeling in other parts of his body. After splashing his face with cold water and drying it off with a hand towel, Linc reached for his toothbrush.

He thought of his mom and all the hell he'd raised about having to brush his teeth a hundred times a day when he was a kid. Growing up, he was convinced his mother was just plain old evil for forcing all those nightly baths, unnecessary hand washings, and teeth cleanings on him. Now he was grateful. If he was going to step outside the sanctuary of this room, there was no telling who might approach him, and his mama would kill him if he greeted them with stank breath.

He smiled, showing strong, foam-covered teeth and feeling more like himself. He spat out the excess toothpaste, rinsed his mouth with water, and then picked up the hotel's free mouthwash sample. His mama would be pleased. Roxanne had always told him he was a mama's boy who was just trying to act hard. Maybe she was right.

The first thing Linc noticed when he entered the Lobby Lounge, which was the most casual of the hotel's restaurants, was that a lot of people had started their Saturday night partying a little early. He waved to a few of his teammates, who not surprisingly had attracted a crowd. Linc asked for a table away from the bar. He shook his head when they gestured for him to come over. Though he hadn't wanted to stay holed up in his room all night, he also didn't feel much like socializing, either. He happily accepted a table near the back of the restaurant. Linc drank a Coors while he waited for his meal to be prepared. Not his usual brand but when in Rome . . . He turned the glass up to his lips. It was half-empty when he put it back down on the table. Not bad, he thought. It probably would have been even better if it hadn't been diluted by the lingering taste of mouthwash.

Linc dug into the complimentary basket of tortilla chips and salsa. An alarm went off in his tongue and his eyes watered. The salsa was hot—just the way he liked it. He took another gulp of his beer and flagged the waitress down the next time she passed by with a tray of food for another table. He asked for another beer and a large glass of water.

Deciding he'd better slow the pace until she came back with his drinks, Linc picked up the magazine about local attractions and events. He'd snagged it right before leaving his room, figuring that it would give him something to do while he was eating and send out a message to his friends that he wasn't looking for company. They, unlike the media, had been really good about giving him some space. He wanted to avoid conversations about Jamal that would cause his concentration to suffer, the kind of conversations that were guaranteed to bring tears and never ending disbelief. Like Roxy, he was still trying to understand how this could have happened. How could he have missed physical signs that Jamal was working his body too hard? The words on the page blurred as Linc's eyes misted. He just couldn't let himself completely grieve until after the season was over. Not until after he'd honored Jamal by realizing his lifelong dream. That's all the Championship Bowl meant to him now. A way to honor his friend. Afterward, there would be time for tears.

Water and a second beer had materialized out of thin air. Linc didn't remember seeing the waitress come over. He tried to shake off his funky mood and focused again on the magazine. He'd been to Denver what? Five or six times? And he'd never been to most of the places they were talking about, he realized with some regret. People thought the life of a professional football player was so glamorous. They just didn't know. Yeah, he got to travel to a lot of interesting places, but most of his brief time there was spent at the airport, in the hotel, on the field, or in a jet-lagged stupor.

The glossy paper crinkled as he turned the pages. Denver had a museum that told about how the African American cowboys contributed to the great cattle drives? He didn't know that and he'd been a history major in college. He would have loved to visit the Black American West Museum or even Buffalo Bill's grave and museum. That fat rich lady from the *Titanic* movie, Molly Brown, her house was just a few blocks away.

Linc set the magazine aside when the waitress placed a rack of ribs in front of him that must have come from a pretty hefty cow. The thing was huge, but Linc had always loved a challenge. He quickly slathered it with the extra barbeque sauce that he had requested. His mouth watered in anticipation when the meat fell off the bone when he tried to cut the rack into more manageable pieces. Not trying to front, he set the knife and fork down and used his fingers. Linc's eyes rolled back in his head and he moaned in appreciation of the first juicy bite. The meal came with fries, coleslaw, and baked beans. He dug in and finished in a matter of minutes.

After cleaning most of the sauce off his fingers with several wet napkins, he reached for the magazine again while he waited for the waitress to return with the check. Seeing all that there was to do in Denver, Linc promised himself that the next time he came, he would try to experience some of the local flavor, even if it was just taking a tour of the Coors Brewery or trying check out a Denver Nuggets or Colorado Avalanche game.

His spine momentarily stiffened when a flirty female voice cooed, "Hey, Mr. Quarterback, if you're thinking about dessert, how about a l'il taste of Honey?"

Linc didn't know why he was so astonished to see Honey Brown standing next to his table. She looked pretty much as he remembered her, only her hair weave was bone straight and much shorter, stopping about a half foot past her shoulders. The first time he'd met her, the ends of the braided weave had teased her firm, rounded behind. She had on a shiny gold pantsuit with the zipper opened practically to her navel. He looked down at her feet. Five-inch gold-and-black platform shoes. She was without a coat, so he assumed she'd been there for a while. Probably over at the bar watching him the whole time. The thought pissed him off. Linc frowned. "What are you doing here?"

"Do you even have to ask?" she said before snagging the chair across from him. "I came looking for you."

Somewhere in the back of his mind, he'd known this could happen. But he'd wanted to believe that she'd just vanished back to whatever rock she'd crawled from under now that Jamal was no longer around. "How did you even know where to look?" he asked. Not that where the team was staying was a big secret.

She laughed then. "Are you kidding? Y'all stayed at this hotel the last time you were in town. And besides, some of your friends"—she looked over at the crowded bar—"must have remembered what a good time they had in Cleopatra's Lair last year. They been in there every night since they got here." She reached over to stroke his cheek, and instinctively Linc jerked back.

If she was offended, she didn't show it. Instead, she boldly met his eyes. "How come you haven't paid me and the girls a visit?"

Now who was kidding whom? If Honey was interested in seeing him, it wasn't 'cause she found him so irresistible. The first time he'd met her, she hadn't given him the time of day. She had been too busy hitting on Jamal. He was not going to play games with this woman. "What do you want, Honey?"

She laughed softly because a dumb question like that deserved to be mocked. "Linc, Linc. You know what I want. I want what's mine and little Jamal's."

Behind her head, he could see Steve Carter and Adam Parisi, the backup quarterback, giving him the thumbs-up sign and generally acting stupid. Steve started pumping his pelvis back and forth. *Great. They think I'm gonna get laid.* Honey was trying to screw him, all right, but not in the way they imagined.

"In case you haven't heard, Jamal is dead. So why are you bothering me?"

"Yeah," she said softly, but her eyes were calculating as ever. "I was sorry to hear about him."

Linc rolled his eyes. He just bet she was sorry. She was probably thinking her free meal ticket had been snatched away. "Jamal's dead. So, I repeat, what do you want from me?" His tone was stone cold.

She tried to win him over with a smile. He guessed the blatant invitation in her wine-red lips and the goodies she so casually displayed usually knocked men to their knees. Unfortunately for her, he was already sitting down, so he was not about to fall for anything. In fact, even if he'd been standing, he probably would have been immune. He found Honey's behavior somewhat pathetic. If she didn't have much else going for her, no wonder she used her sexuality like a tool.

Linc leaned back in his chair and waited. This was her show.

Her lips had formed a little pout, as if she wasn't used to her charms failing. "Order me a drink and I'll tell you," she promised.

After the waitress brought over her lime daiquiri, Linc continued to wait her out as she peered at him over the rim of her glass and wet her lips.

He sighed. He supposed she just couldn't help trying to seduce. Trying to fog a man's senses so that he didn't know which way was up probably came to her naturally, like eating or going to the bathroom. It was just something she did.

He was relieved when she finally came to the real reason she'd tracked him down.

"I know you think I'm a conniving bitch," she said.

He didn't contradict her.

"But I do have a heart. The money Jamal—or should I say you—sent me is long gone . . ."

Linc's hand balled into a fist where it rested on his thigh. When Jamal had told him about that phone call to Honey, the call that he expressly asked him not to make, he felt like decking him. But what was done was done. So he, like an idiot, agreed to send Honey a five-thousand-dollar check because Jamal didn't want to risk Roxanne finding out that he'd suddenly withdrawn that kind of money. And Roxanne would notice because even though she was rich, five thousand dollars was still big money to her. Now, by the gleam in Honey Brown's eye, he could tell that five thousand dollars hadn't been nearly enough to quench her greed. But that was too bad. She wasn't getting another dime out of him or Roxanne until she produced some DNA.

"I was just about to fly to Baltimore for the blood tests"— Yeah, right, Linc thought—"to settle this whole mess once and for all, and before I could get myself together, Jamal died."

"And then what?"

"Well, then I didn't know what to do. I mean, little Jamal deserves his share of his daddy's estate. Just what is his share?" she casually threw in. As if he was really supposed to believe that this was the first time she'd wondered about specific dollars and cents. Linc ignored the question and not just because he didn't know the answer.

Honey smiled and shrugged. "So anyway, I know Jamal's wife must be going through a lot, so I thought I'd wait a little bit before telling her about the situation."

Linc felt something clutch his heart. He didn't want Honey anywhere near Roxy. His voice was low and lethal. "Until you have proof that Jamal is the father of your baby, I want you to keep your mouth shut."

"C'mon, Linc. I figured I could go to Roxanne—that's her name, right—on the down low. You know, woman to woman, and we could work out an arrangement between the two of us. I gotta think of my child. Besides, how am I supposed to prove Jamal's the father if he's dead?"

"Hell, if people can prove that Thomas Jefferson fathered children with a slave over two hundred years ago, I think there are ways to find out if Jamal is your son's father. Just let me talk to his lawyer about it. In the meantime, you are not to approach Roxanne Steele. Not in person, not by phone, letter, fax, or e-mail. Don't contact her. Am I making myself clear?"

"Perfectly," she said before finishing off the last of her daiquiri. "But let me make something clear. My child cannot live on love alone. He needs food, diapers, and a roof over his head."

"You just told me not five minutes ago that you are still working. So don't try to sell me some sob story, because I ain't buying it."

"Well, maybe you aren't, but the tabloids might."

Was this heifer threatening him? She didn't know who she was messing with. Did she think she had the patent on scheming? He grew up around some desperate and sometimes vindictive women who could take her to school on the art of scheming. So little Miss G-string was trying to up the ante. Well, all right. He could play poker with the best of them. "You do what you feel you got to do," he told her. "But you think real hard and long before you do it. The money the tabloids toss at you will be peanuts compared to what you could have gotten if you just waited and went about this the right way. And also think about this. Jamal's wife is one of my oldest and dearest friends, and she's in a fragile state right now. If you have anything to do with causing her more pain because your short-term greed got the best of you, I'll see to it that you get next to nothing, even if I have to pay the lawyers myself to battle you."

Honey listened in silence. She gave him a thoughtful look or two.

Jamal pushed his plate forward, placed both elbows on the table, and rested his hands beneath his chin. He shot her a level look. "Now, are you sure you want to go to the tabloids, or do you want to do the right thing and give Roxy some time to get over the shock of her husband's death?" he asked. And time to resolve the drug-use allegations. And time to get rid of that numbness that had stolen over her.

"How much time does this precious, delicate broad need?" Honey snapped, clearly not happy with being hit with counterthreats.

"Six months."

"Six months! Oh, hell, no. I'm not living in limbo for six months."

"All right, three months, then."

Honey didn't answer him. Instead, she turned around in her chair. Her eyes searched the bar. Finally, her gaze met that of a little guy who looked out of place among the football crowd. He left his drink on the bar and hurried over.

What the hell is going on? Linc wondered. "Honey, who is that?" he asked right before the guy got to the table.

"That is my lawyer."

Who was he? The closer? Honey came at him first, trying to coax him with flirtatious smiles and endless cleavage. When that didn't work, she brought in shyster to finish the deal.

Honey grabbed the guy's hand and yanked him to her side. "Coop, he's trying to stall. He wants me to wait three months before we tell Jamal's wife. What do you think?" She quickly summarized their entire conversation.

"Coop" looked to be somewhere between thirty-five and forty-five. The brother had one of those steep V-shaped receding hairlines. The cheap suit he wore looked a little too big at the shoulders, yet was too formal for a Saturday night at a hotel bar. He was as nerdy-looking as they came. Jamal wondered where Honey had found him. Probably at the club. He looked like the kind of guy who would be stupid enough to turn his entire paycheck over to a stripper because he *thought* they were in a relationship when in reality paying her for a private dance was about as close as he was gonna get. Like the old Doobie Brothers song said: "What a fool believes." Coop was apparently seeing what he wanted to in Honey.

Linc watched as Coop gave Honey's hand a comforting squeeze. He bit his lip to keep a smile at bay. Did the guy really think Honey was some meek little thing in need of protection? If so, he was dumber than he looked. Honey could take care of herself.

The man extended his free hand to Linc. "Cooper Gates," he said. "And no need to introduce yourself. Congratulations on your win today, Linc."

He did not invite the man to sit down and was not interested in small talk. Linc said, "So do we have a deal or not?"

"Three months," Cooper said, as if mulling it over. "I think that's a reasonable amount of time to allow Mrs. Steele to grieve."

The tension seeped out of his body. Honey Brown was a loose cannon. He wondered what she would have done if he hadn't happened to have a game in Denver this weekend. Would she have contacted Roxanne directly? He hoped not, but thank God he was able to buy Roxanne a few more months to heal before Honey inflicted a new wound. He was also more convinced than ever that Honey and her shyster lawyer were not on the up-and-up. They could have forced the issue of paternity testing, but they didn't.

He couldn't help but wonder why they were being so accommodating.

Linc returned to his room shortly after Honey wiggled and jiggled her way out of the restaurant. He tried watching TV. He tried reading the magazine he'd taken down to dinner with him. But any interest that he'd developed in Denver had evaporated. Now, with the lights off, he rolled onto his side yet again and punched his pillow and readjusted it under his head, all the while knowing it wasn't the pillow's fault he couldn't get to sleep.

A little after midnight, the jangle of the phone near his ear made him jump. He reached over to pick it up, wondering which of his fellow teammates had gotten liquored up at the bar and was calling to invite him to join in on all the supposed fun.

Well, they can forget that, Linc thought, as he barked a "yeah" into the phone. *Look what happened the last time me and the fellows decided to have a good time in Denver.*

"And a cheery hello to you, Lincoln," Roxanne said. "What kind of way is that to answer the phone? I know yo' mama taught you better."

"Roxy?" She'd been on his mind all day and night, especially after the pact he'd made with the devil also known as Honey Brown, but he hadn't expected her to call. Not at this time of night. It was around two o'clock in the morning back home. "What are you doing up?" he asked. "Is everything all right?"

"No, everything is not all right," she said.

It was a reply that had Linc shooting up straight in the bed, mindless of his aches and pains. Where were his pants? His shoes? Had planes at Denver International stopped flying for the night? Maybe there was a red-eye flight he could take. "What's wrong?" he thought to ask amid myriad plans for getting back to her that raced through his head.

Then she laughed. "What's wrong is you didn't even bother to answer the message I left you."

Linc turned then to stare at the red message light that glowed and flickered in the dark. Damn! He'd never gotten around to listening to anybody's message. Never mind calling them back. Linc wanted to kick himself. If he'd known Roxy had been trying to reach him . . .

"I guess, now that you're the winning quarterback of the best football team in the Eastern Conference, you're too good to remember all the little people like me."

She injected this poor-pitiful-me quality to her voice, which brought a smile to his face. Linc flopped back against the same pillow he'd been beating only minutes ago. Everything was OK. Roxy was just giving him a hard time, as usual. This was the way it was supposed to be.

"Sorry about that, Rox. It was nothing personal."

"Uh-huh. I bet you were so busy celebrating that you forgot that some of us who caught the game on TV might have wanted to congratulate you, too."

"You watched the game!" he said, unable to control his surprise and pleasure.

"Yes, I did," she replied.

Linc noticed the huskiness in her voice. "You OK?" he quickly asked. Roxy was gutsy. Watching the team play without Jamal had no doubt torn her up inside.

"I'm fine." Silence. "It was just hard, you know."

"Yes. It was hard for me, too. But I felt like Jamal was there with me," he said. He felt stupid. He wasn't much of a religious or spiritual person, but he really *had* sensed Jamal's presence today. When she was quiet for a long time, he knew she was crying.

He wished he could be there with her. Roxy was an emotional person in a lot of ways, but she never let her pain show with the same abandon that she did other feelings like joy, concern, and love. She was always trying to push away the pain. That's why she'd watched the game today. She'd done it because Jamal would have wanted her to. *Because I wanted her to.* She was very attuned to the people she cared about, and surely she had sensed his disappointment when she missed the last game, even though Linc had tried not to let it show. "Roxy, thanks for watching the game. It means a lot to me."

A long sigh. "I wanted to do it. You know I love you, and I want to support you in everything you do. That's what friends are for."

Linc rubbed the back of his neck. *Friends?* Why did the word suddenly sound so inadequate? In fact, he felt suddenly and irrationally insulted by it. "You make it sound like a little thing, but I know it had to be upsetting to watch—"

"I'd do just about anything for you, Lincoln. You're a sweetheart. A champion among men and apparently a champion among quarterbacks," she said, reverting to a lighter tone. "You know, I'm gonna make you a celebration feast when you get home."

He shook his head in the dark, as if she could see him across the thousands of miles. "Nope. We'll go out to celebrate. Tell your mama to go out and buy a new outfit. On me, of course."

"But—"

"No buts. You're always feeding me. Now it's my turn. And it's two o'clock in the morning. Why are you still up?" As if he didn't know. She still wasn't getting much sleep. He was going to take her to see a doctor about it when he got home.

"I tried to sleep. But I felt restless. After tossing and turning, I finally realized that I just wanted to hear your voice. I wanted to tell you that I was thinking about you and happy for you. So I called. I hope you don't mind."

Linc could felt his heart expand and grow full. Roxy had no clue just how much her words affected him. Had no idea just how special she was to him. And as much as he didn't want to admit it, he was feeling more than friendship toward her.

Linc kept those feelings to himself. Instead he said, "Well, the call is made, so you go ahead and get some sleep now. And no, I don't mind. You can call me anytime. Day or night."

What else could he say? Only a real dog would try to push up on her now. Clearly all she needed and was looking for right now was a good friend. That was him, good old, reliable, but not to be taken too seriously, Linc.

Chapter
15

Roxanne's hand hovered over the phone. Then at the last minute she pulled it back. She sighed, frustrated at her cowardice. It had been two days since Gayle's husband had called to say that Gayle had delivered a healthy baby boy. Maxwell Jamal Atwood. That was a lot of name for such a little boy. Six pounds, five ounces. Mother and baby were doing just fine. Reggie had tripped all over his words, trying to describe what it was like to watch his son come into the world. Words like *beautiful, miraculous, exhausting* gushed forth from a man who, though not as stuffy as his job title, accountant, might imply, was not prone to rattling on, either.

He didn't mean to hurt her with his happiness, and Roxanne did nothing to stop him. He was contacting all of Gayle's close friends to tell them the good news. Being a proud father was normal.

She was the one who was being weird. Time moved like a glacier, so slowly that it was not visible to the naked eye. It was February. She could barely remember Christmas. She hadn't done any shopping. For the first time in her adult life, she had not put up a tree, and though she'd been willing to go to St. Louis, her mother hadn't thought it was a good idea to be around so many people so soon, even if it was family. It didn't take much to persuade Roxanne to stay put. New Year's Eve was another night she'd just as soon forget. For the past six years her resolutions had revolved around Jamal and their life together. This time the promise and possibility that came with the start of a brand-new year were missing for her. What she wanted, she couldn't have. Jamal. Their child. Their future. Happiness.

Unending happiness was a lie. Happiness was a fleeting, elusive thing. Like the brass ring Roxanne tried to grab every summer when Grandma Reynolds would take them to the local amusement park or a traveling carnival. Roxanne would always head straight for the merry-go-round. While half hanging off a wooden horse, she would stretch out as far as she could, trying to grab the brass ring. She reached out for it as she whirled by, the bobbing up and down of the horse only making it harder. Sometimes she grabbed only air; occasionally her fingers made contact with that precious metal, only to slip off with a fist full of nothing. Despite the forward momentum of the ride, on a rare, rare occasion she managed to clasp it securely and pry it from the stingy slot that held it in place. The sheer joy of winning against all odds would take over as she waved it around and proclaimed, "I got it. I got the ring. I won."

How was it that she always forgot about the part where she didn't get to keep the brass ring? She *always* had to give it back when the ride was over. And it was funny how it hadn't mattered because the *only* ride that interested her at the amusement park was the merry-go-round. She had fantasies of one day sneaking past the ride attendant. One day she'd smuggle the brass ring and take it home with her. But that day never came.

What kind of person would take almost thirty-six years to real-ize that you didn't get to keep the brass ring? she wondered. Today the thought of merry-go-rounds only made her sad and disillusioned. Today Roxanne hid out in her messy little office waiting for the next interruption or request for assistance and afraid to witness the happiness of one of her closest friends.

She sighed and tried to stop feeling sorry for herself. She might not be happy, but did that mean she had to begrudge other people their happiness? Had Gayle traveled four hundred miles pregnant and all to be with her when Jamal died?

She reached for the phone again. This time her hand actually made contact with the hard, cool plastic. *Just pick up it up, damn it, Roxanne. Stop being so selfish. Call your friend and congratulate her!*

It wasn't that she didn't want to. She was afraid to. She just wasn't sure she could do it without falling apart, and she didn't want to spoil Gayle's happiness by making herself the focus of attention.

Squeezing her eyes to shut in the tears, Roxanne let out a shuddering breath. Not a living soul knew how she'd prayed during the weeks following Jamal's death that her period wouldn't come. *Still reaching for the brass ring, you idiot!* Roxanne felt a strong urge to slap some sense into herself. Hot tears escaped their prison and splashed on her cheeks.

She'd been a fool to hope that Jamal had left her one last gift. Something precious and wonderful so that she'd always have a little part of him. The way that Gayle would always have a little part of Reggie through Maxwell. Maxwell Jamal.

Roxanne had been speechless when Reggie told her the baby's name. She had no idea Gayle had been thinking of naming the baby after Jamal. She hadn't said a word. Once Roxanne recovered from the shock, she had mixed feelings. On the one hand, she was touched that Gayle and Reggie had included her in this way. But on the other hand, every time she saw the little boy—and she would have to see him eventually—she'd be reminded of Jamal.

She'd sent flowers, and a big teddy bear from F. A. O. Schwartz had been ordered. There was nothing left to do now but call. She thoughtfully patted the phone a couple of times before reaching over to snag a facial tissue. She wiped away her tears and then blew her nose. When she was done, Roxanne crumpled the tissue and dropped it into the wastebasket next to her desk.

Children's laughter echoed off the walls as they chased each other down the hallway of the Center. The shrieks and giggles made everything inside her tighten.

Was she destined never to hear the sound of her own child's laughter? Would she always be the godmother, the aunt, and teacher? Was that God's plan for her? If so, why did he have to leave her yearning for more? It was cruel to leave her wanting more.

She pushed back from the desk. She would call Gayle . . . tomorrow. Today was Valentine's Day.

That was what all the running and giggling was about. The Center was throwing a Valentine's Day party for the grade-school kids. And Roxanne should be helping out.

She left her office, determined to shake off any remnants of self-pity. She might not have *everything*, but she had plenty. Making Hope Springs a success would keep her hands and her mind busy.

She was depending on it.

Screeches from a poorly played violin and the metallic jingle of tambourines competed for dominance when she reached the basement of the Center. After spending the fall begging for used instruments, they finally had enough donations to start music lessons. Marita was a genius. The basement was the best place to stash these budding musicians. When the violin shrieked yet again Roxanne smiled and hoped that maybe one day they'd be able to soundproof the rooms.

Despite everything else, things were going well at Hope Springs. The music program was really popular. It had just started in January, and already there was a wait list for lessons. The kids really loved their percussion. Anything that involved banging and clanging. She would have to see about getting more drums and another piano—though only the Lord knew where she was going to put it.

Unable to resist, she poked her head into one of the rooms. Eight kids, five girls and three boys, were lined up in two rows watching intently as Carolyn showed them how to play the tambourine. Carolyn was one of several student volunteers from the Peabody Conservatory of Music. Carolyn held the tambourine perpendicular to the floor in her left hand. She shook it quickly back and forth. Once it was shoulder height, she tapped it with her free hand and then repeated the move on the opposite side of her body. Like little parrots, the kids followed her movements with their own.

Spying her in the doorway, one of the girls, Rashida, broke away and streaked over to Roxanne. Rashida was as wide as she was high but moved pretty good on her sausage-like legs. Her fat, loosely braided pigtails flapped as she ran. She skidded to a halt in front of Roxanne.

"Mrs. Steele. Look at what I can do!" she cried. "I can make the letter H."

Roxanne clapped enthusiastically. "That's great, Rashida."

"I can make an A . . . and, umm . . . a C, too." She proceeded to show her those moves as well and threw her womanlike hips into it.

Roxanne didn't doubt that Rashida could go through the entire alphabet if she let her. But she had work to do. "Thanks for the demonstration, Rashida. Now, go on back over with the rest of the class."

The little girl obediently ran back over and took her place in line. Roxanne didn't know what letter they were supposed to be working on, but Rashida jumped back in without missing a beat.

Roxanne waved to Carolyn and backed out of the door and right into her mother.

Gentle hands grasped her shoulders to steady her. "Look out, Roxy," her mother warned.

"Oops, sorry," Roxanne said. Once her mother let go of her shoulders, she turned around to face her. "I was just coming to help out with the party."

Her mother looked good as usual. Her eye shadow perfectly matched the green of her shirt. A silk shirt, Roxanne noted. Her mama was taking a big chance strolling around this place all dressed up. Kids weren't known for their hygiene or for keeping their hands to themselves. But her mama was good-natured. She'd forgive a little grime on her brown suede skirt.

"Too late," Dot said, and wrapped an arm around Roxanne's waist.

"Too late for what?"

"Too late to help with the party. It's all over except for the cleaning up."

"Aw, man." Roxanne tried to fake disappointment. In truth, she'd holed up in her office most of the day because she had no desire to witness all the Valentine's Day hoopla. She also didn't want her gloominess to bring anyone else down.

She sighed. She knew that anniversaries, birthdays, and certain holidays would be hard for a while, especially the first year. But there were so many of them. So many reminders of what she'd lost and would never have again.

She thought it was a smart move on her part to stay in her office with her box of Kleenex nearby. Nobody wanted to see tear-stained cheeks and sad eyes on Valentine's Day.

This holiday belonged to lovers and romantics, like her mother. Dot had a bounce in her step. Something or someone had her eyes sparkling. "You look nice, Mama," Roxanne complimented her.

"Thanks, baby."

Her mother smelled good, too. She must have just spritzed herself with perfume because Roxanne didn't recall the scent being so noticeable a few hours ago. "You got a date?"

"No . . . no," she said, then gave a conspiratorial wink. "I got dates. Plural."

"Plural?" Roxanne was only mildly surprised. Her mama was a fast worker.

She'd vaguely noticed that there were a lot more middle-aged men hanging around the Center since her mama started helping out. Maybe that's why she'd lasted as long as she had. Her mama usually lost interest in things fast, and frankly, Roxanne was surprised that she hadn't gone back to her life in St. Louis after a couple of weeks.

Not that she was in a rush to see her mother gone. Once she stopped trying to raise a smile out of her, they got along great. Her mama had been like a breath of badly needed fresh air around this place. She'd picked up the slack when Roxanne's own energy flagged. Her mama had made it her mission to recruit some of the stressed-out grandparents to the Center. She'd lured them with card parties. Spades, tonk, and bid whist. Then once she had their attention, she told them all about the Center's self-improvement programs. At least three of the people who had signed up for the GED preparation class could be traced back to her mama. And a lot more had taken up pottery, knitting, gone to the First Aid for Family Finances class, and joined the reading group.

In response to the look on her daughter's face, Dot didn't laugh. She giggled like a woman her age divided by three. She squeezed Roxanne tighter around the middle. "I'm going out to dinner tonight with Craig Euston. But it's *dates* if you count Mr. Moseley, you know, the Toothless Wonder. He took me out to lunch today."

Roxanne allowed herself to be pulled into the empty rec room. All of the kids had disappeared, either off to other center activities or gone home for dinner. It was close to six o'clock. Red and white streamers looped above their heads. Hearts and cupid cutouts were pasted on the wall.

"Me and Moseley didn't go far. Just down the block to Eat-Mores. Roxanne, I tell you, that man must have razor-sharp gums. Can you believe he ordered a pork chop?" her mother exclaimed. "He gnawed on that thing till there wasn't nothing left but gristle." Her amused laughter rang out in the empty room.

Her mother was shameless. She would do just about anything for a little male attention. Mr. Moseley had to be about eighty. Of course, they hadn't gone far. He couldn't get around without one of those motorized wheelchairs, for God's sake. And Toothless Wonder was about right. Mr. Moseley had some dentures somewhere, like maybe in his pants pockets or at home in a jelly jar, but he hardly ever had them in his mouth. What was her mama gonna do with old Mr. Moseley? Now, Craig, with his wavy hair and big dark brown eyes, was closer to her mama in age, but he sniffed around women like a dog at a fire hydrant. But unlike the dog, he wasn't too particular about who'd been there before him. Any old hydrant would do.

The hem of her mother's skirt stopped a couple of inches above the knee. Her mother's long legs and trim figure would probably get most men's motors running. But she was too trusting. Didn't she realize that Craig Euston saw himself as some kind of middle-aged mack daddy? He even had one of those gangster lean pimp walks. Roxanne was tempted to warn her mother. But what could she say? Her mama knew her way around men. She'd seen a thousand and one varieties in her day. Matter of fact, she could probably write a book on the subject.

Roxanne asked another question altogether. "Where y'all going for dinner?"

Her mother picked up a broom and began sweeping up. A small pile of candy wrappers, discarded envelopes with small sneaker prints on them, plus the usual dirt and grit started to form.

"I'm not sure. Craig mentioned some Italian restaurant in Fells Point. But I can't remember the name."

"That's nice," she said. Roxanne brought a chair over. She needed to stand on something in order to pull down the taped-up streamers.

"Be careful," her mother said.

Funny, that was the exact warning Roxanne wanted to give her mother.

Dot stopped sweeping. She came over and put a steadying hand on the chair. "What are your plans for tonight, Roxy?" she asked her daughter.

Roxanne used a fingernail to edge up the Scotch tape that was holding the crepe paper in place. "Don't have any."

Dot frowned. "Really? I thought Linc might come over and keep you company."

"Why would you think that? It's Valentine's Day. Maybe Linc is taking his sweetheart out tonight." Maybe that's where he'd been all these other nights, too, because she certainly hadn't seen much of him.

The same week that they'd won the game in Denver, the toxicology report had come back, and just like Linc had promised, Jamal was clean. The only thing in his system had been ibuprofen. She tried not to be too bitter when the retractions were buried on page twelve and not front-page news like the accusations. She, her mother, and Linc had gone out to dinner that week, and it had been a double celebration. She'd seen very little of him since. She tried to remind herself that he'd been busy. The team did win the Championship Bowl, and he'd been in demand for interviews and commercials ever since. Linc was riding high on a horse called success right now. And he deserved it.

Then why you got such an attitude about him not being around? a little voice inquired. Another voice just as quickly replied, *Because he's never been so busy that he didn't have time for me.*

Because she missed him, she felt compelled to deny it. "Mama, don't you think I'm kinda old for a baby-sitter," she said as she climbed down from the chair. She was so busy balling up the streamers that at first she missed the hurt look in her mother's eyes. When their eyes met again, Roxanne felt like an ungrateful brat for snapping at her mother.

"Well, honey, I wasn't saying you needed a baby-sitter," Dot explained. "I just don't like leaving you alone in that great big house. I know Valentine's Day's got to be hard for you."

Guilt prevented her from answering. Her mama was just trying to look out for her. And how had she thanked her? By sassin' her, as Grandma Reynolds would say. "Mama, I really appreciate your concern . . ." Roxanne started her apology. And she did appreciate it because it was something her mama hadn't showed much capacity for when Roxanne was a little girl. Not that she didn't care. It was just that most of the time she was so self-absorbed, she didn't notice. Roxanne stopped feeling hurt and neglected the day that she finally realized that it never occurred to Dot that her children had worries or fears or desires. She just saw kids as funny and cute and an obstacle to her being able to go out and have fun whenever the mood struck her, which was often.

Roxanne hadn't understood it then, but now she could see it clearly. Her mama had been just a kid herself when she began popping out babies. Was it any wonder she hadn't been ready to put her desire for fun on the back burner?

Roxanne dropped the crumpled ball of paper on the floor. Maybe her mama had finally grown up. She was still here. She was trying. There was no denying that her mama had dropped everything to be there for her when she needed her. She hadn't been running around with men either since she'd gotten to Baltimore.

"Roxy, are you all right?" her mother asked when she showed no signs of retrieving the crumpled mess on the floor. "Maybe I should stay home tonight."

Her mama still wasn't very good at being noble. Her offer ended on a hopeful note. Roxanne smiled and let her off the hook. "No, no. I want you to go. And you tell Mr. Euston, he better treat you right or he's gonna have to answer to me."

Roxanne kicked the paper aside and reached for her mother, enveloping her in a tight hug. Her mother was skinny. She could feel the delicate bones in her back. The arms that returned her embrace were full of love, though.

Dot planted a kiss on the side of Roxanne's head. "I still don't like the idea of you being alone. Is there anybody else you might want to hang out with, since you think Linc is busy?" Dot asked.

"Mama, didn't I just tell you to stop worrying about me? I can get through a couple of hours on my own."

"Well, if you're sure . . ." Dot said, pulling back to search Roxanne's eyes.

"I will be fine," Roxanne replied, her eyes brimming with a confidence that she didn't feel.

Dot must have seen something reassuring or something that she wanted to see, because she finally relented. "OK, then. Do you mind finishing this up on your own, baby? Craig is supposed to pick me up out front at six forty-five, and I want to freshen up a little." She tucked back a couple of wisps of hair that had come loose while she'd been cleaning up.

"You already look gorgeous," Roxanne assured her. "But if you really need to ask the mirror, mirror on the wall who's the fairest of them all one more time, then be my guest."

"Thank you, Roxy," Dot said, giving her a quick hug. "Why don't you give Linc a call before you leave, though? Maybe you could meet him downtown somewhere."

Roxanne shook her head. Her mama just would not quit. She was not calling Linc. If he'd been thinking about her, he would have already called. *Stop being childish*, she chided herself. *Since when have you paid attention to who called who last? It all evened out in the end. Didn't it?*

"It used to," she muttered to herself and then hated how juvenile she sounded. Linc didn't owe her anything. He'd been a good friend for thirty years, and she was trippin' because he'd been incog-Negro for a couple of weeks. But still it wasn't like him not to call, and she hadn't heard from him in three days. Maybe he did have a date. But if so, why hadn't she heard about it?

She shook her head. No way. Valentine's Day was a big deal, and Linc wouldn't spend it with anyone unless it was serious. And the boy didn't have a serious bone in his body. His longest relationship had lasted less than a year. And even then it was obvious to her that Linc had lost interest around the sixth month. In this past year she couldn't think of anybody he'd gone out with more than once or twice.

So then why couldn't he squeeze me into his schedule tonight? He has to know how much I'd be missing Jamal today.

"Get over yourself, Roxanne Steele," she ordered. "Is Linc supposed to be thinking about you every second of the day? You're only obsessing about him now because it seems like he's not thinking about you."

She suddenly realized she was talking out loud. *Great, now I'm talking to myself. Guess it won't be a problem until I start answering myself back.*

Chuckling at her own irrational behavior, Roxanne got back to the task at hand. Not that there was much left to do. Somebody had already cleared away the food. She pushed the pile her mother had made onto a dustpan and emptied it in the trash can. Next, she began rearranging the tables. For some reason unbeknownst to her, all the tables and chairs had been pushed up against one wall.

She had her hands on her hips, surveying her progress, when Pedro Garcia shuffled into the room. He had to shuffle because the pants he wore were bunched at the ankles, covering most of his sneakers. He had on a plaid flannel shirt that also looked a size or so too big. But that six-year-old face was just perfect. His eyes were so dark they almost looked black, his hair was a wild mass of dark brown waves, his skin was golden cream, and he had the deepest dimples when he gave one of his shy smiles. Not that the dimples were showing now. His dark eyes were somber as he quietly approached her.

"Hey, Pedro, what are you still doing here?" she asked.

Stopping a few feet away, he told her, "Today is Valentine's Day."

"Yes, I know," Roxanne said.

"You missed the *par-tee*." He stressed the last syllable, reminding her that English was his second language.

"I know. I'm sorry about that," Roxanne said. "Did you have a good time?"

He shrugged and looked down at his scuffed-up shoes. "We played . . . Mailman."

Roxanne smiled. The name of the game was Post Office. It was an old game that even she had played back in the day. It was a way for kids to exchange Valentine's Day cards. The teacher always saw to it that everyone got at least one or two cards. There was always one from the teacher, each student had to give a card to someone whose name they pulled, and then the rest of the cards could go to their true loves, which in second grade usually meant her girlfriends and an occasional boy.

When Pedro continued to glance from her to his shoes and back, she wondered what was up. "Did you forget something?" she asked. She looked around. She hadn't seen any coats or gloves or books, the usual things that kids lost track of.

He held her gaze and slowly reached into his pocket. He came out with a grubby-looking small white envelope. "You didn't come to the *par-tee*," he repeated, and held it out to her.

A Valentine's Day card. Her eyes misted just at the sight of it. Roxanne couldn't control the slight tremor in her hand when she accepted the wrinkled envelope. She carefully pulled out the heart-shaped card. *"Will you be mine?"* it read.

She bent to pull him in for a hug. He was precious. This was why she loved children. They could touch the heart with the simplest of gestures. And here she was feeling that nobody cared about her on Valentine's Day. She couldn't have been more wrong.

"Oh, Pedro," she said, trying to keep the tears at bay. "I would love to be your valentine," she managed to choke out. Behind his soft halo of hair, she dabbed her eyes, not wanting to scare the child by crying a river all over him.

Chapter

16

Burning logs crackled in the limestone fireplace that was the centerpiece of the den. Next to the kitchen, it was Roxanne's favorite place in the house. The sectional couches had a Southwestern design, and the maple floor was liberally sprinkled with Navajo rugs. The soft draperies, which framed a side view of the property, were hung from rusted iron drapery rods. An antique metal coffee table and a glass end table from Ikea helped to create the feeling of combining the old with the new.

The dancing flames were somewhat hypnotic, and Roxanne could feel herself falling under their spell. When she caught herself nodding off, she forced herself to focus on her mother's favorite television show. Tonight's story line was something about the main character having an affair with not one but two of her stepsons.

Roxanne smiled at the mother, who was curled up next to her date for the evening. Her head was on his shoulder, and she was holding a throw pillow across her lap. Curtis was a good-looking man, with salt-and-pepper gray hair, light brown skin, a mustache, and small rectangular-framed glasses. He wore one of those Mr. Rogers-like cardigans and a pair of dress slacks. He looked at home, too. His arm was around the back of the couch, lightly brushing her mother's shoulders, and his legs were stretched out in front of him and crossed at the ankles. He'd taken his shoes off, and Roxanne could see where his socks were frayed at the heels, not riddled with holes yet but getting there.

Though her mother had invited her to watch the program with them, Roxanne suddenly felt like a third wheel. She picked up her dessert fork and empty ceramic plate off the end table. "I think I'm going to load the dishwasher and then head up to bed," she announced. "Curtis, Mama, can I get you anything else to drink? Another piece of pie maybe?" Her mama had made these slammin' sweet potato pies. Between yesterday and today, Roxanne had already had four slices. Her mama had made such a fuss at this sign that Roxanne's appetite was returning to normal.

"No, thank you," Curtis said. "I couldn't eat another bite." He patted his stomach. There wasn't much of a bulge for a man in his late fifties or early sixties. "Your mama is a hell of a cook. I'm gonna have to join a gym if I keep taking my meals around here."

Actually, Curtis had only been over to the house twice. He was the brother of a friend, one of the few men Dot hadn't met at the Center.

"Well, I know how to help you burn off some calories, and you don't have to join a gym to do it," Dot purred.

"Mama!" Roxanne said. She couldn't believe she was talking to him like that in front of her.

"Dot," Curtis said with a chuckle, "I think you're embarrassing your daughter."

Dot gave him this coy "Who me?" look. She turned to look at Roxanne and then peered into Curtis's eyes. "What?" she said, smiling. "I was only going to suggest that you volunteer down at the Center. Chasing kids around all day is guaranteed to burn the calories off."

When Roxanne sucked her teeth and rolled her eyes, Dot asked, "What did you two think I was talking about?"

"Not a thing," Roxanne said, while reaching for their empty dishes. "I'm going to take this out to the kitchen. Y'all have a good rest of the evening."

Roxanne had loaded the dishwasher and was wiping down the counters when her mother trailed in a few minutes later. Her mama was looking as starry-eyed as a sixteen-year-old, and most of her lipstick had mysteriously disappeared.

"I just put the pie in the fridge. Did you or Curtis decide you wanted some more?"

Her mama looked like an aging Alvin Ailey dancer as she practically twirled around the room in her bare feet. Roxanne had on fuzzy slippers and missed the Navajo blanket that she'd left on the couch. Obviously, her mama had something else to keep her warm. When her dance recital was over, she sank into the nearest chair and stared out the French doors with her hand resting under her chin.

"Earth to Mama. Earth to Mama. Please respond if you can hear me," Roxanne finally said. "Mama, did you forget you have a date waiting for you?" she reminded her.

"Oh, he's gone . . ." Dot said. "He didn't want to overstay his welcome. Said he didn't want you getting the wrong idea about him."

"It ain't him I'm worried about," Roxanne teased. "You're a regular man eater. Whatcha doing drapin' yourself all over poor Curtis?"

"Humph," Dot replied, not missing a beat. "If I'm drapes, then he can be my rod anytime."

"Mama!" Roxanne cried, and this time she wasn't faking her shock. *Just how childish would I look if I stuck both fingers in my ears? I am not hearing this. I mean, if it was Cynthia or one of my other girlfriends, well OK, but my own mama!* Roxanne thought she'd heard just about everything come out of her mama's mouth, but this one took the cake.

Noticing her expression, Dot added, "Calm down, Roxy. I was just flirting."

"Is that how all your lipstick got missing? By just flirting?" Roxanne said with a stern look, but she could appreciate the humor in the situation. It wasn't like she hadn't seen her mother gaga over a man before. She just hadn't heard her put it into words so bluntly.

"OK, so I was doing a little smooching, too," Dot admitted with a grin.

"Uh-huh," Roxanne said. She put the sponge on the rim of the stainless steel sink and then walked over to her mother. She hugged her from behind, and Dot put her hand up to hold Roxanne close to her. Roxanne leaned in and whispered close to her mother's ear, "Well, get in a little smooch for me, too. Curtis is a cutie."

Dot laughed. "Who you telling?"

Dot proceeded to tell Roxanne all about Curtis's finer qualities. He worked for the post office. He had been married for thirty years until his wife had died of breast cancer seven years ago.

Roxanne hid a smile. Her mama was already sizing him up. She also mentioned that he had two grown sons. The virtuous Curtis didn't smoke, either. He drank, but Dot had checked this out with his sister, who swore he'd never had a drinking or drug problem.

Roxanne took a seat across from her. "Dang, Mama. I'm surprised you didn't get his fingerprints so you could take them down to the local police station to have them run a background check."

Cocking her head to the side, Dot challenged, "And what makes you think I haven't?"

Roxanne's laugh was delayed for a minute, since she didn't know if Dot was kidding or not. Then her mother winked. Wow, Roxanne thought, Mama is really changing. A guy's background and credentials weren't something her mama had ever worried about. Look at how just a few weeks ago she'd gone out with that slimy Craig Euston. Speaking of which . . .

"Mama, you sound mighty interested in Curtis. What about Craig and Mr. Moseley? What happened to them?"

Dot rolled her eyes. "Now, I was just trying to be nice to the Toothless Wonder. You know, keep the old man's heart going rat-a-tat-tat. As for Craig?" she scoffed. "He was just someone to spend Valentine's Day with. He wanted to take me out to dinner, and I didn't have nothing better to do . . ." She didn't bother finishing the sentence, as if what she had said thus far explained it all.

Despite her sweet and sunny disposition, if her mother had been a contestant on that show *Survivor*, she would have won. She generally got what she wanted.

And Roxanne had to admit she was relieved that her mama was finally thinking some things through for a change. It was nice to sit around the kitchen table on a Saturday night teasing her about men and sex. Most people couldn't have that kind of conversation with their mothers. Her mama had never been afraid to let anybody see that she was a person, not a just a mother or someone's daughter or the poorly paid cashier at the supermarket checkout. Her mama was a one-of-a-kind original. She didn't let something like a role or job title hem her in. Maybe that's why folks down at the Center had taken to her. She was "people." Her sense of humor and optimism were great. Her mama was always coming up with new ideas. Many of them impractical, but at least she was interested and involved. At some point, Roxanne wanted to talk to her about paying her because she was putting in a lot of time at Hope Springs and had made a difference, especially in recruiting people around her age.

Dot was smiling to herself and gazed out into the night again.

Roxanne might as well accept it, there would always be a bit of the little girl in her mama. And she couldn't fault her for being an optimist, she had been accused of that herself a time or two. But if her mama was becoming more mature and less spur-of-the-moment about how she lived her life, maybe they could be friends.

Staring at her mama's profile, Roxanne realized that's all she had ever wanted, for her mama to be a friend *and* mother.

Roxanne opened the front door just a crack and stuck her arm out. It had been pouring since last night. The April showers had gotten a head start. It was still mid-March. The sleeve of her chenille robe was immediately soaked with freezing rain. "Yuk!" she cried, as she tried to locate the newspaper without getting too much of the rest of her wet. She knew the paper was there because she'd heard the thunk all the way in her bedroom when it bounced off the front door. She also heard a car pull up and then drive away. If the paper had landed in the soggy grass somewhere and she had to go out in this downpour, she was going to kill the newspaper boy. Newspaperman would be a more apt description. After all, Ralph did have a beard and drove an old Buick.

Her fingers searched around blindly before snagging the edges of a plastic wrapper. Roxanne latched on to it, then jerked it through the small opening. She held the paper away from her body as she padded down the hallway in her house shoes toward the kitchen. She told herself to be grateful that Ralph had wrapped it in plastic. She also made a mental note to mop up the water trail she was leaving.

But not until after she'd made herself a cup of hot tea.

Roxanne heard but did not see her mother come into the kitchen. She was too busy, perusing the Sunday circulars. She saw a coupon for adult diapers and picked up her scissors.

"Roxy, what on earth are you doing?" Dot cried, then tossed the sports page and the classified ads on the floor so that she could sit down.

Roxy glanced up then refocused on the task at hand. The clicking sound of metal meeting metal followed Dot's question. When the coupon fluttered to the table, Roxanne looked up again and said, "I'm clipping coupons."

Dot lifted the lid off the teapot, peered inside, shuddered, and then replaced the lid. She was not a tea drinker. Coffee with plenty of caffeine was her wake-up call in the morning. "I can see that, Roxy. But why? Did you forget that you're rich?" she reminded her as if she was talking to an idiot. "You don't have to clip coupons anymore."

"How do you think the rich stay rich, Mama?" Roxanne countered. "They try not to pay full price for things if they don't have to. They bargain and negotiate and save."

"If you were talking about a big purchase like a house or something, I could see it but . . ." Dot reached for the nearest coupon. Her eyes widened in surprise. "What do you need with adult diapers? I may be getting older, but I ain't *that* old."

Roxanne carefully eased the coupon out of her mother's hand so as not to rip it. She stuck it in an envelope with some others that she'd already cut. "Stop being silly, Mama. That coupon isn't for you or for me. I thought I'd take the coupons to the Center. I meant what I said about poor people being the last ones to use something that could help them save a buck or two."

"More like a penny or two," Dot argued.

"Pennies add up. You have three kids, you should know that," Roxanne told her, then teased, "Or are you so old that you can't remember that far back?"

"I ain't so old that I can't whup your behind for getting smart with me," Dot warned her.

Roxanne took it for the empty threat that it was. Dot hadn't been much of a disciplinarian. But Grandpa George and Grandma Reynolds more than made up for it. They'd lit up her behind on quite a few occasions.

When Roxanne would have searched for another ad to cut, Dot prevented her. She rested her hand on top of the one that held the scissors. "Seriously, Roxanne, you've got to stop this."

Surprised, Roxanne met her eyes. "Stop what?" she asked, genuinely confused. "What are you talking about?"

"Every other word out of your mouth is the Center this or the Center that. Everything you do revolves around that place."

Roxanne tugged her hand from beneath her mother's. She put the scissors on the table. Where had this come from? Since when did her mother have a problem with Hope Springs? "Mama, the place isn't going to run itself. In case you forgot, I don't have Jamal to help me anymore."

"Don't give me that. Now, tell the truth, when Jamal was alive, did you sit around on a Sunday morning clipping store coupons?"

Roxanne's lips thinned and she lifted her chin a notch.

Dot seemed not to notice the warning in her daughter's body language. "The people at Hope Springs do not need you looking after them every single second of the day." She added more gently, "Sweetheart, I think you're bored and restless. You need to spend time doing something else besides slaving away at Hope Springs." When Roxanne opened her mouth to protest, her mother said softly, "Believe me, that place has got more helping hands than it knows what to do with."

With a sigh Roxanne asked, "What would you suggest I do, Mama?"

"Have some fun. Take a trip. Go shopping. Brighten this place up."

Frowning, Roxanne immediately took offense. "What's wrong with this place? I love my house."

"Calm down," Dot said, "Ain't nothing wrong with the house itself. But some of the rooms . . ." her voice trailed off.

"What's wrong with the rooms?" Roxanne said, striving to appear open-minded but thinking her mama was pushing her luck. This house was more luxurious than any place either one of them had ever imagined being in, let alone owning. Yet, her mother had found something to criticize, which wasn't like her. So, Roxanne was definitely curious if nothing else.

"Well, since you asked . . . the dining room for one thing. It looks like a museum. Somewhere you'd expect to find dinosaur bones on display."

"Thanks," Roxanne muttered. She wasn't too thrilled by the lack of warmth the dining room projected, either. What her mama was saying only made her mad because it was true. Even Jamal used to say the same thing.

"And the room upstairs—"

"Which room upstairs? There are about five rooms upstairs," Roxanne reminded her.

Suddenly, Dot's eyes grew uncertain. She fixated on a point to the left of Roxanne's shoulder, which had Roxanne turning around to see if some critter had scampered across the wraparound porch. Nothing was there. Her mother appeared lost in thought in the silence, which was starting to feel a bit drawn out. When she finally looked at Roxanne again, there was a hint of fear and pleading in her expression. "Honey, now, don't get mad. But don't you think it's time you did something about the . . . about the nursery?"

The nursery? Roxanne's gut twisted into a knot of pain. She hadn't been in the room that was *supposed to have been* the nursery in weeks. She used to go in there in the days following Jamal's death back when she was torturing herself with "what-ifs." But she quickly realized she couldn't inflict that kind of pain on herself and still be able to function. That room held nothing for her. She wouldn't be using it anytime soon. Maybe never.

Her hand massaged the tight knot in the middle of her belly. She found herself preoccupied with the way her mother chewed at her bottom lip, the way her concerned eyes were searching her face. Leave it to her mama to put the truth out there on the table.

There was no baby. And there were zero prospects for a baby. Roxanne couldn't imagine ever putting herself through conception hell again. She couldn't even imagine another man taking Jamal's place. *So what do I need a nursery for?* She asked herself. *The simple answer? I don't.*

Her mama was right as mamas were prone to be. She needed to do something about the nursery. Roxanne decided then and there to check with Gayle to see if she wanted any of the furniture. The rest of it she could take to the Center. It wasn't like she'd bought clothes or anything. Roxanne tried to breathe through the pain in her stomach. As for the room itself, she would have to change the decor completely. The Beatrix Potter motif would be cute and fitting for a little boy or a girl, but keeping it there would only remind her of what she didn't have. She had painted the walls pastel green with white trim and had done the stenciling herself in the evenings and on the weekends when Jamal had away games.

It had all been for nothing.

Seeing the tears in her daughter's eyes, Dot felt awful. "Roxy?" her mother said. "Sweetheart, I'm sorry if I stepped out of line . . . I guess, I see you pushing yourself so hard at work. It's like you forgot there's more to life . . ." Something like pain flickered across her face, robbing it of its usually carefree expression. "You know what, sometimes your mama gets diarrhea of the mouth. Just forget I ever said anything . . ." she pleaded.

"Shush . . . Mama, it's OK," Roxanne told. "You got it right. I needed to hear the truth." She swallowed the lump that had moved from her stomach to her throat and silently added, even if it hurts like hell.

Dot's shoulders slumped with a mix of guilt and relief. She was glad Roxy wasn't upset with her, but it bothered her that Roxy felt bad for causing her mother even a second of distress.

Roxanne gave her mother a smile to show that all was forgiven, all the while feeling that *she* was the one that should be apologizing, not her mama. "So tell me, Martha Stewart," she said, "what suggestions do you have for revamping the dining room and the nursery?"

Dot's eyes lit up like the top of the Empire State Building. She scooted her chair closer to Roxanne's. She started pawing through various sections of the paper until finally Roxanne asked with a trace of amusement in her voice, "Mama, what are you looking for? Maybe I can help you find it."

"The circulars from the furniture stores," she explained distractedly. "Did you throw them away? 'Cause I was thinking . . ."

As her mother thumbed through the home section of the paper to get decorating ideas, Roxanne got up and walked over to the kitchen counter. She measured enough coffee for half a pot and put it in a filter. She filled the glass carafe with water. If her mama was gonna work this hard on her behalf, the least she could do was make her some of the coffee she loved so much. Roxanne's heart felt a little lighter. It was comforting to have her mama around to look out for her. Finally.

* * *

Etienne tossed a large navy duffel bag onto the threadbare bedspread. He walked over to the dresser, which had been scarred by deep grooves and black splotches where it had been used as an ashtray. He jerked open the top drawer and scooped up a meager supply of underwear, socks, and T-shirts. He quickly stuffed them in the duffel bag and gave the room a quick inspection to see if he'd forgotten anything. Not that there was much to forget. Most of what he'd acquired since coming to this country had been left behind at his old apartment in St. Louis; his furniture, the CD player, even the pictures on the wall. Things he'd worked so hard for. Etienne stood in the center of the small, dank smelling room as a helpless frustration threatened to suffocate him.

After that disastrous interview with the INS, his life had been turned upside down. He couldn't go back to his job. How could he with a false social security number? His cousin had given him the name of an immigration lawyer. He was an extremely busy man, so Etienne had to make due with speaking to Salvatore Hershberger over the phone. Etienne told him of his desire to seek political asylum. That was the easiest way to buy some time. The U.S. government had to investigate such a claim. He couldn't believe it when Hershberger told him that there was a good chance he might be deported first and then he'd have to apply for political asylum from Haiti. This was all because he'd entered the country under an assumed name and then tried to stay here by marrying an American. "If you'd just asked for political asylum in the first place," Hershberger had told him, "you wouldn't be in this mess."

Etienne wanted to scream at him, "Where do you think I come from? Cuba?" They didn't let Haitians into the country with the same degree of welcome. He had feared he would be sent back on the first available boat or plane. Whichever was fastest. And he didn't want to meet the same fate as others who had tried to escape persecution and failed. Violent, sometimes protracted deaths. No, that would not be his fate.

The only reason he hadn't been deported on the spot was because Dot denied that the marriage was fake, and he tried to convince the INS that he and Dot had argued shortly before the interview and that was why Dot was acting like she didn't know anything about him. She was angry and trying to hurt and embarrass him, he had lied. He thought they had bought it. But in his experience, government types didn't always keep their word. He skipped town because he didn't want to be around in case they changed their minds about the second interview. It was coming up in just a few weeks. Even with the marriage to Dot, Etienne had never felt certain that he would be allowed to remain in this country. He had saved most of his money just in case he ever had to disappear in a hurry. That time had come.

When he had run out of friends to turn to—friends who were in this country legally and who didn't want the INS breathing down their necks—this rent-by-the-hour, -day, or -week motel had become his temporary home. A teenage girl with a colicky baby had moved in next door. The child had squalled continuously for two days and nights. An alcoholic trucker who brought home a different whore every night occupied the room on his other side. Honking horns and high beams from cars erupted at odd hours. His neighbors and his situation kept him awake, gritty eyed, and on the verge of panic.

This was not the America he had dreamed of. Still, he could not return to Haiti. As a student he had protested against the current leadership, but they had come to power anyhow. His life wouldn't be worth a damn if he showed up in Port-au-Prince.

Dot was his last chance. His only chance. He had to convince her to give their marriage one last try. She was a nice lady. Though she had asked him to leave her alone, he believed that was her grief talking. He shouldn't have tried to talk to her about this so soon after her son-in-law's death. She used to brag about the celebrity son-in-law all the time. She had been so proud of him. She couldn't have meant it when she told Etienne to stay away. Dot was simply trying to fulfill her duty and comfort her daughter. He shouldn't have approached her . . . it had been too soon after her loss.

But surely, four months was a reasonable amount of time to grieve. Etienne smashed down the clothes with his hand so that he could ease the zipper up. He slung the bag that held all his worldly possessions over one shoulder. He opened the door of the room and stepped out in the early morning mist of the Ozarks. The damp air teased his nostrils.

Very soon he would be in Baltimore. With his wife.

Chapter

17

Chaos met Roxanne at the entrance to the community meeting room. A smart woman would have taken off before anybody noticed her. But Roxanne was too busy staring to think about that. There were about twenty-five to thirty kids running around like they were hyped up on caffeine, sugar, and adrenaline all combined. Books, backpacks, and notebook paper covered the floor like mismatched rugs. The noise could give a person a headache.

Roxanne squared her shoulders and moved a little farther into the room. By some stroke of bad luck, three of the six tutors hadn't been able to make it today. Dawn had car trouble. Alisa had a sick baby to take care of, and Dulin had his psychology licensure exam coming up in less than week. He was the one that usually organized the tutoring sessions and kept the kids in check, but Dulin hadn't been around much in the past month.

A sponge football whizzed by her face. Roxanne ducked. She shook her head and gave a rueful smile. She had wanted the tutoring program to grow, and now she had her wish. She had gone with Linc's suggestion that the sports, games, music lessons, and other recreational activities be contingent on two hours of homework or reading time per week. After their initial grumbling, the kids got used to it. Now the challenge was finding enough volunteers to meet the demand. A lot of people were still at work in the late afternoon.

Jean and Amy, two retired social workers and "roommates," had shown up on time like they always did. And her mama's new boyfriend, Curtis, was there, but since he was new, it wasn't fair to put him in charge of bringing order to this bedlam. Though her mama had persuaded Curtis to be a tutor, she was not one herself. And Roxanne didn't expect her to be, since her mama's attention span was nonexistent. In many ways, she was worse than a lot of the kids. Her mama was best with the social and recreational stuff. Dulin, who spoke with a quiet authority and whose six-foot-four-inch presence added to the effect, usually had no trouble rounding up the kids. Jean and Amy were as sweet as could be, but were more likely to meow like a couple of house cats than roar like lions—which was sometimes necessary to get the kids attention.

Roxanne had no choice but to take control if any tutoring was going to happen today. Then she was going to get on the phone and see if she could round up a few more tutors. One little boy was chasing his sister around one of the tables. Roxanne snagged him by the back of his shirt. When he couldn't jerk free, he turned around to see who was spoiling his fun.

"Have a seat, Kevin," Roxanne said.

"Aw man," he said before reluctantly obeying.

His sister's screeching stopped once she realized she was no longer being chased. Roxanne pointed to a seat. Just then a couple of teenagers hopped up on the stage at the front of the room. Roxanne frowned. They weren't even supposed to be here. The tutoring sessions were done by grade. Roxanne looked at her watch. It was time for the fourth through sixth grades. Some of the younger kids had gathered around of the stage to see what was up.

Roxanne began walking that way. One of the boys had short twists in his hair. He picked up a wireless mike from the lectern and turned it on. "Listen up, y'all, me and my boy, Spike, got a little rap and it goes a little somethin' like this. Do it, Spike."

The crowd around the stage increased in size in a matter of seconds.

The lanky Spike, who must have gotten his name for his height, took the mike.

"We be your future young biz execs.

Rockin' three-quarter Nikes with the Echo sweats."

He handed the mike back to his friend. From then on they kept switching off every other line.

"Say my generation doomed?
But we exempt from this mess.
Not everyone is dumb and flunk a SAT test.
Don't need no tutor or Hooked on Phonics.
We ain't talking slang, we exercisin' our Ebonics.
So what's the sense of having a phat GPA that you don't use.
But it don't mean drugs and women we will ever abuse."

Roxanne frowned. The boys had made a few good points, but telling the kids they didn't need a tutor? What was up with that? She reached the edge of the stage. "OK, break it up, everybody," she said. "Find yourself an empty seat at a table and take out any homework that you've brought with you."

The kids didn't even look her way. She might as well have been talking to the wall. Fine, thought Roxanne, if they wanna play it like that. She could speak their language. She skipped up the three steps leading to the stage. When she got to the wanna-be MCs, she tapped the one holding the mike on the shoulder. Both of the boys jumped. Apparently, they were so into their rap, they hadn't seen her coming. She held her hand out for the mike. The one with twists in his hair gave her a grin, and with a little bow took a step back.

Mike in hand, she turned and faced her audience. The kids had finally quieted down. They stared up at her with big, curious eyes and open mouths. Roxanne took a deep breath, then let it flow.

"My name is Roxanne and I am the boss. Get your butts to a table or pay the cost. I know you like b-ball. You wanna shoot pool. That ain't gonna happen unless you master school."

"You go, Mrs. Steele," one of the kids encouraged her. "Rock the house."

Roxanne cupped her hand, holding the mike close to her mouth, and made human beat box noises in true old-school fashion. "Is this mike working? Didn't y'all hear? I said get your behinds to a table. Get your butts in gear. I've asked you once. Don't make me have to ask you twice. Better get moving or what happens next won't be nice."

Roxanne had no idea what she'd do next, but the kids must have been imagining something awful because before she could cross her arms and lean back in the usual MC pose, the kids had scattered, running to tables like this was a game of musical chairs. By the time the sound of chairs scraping the tile floor had subsided, her fellow MCs had wisely disappeared. Roxanne made a mental note to deal with those two later.

Then she grinned and felt quite pleased with herself. She might try this rapping stuff more often, if it produced obedience like this. Her fellow tutors flashed her smiles of gratitude.

Someone in the rear of the room clapped loud enough to be heard over the chatter and giggles of the kids. Roxanne's eyes followed the sound.

Linc. What was he doing here? Linc hadn't been around in a few weeks. He gave her a thumbs-up sign and a big grin.

They met each other in the middle of the room. Roxanne flung her arms around him and gave him a tremendous hug.

Linc thought guiltily, it shouldn't feel this good to hold her. Roxy was one of those three-minute huggers. "Hey, MC Roxy, you trying to crack a rib or two," he joked.

Roxanne playfully slapped him on the chest as she stepped back. "It would serve you right if I did," she said. "Do you know how long it's been since you showed your face around here?"

Another flash of guilt. "I don't know how long it's been, but I got a funny feeling that you're gonna tell me."

Roxanne's hands were on her hips. "It's been three weeks. Twenty-one days. Not that I'm counting or anything," she informed him. But she had been counting the days because she'd been counting on him. Not just to help out around Hope Springs but to be there in case she needed him. When Jamal was alive, Linc had been in and out of the house like he lived there. He even had a key. The same for Hope Springs.

Linc shifted and wondered what Roxy was thinking. She was never quiet for no reason. She was probably waiting for an explanation as to why he'd done a disappearing act. And he'd give her one. Not the truth but an explanation nonetheless. What she wasn't going to hear was that he was inexplicably hot for her and hating himself for it. She wouldn't hear that he'd stayed away because he'd didn't trust himself not to blurt out those feelings because they were his problem to deal with. Not that staying away had helped any, because without realizing it, he had reached out for her. His body had a mind of its own. Somehow, he'd grabbed her hand and was pulling her closer to him.

Linc looked down in amazement, where his hand trapped hers. Her hand felt small, soft and warm in his. He felt the slight pressure where her short, neat nails dug into his palms. He noticed the slight rise and fall of her chest beneath the sweater she wore. Her eyes behind the wire frames were watching him, still playful but waiting for a response. Her unpainted lips quivered slightly as if on the verge of asking a question.

He abruptly let go of her hand. Until a few months ago, he would have thought it impossible to be this drawn to any woman, to feel so much in the most innocent of touches. And to think he used to tease Jamal about being whipped. He gave himself an invisible shake. *Answer the woman's question, Linc.*

He sighed dramatically. "It's so hard being a superstar," he lamented. "So many endorsement deals pouring in, so many contracts to consider, so many autographs to sign."

"Oh, no wonder I haven't seen you then," Roxanne said, pretending to feel sympathy for him. "How silly of me. I should have had your people call my people, and then maybe you could have penciled me in," she suggested.

A dangerous glint had come into her eyes. Before she could put him in his place, he threw up his hands in mock surrender. "Now, girl, you know I was just playing," he said. "Roxanne Steele will never be penciled in." How could she be? When Roxy was already in his book, drawn deep into the soul of who he was in permanent marker. There was no erasing that.

Roxanne noticed that a lot of the kids were looking their way rather than focusing on their studies. Having famous football players around the Center was nothing new, but the awe never quite wore off, either. So Mr. Superstar needed to either roll up his sleeves and get to work or get going before he became a major distraction. And it didn't take much with this bunch. Homework was the last thing they wanted to be doing anyhow.

"Now that you're done with your weak . . . excuses"—she had started to say weak-ass excuses but didn't want to set a poor example for the kiddies—"Do you plan on doing some work around here or just stand there looking all manly and good looking?"

Linc did a double take, and Roxanne almost slapped a hand

over her wayward mouth. Manly and good-looking? Had she really said that? She meant to say something about him looking famous. Then she shrugged off her momentary embarrassment. Obviously, she was so happy to see him, she was babbling.

And damn it, if it wasn't good to lay eyes on him. It had been too long. "Don't just stand there with your chest all puffed out 'cause I gave you a compliment," she told him, acknowledging what she had said but playing it off just the same. "We really could use help with the tutoring program today. You wouldn't believe how short-staffed I am."

She'd actually noticed that his chest had swelled? Amazing. But thankfully, she misunderstood the reason why. It wasn't because he was so full of himself. It was just the result of the involuntary breath he took because he couldn't believe what Roxy had just said. *But remember, buddy boy, her next words deflated you like a near-bald tire after it rolled over a thumbtack.*

The comment about his looks hadn't meant anything. Linc cursed himself for thinking that it had. Roxy had always been a big flirt. She didn't even know she was doing it. Jamal claimed it never bothered him. He knew where Roxy's loyalties lay. Besides, Jamal had once observed, she flirted with everybody.

With everybody except me, Linc thought, *and this time was no exception. Look at how quickly she shot you down.* Linc tried to control his expression. He didn't want any of what he was feeling to show in his face. If Roxy had noticed his chest swelling in response to something she'd said, Linc realized he was gonna have to be a lot more careful around her. She knew him too well. Swallowing his disappointment, Linc said, "Not only am *I* here to work, but I brought help with me."

"Bless you, Linc," Roxanne said, "I could kiss you."

Linc licked his desert dry lips. If only she knew how welcome that kiss would be.

"So which of your teammates did you bring?" she asked. "And where is he?" Roxanne's eyes searched the room, as if she expected to find a football player hiding under one of the tables. She'd been so happy to see Linc, she'd almost forgotten that other people were in the room with them—including the kids.

"Well, what did you do with him?" she asked when she didn't spy any burly football players lurking about.

"Actually, it's a her not a him," Linc said. "Football players aren't my only friends, you know."

Roxanne didn't attempt to hide her surprise. This certainly was news. Linc didn't have any women friends that she knew of. He was the type of guy to whom women "friends" usually meant girl-friends or ex-girlfriends. *She* was the only woman Linc had as a friend who hadn't been an ex-girlfriend. Roxanne gave him a con-sidering look. She was itching with curiosity about his new friend.

"I stand corrected," she said. "So where is *she*?"

Linc groaned. "With your nosy mama. Last time I saw Dot, she was dragging Desiree into the staff room, talking about getting her a cup of coffee. If I know your mama, what she's probably giving her is the third degree and basically getting all up in her busi-ness . . . and mine." Dot Miller and his mother were fast friends. Linc wouldn't be at all surprised if there was a message from his mother on his voice mail by the time he got home. Finding him a proper wife was his mother's main goal in life these days.

As they headed toward the administrative offices, Roxanne said, "Why you looking so nervous. What kind of skeletons does the woman have in her closet?"

"Now, don't you get started, too," Linc begged. "Desiree is just a friend."

Yeah, right. Roxanne wanted to meet this woman herself. Men could be so gullible sometimes. Linc was really hot property right now, and she didn't want some hoochie taking advantage of him.

When they walked into the room where volunteers and staff went to chill out and get a moment's peace, her mother was indeed plying a woman with coffee; but if appearances meant anything at all, this woman was no hoochie.

Linc called to her and she stood up, and up, and up. Damn, she was tall. Almost six feet tall. Roxanne felt like a runt next to her. And she was stunning. She had the body of a gazelle, lean and graceful-looking. Everything about her screamed class, not hoochie mama, and rather than feeling relieved, Roxanne felt unsettled. Desiree wore a double-breasted camel-hair jacket and slacks with a brown silk blouse. Shoes with pencil-thin three-inch heels covered her somewhat large but narrow feet. Her thick, dark brown hair had a center part, was combed away from her high forehead, and stopped an inch or so past her shoulders. No wonder she hadn't heard from him in weeks, Roxanne thought. He's probably been holed up with this Amazon somewhere.

Desiree's smile was completely genuine as she reached out to shake Roxanne's hand. "Mrs. Steele, it's so good to meet you. Lincoln had told me so much about you."

Lincoln? Nobody called him that except me and maybe his mama, and only when we're really trying to get his attention.

Belatedly remembering her manners, Roxanne said, "Please call me Roxanne."

"Or you could call her MC Roxy," Linc joked.

Warmth flooded Roxanne's cheeks. He used to embarrass her like this all the time when they were kids.

"MC Roxy?" Dot repeated, looking from her daughter's mortified face to Linc's grinning one. "What is he talking about?" Desiree was looking puzzled as well.

"Well—" Linc began but never finished when he got a load of Roxanne's warning glare.

"Nothing, Mama. Ignore him," Roxanne said. She turned her attention to Desiree again. "Even though Linc never properly introduced you—'cause he has no manners—I already know your name is Desiree. Pleased to meet you, too."

"I was so sorry to hear about your husband. Jamal was a really wonderful person," Desiree said.

Roxanne was about to nod and murmur the automatic "thank you" that followed condolences by a stranger, but something in Desiree's voice, a sincerity that shone in her big brown eyes had Roxanne asking, "Did you know Jamal?"

"Desiree works in the marketing department for the team. I thought I told you that."

Roxanne heaved a sigh and flashed him an annoyed look. When was he supposed to have done that? Five minutes ago, she hadn't even known Desiree existed.

"It's Desiree's job to find new sponsors and advertisers for the team. She's been an account executive with the team for two years, but moved here from Cincinnati. She has always loved sports. Played on her college volleyball and basketball teams. She always knew her dream job would involve working with athletes. She's not married and she doesn't have any kids."

This bio came from Dot, not Linc. Roxanne slowly turned her

head to stare in amazement at her mother. She couldn't have been alone with the woman for more than a few minutes. Yet, if asked, her mama could probably supply Desiree's favorite season, where she lived, and the names of her two closest friends. Her mama could pick people for information faster than a thief could pick a lock. It was ridiculous.

Dot missed Roxanne's incredulous look. She was too busy smiling at Linc. "What I can't understand is why a fine, young thing like her hasn't been snapped up. I mean she's beautiful and smart. A man would have to be just plain crazy not to notice."

Linc smiled and said nothing. He caught Roxanne's eye and gave her an I-told-you-so look. Dot's attempts at matchmaking were as blatant as his mother's. And why was Roxanne looking so . . . so . . . well, he couldn't actually figure out how she was looking. Her head was cocked to the side, and her lips were tight and kind of twisted, like she was mad about something.

Desiree gave a little laugh. "Dot, you must have been a detective in another life. Or I'm just a big blabbermouth. I didn't realize I'd told you so much about myself."

"Don't blame yourself, Desiree. Dot, here, is as nosy as they come," Linc told her.

Dot drew herself up to her full five feet eight inches. Yet, Desiree still had her beat by several inches. "You and Roxanne are like two peas in a pod," Dot said. "Just because people find me easy to talk to, doesn't mean I'm nosy."

Desiree put a friendly arm around Dot's shoulder. "Lincoln, stop picking on my new friend. Dot is not nosy. Besides, my life is an open book."

Roxanne's ears perked up. An open book? Is that right? Then what page did the story of you and *Lincoln* start on? Obviously, they'd known each other a long time if she'd worked for the team for two years. How come Linc had never mentioned her before? Roxanne felt a little hurt. Linc always told her about the women in his life. Just as he always knew about the men in her life. He was like one of her girlfriends in that respect. Linc's tales of woe were usually about how to get rid of someone, and Roxanne's basic theme had been how to find someone worth keeping. Someone like Jamal.

"Desiree, you mentioned that you knew Jamal. How come

we've never met before?" Roxanne asked and hoped it didn't sound as rude to Desiree as it did to her. The question was also directed at Linc, who gave her a strange, slightly confused look.

"Well, I work for the front office and really don't have all that much direct contact with the players, unless I'm working a deal that calls for it. Like if a sponsor specifically requested a particular player, then I'd set that up directly or via his agent, if necessary."

"Oh," Roxanne murmured, feeling frustrated. That didn't tell her anything. When had she and Linc become such fast friends, then? And why did she care so much? It was really none of her business. Linc was a big boy. He hadn't asked her to cluck over him like a mother hen.

"So, I worked with Jamal a couple of times. He really enjoyed a love-love relationship with the public. I never heard a bad word about him. It was all good," Desiree said.

"Until he died," Roxanne said in a tight voice. Even now, it pissed her off that at the very end a few publicity-seeking media outlets just had to come up with something negative. His sterling reputation would be forever tarnished by "allegations" of possible drug use.

Linc knew the second that Roxy began to retreat within herself. Her arms had come up to hug herself as if suddenly chilled. Her eyes had a faraway look that hadn't been there a minute ago. He wanted her to come away from that dark place she'd gone to. He wanted her back. Unable to stop himself, he laid a hand on her forearm.

At his touch, she glanced up in surprise. He didn't say anything, just studied her intently.

Roxanne sighed. She had thought she was doing well. Lately, she'd been feeling more like her old self, thanks to the passage of time and her mother keeping her occupied. But it didn't take much to trigger memories of Jamal. "I got to get back to the kids. They are supposed to be studying, but I never know how long that will last. Desiree, I know Linc dragged you down here. But don't feel obligated to do anything."

"Oh no, I invited myself," Desiree assured her. "Lincoln always has good things to say about Hope Springs, and I asked if I could tag along. I'd be more than happy to help. What do you need me to do?"

Desiree is a nice woman, Roxanne acknowledged. Then wondered why she was having such a hard time feeling nice toward her. Something inside her responded to Desiree on a mean and small level. And for absolutely no reason. Roxanne tried to let go of whatever it was. She said, "Well, basically the tutors help the kids with any homework they bring, and if they have no homework, they're supposed to bring a book to read. Sometimes, they take turns reading from their books, and the tutors help them with pronunciation or ask them questions about the book to make sure they understand what's going on."

"No problem. I can handle that," Desiree said. "I love kids."

"Did you hear that, Linc? Desiree loves kids. Ain't that something?" Dot said with a wink.

Her mother was starting to work on her nerves. "Mama, don't you need to be setting up for the parenting seminar?" Roxanne reminded her.

"Oh, I got plenty of time before that starts." Roxanne shot her a pained look, and Dot quickly added, "But . . . but I suppose I could go ahead and get the chairs, the overhead projector, and everything set up for Mr. Gaines."

"Thank you, Mama. That would be great." Dot left the break room first, and the rest of them filed out after her.

Desiree hadn't been kidding when she said she liked kids. And the feeling was mutual. Roxanne felt an irrational jealousy as she watched her captivate the kids. She was working with a group of five. One little girl with a bad case of the sniffles stood in front of Desiree with her head pressed against her torso as Blanca Charriez read from a book. Desiree didn't seem to mind getting snot smeared on the silk blouse that Roxanne had been admiring earlier. Her hair was no longer neatly combed. In fact it was a mess, sticking every which way. Either Desiree didn't know it or she simply didn't care, because not once had Roxanne seen her make a move to pull it back or tamp it down. Desiree was just the kind of woman that Roxanne usually liked. Down to earth, patient, and approachable. And she loved kids. But for some reason, those very qualities were annoying to her, which made no sense because most people thought *she* was down to earth and approachable.

"Mrs. Steele, is this right?" Roxanne forced herself to pay attention to her little group.

"Is what right, Christine?" Roxanne said, reaching for the pencil-smudged paper the nine-year-old held out to her. By the time Roxanne got the tutoring session organized, everybody else got the easy stuff. She got stuck with math.

"Did I shrink the fraction?" Christine wanted to know.

The fraction Christine had started with was $6/18$ and she was supposed to be reducing it to its lowest terms. She'd divided by two to get $3/9$. "Almost, sweetie, you just have to reduce it a little teeny, weenie bit more," she said, holding up her thumb and forefinger showing only the tiniest space between the two.

Christine groaned and made an ugly face. "This is hard. I hate fractions." Roxanne didn't much like them, either. But she gave Christine an encouraging smile and showed her the easiest way to solve the math problem.

The girl whipped out her chewed-up pencil with its dirty stub of an eraser. "So I divide the top and bottom by six?" she said.

"That's right." Roxanne nodded. "You're looking for the greatest common divisor. The biggest number that both the numerator and the denominator can be divided by."

After a minute of intense concentration, Christine scribbled something and held it up for Roxanne to inspect. "Is it right now?" she asked. Speaking of fractions, her voice held one-half hope and two-fourths frustration.

"One-third!! That's as low as it gets. You go, girl. I knew you could do it, Chris!" Roxanne exclaimed.

"Let me see." The paper was suddenly wrenched from her hands. For a big man, Linc moved very silently.

"Oh, yeah!" he boomed. "This is definitely a touchdown. Ain't nothing left to do but the Touchdown Tango. Everybody up," he said to the other kids sitting at the table. "Y'all know how it goes."

And that was it.

The calm that Roxanne had worked so hard to create was over in a matter of seconds. Of course, they knew what he was talking about: the crazy little in-your-face dance that the Baltimore receivers did to mock the other team's defense when they had a big scoring play. Every child at her table was following Linc's lead as he took them through the head-swiveling, inward-knee-rotating movements that was a cross between the dance called the Snake and an epileptic fit. All the gyrating brought back memories of Jamal. Happy memories for a change. The kids at the other tables hadn't joined in yet, but they looked about ready to.

"All right. All right. That's enough celebrating," she said, shooing them back into their seats. "Thanks a lot," she told Linc when everybody finally settled down.

"No problem. I'm here to help," he said, grinning in the face of her annoyed expression.

Roxanne pulled him over to the side near a wall. "You're supposed to be helping your group. What are you doing over here, besides stirring up trouble?"

"My group is doing social studies. Mostly just reading. They really didn't need any help. And since math was never your best subject . . ." He shrugged.

"You got a lot of nerve, Linc. Math might not have been my best subject, but at least *I* was good at something."

"Ouch, that hurt," he said. "Maybe I had an undiagnosed learning disability."

"I don't think so. You just had a bad case of being lazy and a talent for finding girls who were willing to do your homework for you."

He shook his head. "I still can't believe you told Miss Clarke about that." Miss Clarke had been their teacher in third grade. She was pretty on the outside but hard as nails on the inside. Thinking back, she kind of reminded Linc of Roxanne's friend, the beautiful Monique.

"I did it for your own good," she told him, sounding all prim and proper. At just that moment, Desiree looked up and waved. Her broad smile said she was having a ball. "I guess it didn't really work, since you still have women doing your bidding."

"What do you mean?"

"Look at Miss Desiree over there. She's close to winning the 'Tutor of the Day' award, and you're just shootin' the breeze."

"It's not like I put a gun to her head and forced her at gunpoint," Linc quipped. "She asked to come, remember?"

"I just bet she did," Roxanne drawled. How old was he, thirty-six? How good-looking and famous did he have to be before Linc realized he didn't have to do much to get a woman to jump through hoops for him? Men could be so dumb, sometimes. "I bet old Desiree would do just about anything you asked her to," she said.

Now Linc frowned. At first he thought she was joking, but it was starting to sound like bitchiness to him, which was not like her. "Why don't you like Desiree?" he asked flat out.

Roxanne's head shot up at his tone. "Don't get all huffy. I like your lady friend—from what I've seen of her. She seems nice. I'm just wondering why you've kept her such a secret, that's all."

Is that what was bothering her? She thought he had this big romance going on, and he'd left her out of the loop? In a way, she was right. He did have "a thing" for someone—*her*!! He wished it was Desiree and he wasn't proud of himself, but he'd tried to make it Desiree. He'd known for a long time that Desiree was attracted to him. She wasn't obvious about it. She didn't flirt. It was her interest and attentiveness whenever their paths crossed that clued Linc in. Linc had been flattered. What normal man wouldn't be? Desiree was an attractive woman. But he had felt no urge to make a move on her in the past. But with the team winning the Championship Bowl, they were working together a lot more—riding the wave while both he and the team were still hot 'cause who knew what the next season would bring—and he'd asked Desiree out on a couple of dates. And they were real disasters, at least from an attraction standpoint. She was good company, but he didn't want *her*. He wanted Roxanne, and he surprised himself by being gentleman enough not to use Desiree as a stand-in because he couldn't get the real deal. Five, ten years ago, and it would have been a whole different story.

He'd told Desiree as gently as he could—rejection was never a completely pain-free experience—at the end of their second date that he only felt friendship for her. Desiree was honest enough to admit she was disappointed but mature enough to say you could never have too many friends. So, they did hang out some. Despite her cool elegance, she really was something of a tomboy. The first person he'd shot hoops with since Jamal died. Desiree was like a buddy to him. But Roxanne seemed to have gotten the wrong impression somehow. "Roxy, you're starting to sound like your mama . . . and my mama for that matter. Desiree and I are just friends—"

She shrugged. "If you say so."

Linc felt his hackles rise. He felt like shouting "I can't even see another woman as a woman because of you!" This was the most honest he'd been with her in months, yet she was treating him like he was a liar. "Roxy, it's the truth," he repeated.

Again she shrugged. "You don't have to explain *anything* to me," she insisted.

"Damn right, I don't, especially when I've already explained and you chose not to believe it." He grasped her by the elbow and nudged her a little closer to the wall so that their conversation wouldn't be heard. "What is wrong with you? Why are you acting like this? As much as you're always looking for new volunteers around here, I thought you'd be grateful to have an extra pair of hands."

"Just like I'm supposed to be grateful when my so-called best friend goes missing for weeks, just when I need him most, and then he comes blowing back in when it suits him?" she said. She snatched her elbow out of his loose grip. "Oh, excuse me. You came with a *volunteer*, so I guess that makes it all better."

Why was she picking a frickin' argument? None of this made any sense. "Roxy, I'm sorry if you feel I deserted you. I warned you before the play-offs even started that things could get hectic—"

"Not too hectic for you to get yourself a new girlfriend."

He threw up his hands in disgust. "OK, that's it. I'm out. I can't talk to you when you're acting crazy. I don't know what you've got against Desiree. But I will figure out some way to let her know that her help isn't wanted around here. And when you figure out what bee flew up your butt, feel free to give me a call."

Linc turned away as if he couldn't stand the sight of her a minute longer. He had called her crazy and Roxanne couldn't argue there. She had picked and picked at him, even though he kept telling her to stop. If Linc felt confused, it was nothing compared to what she felt. She was the one who instigated the whole thing. And now she was left shaking inside. Linc had never ever walked away from her in anger. If Grandma Reynolds had been here, she would have told Roxanne that she was "acting like a pure-D fool!"

She leaned against the wall for the support she usually expected and got from Linc when she was feeling unsteady. Linc wasn't thinking about her now. Or at least he wasn't thinking too highly of her at the moment. But who could blame him? She wasn't too thrilled with herself, either. Roxanne watched as he tapped Desiree lightly on the shoulder to get her attention. She had a feeling Desiree would look her way to say good-bye.

Roxanne averted her eyes.

She wasn't going to be able to face Desiree or Linc until she figured out what bee had flown up her butt. And why.

Chapter

18

Roxanne sneezed and tried to lock her legs at the same time, so she wouldn't tumble off the stepladder she was standing on. Her mama was over by the window measuring for curtains, and Curtis was using a steamer to loosen up the wallpaper in what used to be the nursery. At Roxanne's loud sneeze, they both said, "Bless you," without stopping what they were doing.

It was Good Friday, and they'd closed Hope Springs to make for a long Easter weekend. Roxanne hadn't wanted to, but her small staff outvoted her. Such were the drawbacks of running the place in a democratic fashion. Privately, Roxanne suspected that her mother had been behind the little rebellion. She'd been trying to get Roxanne to slow down at work. But it appears she had a second motive; to make a real dent in redecorating the nursery. The three of them had been at it since around ten o'clock this morning.

Roxanne sniffed then yanked off another panel of wallpaper. She reached for a scraper to get at a piece of paper that stubbornly clung to the wall. She sneezed again. She was allergic to something. It could be all the dust or maybe even the adhesive on the wallpaper, but she was determined to stick it out. She needed all the scraping, tearing, and measuring to take her mind off the argument she'd had with Linc two days ago. Roxanne hadn't called him because she still didn't know what she'd say. She knew she ought to apologize, because she'd definitely been acting like a first-class bitch. She just didn't know what she'd say beyond sorry.

She crumpled the paper and it joined a growing pile at the foot of the ladder. Besides, she was mad at him, too. She'd been to hell since Jamal died and still had not completely made the journey back. That should have counted for something. That should have made Linc a little more understanding at least.

If he cared then he would have been here to hold her and be her friend when the moving truck came and took away all the toys and furniture she'd bought in anticipation of a child that was not meant to be. She was trying hard to find comfort in the knowledge that other children would get to enjoy them. But still her heart ached. Roxanne longed to be around someone who could have predicted, who would have instinctively known that her heart would tear and twist every time she listened to her mama's cheerful plans to erase any trace of the family she thought she'd have with Jamal. If Linc had bothered to come around, he would have seen through her fake enthusiasm, would have acknowledged the pain that she didn't want to own. Instead, he was off pouting because she'd gotten pissy with him—one time in their lifelong friendship.

Roxanne tugged at the next strip of paper, trying unsuccessfully to hold off another sneeze. The more she thought about it, she wasn't the only one who needed to be handing out apologies. Linc owed her one, too, for being such a lousy friend lately. As much as she loved her girlfriends, they didn't understand what Jamal meant to her and Linc did. He should have been there for her, football or no football.

But he wasn't even in town. Her mama had scared her awake this morning when she came running to Roxanne's bedroom, squealing about Linc being on the *Today Show*. She'd jumped in bed with Roxanne and turned on the TV. And there he was, looking larger than life and charming as hell. Dressed in jeans, a muscle-gripping black shirt and a blazer, he was chatting with Katie Couric, looking as casual as he did when he lounged around her kitchen trying to sample the food while she was cooking it. Linc had always been more at ease with the fame than Jamal. Though it was months after the Championship Bowl, America still couldn't get enough of him. He was telling Katie that he had stops at the

Daily Show, a fund-raiser for the A Better Chance scholarship program, and last but not least a photo shoot for *GQ*. There was nothing about his clean-shaven face and crystal-clear eyes to suggest that he'd lost a wink of sleep over the argument they'd had the other day. And why should he? In between all his public appearances, he probably had Desiree to distract him from all his worries, Roxanne concluded bitterly.

She put down the scraper and climbed down from the ladder. Why was she back to who Linc was screwing? It was none of her business. She started to gather up the scraps of paper that she'd thrown on the floor.

"All done over there, Roxy?" Her mother asked.

Roxanne dumped the torn wallpaper in the large trash basket Curtis had brought up to the room. "Not quite," she said, sounding much lighter than she felt as she gave the mutilated rabbit-themed wallpaper one last glance.

"Curtis, honey, would you find me the metal tape measure? This cloth one isn't long enough to measure the length of the window," Dot cooed.

"No problem, sweet cakes," Curtis said. He had been working on the wall adjacent to where Roxanne was. Curtis put the steamer down and started searching through the box of supplies they'd hauled up to the room. "Here you go, baby," he said, holding the silver case out to Dot.

"Thank you, honey bunch."

Roxanne watched the little interchange and mumbled, "The sugar in here is so high, y'all 'bout to put me into a diabetic coma."

"Did you say something, Roxy?" her mother asked.

"Nope. I was just thinking what a cute couple you and Curtis make."

Dot laughed delightedly and grabbed Curtis by the forearm. "You hear that, Curtis, we're cute."

"Naw, you're the cute one," he said. "I'm just here. You make me look good."

"Oh, Curtis, that's so sweet. Bend down here so I can give you a big old kiss."

Lord have mercy, what had she started? Roxanne turned away and repositioned her ladder. *Well, you better get used to it, girl, because your mama and Curtis definitely have "a thing" going on.* And despite her childish embarrassment, Roxanne was thrilled. If anybody deserved to find a good man, it was her mama. She had to have gone through her allotment of bad ones. It had been a tough year on the Miller women when it came to men. Jamal was dead. Jimmy was sick. And Denise . . . well Denise was following in mama's footsteps when it came to men. Hers were usually the slam-bam-thank-you ma'am type.

Roxanne ventured a peek at her mama and Curtis. He was kneeling at her feet, holding the tape measure steady so she could measure the window. He playfully copped a feel on her calf. Dot giggled and skittered away.

Roxanne leaned back against the ladder. If her mama could change, than maybe there was hope for Denise, too. Maybe there was hope for all of them.

A minute later Dot announced, "I can't wait until we get the wall painted, and buy new furniture and curtains. This room is going to be so beautiful. You just wait and see," she declared with a wink in Roxanne's direction.

Ever since Roxanne had given her mother permission to redo the room, she was a woman on a mission. Roxanne had no doubt it would be a gorgeous room when her mother finished with it. Even when they were living in crummy apartments, her mama had subscribed to magazines like *Better Homes and Gardens* and *House Beautiful*. Roxanne was just happy to be in a position where she could allow her mother's interest in decorating to blossom.

Curtis arched his back. "So, girls, I think after we've cleaned the walls with damp sponges and smoothed any scratches out with spackle, I'll slap some primer on it. Give it a couple of coats of paint, and it'll be good to go. I can tell that sweet cakes is just itching to get to the real decorating part."

"You got that right, sugar," Dot said, then began to outline her vision for the room. "We're gonna put a queen-size bed on the south wall. An upholstered chair and ottoman will go next to the window. I thought we might put a small table in the space between the chair and bed. I mean, don't you think that's a nice touch rather than a nightstand?" she asked, but didn't wait for a reply. "Of course, if we have a table on one side of the bed then we need one on the other side to even it out. Then maybe we could put an armoire over here in this corner. It could be used as an entertainment center. All we'd have to do is put it at an angle so that you could see it from the bed or the chair. At the foot of the bed, we could put a chest."

"Mama, if it's a guest room, what do they need a chest for? They ain't coming to stay forever."

"All book sense and no common sense," Dot sighed dramatically. "You can store blankets and linen in it, silly."

"Well, e-x-c-u-s-e me," Roxanne replied, trying not to laugh at her mother's exasperated tone.

Dot surveyed the room. Her hands were on her hips as she looked around. Roxanne suspected that her mama was not seeing the same barren and stripped space that she was.

Dot said, talking more to herself than to Roxanne or Curtis, "We want it to be comfy, not all bo-ring, like a hotel room . . . but at the same time, we don't want to clutter it too much. And I just don't know what I'm gonna do with this window. I really have to think about this. I don't want to screw up the window treatment. I mean, the view of the backyard is gorgeous. You get to see the gazebo and the greenhouse. In the fall when the leaves turn, it's gonna be beautiful. And it faces west, so you'll get a lovely sunset. But maybe too much sun during the day. I heard about this transparent film that you can put on the window to reduce heat, glare, and keep the sun from fading the fabric on the furniture. Maybe we should get some of that."

Roxanne felt her mother's enthusiasm lift her own spirits. "Mama, this is your little project. Do whatever you want. Pick out the linen, the carpet, the curtains, whatever. I trust your judgment."

Dot sputtered a surprised "Really?"

OK, so Roxanne had a few qualms at the beginning. Her mama could be a bit flashy in her choice of clothes, but she'd always had a nice-looking home. No plastic slipcovers or vibrating beds. Besides, Roxanne had a little secret of her own. When her mama was done creating the perfect "guest room," Roxanne was going to invite her to move into it permanently. Her mama's zest for life was contagious enough that it was slowly resurrecting her own comatose spirit.

She needed her.

Roxanne was finally seeing the person her mother could have

become if poverty and lack of education hadn't held her back. And she was a beautiful sight to behold. Just like this room would be once her mama was done with it. "Mama, really. I'm convinced this room is gonna be a work of art. You'll be the B. Smith or Martha Stewart of Baltimore. I've got some contacts, maybe you could start your own decorating business, or if not that, at least teach a class at the Center. 'Cause I know you're an expert at decorating on a shoestring budget."

Dot threw herself into Roxanne's arms. "Oh, Roxy, girl, you're about the best daughter a mama could hope for." Before the words were even out, Roxanne could hear the tears in her mama's voice, and she felt herself choke up in response.

Over her mother's shoulder, Roxanne included Curtis with a watery smile. He chuckled and shook his head. He probably thought they were two crazy women. And if mama didn't stop crying all over her, she was gonna scare off the best man that had come her way in a long time.

As if on cue, he looked at his wristwatch. "Dottie, it's almost five o'clock. I need to change and then get over to my son's house." At Roxanne's curious expression, he added, "We're going to Mass."

Like St. Louis, Baltimore had a large number of African American Catholics. But Roxanne hadn't known Curtis was Catholic. And practicing, too. Score another point for Curtis. "Oh, that's nice. Mama, are you going, too?"

"I don't think so. I ain't one to go to church on a Friday night." She tossed an apologetic smile Curtis's way. "Besides, we had a busy day. These old bones are tired. But when I get back, why don't we look over some linen patterns? I'll still have enough energy for that," she promised Roxanne. "In fact, there's this one called Rose Rhapsody that I absolutely love." She paused and eyed Roxanne doubtfully. "*You* might not like it 'cause it's a floral design. But," she added in her most persuasive voice, "I know you'll love the colors. It's a blend of rose, burgundy, cream, taupe, and green and—"

"Mama, I already told you, do your thing. So why don't you drop Curtis off, and I'll fry us up some fish for dinner. Doesn't that sound like an appropriate Good Friday meal?"

"Um . . . that does sound good. And then after dinner maybe

we can look at furniture. I can't decide between a Club chair or a Queen Anne chair. I was thinking about putting a mirror on the wall behind the chair, then on clear days it could reflect the back-yard scenery. And are you sure you want to keep that neutral color for the paint? Of course, we've got to have some decorative pillows for the chair and the bed that will pick up the colors in the linen. You have to tell me what you think . . ." Not that her mama had paused long enough for Roxanne to get her two cents in.

If her mama had, she would have learned that Roxanne was thinking that Dot was so into finishing this room that she wasn't going to stop talking about it until her vision became a reality. Roxanne just let her go on until she'd shared all her major ideas.

After they left, the house felt unnaturally quiet without her mother's tickling laughter. Knowing she'd be back in an hour or so, Roxanne decided to work a little longer on the room. Only one wall was still covered with the old wallpaper. Roxanne hurriedly began ripping it down while it was still loose and damp from the steamer. She had a great time running from one panel to the next, like she was doing circuit training. It didn't take much strength to pry the paper from the wall, but she was breathless from all the running to and fro. The walls were devoid of wallpaper except for a few stubborn spots. A little more scraping was in order, she concluded.

Roxanne suddenly sprinted down the hall to one of the other bedrooms. She returned with the boom box that she kept for guests who couldn't fall sleep or wake up without music. She plugged it in. She started to turn on the radio but noticed that the CD changer button was lit up. She pressed play then began to hum and bop along to Macy Gray. True, Macy was singing about sex and dysfunctional relationships for the most part, but her voice was so interesting and the beats so funky, it was easy to tune out the words.

Another fit of sneezing seized her. "Damn," Roxanne swore, annoyed that her groove had been disrupted. *Maybe if I let in some fresh air,* she thought. Her mother was right about the amount of light this room got in the afternoon, and it was a long window. The hundred-year-old house had eight-foot ceilings. The window started about a foot from the ceiling and stopped about two feet from the floor. Roxanne sat down next to it and threw open the sash.

The lawn service had been over to cut the grass this morning. It smelled like spring. The daffodil bulbs she'd planted had survived the winter, and the entrance to the greenhouse was surrounded by a burst of yellow. Roxanne rested her elbows on the windowsill and took a deep breath, filling her lungs with the fortifying, crisp air. With the thick surrounding of trees at the back and to the side of the property, it was hard to believe that she was still in the city. This would be a great evening to sit out on the back porch with a nice mystery and watch the sun go down, Roxanne thought.

Suddenly inspired, Roxanne decided that was exactly what she was going to do. When was the last time she'd felt the urge to just chill? She couldn't even remember. And that was truly sad. She leapt to her feet. It was time to stop moping around and working to the point of exhaustion. That's not what life was supposed to be all about. Jamal wouldn't want her dragging through life like she was just waiting to die herself. In fact, he would probably turn over in his grave when he saw just how hard she'd been driving herself these past few months.

Roxanne stopped by her bedroom to pick up a shawl and a psychological thriller that she'd abandoned months ago. She still couldn't bring herself to read the historical romances everybody used to tease her about. She entered the wraparound porch through the French doors off from the kitchen. For a brief moment she wavered. Maybe she should just start dinner. Then she told herself, get real. Though Mama had said that she'd be back around seven, that really meant anywhere from seven until nine. Fish only took a few minutes to fry, and Roxanne wasn't all that hungry herself. Starting dinner could wait until her mother actually showed up.

Roxanne plopped down in a wicker lounge chair. Her mother had Curtis bring the patio furniture out of the basement storage room, but Roxanne had yet to use it this spring. The smell of freshly cut grass was even stronger out here. It was so peaceful. A slight breeze ruffled the rows of tulips that ran parallel to the path from the porch to the greenhouse and gazebo. Birds were shouting evening greetings, and the sun was peeking over the tops of the trees. Her bookmark had been placed in the middle of chapter three. She had no recollection of what the stalker had done in chapters one and two, so she started over at the beginning.

Roxanne drew the shawl over the front of her chest and curled on her side with the book. Despite her intentions to watch the sunset, she was asleep within minutes.

And she dreamt.

It was back when she'd first moved to Baltimore; she was still teaching. Linc had called her up in the middle of the day and asked that she meet him at his place after school. He'd told her he needed a favor, but was all mysterious about it. She had hurried over thinking he was in trouble. But Linc's favor was that she fly to New York with him to pick out a tux. He'd needed one for some sports award show that was coming up. Roxanne was not used to this kind of jet-set lifestyle. She was just a schoolteacher. And schoolteachers didn't fly up to New York to have private showings of designer tuxedos. She told Linc he was crazy. She'd thought his favor was some kind of emergency. But how could she have forgotten that Linc couldn't be serious—about anything. Besides, she told him, I need to be here in Baltimore—with Jamal, her husband. They had plans for a community center, a new house, and lots of babies . . . Then Jamal appeared out of nowhere. He already had on a tux, the one he had worn to their wedding. He held a small overnight bag in his hand. He extended it to her and said, "Go to New York. Have fun." They argued about it. He kept pushing the bag toward her, and Roxanne kept insisting she should stay with him. Linc was old enough to shop for his own clothes. Finally, Jamal tossed the bag to Linc and said, "Take her. I'll be right here when you get back, Roxanne." She turned around to argue some more, but he was gone. She could still hear his voice, though. "I'll be right here," he kept saying. "I'll be right here." She started running from room to room in Linc's condo, but she couldn't find Jamal.

Roxanne tossed from side to side on the chaise lounge. In her sleep her fingers clutched at the gold band she wore on a chain around her neck. A hand touched her shoulder, whether to wake her or calm her Roxanne had no idea, because she still clung to the dream. She still searched for Jamal. A male voice called her name, and that did register. She turned toward the sound.

"Jamal?" she said, still hopeful. Someone was bending over her, his hand on her arm. It wasn't Jamal. "Linc?" she said, struggling to move into a sitting position. She blinked, trying to clear her vision. Linc was in New York.

This man didn't smell like Jamal or Linc. He smelled of strong cologne and cigarettes. A fissure of fear snaked her spine, and she became fully awake then. He was young, maybe in his early twenties, and he hovered over her, his face barely inches from her own. Dark circles under his eyes marred his light brown skin, and an uneven beard suggested he hadn't shaved in a couple of days. Though his clothes were a bit baggy on him, they looked relatively clean and of good quality. But that didn't mean he wasn't deranged or something. Roxanne used her hand to shove at his chest. She tumbled backward off the chaise and away from him.

"Who are you? What do you want?" she demanded, hoping she sounded brave, but shaking from head to toe.

For the first time in her life, Roxanne wished she lived in a gated community. Jamal had suggested it when they were talking about buying a house, and she'd laughed in his face, confident that despite his fame they were no more likely to be victimized than anyone else. Now she wasn't so sure. This was not the kind of neighborhood where people just wandered in off the street. It was completely residential—no stores, office buildings, or restaurants. *Where had this man come from?*

"If you don't leave right now, I'll scream so loud, it'll bring the whole neighborhood over here," she warned. Roxanne opened her mouth wide, as if to follow through with the threat. Not that it would do her much good. Of course, she'd made a point to meet her neighbors, but she'd never heard a peep from them when she was at home. An acre of land and the same trees and shrubbery she'd been admiring earlier separated them.

"Wait, Roxanne," he begged, his expression becoming as fearful as hers.

He had called her by name. Roxanne paused to peer at him more carefully. Something about him did look familiar. "Do I know you?"

"Yes, yes, I'm Etienne," he said. When she showed no signs of recognition, he hastily added, "We met last fall. In St. Louis."

"Etienne?" Roxanne felt herself relax a little. But not completely. She did remember meeting him, but that didn't explain what he was doing here in her backyard. Thousands of miles away from St. Louis. "You were at my sister's place. You're my mother's . . . my mother's *friend*," she acknowledged, but still on guard.

Etienne shook his head. "No, I am not your mother's friend," he corrected. "I am your mother's husband."

Chapter

19

The sun had disappeared by the time Dot got off the Beltway. She'd spent a little more time at Curtis's than she had intended to. She smiled into what light was left of the day when she remembered Curtis's praise.

"Dottie, I haven't felt this close to a woman since my wife passed away. You've brought a lot of joy into my life."

She hadn't been expecting that kind of declaration. She and Curtis didn't talk about the past much. He hardly ever shared specific memories or stories about his wife. And Dot wasn't about to bring up any of her past mistakes. She didn't want Curtis to know about them. Didn't want him to think less of her.

Her life was starting over here in Baltimore. A new beginning. What happened yesterday was not important. A line from a seventies song popped into her head. *Yesterday's gone. Yesterday's gone.* Her sentiments exactly.

Dot sighed. She hated to leave Curtis, but he had to meet his son. She would have liked nothing better than to spend the evening curled up in front of the TV with him. But he had to go, and Roxanne was expecting her back home for dinner.

While Curtis hadn't come right out and said he loved her, she had a feeling he wasn't far from it. Knowing that for once she and a man were on the same wavelength left her feeling pretty happy, even if she couldn't be with him tonight. Dot was humming along with the music that blared on the car's radio and driving a little faster than the posted speed limit as she headed the silver Volvo toward home. Roxanne called her a speed demon, but Dot laughed at the description. She loved to go fast, and something about this boxy car made her feel like she was in her own little protected cocoon. Even in some of her old rattletraps, she hadn't gone slowly but she wasn't reckless, either. At least not anymore.

She did tap the brakes, though, before turning onto Roxanne's tree-lined street. She always liked to play a little game to see how far away from the house she could be and still get the garage door to open. Dot reached up to press the remote that was attached to the visor on the driver's side when she got about two houses away from home. Nothing happened. Not that she really expected it to. Two or three more houses could have been built on the area that separated Roxanne from her closest neighbor.

Every time Dot caught sight of the houses—no, make that mansions—in the historic part of Towson, she felt like she was in a dream. Whoever thought her little Roxy would end up living in the lap of luxury. And Dot was so proud of her because having money hadn't changed her a bit. She still had the same old friends, like her girlfriends from college and Linc. Maybe tonight would be a good time to find out what had happened between those two at the Center the other day. When she'd gone down to set up for the seminar, everything had been fine. Then the next time she saw him, Linc blew by her, looking mad as hell, and Desiree was running to keep up. And Roxy had been acting funny, too. She said she didn't know what his problem was. And Dot hadn't seen any of his phone numbers on the Caller ID lately, either. When she'd mentioned it to Roxy, she seemed unconcerned, which was not like her. If something was wrong with her family or friends, Roxy was usually right up in the middle of it, trying to set things straight. Look at how she'd deeded them the house in St. Louis, and LaToya had told her Roxy was paying for Jimmy to be treated by one of the best oncologists in the city.

Roxanne was a fine person, but Dot couldn't take much credit for it, though. Her own parents pretty much raised the girls.

Dot hit the remote again when she was a few feet away from the driveway. The door to the three-car garage slowly lumbered open. A sad and painful event had brought her and Roxy together again. They'd been given a second chance to be like a mother and daughter were supposed to be. And Dot was determined to get it right this time. She pulled into the garage, turned off the radio, and then the ignition. She opened the trunk to take out the groceries she had picked up on the way home.

Dot sniffed the air as soon as she entered the house. She didn't smell anything except the scented candles and incense Roxy was always burning. She'd been expecting to smell and hear catfish frying. Darn, she was ready to eat now. She hoped Roxy wasn't still working on that room. That girl pushed herself way too hard. She decided to get rid of the groceries first, and then she'd drag Roxanne downstairs.

Once in the kitchen, she quickly emptied the bag. She frowned when she saw that the milk expired in about three days. She was mad with herself for forgetting to look. She inspected the half and half. At least that would be good for two weeks. Dot was about to put a pint of coleslaw in the fridge when Roxanne showed up.

"Hi, sweetie, I stopped by the store to get some coleslaw to go along with the fish," Dot said.

The welcoming smile died on her lips when she saw how Roxanne looked. She was still wearing the same dusty pale blue overalls. But her eyes were flat and unreadable, looking past her. Then she leaned her head against the doorjamb. Her arms were hugging her waist as if she had cramps or something.

Alarmed, Dot put the coleslaw on the table and walked over to her. She pushed her daughter's hair off her face and touched the back of her hand to her forehead. She didn't feel warm. "Are you all right, Roxy?" Dot asked, her eyes full of concern. "You look about ready to fall on your feet. Don't tell me you been working on that room ever since I left."

Roxanne shook her head, then stepped around her mother and walked over to the island in the center of the kitchen. She braced her hands against the edge of it and stared down at the tiles on the floor. "No, Mama, I finished with the wallpaper a little while after you left," she said in a low voice.

Even though Roxy didn't have a fever, Dot was worried and feeling a little guilty for pressing Roxanne to help with redecorating the room. She had probably overextended herself to the point that she wasn't feeling well. "Then, why you looking so beat? Why didn't you take a shower and change your clothes? If you're not feeling well, why didn't you go lie down?"

Roxanne looked up then. "I couldn't do that, Mama," she said.

"Why not?" Dot hoped Roxanne hadn't felt obligated to stay on her feet just because she'd promised to cook dinner. She could fend for herself.

"Because I've been too busy getting acquainted with your husband to do any of that, Mama," Roxanne stated, her eyes expressionless.

Dot's throat closed up on her. She managed to choke out, "My . . ."

". . . husband," Roxanne finished for her. "Or at least that's what Etienne called himself."

Dot wanted to go over to her. To explain. The distance in Roxy's eyes held her feet rooted to the spot. It was like trying to walk through quicksand. Her legs felt heavy and her whole body was sinking. The yesterday she wanted to forget had caught up with her.

"Did Etienne call here?" Dot asked.

"Call?" Roxy laughed. "No, Etienne *is* here."

The blood drained from Dot's face. Etienne was here? "What!" she cried.

"Yeah, that's what I said when he told me that you two were married and that you'd run out on him," Roxy said. "Since he's your husband and all, I thought you would have recognized his car on the front drive."

Dot stared at her daughter. His car? It was dark out, and the garage was off to the right of the front drive. She hadn't even looked that way. Why would she? And Etienne was the last person she'd been expecting to see. "Where's he now?" she asked.

"Using the bathroom. He asked if he could freshen up. He's been on the road for a couple of days. I didn't feel it would be right to say no, since he's my . . . my stepfather. Besides, he looked like hell. I hardly recognized him as the boy . . . man that I met last fall. He seems real eager to reunite with his wife, though," she added dryly.

Dot blushed. "Roxy, please don't be mad at me." Roxy had never spoken to her so coldly. Dot wanted to run and hide from the bitterness in her daughter's voice. *What kind of lies had Etienne been telling that would have Roxanne so mad at her?* "Listen, honey. I don't know what Etienne told you, but there are always two sides to any story," Dot said, hoping for a chance to explain.

Roxanne walked over to the kitchen table and took a seat. She pushed out a chair and gestured for Dot to sit as well. "I'm listening."

Dot told her the whole thing, about agreeing to marry Etienne to help him get his green card and how she'd had no idea that he'd entered the country illegally until that meeting with the INS.

Roxanne's lips were pursed, and she rested her chin under her clasped hands. "So you were just being a Good Samaritan and got caught up in something? That's what happened?"

Dot vigorously bobbed her head. "Yes, baby. That's exactly what happened."

Roxanne didn't say anything. But one thing she knew for sure . . . her mother was not that selfless. Up until recently, she didn't even put herself out for family unless there was something in it for her. She had to be guilted into taking care of Grandma Reynolds. And even then she hadn't done much. And she hadn't done anything that Roxanne could see to ease LaToya's burden this past year.

Why was she bothering to deny the truth?

Her mama had wanted that boy, and she thought if she helped him out, it might lead to something. Her mother was so obvious when she set her sights on a man. Had Etienne seen this and used her, too? Roxanne let out a shuddering breath. She needed to stop trying to figure out what had motivated either one of them. Who knew what went on between two people? And would it really make a difference if she knew why her mama had agreed to this cockamamy idea?

Roxanne sighed. "Even if I believe you, and that's a big if, why am I just hearing about all this, Mama? You've been living here for months."

"Roxy, I couldn't tell you. The timing wasn't right . . ." she hesitated, reluctant to bring up painful memories of what it had been like for Roxanne right after Jamal had died. But there was no way to avoid the subject if she wanted Roxanne to understand why she'd done what she'd done. She took a deep breath, then continued. ". . . All this happened right before Jamal died. You had your own stuff to deal with. This situation with Etienne was nothing compared to that." She nervously watched her daughter to see how she was dealing with what she'd just said.

Roxanne nodded and Dot felt a moment of relief.

Then Roxanne said, "I can appreciate that, Mama. Thanks for thinking of me. But that was December. It's April. When *were* you going to say something?" Her eyes narrowed. "Or maybe you weren't? Were you just hoping Etienne would disappear? Etienne told me how rattled you got at the INS interview. Did you stay in Baltimore out of concern for me or because you were running scared?"

The swift denial that Dot was about to make caught in her throat. Her eyes pleaded with Roxy's. Finding no bending there, she finally said, "It wasn't like that. You make it sound like I planned to use you . . ."

No, her mama had just "unintentionally" used her. And she found that very hard to forgive. Roxanne felt like a sharp blade had been rammed into her back.

". . . I was so scared the week after the INS, I didn't know what to think. I still didn't know what I was going to do, and then Jamal died. I came here because I wanted to be with you, sweetie. And then we were getting along so well . . . and I knew you needed someone. I wanted to be here for you. Then I realized that I loved working at the Center. There was nothing to go back to St. Louis for . . ."

"Except a husband," Roxanne reminded her. Why had she ever thought she could trust her mother not to hurt her? When would she learn? "Mama, why don't you just tell the truth. Jamal's death gave you a reason to stay away from St. Louis. It was *convenient* for you to stay here to look after me. If the INS hadn't been on your case, you probably would have been long gone. I guess you would have been out of here like a shot once Etienne finally got deported."

Dot began to cry. So many times she hadn't been there for her kids, for her family. She could understand why Roxy didn't believe her. And what she was saying had been true . . . at the beginning. But she had changed. "Roxy, don't say that. I love spending time with you. I've never been happier in my life. I feel like we're finally getting to know each other."

Roxanne stared at her mother's bowed head in amazement. "How can you say that when you didn't even bother to tell me that you had a husband? That you were in trouble? And what about Curtis? Does *he* know he's dating a married woman?"

Dot looked up in alarm. She hadn't thought about that. Her whole body went cold with fear. This thing that was growing between her and Curtis was as close to wonderful as she'd ever been. What *was* Curtis going to think of her? Could he forgive her or would he feel betrayed and lied to like Roxy? She should have started the divorce process or something. She could have told him she was separated, which was the truth.

Overwhelmed by her poor choices, Dot buried her face in her hands and sobbed. Oh, God, she'd really screwed up this time.

An eternity went by and then she heard a deep sigh escape Roxy. She felt a hand on her shoulder. "Mama, stop crying. Please," Roxy said. "I'm sorry I yelled at you. It'll be all right."

Dot looked up with watery eyes. Roxy looked weary but not nearly as angry. She reached for her daughter's hand and clung to it. "I'm sorry, too, Roxy." She raised Roxanne's icy hand to her lips and kissed it. "What am I going to do?" she wondered despairingly. Hot tears splashed on their joined hands.

That was a good question, Roxanne thought as she heard Etienne's footfalls on the stairs. She reached for a fistful of napkins and held them out to her mother. "Dry your tears, Mama. We'll figure something out."

The Miller women always did.

Leaving her mother at the table sopping her tears, Roxanne went over to the refrigerator.

Roxanne took out something in a plastic bag. She then removed a white paper-wrapped package from the bag.

Dot grabbed a couple of paper napkins. She blew her nose noisily, then watched as Roxanne walked over to the cabinets and tossed the package on the countertop next to the stove. She reached up to grab a skillet that hung above the sink.

Roxanne's behavior was strange to her. Out of place, given what they'd just been talking about. Dot asked, "What are you doing?"

Skillet in hand, Roxanne turned to face her. "I'm going to fry this fish. Then I'm going to figure out how to get you out of this mess."

That should be a real interesting endeavor, because Roxanne did her best thinking when her stomach was full, and right now the thought of eating made her queasy.

Chapter

20

Dot gnawed on nails that were already bitten to the quick while she waited for the burly uniformed guard in the gatehouse of Linc's condo to announce her unexpected arrival. She probably should have called first, but Linc was family, she reasoned. The guard had turned away from her and was speaking into the phone. Dot stared at the three luxury towers that overlooked the harbor. The place had its own private park and fitness center. Dot had been to Linc's several times, but she also marveled at how far in life "Big Head Linc," as she used to call him, had come. In their old neighborhood, it was a minor miracle when the cops could be persuaded to come out to investigate the sound of gunfire. Now Linc had gatekeepers, a concierge in the lobby, and private security for the buildings and grounds.

She was impressed but Dot was fast learning that all that stuff plus money to boot couldn't guarantee happiness. Roxy was showing her that, and that's why she desperately needed to talk to Linc. Someone needed to look out for Roxy. And her daughter was too coolly pissed off right now to let her be the one.

The guard gave her the thumbs-up sign and the gate lifted.

Dot drove through.

Linc threw back the single sheet that until a minute ago had been draped across his lower torso. He jumped out of bed to hastily search for something to put on. He sniffed the armpits of a T-shirt that had been lying on the floor. It didn't smell too ripe so he pulled it over his head. He pulled back on the wrinkled jeans he'd worn the day before. Linc ran a hand over his head. It was cut so short right now a comb had no effect. Still groggy, he didn't have the presence of mind to go looking for a brush. *GQ* magazine probably wouldn't think much of their Man of the Year if they could see him right now, but it was better than shocking the hell out of Roxy's mother by answering the door butt naked.

The guard's call had interrupted some needed and much deserved sleep. It was almost eleven o'clock in the morning, but these days Linc caught some Zs when he could. The last media blitz had left him exhausted. He was looking forward to a full week with absolutely nothing on his schedule. He knew eventually he'd make his way over to Roxy's or Hope Springs to find out what he'd done to make Roxy hiss at him like a cornered cat.

This past week, he'd ached with missing her. He'd started to pick up the phone a million times but didn't want to talk about their argument over the phone. She'd been acting crazy, and his response hadn't been much better. But damn it, she had pissed him off. He hadn't seen her in ages, and then she starts tripping for reasons that were a mystery to him.

As much as he wanted to put things right, Linc hadn't dared check his voice mail while he was in New York. It was hard enough to summon smiles and easy conversation on demand, without having confirmation that Roxy hadn't given him a second thought since he walked out on her. Instead he threw himself into the round of interviews, receptions, and parties in his honor to keep his mind off of her.

When he got back to Baltimore, just as he suspected Roxy hadn't left any messages. He decided he hated voice mail. At least with an old-fashioned answering machine, he would know if someone had called, changed their mind, and then hung up. He could have clung to the fantasy that Roxy was that someone.

Linc couldn't stand the emotional state of poverty he'd been living in since they had gotten into it. And with Dot due to arrive on his doorstep any minute, Linc had a feeling that he and Roxy would be talking sooner rather than later.

He was also worried. Though she was welcome anytime, Dot had never just "dropped by."

There was only one other apartment on this floor. Linc had left the door open a crack and was putting on a pot of coffee by the time Dot showed up.

After a small knock, she let herself in and Linc left the kitchen to greet her. He caught up with her in the foyer. She was just a couple of steps inside the doorway.

He frowned when he saw her. Like him, Dot looked like she'd started the day before she was ready to face it. She wasn't wearing any makeup. Not even lipstick. Her normally golden skin was an unhealthy dull yellow. Linc wasn't sure if this was her natural coloring. He couldn't remember seeing Dot without at least a little makeup on. He hoped this wasn't what she looked like underneath. Certainly, her eyes were never overly bright, like she'd had a toke or two. Her clothes looked all right, though. One of those velour jogging suits that she wore around the house—but usually not in public. And she must have been in a rush, because her hair was stuffed under this polyester, turban-looking thing.

Her eyes met his and grew even brighter as tears began to gather in them.

Linc felt his gut tighten. "Dot, are you—"

"Oh, Linc," she uttered with a sigh and threw herself into his arms. Like her daughter, Dot was a touchy-feely type. He was used to a quick squeeze and release from Dot along with a peck on the cheek, but in this moment, she was holding on to him like a lifeline.

What the hell was wrong? he wondered. Spying the still open front door, Linc used a free hand to push it closed.

"Dot, why don't you come into the living room and tell me what's up?" he invited in a gentle voice. He kept an arm around her waist to guide her there.

Dot sat down on the couch. She fiddled with the zipper of the small leather purse she set on her lap. Then she opened it and took out a pack of cigarettes and a lighter.

Linc stared in surprise. He thought Dot had given up cigarettes years ago.

"Do you mind?" she asked him but looked very much like she'd break in two if she didn't get to smoke her cigarette.

He nodded his permission, feeling more apprehensive by the minute. He retrieved the ashtray that he kept hidden in a cabinet in the entertainment center. A cloud of gray-white smoke circled Dot's head by the time he handed the ashtray to her.

Linc took a seat in the armchair, striving to appear calm. "What's wrong?"

Dot immediately dissolved into tears. Her normally pretty face was blotchy within seconds.

Damn it, all he did was ask her a simple question. Why couldn't she just spit it out? He assumed Dot came here to talk. Instead, she turns into Niagara Falls. What the hell was he supposed to do with a weeping woman? It was pointless to look for a box of Kleenex. He didn't buy stuff like that. If he needed to blow his nose, he just used paper napkins or toilet paper, whatever was handy. But he wasn't leaving this room, not even for a second, until he found out why Dot was crying. He hoped it didn't have anything to do with Roxy.

"Is there something wrong with Roxy?" he said, trying to keep the urgency out of his voice. Dot was upset enough without having him push her even closer to the edge.

She looked up then. Her eyes were red from crying.

"Everything is wrong, Linc. I've messed up everything." She cried even harder after that unhelpful bit of information.

He moved over next to her on the couch. Feeling awkward, he gently grasped her by the shoulders until she was facing him. "Dot, I want you to take a deep breath. Try to calm down. Then I want you to tell me exactly what the problem is," he said, trying to keep his tone as even as possible.

Linc watched and waited as she struggled to do as he had asked. At first the deep breaths sounded like hyperventilation to him. Eventually, they slowed down with longer pauses in between. In the absence of a handkerchief, Dot wiped at her tears first with her fingertips and then the back of her hands. She tried to dry her tear-dampened fingers on the fabric of her pants. She sniffed hard like she really needed to blow her nose.

By now Linc didn't care if a whole wad of snot came shooting out. He wanted to know what the hell was the matter.

"OK, that's better," he praised her for pulling herself together.

"Now start from the beginning and tell me what this surprise visit is all about."

And so she did.

". . . so she's helping me even though I can tell she hates me for getting into this mess," Dot said, her voice quavering.

Dot had to be exaggerating. Linc didn't believe Roxy was capable of hating anyone. Though he could understand why she'd be pissed. He had listened to the whole story about the INS. It didn't surprise him a bit. Dot was impulsive like that. She'd never been one to think a plan through. Most of the time, that childlike spirit was sweet, endearing. But this time, her shortsightedness had brought trouble to Roxy's doorstep. And he'd bet his last dollar that it was hurt and a sense of betrayal that was eating away at Roxanne, not anger about the situation itself. Dot was frequently in the middle of a crisis of her own making. Though he hadn't spent a lot of time with Roxy lately, any fool could see how grateful and pleased she'd been that Dot wanted to stay in Baltimore, wanted to be with her. Now she had found out that Dot had an ulterior motive.

The thought of Roxanne feeling used and hurt didn't sit well with him. Not at all.

How could Dot be so reckless with Roxy's feelings? In all the years he'd known her, Roxy hadn't said one bad word against her mother. No more than the usual, "I want to stay out later than she will let me." Or "Why can't we get a color TV when everybody else in the neighborhood bought one ten years ago." In fact, the feud about the black-and-white TV was the only on-going beef Roxy *ever* had with her mother. And that was back in the day. Roxy had never complained about all the boyfriends or her mother's party-girl ways.

"I never wanted Roxy mixed up in this. My girl has such a big heart," Dot said, as if amazed by it. "Too big sometimes," she murmured almost to herself. She leaned forward to tap the end ash of her quickly burning second cigarette on the ashtray. "Can you believe she let Etienne stay the night at her house? The next day, I begged her to stash him in a hotel somewhere. What if Curtis stopped by the house and wanted to know who he was?" she fretted.

Linc didn't know who the hell Curtis was. He assumed it was one of Dot's boyfriends. She usually had a string of them. He really felt like telling her, "You should have been thinking about that when you started dating the man without telling him you were married." It would have served no purpose, though, except to make her feel even crappier than she already did. So he kept his criticism to himself.

"I told her that I love it here," Dot said, then rubbed away tears again with her fingers. "I want to stay in Baltimore with her, but I don't think she believes me."

Imagine that.

"Roxanne is mad at you? That's why you came running over here? Dot, believe me, she'll get over it."

"No," she said, shaking her head. "It's not just that. Is that all you think I care about? You must really think me a foolish, selfish woman."

Actually that's exactly what he was thinking. So far, all she'd focused on was how much her screw up had cost her. He chose not to answer her question. Dot really would not want to know what he thought of her right now. "Is there something else?" he said with a sigh.

"Of course there's something else," Dot said, sounding a little aggravated. "It's Roxy. I'm scared for her. She was just getting her appetite back, and now she's not eating again. The only thing I've seen her put in her mouth in the last few days is hot tea. Cups and cups of the stuff. Not even a slice of toast has passed her lips."

When Linc looked skeptical, she added. "I'm not lying, Linc. She hasn't eaten for days."

Shit! Not the loss of appetite thing again. What was Roxy trying to do? Punish herself for trusting her mother? Did she see herself as some kind of fool for allowing her mother to get close to her? Linc inhaled deeply and then let it out in a rush. Somebody had to make Roxy see that she hadn't done anything wrong. It was everything and everybody around her that was fucked up. Starting with Jamal, then him, and now her mother.

"And another thing, not only is she working long hours at the Center, when she's at home she holes up in her office. This time of year, she's usually in the greenhouse or doing some gardening. But she's not doing any of that. And she's completely lost interest in the room we were redecorating. Sometimes I'll knock on the office door, and she doesn't even bother to answer. I don't know when she sleeps. I've tried to stay up to make sure she gets to bed all right, and I've never outlasted her once. To tell you the truth, I don't think she *is* sleeping. And . . ."

Linc braced himself. There was more?

". . . I think something's physically wrong with her. I just don't know what. I was doing some cleaning around the house, and I found antacid pills and stuff to coat the stomach. I don't know what could be wrong with her stomach, she hasn't eaten anything. I tried to talk to her, but she said she was fine and had work to do. That's when I decided to come over here. Linc, what should I do?" she asked.

Linc didn't know what Dot was going to do, but he had some ideas of his own. The smell of coffee had permeated the room. He'd forgotten all about the pot he'd put on. But that was just as well, he wouldn't be offering any to Dot anyhow. Apparently, he needed to pay a little visit to Roxy and find out why she was so determined to make herself sick.

The door hinges of her home office creaked as someone opened it wider. Roxanne had meant to lock it. That was the only way to keep her mother out. And she needed to put some oil on that door. Someday. She didn't look up from her computer screen, no point in encouraging her mama to come on in. "Mama, I can't talk now. I'm busy working."

"Working on what?" Linc asked.

Startled, Roxanne accidentally clicked the mouse. An irritating sound effect bleeped at her because she had tried to move ten of Hearts on top of the Jack of Diamonds in her latest game of Free Cell. She had long ago given up on getting any work done. She hadn't slept well the past couple of days, and her concentration was shot.

Frowning, she glared at Linc. "What are you doing here?" she asked.

He moved farther into the room, and when he tried to look at what she was working on, Roxanne hastily exited the program. "Your mother told me about her situation. She's worried about you and I thought you might need me."

"Well, you thought wrong," she told him. "Mama shouldn't have bothered you. Where is she anyhow?"

Linc shrugged. Dot had suggested that it might be better if he talked to Roxanne alone. He assumed she'd gone over to the Center or maybe to her new man's place.

Roxanne wished he'd sit himself down and stop towering over her. And wait until she got her mama alone. It was just like her to drag somebody in to clean up after her and then leave. Roxanne would see her through this INS mess, because despite everything, she was still her mother. But she refused to pretend that they were tight. Not when her mama had been lying to her the whole time she'd been living under her roof.

She could go fetch Linc all she wanted, but not even he could fix the disappointment she was feeling. Besides, she was feeling pretty disappointed in him, too.

She needed to stand so she wouldn't feel so dwarfed by him. Roxanne got out of her chair and walked over to a bookcase. Once she got there, she pretended to search for a book. "I have everything under control," she said, turning to look at him when she'd stalled for as long as she could. "Monique has given me the names of some immigration lawyers. She really doesn't think Mama has anything to worry about. Her situation with Etienne is such small potatoes in the grand scheme of things. The INS has bigger fish to fry, like potential terrorists who are in the country on student visas so they can learn their bomb-making skills at our colleges and universities or whole shiploads of people who if they survive the journey will be forced into virtual slavery."

"I see," Linc said, taking in the dullness in her eyes, the edginess of her movements. He walked up to her and took the book out of her hands. She was mauling it. He briefly glanced at the title before sticking it back on the shelf. *Their Eyes Were Watching God*. He hoped to hell she wasn't reading that. Zora Neale Hurston wasn't exactly reading that lightened the heart.

She'd moved away from him again and leaned with her butt against the edge of the desk. Half sitting and half standing.

He followed and stopped in front of her. "If you're not worried, then what do you need a lawyer for?"

"I'm going to try to help Etienne. He makes it sound like he'll be killed if he goes back to Haiti, and I think it would be cold-hearted not to offer to help. It's not like I don't have the money to do it."

"And who is gonna help you?"

"Help me?" she said with a frown. "I don't need no help."

"Right. Is that why your Ebonics just slipped out? Miss 'I don't need *no* help.'"

Annoyed, she sucked her teeth and sighed her disgust before responding. "What are you now, an English teacher?"

"No, I'm just trying to be a friend. I made a joke. If you were truly OK, you would have laughed instead of biting my head off."

"Lincoln Weaver, you have a lot of damn nerve coming in here talking to me about friendship. Where was your friendship these past few months? Where were you when I had to get through Valentine's Day alone? You know it's one of my favorite days of the year. How could you not know how sad I'd be? I spent most of it remembering the Valentine's Days that Jamal and I had spent together . . . and crying about the ones we'd never get to share . . . And then there's Jamal's god-awful family. Do you think I've heard a peep from them once they were satisfied that Jamal left them something in the will. And I tried . . . I really tried to reach out to them, and they shut the door in my face. Just like you've shut the door."

Hot metal spears of guilt pierced his heart. "Roxy, all you had to do was call, and I would have been here. I have not shut the door on you. Baby, believe me." He tried to reach out for her, but she evaded his touch by sliding down to the other corner of the desk.

"I shouldn't have had to call, Linc. You know me better than anybody. You should have been here, but you were too busy being the Great American Hero. Too busy to fit me in between your interviews, photo ops, and your new girlfriend. By the way, how is Desiree?"

"Desiree?" he repeated, not following the swift change of topic. What did Desiree have to do with anything? Maybe Dot had been right; Roxy was very close to losing it.

Not buying his confusion, Roxanne added, "Did Desiree enjoy the trip to New York? I mean, you did take her with you, didn't you?"

"Yes," he slowly replied, "Desiree was in New York. But I didn't take her *with me*. She was there doing her job. Besides, sounds like you're pissed at me about stuff that ain't got nothing to do with Desiree. Basically, you're saying I've sucked as a friend these past few months."

"Are you saying I'm wrong?"

She looked like she'd sock him one if he dared say yes, and he had no intentions of doing anything to get her back up any higher than it already was. To his dismay, he was feeling a little turned on by all the heat coming from her—which was further evidence of how messed up he was. But he found her anger compelling because it was real, and most importantly it was deserved. She had come to rely on him over the years, just as he had relied on her, and it was only natural that she'd expect him to make her a priority. And because he couldn't control his attraction to her, he'd left her high and dry. No wonder she was pissed. He'd be pissed, too.

"Listen, Roxy. I wouldn't dream of contradicting you. I'm guilty as charged. So go ahead and finish telling me off," he invited. "Throw in a few cuss words, too. I know you want to. The Ebonics have already come out."

"Enough about the Ebonics," she cried. But Roxanne felt some of the fight seep out of her. She almost laughed but stopped herself because she was still mad at him. How did Linc do that? How did he influence her emotions so easily?

"I'm done," she announced. "You're an a-hole—I'm trying to clean up the foul mouth—but I don't want you coming over here just because my mother begged you to."

"C'mon, Roxanne, it wasn't even like that. You know you're my girl. Nobody has to beg me to spend time with you." He wondered what Roxy would do if he told her just how much time he wanted to spend with her. Every waking moment and her face in every dream.

And still that would not be enough of her.

"That's what you say, but where have you been? Why haven't you been here for me?"

That was one question he didn't want to answer. "Roxy, I'm not sure myself," he lied. He shrugged. "I'm still trying to figure it out. It's partially not wanting to deal with my own feelings about Jamal's death—"

"But, Linc, we could have helped each other through it!" she cried. She touched his arm as if to console them both through the physical connection.

Linc glanced at the warm hand that rested on his forearm. He shook his head. He wasn't sure Roxy would understand or appreciate the kind of comfort he wanted from her. He wanted to sink himself into her and get lost in the softness and heat of her. "It's partially about the flood of attention that came my way after winning the Championship Bowl. And then it's a lot of stuff that I've yet to sort out."

When she still looked at him as if waiting for more, Linc said, "Sometimes a person is just plain confused. For example, can you tell me why you were determined to piss me off the other day at the Center? Why were you so phony with Desiree when all she was trying to do was offer her help?"

Roxy flinched. She *had* been a bitch that day. She could have given her good friend, Monique, a run for her money. Then she realized that Linc had done it again. He turned the conversation on its head. Now he was the one demanding explanations, not her. "To be honest, I was jealous," she admitted.

Jealous? Had he heard her right? Linc's heart soared. Maybe there was hope for him and Roxy after all. A little grin pulled the corners of his mouth upward.

What was he grinning about? she wondered. Here she was admitting to some less than fine qualities, and he thought it was funny. "I'm not proud of it, but I was jealous because I hadn't seen you in weeks and when I do, you show up with some woman in tow. And I don't even know who she is, but she seems to know more about what's going on in your life than I do. Since she was there with us at the Center, I knew I wasn't going to be able to talk to you alone. You know, just to catch up and stuff. So I was frustrated and irritated. Then, to top it off, she kept calling you Lincoln. What was up with that?"

He laughed then. She really *was* jealous. Maybe not exactly for the reasons he'd hoped, but clearly she missed him and she didn't want anybody taking her place in his life. As if that was remotely possible.

"OK, so I'll tell Desiree to stop calling me Lincoln. Anything else?"

"That's not the point and you know it. Desiree was acting and sounding all familiar with you, and I couldn't believe you hadn't told me you had a new girlfriend. I'm your best friend. I'm supposed to know these things," she muttered. She lowered her head. It was embarrassing to admit feelings that she thought were childish. And she wasn't even sure they were one hundred percent true. Was it just the jealousy of a friend? In the past, she would have come right out and said so and not act all hostile the way she had.

God love her, and he did, too. Roxy was precious. Linc used two figures to lift her chin so their eyes would meet. "Roxy. You *are* my best friend. The reason you hadn't heard about Desiree is because there is nothing to tell. She is not my girlfriend or anything close to it. And she certainly isn't taking your place as my ace boon coon, my home girl, my sidekick, and general partner in crime."

She sighed and wrapped her arms around him. "Thanks, Linc. I guess I've been acting pretty immature. In my heart of hearts, I knew you cared. I guess I just needed to hear the words."

Linc didn't respond. He was too busy noticing the changes in her body. He could feel the sharp bones of her shoulder blades and rib cage. He had held and been held by Roxanne many times. And she was supposed to be ripe and lush. Not a bag of bones. Suddenly he was furious. With himself. Like Roxanne said, if he'd been around, maybe he would have seen the changes she was going through. If he hadn't been so afraid that touching her would set off fireworks in his groin, maybe he would have noticed the weight she had dropped. It had only been two weeks since he saw her at the Center! She hadn't felt this fragile then. But she'd already lost some weight since Jamal died, he reminded himself. He should have been watching out for her.

He bent down and tenderly kissed the top of her head. She pulled back. The smile she gave him was questioning.

"What was that for?" she asked. "I thought you'd be kicking me in the butt right about now for being an idiot."

He sidestepped her question. "Why would I do that? We're both idiots and that would mean you'd have to kick me in the butt, too. And we don't have time for that because you've got to pack."

She took a step back from him so that she could see his face more clearly. "Pack? For what? I'm not going anywhere."

"Oh, but you are," he assured her. "You and I are going away for a few days of rest and relaxation. Your mama told me that you haven't been sleeping or eating, but I had to see for myself. Just look at you," he said, encircling her bony wrist with his hand. When she started to protest, he said, "Don't say a word. You need to get your energy back and get some meat on your bones. What would Grandma Reynolds say if she could see you? I can hear her now, 'Oh, Lord, my Roxy is just wasting away to nothing.' And she'd be right."

He was talking crazy. "Linc, I can't go anywhere. Mama has to be back to St. Louis for the INS hearing next week. I think I should be with her. You know how flustered she gets."

"Not a problem, we won't be gone that long," he said. "Just a few days," he promised. "You need a break. I need a break. And I think it would do us both some good to spend time with each other."

She tried another tack. "I can't just up and leave Hope Springs."

"You can and you will," he told her. "Don't argue with me, Roxy, because I will win." His arms were crossed in front of his chest, and he stood with his feet planted like a sturdy oak. It was a challenging stance. You're gonna have to get through me to get out of this trip, he seemed to be saying.

Though he let her have her way most of the time, when Linc put his foot down about something—like he was doing right now—she didn't stand a chance. He had her beat in the stubborn-as-a-mule department.

Oddly, Roxanne felt a small thrill shoot up her spine. When was the last time she'd done something on the spur of the moment? Too long ago to remember. "Where are we going?" she asked, suddenly breathless.

"It's a surprise." It was a surprise even to him. He had no clue. He just knew that he needed to be alone with Roxy and that he was determined to take better care of her. Strictly as a concerned friend, of course.

"But how will I know what to pack, if I don't know where I'm going?" she asked.

He tapped this watch. "Time is a-wasting, Roxy. So pack the

basics and anything you don't have we can buy when we get there."

He wished Roxy would get a move on and stop questioning him. He had a lot of work to do. If she'd ever take her behind upstairs, he could place an emergency call to his travel agent, and talk to Dot and Roxy's assistant over at Hope Springs about taking charge for a few days. Then he'd have to think up a good explanation as to why his own bags weren't packed when they stopped by his place. But that was the least of his worries. He'd cross that bridge when he got to it. First, he had to figure out where they were headed for this little vacation.

Roxanne grinned at him. A slow-moving excitement began to replace the emptiness that had taken hold of her. She couldn't believe they were going to just skip town like this. It was so thrilling. And damn and bless him, too. He wasn't going to give her one hint. She loved surprises.

"Are you still here?" he said, penetrating the fog of anticipation that had temporarily immobilized her. "Maybe I should just go upstairs myself and throw some of your holey drawers into a suitcase."

It was a threat, not a joke. Linc would do it, too. Just to laugh at her embarrassment.

Her face felt hot. The image of Linc's big hands touching the wispy lingerie she wore under her very ordinary-looking clothes finally had Roxanne bolting for the door.

She noticed that he was right behind her. "Don't even think about it," she warned. "'Keep your filthy paws off my silky drawers.'"

Linc roared with laughter. "Didn't you steal that line from a song from the movie *Grease*?"

"Don't worry about where I got it from," she threw over her shoulder as she floated out of the room. "Just stay here. I can pack my own stuff. Thank you very much," she said.

When she rounded the corner, she chuckled. Damn Linc for having such an excellent memory. She'd made him go to that movie three times when they were teenagers. He made her pay for his ticket the second and third times. He thought she was crazy for going to see a movie where she already knew what was going to happen. It had been worth it to her, though. She'd thought that Danny and Sandy were the ideal romantic couple because of the lengths that they were willing to go to please the other person.

There was nothing vaguely romantic about this gesture that Linc was making, but it made her heart flip-flop just like it had done as a teenager every time she watched *Grease*.

Chapter

21

"C'mon, kid, give your mama a break," Honey begged the crying baby. He had been at it for the past hour. "Hush, now, Junior. I know you ain't hungry. I've fed you, changed your diaper, and sang to you. What more could you want?" she asked, peering down at the squalling baby as if she really expected him to answer.

He didn't.

She continued to walk the floor with him. She usually left Junior with her neighbor down the hall, Mrs. Rodriquez, while she was working and didn't pick him up until early afternoon. But not today. Mrs. Rodriquez was driving down to Pueblo to help with her niece's bridal shower. So she'd brought Junior over at six o'clock in the morning. Honey switched him from the left side of her body to the right. At almost nine months, he was big for his age. Twenty pounds. And he was driving his mama crazy.

It didn't help that the Lair had been busy the last few nights. Some type of dentists' convention was in town. What a horny bunch of losers. But fixing people's raggedy ass teeth must pay well because her G-string had been stuffed with cash by the time she strutted off the stage.

If she had to kiss one more balding head or act like she was actually attracted to one more middle-aged Herb, she would have pulled the weave right out of her head.

"What a way to make a living," she muttered to the still crying baby.

There was a time when she could have made some extra benjamins by going back to a hotel with one of them. But she couldn't do that anymore. Not with a baby to come home to. Besides, she had to be careful. She didn't want to give the other side even more reason to question her character. Being a stripper was suspect enough.

She was probably being paranoid. She hadn't heard from Linc or Jamal's schmuck agent in months. Mark Krautheim. She had never met the man, but she could tell he looked down on her just by the tone of voice he used when they had talked.

Honey reached into her robe pocket and took out a linty pacifier. She put it in her own mouth to clean it off, then stuck it in the baby's mouth. He didn't even stop crying long enough to see what it was. The pacifier fell out of his open mouth and landed at her feet. She sighed then stepped over it. She also sidestepped baby toys and shoes she'd kicked off when she entered the apartment in the wee hours of the morning.

She walked over to the dining room table. Unopened bills and plates that hadn't made their way to the kitchen sink were scattered all over it. She'd never been much of a housekeeper, but with a baby around and little to no help, it was impossible to keep the place clean. What she needed was a maid. A maid and a live-in nanny. Then maybe she could get some sleep. She bet the widow Steele had a maid. Delicate, breakable, Roxanne Steele. She had all kinds of help that she didn't even know about. Everybody seemed to think she needed protecting.

Who was she? A black princess? Honey didn't think so. Miss Thang took a crap and woke up with bad breath just like the rest of us, whether her "protectors" wanted to believe that or not.

And nobody gives a shit about you, Honey Brown. That's why you have to look out for number one. Linc Weaver hated the sight of her. And that stuck-up agent, lawyer, whatever, always seemed to have a hint of superior amusement in his voice whenever he talked to her. Like he was trying not to laugh in her face. Like he knew "her type." She grabbed her cigarettes, took one out, and lit it. Blowing out a stream of smoke then absently waving it away from the baby's face, she thought, who did Mark Krautheim think he was anyhow, looking down his nose at her? How was he any better? He was a leech who earned his dough by peddling someone else's talent.

At least people knew what they were getting with her. Flesh for fantasy. When she shook her ass in a man's face and he decided to reach for his wallet, it was just business. Was it her fault that some fools thought it was personal? Like that damn Coop. She'd given him a little bit, and now the fool thought he was in love. Well, at least she'd got free legal services out of it. Not that he was much of a lawyer. More of an ambulance chaser. She thought all lawyers made big bucks, but hell, she earned about as much as Coop did. And if he didn't get her some money out of this soon, she was gonna fire his ass and get someone who could play with the big boys. If they had to go to court, Linc had promised to fight her tooth and nail. Coop would be way out of his league. Probably already was.

Junior's cries had quieted to whimpers. Honey shoved some unfolded laundry to the side and took a seat on the couch. She was dead on her feet. She usually wasn't up before noon. She smoothed his baby soft hair. Mrs. Rodriquez had put him in one of those cotton sleepers with the footies. He was wriggling those fat little feet right now and staring at Honey. She rubbed his stomach then tugged on a covered foot. He grabbed her hand and Honey smiled at him. She put out her cigarette in an already over-flowing ashtray.

He was cute when he wasn't acting up. Maybe he was cutting a tooth or something. Too bad she wasn't on speaking terms with her mama. If nothing else, the woman had popped out enough babies—eight of them—she'd know what all his crying was about. But Honey had left her mama and Alabama and never looked back. Not when the woman who was supposed to love and protect her had turned a blind eye to what that bastard of a husband of hers had been doing to Honey while she was working at the local Wal-Mart.

While the cat's away the mouse will play. Well, Honey Brown would never be a plaything for another rat. If anybody was going to be running the game, it would be her.

And she was getting really sick of waiting for Jamal's "people" to get back to her. Linc had asked for three months, and it had been three and a half. She'd been more than fair. Fairer than anybody had been to her. Fuck this shit, Roxanne Steele better be ready because she was about to burst her little bubble.

Honey's address book was next to the phone. She looked under the K's. She picked up the phone and punched in a number.

"Krautheim and Associates," a generic female voice greeted her. "How may I direct your call?"

"You may tell Krautheim to get his ass on the phone. Honey Brown wants to talk to him. And he'll sincerely regret it if he doesn't take this call immediately."

"Mr. Krautheim is with a client at the moment. What is this call in regards to?"

"None of your goddamn business. Is your name Mark Krautheim?" There was a shocked pause. Honey smiled and bounced Junior on her knee. He had finally quieted down. She bet Krautheim and Associates didn't get calls like this every day. She decided to help the receptionist get her priorities straight. "Listen, girlfriend, if you don't put this call through, you'll be regretting it tomorrow after he fires your ass. Trust me, he'll know why I am calling."

Another pause. This one shorter than the last. "One moment, please," the woman said, her voice a lot more snippy than it had been when she first answered the phone.

Seconds later Mark Krautheim's totally fake, cheery voice came over the line. "Ms. Brown, long time no hear from. You must have put the fear of God in poor Mitzi," he joked. Honey could imagine him smoothing his tie and striving to appear relaxed. "She told me it was urgent that you speak to me. What's up?"

He was trying to sound pleasant and at ease about hearing from her. Like they were buds or something. He was a smooth one all right, but Honey had seen smoother. He wouldn't have interrupted a client meeting—that's assuming Mitzi hadn't been lying— if he wasn't just a little worried about this call. "Listen, Krautheim. I need to get ahold of Linc Weaver and settle this paternity thing. Did you people think I would just go away? Crawl back under the rock that you're so sure I came from? My boy is growing up in a lousy one-bedroom apartment while his daddy's wife is living in the lap of luxury. And I'm not having it."

"Well, what is it you need? Maybe I can help you?"

Honey laughed. Like he'd been helping her? "The only person I want to talk to is Linc . . . or," she said after a pause, ". . . maybe I should contact Roxanne Steele directly. In fact, she should be pretty easy to find. I'm sure she's over at her little charity helping all those less fortunate than herself. And that would be pretty damn near everybody, including me. I think it's about time she knew what her husband did besides catch touchdown receptions the last time he came out to Denver."

Mark Krautheim stopped smiling. This was the first time Honey had threatened to contact Jamal's wife. He knew that was the last thing Linc or Jamal had wanted. Personally, he didn't see what the big deal was. Jamal wouldn't be the first athlete to engage in a little extracurricular activity. But Linc was also his client, and he was hot property right now. Always thinking to the future, Mark didn't want to piss him off.

"Calm down, Ms. Brown. There's no need to bother Mrs. Steele. I'll try to get ahold of Linc and then call you back."

"Don't dick me around, Krautheim. I'll be expecting a call within the hour. I got better things to do than sit by the phone." She slammed the phone down in his ear. Being put off, lack of sleep, and an unhappy baby had her crankiness running at an all-time high. The next voice she wanted to hear was Linc's.

Junior had finally fallen asleep. She carried him to the bedroom and placed him on his back on the unmade bed. "That's right, sleep," she cooed to him. "You don't need to cry no more. It's time for you and Mama to get paid."

She pulled the covers over him. Though she longed to join him, she couldn't. She wanted to be clear-headed when Linc called. Honey dragged herself back out to the living room.

Excited about finally taking action, she found herself restless as she waited for the call. She turned the television off after five minutes. Who cared about the weather report? She was in the middle of washing a week's worth of dishes when the phone rang.

"Hello?"

"Hi, Ms. Brown, it's Mark Krautheim."

She felt a moment of disappointment. She'd hoped to talk to Linc directly. But Mark had said he'd call her back. She finished rinsing the plate she was holding, turned off the tap, and put the dripping plate in the dish rack to drain. "So what's the good news," she said.

"Actually, I'm afraid I have bad news . . . I wasn't able to get ahold of Linc."

Honey banged her wet fist on the counter. Bullshit.

"I know what you're thinking. But honest to God, I tried him everywhere. I even called Roxanne Steele's place. I've left messages all over town. It's like he's disappeared off the face of the earth."

She leaned back against the counter, the phone pressed tightly to her ear. She had wanted to do all this on the down low. But these people weren't taking her seriously. She'd have to show 'em better than she could tell 'em. "Well, that's too bad. Linc didn't keep his side of the bargain," she said in a tight voice. "Now he'll have to live with the consequences."

"Honey," he said, his anxiety making him forget to address her as Ms. Brown for the first time. "What do you plan to do?"

"That's for me to know and you to find out." For the second time that morning, she hung up on him.

Chapter

22

"Linc, where are we going?" Roxanne asked for the hundredth time since the plane had touched down at Bradley Airport in Hartford. The guy at the rental counter had given Linc a map, but when they got ready to talk directions, Linc had ushered her to a chair. He and the man conferred in hushed tones, so she was still clueless.

Linc smiled. Roxy certainly was a persistent little thing. "I'm not telling you, so you just sit back and enjoy the ride."

"That's easy for you to say. You're not the one being abducted," she mumbled. In fact, he looked at home behind the wheel of the big old rented Navigator. Men and their cars! Good thing this metal monster had running boards—lighted ones at that—otherwise she would have needed a step stool just to get into it. Besides, it was just the two of them—what did they need with an SUV that had three rows of seats? Maybe Linc planned on picking up a few hitchers along the way to . . . wherever.

Roxanne stared straight ahead, but the growing darkness didn't give her much to look at. The wheels of the car churned through the rolling countryside. Linc said they had another fifteen minutes before they got to their hotel. She assumed it was a hotel. Obviously they were going someplace out of the way because if Boston or New York or even one of the smaller cities of the Northeast had been his destination, they could have flown directly there and Linc wouldn't have needed a rental car. Based on the highway signs, she'd figured out that they had driven south then east. But she didn't know her New England geography well enough to take a guess as to where. She knew that east was toward the ocean. There were lots of small towns along the coast.

"Won't you at least give me a hint?" she pleaded with him.

Linc took his eyes off the road. In the faint light, he could see her glaring at him from behind her glasses. Her full lips were pouting like a child's. Roxy was cute when she was frustrated, he decided. "OK, all right," he sighed. "I give in."

Finally. Roxanne eagerly waited to get the lowdown.

Struggling to keep a straight face, Linc informed her in a stage whisper. "We're going . . ."—a dramatic pause—". . . somewhere you can get some rest and relaxation."

"Well, hell, that don't tell me nothing," she snapped.

"Exactly. So stop asking." He loved teasing her. She was so easy to rattle.

Roxanne sighed, slumped back in the seat, and tried to master her curiosity.

Linc eventually turned onto Route 32 North. About two miles down the road he passed a series of high hedges, then turned into an almost hidden drive. A sign announced the Spa at Northwoods Inn.

"We're staying at a spa?" she squealed.

"Ding. Ding. Give the little lady a prize. She got it right on the first try. Of course, it didn't hurt that the sign said as plain as day, *Spa*."

Roxanne punched him in the arm for being a smart ass. Her fist bounced off a rock-hard biceps, and she felt the impact as far as her elbow. He didn't even flinch.

"Let's hope that a little R & R curbs your tendency toward violence," Linc quipped when he saw her shake her arm then massage the back of her knuckles. "I haven't been here before, but this is supposed to be one of those pampering spas, not a fat farm where they starve you." *She'd been doing a pretty good job of that all by herself.*

Roxanne leaned back against her leather seat. The road they were on was narrow and winding. Tall trees on each side of the road formed an umbrella for cars passing this way. But they also blocked out the moonlight and made her a little nervous. As much as she loved the changing colors and smells of nature, she'd always been a city girl at heart.

There was safety in numbers.

They turned a corner and suddenly, a large Georgian-style red-brick building appeared. After the slightly eerie drive down the lane, Roxanne welcomed the warmth of the lights and the signs of life beyond the inn's white shutters. She leaned forward to get a better look. She had always wanted to go to a place like this but had never found the time. Though she'd been to hotels that had spa services, she was pretty sure that was not the same thing.

A uniformed valet attendant opened her door for her. Roxanne was further impressed when a doorman greeted them with a cheery "Enjoy your stay at Northwoods."

Linc followed her into the elegant lobby. Parts of the marble floor were covered with Oriental rugs and plush couches with chintz upholstery. Glittering chandeliers hung from the ceiling. Flower vases with bird of paradise, spring flowers, and assorted greenery sat on antique tables. Mirrors and murals created an intimate glow.

She reared her head back at the sight of people sitting around in thick white terry cloth robes and slippers like they were settling down for a relaxing evening at home. She moistened her dry lips in envy when a waiter delivered glasses of white wine to a robe-covered couple. Roxanne liked the casualness of it. She even saw some "family" besides Linc and herself. Up until now she'd been a little worried that this would be a stuck-up joint and that she would feel out of place.

Linc had made a good choice. She hadn't seen a roomful of people this mellow since one of the guys on her floor back in college had decided to share his homegrown weed with the rest of them. Her weed-smoking days were long gone, but she wanted some of whatever her fellow patrons had been having.

Drinking in their contentment, Roxanne felt her own weary muscles start to loosen. It had been a long day of rushed packing, last-minute instructions, and unexpected travel. She wondered if the massage therapists were still on duty. She could certainly use a rubdown.

Instead, she turned to Linc. At some point he had taken her hand, and they were next in line at the registration desk. She asked, "Is the bellman getting our luggage out of the car?"

"Yes, but we're not staying at the inn."

"We're not?" she echoed. But in the car Linc had told her they were going to the spa. Had she misunderstood him?

Seeing her confusion, he hastily explained. "They have some private villas. Don't accuse me of having a big head. But yours truly is a celebrity, and I want to keep a low profile." He didn't expect that people would bother him too much. His travel agent had assured him this place was used to famous and sometimes infamous guests.

Her spirits lifted immediately. Roxanne hadn't even thought about that. She still saw him as Linc from around the way and probably always would. But she should have known better, though. Jamal also had been recognized when they went out in public. And Linc was practically a household name since the Championship Bowl. There weren't too many magazine covers, talk shows, or television news programs that had missed having his confident mug on them. With all that media attention, even folks who didn't follow football would probably know who he was.

Linc gave his name as Jonathan Lewis. Roxanne smiled but didn't say anything. Jon Lewis had been the lazy-ass head custodian for the chronically broken-down and malfunctioning housing project they had lived in when they were kids. She never quite understood why he used that name when he was traveling.

"Ah, I see that your account has been paid in advance. You have the three-day spa package," the desk clerk said. She then gave Linc a bulging folder. Linc passed it to Roxanne. A quick glance revealed that it contained info about the inn, the spa services, and local attractions. She also told them that a bellman would escort them to their villa.

Before they reached the entrance, they were waylaid by a tall, attractive Hispanic man in his late forties or early fifties. He held out his hand to Linc. "Mr. Weaver . . ." he said, addressing Linc by his real name.

So much for traveling under an alias, Roxanne thought.

". . . I'm Cesar Cardoza, the manager. I apologize for not greeting you personally, but I was buried with paperwork. Nevertheless, I'm so glad I caught up with you. Our clients' comfort and privacy are paramount at Northwoods. Please don't hesitate to let me or my staff know of ways that we can be of service to ensure both," he said, including Roxanne with a dazzling smile. He took Roxanne's hand and gave a slight bow. The gesture was a throwback from another age.

Tired as she was, Roxanne found herself responding to the man's courtly behavior. After all, he *was* a handsome-looking man. Cesar. Didn't that mean "the king" or ruler in Latin? She couldn't quite recall. An old habit of hers, her eyes sought out the ring finger of his left hand. No wedding band. His fingers were long and lean like the rest of him. When she raised her eyes and found that Linc was watching her with a stunned expression on his face, she was busted.

Roxy felt her face grow hot. Well, hell. She was just looking. No harm in that. Was there? Then she wondered why Linc's scowl of disapproval made her so flustered and guilty in the first place.

Linc pried her hand out of the manager's. Roxanne hadn't realized Cesar was still holding on to it. Linc practically dragged her over to the bellman's station.

After tipping the bellman, Linc stood in the middle of the villa's spacious living room. He could hear Roxanne moving about as she went to check out the two bedrooms. He still couldn't believe she had been *checking out* the night manager. This was the first sign since Jamal's death that she hadn't completely lost her interest in men. He should have been glad about it and probably would have been, he silently acknowledged, if she'd been ogling him and not some middle-aged Latin lover. Had Roxanne noticed the answering spark of interest in the manager's eyes? Probably not. But he had, and there would be none of that. The guy was all wrong for her. He was too old, too practiced at sucking up to wealthy women, and besides he lived too far away. Linc had concluded all this from an interaction that was less than thirty seconds long.

Roxanne breezed back into the room. Her already shoeless feet were silent as she crossed the carpeted floor. "This place is wonderful, Linc. I love it."

Linc was gonna have to give Judi, his travel agent, a big bonus. "So it meets your high standards, then?"

Roxanne nodded. "And then some. There's a king-size bed in

one of the rooms and a queen-size bed in the other one. And since you're so damn big, I'll be nice and let you have the master bedroom." Roxanne then described the bedroom in unnecessary detail. The antique armoire, the curved writing desk, and the texture of the fabric on the club chairs.

"By the way, your bed might be a little rumpled," she said, looking guilty as a preacher in a whorehouse.

"And why is that?" Linc asked, raising an eyebrow.

"Well . . . I couldn't help myself," she confessed, twirling the end of one her dreads. Linc noticed for the first time that she'd cut her hair. Rather than ending halfway down her back, the dreads now stopped a couple of inches below her shoulders. It bothered him that he had no idea when she'd cut it. May have been a month ago or yesterday. No wonder she'd accused him of being out of the loop where she was concerned. ". . . The down comforter was so plush-looking, I just had to try it out. And there's this mountain of pillows. I hope you don't mind, but I ate the chocolate that was on your pillow."

"Pig," he accused.

"You told me you wanted me to eat more," she reminded him. She didn't tell him she'd eaten the chocolate on her pillow, too. Linc walked over to the table behind the couch. It held a basket of fruit and a selection of bottled waters. He grabbed two apples. He tossed one to Roxanne and bit into the other. Roxanne took a smaller bite out of hers and licked at the juice that appeared on the surface of the Golden Delicious. She took another bite. Tilting her head, she again licked at the apple's juices before it trickled down to her fingers. The tip of her pink tongue darted out. She smiled at him. "Have you seen the bathroom yet? It's got this big sunken tub. Big enough for two people," she innocently mentioned.

Linc felt his groin stir to life. He was hungry and it wasn't just for food. Down boy, he ordered his overeager erection. Linc moved closer to the table, hoping it would provide some cover, but it didn't even reach knee level.

"Linc!" Roxanne cried.

He froze.

For one mortifying moment, he thought she'd seen the growing bulge in his pants. Then she said, "Did you see the kitchen? It's amazing. They got the good cookware," she declared. And Roxanne knew what she was talking about. To make ends meet when she was a teacher, she had moonlighted at a high-end culinary shop on the weekends.

When he had his body under control again, Linc joined her in the small kitchen. She was nosing around in the cabinets. Other than pots and pans and spices, they were bare. You had to stock the place with food yourself. He took her by her too thin shoulders and frog marched her back toward the living room. "Just because the place comes with a kitchen doesn't mean I expect you to cook. In fact, I'm insisting that you don't."

"What's the matter, don't you like my cooking?" she challenged.

"Stop fishing for compliments. The point is you're not supposed to lift a finger while you're here, and that means no cooking."

"Fine by me," she said, but gazed longingly in the direction of the kitchen. Maybe he'd at least let her make breakfast. There was a gorgeous waffle iron in there. She thought she saw some crepe pans, too. Not that Linc would care. Crepes or pancakes, either would be fine with him as long as there were plenty of them.

"Go take a shower and I'll order us dinner." He was pretty sure the kitchen was still open, but even if it wasn't, Cesar had assured them that he was at their service. And given how the man had been eyeing Roxy, it would give Linc distinct pleasure to have him running around trying to keep him happy. Being a celebrity did have some perks.

"My, my," Roxanne said, "aren't we getting macho in our old age? First you tell me, no, order me to take a shower. What's the matter?" she mock sniffed under her armpits. "Did you catch a whiff of something funky? Never mind, don't answer that. I'm dying to take a shower anyhow. I noticed that the inn supplied us with its own brand of toiletries. I wanna give them a try. But as for your second pronouncement, you're going to order dinner for me? How do you know what I want?"

He gave her a challenging look. "I'm not being macho. I'm just trying to be efficient. Besides, name one thing that you *won't* eat."

Roxanne stared at him. She opened her mouth to say something. Then she closed it. He knew her too well. Without a word, she turned on her heel and headed for the bedroom. She thought she heard him say, "My point exactly," before she slammed the door shut.

Given the time of night, Linc had decided on a light dinner. Club sandwiches with cole slaw. He had a double order. He noted with satisfaction that Roxy's appetite must have caught up with her, because she'd cleaned her plate. They washed the sandwiches down with half a bottle of Chardonnay. Linc needed something to dull his senses because Roxanne sat across from him in a fluffy white robe, and try as he might he couldn't detect any edges of a nightgown or at least a slip strap. Maybe she had on a strapless teddy? Or maybe nothing at all. He tried not to dwell on it too much, but all these possibilities, each one more tantalizing than the next, kept popping into his head.

Linc ate quickly and practically ran to the shower. He needed to cool off.

While Linc took his shower, Roxanne thought about calling home to check on her mother. Then she decided to be good. Linc had already said calling home was a no-no. Neither one of them was to call home, work, or check messages. This was to be a complete escape from reality. He had given her mother the number here in case of a bona fide emergency.

Roxanne would do as he asked. Both of them needed a break. But it was hard not to worry. Though Etienne was on his way back to St. Louis, they still had that hearing or whatever it was called next week.

In an effort to distract herself, she reached for the colorful brochures in the folder they'd been given at the front desk. They had unlimited use of the fitness center and fitness classes. A trainer would work with them to develop an individualized program. Roxanne turned up her nose. That sounded like work to her. They were also entitled to facials, five massages, and either a hand or foot treatment each day of their stay. If the brochures were to be believed, this place was heaven on earth.

She felt a pang of guilt wondering how much Linc was spending on this little getaway. Just how much did round-trip first-class tickets from Baltimore to Hartford cost when you booked them only three hours before the flight, then there was the luxury SUV, and any fool could see this place was pricey. She knew not to ask. First of all, he wouldn't tell her. Secondly, did it really matter? He could more than afford it.

If Cynthia was here, Roxanne knew what she would say, *Girl*

*are you crazy? We all need to be spoiled every now and then—
especially when someone else is footing the bill.*

Just then, her gift horse walked into the room.

"Figured out what you're going to do tomorrow," Linc asked.

Like her, he was wearing one of the white robes that the inn
provided and a pair of cotton pajama bottoms. Roxanne was
struck by how the whiteness of the robe contrasted with his much
darker skin. The veins on the back of his muscled hands stood out
and trailed up past his wrist. She could see no farther because of
the sleeve of the robe. But having seen him in various stages of
undress, she knew Linc was ripped all over.

He approached her with the grace and impatience of a barely
tamed panther. Roxanne admired the way he moved. He was just
too fine to still be alone, she thought. Roxanne didn't get him. She
knew women wanted him. Some time before this trip was over, she
was gonna find out what was the deal on his end.

For now, she'd settle for answering his question. "I think I'll
skip the fitness classes. I'm here to recharge my batteries, not drain
them. Are you up for a hot stone therapy session?"

Linc asked. "What's that? Some shrink throwing hot stones at
me to heal me from all the damage my parents inflicted when I was
child?" He sat down in the armchair. He barely fit in it.

Roxanne scooted over and made room for him on the couch.
She patted a now empty spot, and he shifted places. "No, silly. It's
a type of massage therapy not psychotherapy. Besides, ain't
nobody responsible for how you turned out but you," she told him

"Hmm . . . something tells me that was not a compliment." She
didn't correct him but made a kissy face at him to show she was
only teasing.

In response, Linc had one of those out-of-body experiences,
where he suddenly found himself taking those lips she offered in
fun and grinding his lips into them. His hot breath mingled with
her surprised one, and then she kissed him back with just as much
pent-up passion. Encouraged, his hand pushed aside the robe eager
to find out exactly what she was wearing underneath, if anything.

"So what do you want to do?" Roxanne asked. "Here, take
a look at the brochures," she said, shoving a small pile of them
at him.

Linc blinked. She was still a couch cushion away. The kiss had been in his head? That cold shower hadn't done him any good. He still was hot for her. So hot he was starting to hallucinate.

Roxanne eyed him curiously. "Well?" she asked. He'd zoned out for a minute. No doubt he was beat. He'd put this trip together in a matter of hours and then did the hour-long drive from Hartford. She'd let him hit the sack as soon as they made a few plans—for tomorrow at least. She was kind of wound up herself, so she would probably read for a while. She'd bought a couple of paperbacks at the airport before takeoff.

Linc reached for the brochures she offered. Before this trip was over, he was gonna have to tell her about these feelings he'd been having. Otherwise, he was gonna go out of his mind. But first he wanted her to enjoy herself, because there was no telling how she might feel once he finally told her.

"I assume you'll use their fitness center to get your workouts in. You can do it while I'm getting a massage or something." Linc usually worked out two to three hours a day in the off-season, but he didn't want to risk having someone recognize him.

"I'm gonna try to avoid group activities."

"I want this to be relaxing for you, too," she said, feeling sad for him because he had to travel incognito. He couldn't just do . . . whatever . . . without running into his adoring public. "I know you're just as exhausted as I am, albeit for different reasons."

By the time they went to bed, they had found some activities they could do together, and a few they would do alone. Roxanne called him a wimp. But no way was he letting someone pelt him with hot stones. He was gonna protect his thick hide. He was more interested in the history of the area, so they planned to go into Mystic at some point. He really wanted to see Underground Railroad sites and do the *Amistad* tour. He'd heard they were finished with construction of the famous slave ship in Mystic Harbor.

It was after midnight when Linc crawled between the sheets. The extra-firm mattress barely dipped in response to his two-hundred-plus pounds. With a sweeping movement of his arm, Linc belatedly tossed most of the decorative pillows and rolls onto the floor. He grabbed a real pillow, punched it a few times, and tucked it under his head.

A huge yawn rippled through him. Hard to believe that it had been just this morning when Dot had busted up his sleep. And as much as he longed to sleep in tomorrow and let his body wake up in its own good time, he knew he couldn't. Not if he and Roxy were gonna get through half the activities she'd lined up. She planned to set her alarm for ten and told him not to be surprised if she was gone when he got up. For someone who hadn't been eating for days, she sure did have a lot of energy.

Linc turned on his side, hugged the pillow tighter, and sighed. Still, it was nice to see her excited about something again. And it was nice to be in a bed that accommodated his length. He traveled so much he usually had no problem sleeping in strange beds. So when he had flip-flopped from his left side to his right side half a dozen times, he started to wonder what the problem was. He tried deep breathing. It was a little trick the team's sports psychologist had taught him to help him let go of tension and clear his mind. Not that he had anything on his mind, except how much fun it would be to hang out with Roxy. They hadn't spent time alone like this in years.

Linc inhaled. A familiar scent came into his sleep-deprived awareness. Linc brought the pillow up to his nose. He yanked an edge of the comforter and sniffed that as well. The perfumed oils that Roxy mixed for herself to create her own unique scent had invaded his bed. What had she done? Rubbed herself against every pillow, every inch of the comforter, like some contented kitten?

The image of a fully clothed Roxy was quickly followed by a stark-naked Roxy, writhing and twisting on the big bed.

Linc tried to turn that switch off. And failed. He choked back a moan. He squeezed his eyes tight but the image was in his head, so that didn't help any.

Punching the pillow in frustration, Linc tossed and turned yet again. He had hoped to get caught up on his sleep while he was here. But it sure as hell wouldn't be tonight.

Chapter

23

There was a spring in Roxanne's step as she walked several paces ahead of Linc along the path that led from the parking lot to their villa. The sun had gone down, and the leaves of the trees whistled in response to a slight wind. It was hard to believe that she found the country locale of the inn a little creepy when they'd arrived three days ago. That was before she had seen it during the day. Like its name implied, woods surrounded the inn. What she hadn't been able see at night was that it overlooked the sixteenth tee of a PGA-approved public golf course and a river. The Thames River, she had later learned, like in England. There were several beautiful ponds with fountains on the property. In between treatments or when she was waiting to meet up with Linc, she found sitting by a pond very soothing. The grounds were just as manicured and beautiful as the spa visitors were by the time they left.

That summed up how she felt right now, beautiful and . . . renewed. In body and spirit. She had taken to being pampered like a duck takes to water. They were leaving in the morning, and she didn't want to go.

"Yo, Roxy, what's the rush?" Linc complained, panting to keep up with her. They had rounded up their day of sight-seeing with a trip to Olde Mistick Village. The history buff in him had enjoyed seeing what the New England town was supposed to have been like in 1720. There were also several flower gardens that Roxanne lost her mind over. They must have strolled through them for hours. Mostly, because she stopped to read the little description of every plant and bush. One tulip looked about the same as the next to him. Still, the gardens he could deal with. It was the shopping that had done him in.

Roxanne was determined to buy a souvenir for everybody she'd ever met in her entire life. After depleting all the shops in the village, she descended upon Downtown Mystic. Linc had been reduced to package toter. Apparently, she was OK with spending money as long as it wasn't on herself. They'd left all the packages in the car. No point in bringing them in when they'd be going to the airport tomorrow. Linc figured they should be safe enough. He'd stuffed them under the seats, which is why Roxy had a head start on him.

His dogs were barking. He couldn't wait to take his shoes off. This would be a good time for one of those foot treatments Roxanne had gotten yesterday. Maybe that's why she still had energy to practically skip down the path after all the walking they had done.

"Hurry up, slow poke. I'm starving," she said, turning around to face him. The lines of tension were no longer marring her forehead. Her eyes were dancing and her skin looked healthier, too. Shiny and not as slack. In her hiking shorts and T-shirt, her legs looked skinnier than he'd ever seen them. But it wasn't from lack of eating. Maybe she just needed fresh country air, because homegirl's appetite had returned with a vengeance. Linc just hoped it stayed that way when she got back home. Then maybe she'd fill out, get back the rounder hips and fuller breasts that he was used to seeing.

She whipped a disposable camera from out of her shorts pocket and snapped a picture of him. They had bought several of the cheap cameras the first day. Naturally, Roxy had to take a picture of everything. He hoped she hadn't captured the amusement he had felt at her insistence on getting "the right shots." Who was she with her plastic camera that didn't even have a zoom lens? A female Herb Ritts? The only time she let go of the camera was when she asked a fellow tourist to take a picture of the two of them, like the one today near the Bascule Drawbridge. She was filled with this child-like wonder at the idea of a seventy-year-old drawbridge right in the center of town.

"Hey, don't take my picture when I'm hobbling like an old

man," Linc groused, sounding just like a grouchy old man. "I'm moving as fast as I can. My knees aren't as good as yours. They've hit a lot of unforgiving turf, you know."

Roxanne laughed. She slipped the camera back in her pocket. She put her hands on her hips and waited for him to catch up with her. "Didn't look like anything was wrong with your knees when you saw that snake yesterday," she teased.

"I don't suppose you'll ever let me live that down," Linc said. They had gone hiking, and he had almost stepped on a snake that had been curled up in front of a footbridge they needed to cross. They couldn't go back the other way because it was muddy and flooded out from the previous night's rain. The damn thing looked dead. Roxanne was the one who picked up a fallen tree branch to nudge it to make sure. It slithered down the bank into the creek that flowed under the bridge. Which was fine with him as long as it got the hell away from them.

"Live it down?" Roxanne scoffed. "Not in this lifetime. Linc, you screamed like a girl. 'Snake!' You must have jumped back about a foot. Wait until I tell everybody how a little old garter snake had Mr. Football quaking in his Nikes."

"First of all, I'll deny everything, and second of all, how do you know it was a garter snake? It could have been a python."

A python? Now she cracked up in earnest. "Linc, please. The thing was scrawny and less than a foot long," she said.

"Could've been a baby python," he insisted, searching his pockets for a key to the villa.

After he opened the door, Roxanne said, "Wait! Better let me go first"—stepping in front of him—"in case there's a spider or giant moth in there. I wouldn't want you to get scared all over again."

He smacked her soundly on the butt. And "Ouch!" replaced mocking laughter.

Linc was enjoying this bickering back and forth between them. It was the kind of easy familiarity that he was used to with Roxy. After that first sleepless night, when all he could think about was how much he wanted her, Linc had pulled himself together. Satisfying his lust was not what this trip was about. He had reined in his libido before the tension in him got so high that Roxanne couldn't help but notice it. And what Roxanne noticed, she always commented on. Roxy's own gradual metamorphosis worked in his favor, too. She was having such a good time and was so relaxed herself, she probably wasn't paying him any attention.

Linc kicked off his shoes as soon as he crossed the threshold. Roxanne's feet might not be killing her, but she didn't protest when he suggested that they order room service. After they ordered, Roxanne took a shower. She emerged in a T-shirt she'd bought at the Marinelife Aquarium the first day. It had a big beluga whale on it. She also had on green sweats and no shoes.

Their dinner arrived before Linc had a chance to take his own shower. Maybe he'd opt for a long soak in the two-person tub that Roxanne had rhapsodized about.

He looked over at the dishes the server had uncovered. The bath could wait, he decided as his mouth started to water.

Roxanne was already at the table. "Hey," he said when she dipped a fork into his baked potato.

"Why you got to be so stingy?" she complained.

"I am stingy? Because I won't let you eat up all my food before I get a bite of it?" he said, taking a seat across from her. He deliberately moved his food out of sampling range.

"Fine. Be that way," she said, turning her attention to her own grilled salmon. She rolled her eyes heavenward. "Um . . . this is some good grub," she proclaimed.

"Spoken like a true connoisseur," Linc replied.

"Seriously, this dinner is excellent."

He had to agree with her there. His steak was cooked to perfection. Most chefs thought well-done meant burned or dry. This time they'd got it right. "It's was a helluva lot better than what we had for lunch yesterday."

"Not lunch, high tea," she corrected. "Just like they serve over in England."

"I've been to England a couple of times, and the food was lousy. No wonder the British always look like they're sucking on something sour. It was probably the food." To humor Roxy, he'd gone to "high tea" and had nibbled on those teeny, tiny little sandwiches that had crap on them like cranberry mayonnaise. Good old Hellmann's would have been all right with him. "What's the name of that brick-hard soda bread we had?"

"Scones?"

"Yeah, scones. They tasted like dry, flavorless biscuits to me."

He had needed the vile tasting tea just to wash them down. Later, at the dinner cruise, he'd eaten like a pig to make up for it.

Roxanne shook her head. He was hopeless.

They ate in silence for a few minutes. While Roxanne savored the food, Linc found himself watching her. She dug into her meal with gusto and showed her appreciation with little groans of pleasure from time to time. He wished she wouldn't do that. He found the sound effects distracting, stimulating his imagination in ways that were dangerous.

She caught him watching her. She took a sip of her water. "What?"

"Nothing. I was thinking this meal deserves something better than water," he easily lied. "I say we crack open one of those bottles of that wine we bought." They had done some serious wine tasting at three of the local vineyards. They had left a little tipsy but not empty-handed.

Linc got up from the table. Before he could snag a bottle from the kitchen, the lights went out.

"Whoa!" Roxanne cried. "What happened?"

The waiter had lit one small candle on the table before leaving. Linc could barely make out Roxy's silhouette. "I don't know. Maybe it was a power surge or something. The lights will probably come back on in a few minutes."

"Oh, well, dinner by candlelight is nice, too," Roxanne said. A second later he could hear the sound of cutlery scraping her plate again. Linc carefully made his way over to the kitchen. He opened the kitchen curtains and used the moonlight to read the labels on the bottles. That's when he realized that except for the moon and stars, it was pitch-black outside.

"So what will it be? Pinot Noir, Chardonnay, or a basic white table wine," he asked.

"You decide," she said.

She was taking her chances asking him to choose. He had no idea which wine would go best with steak and salmon. Shrugging, Linc hung on to the Pinot Noir and left the other two on the counter. As he felt his way around the cutlery drawer looking for a corkscrew, the phone rang.

"I'll get it," Roxanne said. The light from the candle danced as she carried it over to the coffee table and picked up the phone. Linc tried to center the corkscrew over the wine bottle in near darkness. A couple of "I sees" later, Roxanne hung up the phone.

"That was the front desk," she explained, holding the candle in front of her to guide her to the kitchen. "A cruise ship dropped an anchor and hit a transformer. All of Mystic and the surrounding areas have lost power. The electric company is trying to fix it. In the meantime, the inn is sending someone over with some lamps and extra candles."

"Well, grab a couple of wineglasses and let's finish our meal before it gets cold," he said between clenched teeth. The less moving around they did the better. He'd just stubbed his toe on a cabinet door, and it was killing. But he didn't dare show any pain. After the snake incident, it would just give Roxy more ammunition.

The hotel staff wasted no time coming over. They left three battery-powered lamps, but Roxanne insisted on simple candlelight during the meal. Around them flames of several glass-covered candles flickered.

"This is really nice," Roxanne said with a contented sigh before raising her second glass of wine to her lips. "Do you think I'll have time for one more visit to the spa tomorrow?" she asked.

"For what?" he asked. "There can't be an inch of you left that hasn't been soaked, waxed, plucked, and polished."

"Hey, I'm just trying to get your money's worth," she said. "You've been so busy playing golf and being a history nerd that you have barely set foot in the spa. Besides, I've only used three of my five treatments. I want to try the Flower Wrap." Roxanne feared she was becoming addicted to the body treatments. This one used a mixture of aloe vera, flowers indigenous to this area, and herbs. It was supposed to cleanse and stimulate the skin while helping treat excess oil, flaking, and dryness. As far as Roxanne knew, she didn't have a problem with any of those things, but it sure was heaven to have her skin moisturized and stimulated.

"Our plane doesn't leave until three. If we leave here by ten-thirty, eleven o'clock, we should be OK."

She leapt out her chair and hugged him around the neck. "Thank you. Thank you." She planted little kisses all over his face and head.

She smelled like tangerines, tangy and sweet. Linc gave her his best poker face. Roxy didn't know she was playing with fire. He was trying to be upstanding and all, but she really needed to keep her hands and lips off of him if that was to happen.

"I'm going to call as soon as we finish dinner," she said, still pressing his head against her cheek. She didn't really expect to have any problems getting an appointment. So far they'd been getting VIP service, and she knew why. Linc. She took her seat again. "I'll try to get a really early appointment," she promised.

The hot stone massage had been nothing short of bliss. The ethereal sounds of New Age music wafted around her in a low-lit room. Firm, skilled hands applied scented oils all over her body. Then smooth heated volcanic stones were placed on her skin, her throat, even on her eyelids, and between her toes. Slowly they soothed, penetrated, and loosened her muscles. The same languor seeped into her bones just thinking about it.

"Linc, I still think you should try the hot stone massage. I'm telling you, I just about had an orgasm right there in treatment room number 16," she confessed. Recalling in her mind's eye how good it felt, she gave a little moan.

Linc almost choked on the piece of steak he was chewing. Roxanne's eyes were closed. She didn't even notice. His eyes watered, and he reached for his wineglass to wash down the hunk of meat that had become lodged in his airway.

Eventually she opened her eyes and gave him a guileless smile. Then she leaned across the table to snag Linc's black forest cake. If he wasn't going to eat it, she sure would.

"I'm done," she announced a few bites later and rose from the table.

Linc stared at her in amazement. Of course, she was done. There was nothing left of their meal but crumbs and the image he had of touching her oil-slicked body with warm stones and equally warm hands. In the meantime, she glided over to the living room and plopped down on the couch.

"Hmm . . . this is the life," she said, propping her feet on the coffee table. "No cooking, clearing the table, or washing the dishes."

"I take it you enjoyed your time here?" he asked, though he already knew the answer.

"For the most part, but I have one complaint," she said.

"And that is," he prompted.

"I don't want to leave. How can I go back home to my hustle-bustle life after all this pampering?"

He got up from the table and walked toward her. She made room for him on the couch. "It doesn't have to be hustle and bustle, you know," he told her. "I am hoping you're going to take it down a notch or two when you get home. I've been worried about you."

She sighed. She got into a cross-legged position and faced him. "I don't know if you brought me here to teach me something, but I have learned one thing. Life can be a grind, something to plow my way through. Or I can try to find my way back to the person I used to be. I don't know if I'll ever be the same person. Too much has happened . . . Still I haven't laughed this much, haven't been this spontaneous in ages," she said, thinking about all the chips she won playing roulette at the Foxwoods Casino. Admittedly, Linc had been urging her on. After playing only the quarter slot machines, on impulse, she had bet a hundred dollars on twenty-nine black—the number of years she had known Linc. It was crazy but she had won.

Roxanne had thought that side of her, the impulsive, risk-taking side, had died with Jamal. Now she knew that wasn't true. Thanks to Linc.

With a small laugh, she added, "And I've never been this self-indulgent. I didn't know I had it in me. So I learned something new . . ."

"And . . ." he prompted.

"And . . . I realize there's no going back. I can only move forward. I just have to figure out where I am headed. I mean, there's Hope Springs, but is that the only place my happiness lies?"

It lies with me! With me! He longed to blurt out. But that would be coming out of left field, and Roxy would think he'd lost his mind. Still, she'd committed to moving forward and that was something. He'd have to be content with that. For now. The past few months were teaching Linc that he had a capacity for patience that he never knew existed. So Roxy wasn't the only one learning things about herself.

"I'm glad you've finally realized you can't keep on doing what you've been doing. You were pushing yourself too hard. That's not what Jamal would have wanted for you." He felt guilty evoking Jamal's name. *Would Jamal want you taking his place?* But then, he wasn't trying to take his place. He couldn't. He only wanted Roxy to see him and be with him for the man he was, not as some substitute for Jamal.

The toe that he'd stubbed was throbbing. He'd slammed it good. Linc reached down to massage it through the thick sports socks he wore.

Noticing the action, Roxanne said, "Are your feet still hurting?"

"My feet, my legs. You wore me out today," he said.

"Sorry," she murmured. She reached down and yanked at his pant leg. "Here, swing your legs up on the couch. I'll give you a foot massage."

Was she serious? "Uh . . . that's OK. It's no big deal," Linc said, trying to maneuver out of her reach. He preferred the physical pain to the kind Roxy's touch would activate.

Ignoring him, she yanked one leg onto her lap. She moved into a kneeling position and his heel rested against her thigh. "Trust me. You'll love it. I used to do this for Jamal all the time. Now, give me your other leg."

When he didn't immediately comply, she cocked her head to one side as if to say, what are you waiting for? Linc reluctantly did as she obeyed; to do otherwise would make her suspicious.

Roxanne peeled off his socks and started rolling his pant legs up to his knees. She trailed a palm down his calf, as if prepping his leg for something.

This was going to be torture.

And he wished she hadn't mentioned Jamal. A foot massage was not the kind of massage Jamal had talked about her giving *him*. And sadly, Linc knew he wouldn't be getting *that* kind of tending to.

"Scoot down to the end of the couch, so you can stretch out," she told him. She picked up one foot and inspected it. "You got some big ass feet," she said.

In his fantasy massage, this was not what he was expecting to hear. She made him laugh. "You volunteered," he reminded her.

"So, I did. I guess I should be grateful they don't stink . . . too bad," she said, wrinkling her nose.

His feet did not stink. Linc chucked a pillow at her. She ducked and it missed.

After that exchange, Roxy became all business. She started by stroking her thumbs from the base of his ankles to the tips of his toes. Then she began gently rolling, rubbing, and squeezing his toes. She gently tugged at each one, slowly stretching it. Linc forgot all about the pain in his big toe.

Roxy was watching his face to see if her work was helping him. It definitely was causing him to loosen up—in ways that even the wine hadn't. Linc lowered his lids, fearful that she would see just how she was affecting him.

He almost purred—yes, that was the sound he made—as Roxy began to roll her knuckles over the ball of his foot. Using both hands, she glided back and forth, tracing a T-shape as she moved from near his toes toward his heel.

"This would probably feel a lot better if I had some aromatherapy oil or massage lotion," she said, a bit apologetic.

Linc murmured, "It feels great. Roxy, if you ever consider a career change, this might be a good one."

"Thank you," she said, then deliberately tickled the bottom of his foot with a fingernail. "But if you got yourself a steady girlfriend or a wife, you probably could get service like this all the time."

Now, why did she have to bring that subject up? He was putty in her hands and she was too . . . too oblivious to notice. "Don't start," he warned.

Her hands worked their way up his calves. Roxanne wished hers could be this solid. Maybe not as huge, but he was all muscle. "Don't start what? I could probably help you out," she offered. And if Linc ever did find someone, she would be a damn lucky woman, too, she thought as she skimmed her hands across the dark hairs on his muscled leg. "What kind of woman are you attracted to?" she asked.

Linc open his eyes then to inspect her face. Was she playing with him? He didn't know, but since she asked, he'd tell her. "I'm attracted to a woman like you."

She stopped then and threw her hands up in the air. "What does that mean? You like 'em short? Educated? A good cook? What?"

"Roxy," he bit out so tersely, Roxanne stopped jabbering. She fell back and landed on her butt.

Linc swung his legs off the couch and moved until he was just inches away from her outstretched legs. "Let me be perfectly clear about this, I'm not attracted to *women like you*. I am attracted to *you*."

He hadn't meant to tell her like this, but it was time she knew. And from the way her eyes had bugged out, he knew he'd shocked her. She toyed with the end of one her dreads. Looking at him as if he'd suddenly grown two heads.

"Linc . . . are you being serious?" She knew he was. He wasn't cracking a smile. He looked uncertain. Like he'd surprised himself. "But . . . you . . . me," she floundered.

"Yeah . . . you *and* me." He was half-afraid she'd take off running. Without thinking, he grabbed her small foot in his hands. Never taking his eyes off of hers, Linc started slowly massaging her foot. But not in the same way she'd been touching him minutes before. His fingers moved more slowly, lazily making circular sweeps in the sensitive center of her sole.

Roxanne stared at him openmouthed as heat shot up her leg. Her skin sizzled where he touched. She felt dizzy. Linc was attracted to her?

"But . . . but . . . we've known each other forever"—her voice filled with disbelief—"and not once did you ask me out." Nor had he touched her the way he was touching her now. His rough fingers felt light as they moved over the small bones of her ankles and feet.

His touch was affecting her breathing. Roxanne couldn't think straight, but didn't tell him to stop, either.

Surprised but mostly curious, she asked, "Linc, is the way you feel . . . something new?" 'Cause if it wasn't, he sure as hell hid it well. And why would he have introduced her to Jamal if he had feelings for her himself? How could the three of them have been such close friends? She refused to believe he was that good of an actor or that she was that clueless. "The feelings have to be new. I mean, how come you never asked me out when were both kids?" Teenagers. Whatever. She'd spent most of her twenties alone or in dead-end relationships. He knew that and not once had he tried to take their relationship in a different direction.

"I didn't ask you out because I knew you would have said no."

She opened her mouth to deny it. The words wouldn't come.

Because what he said was true. She never looked at him that way. But about the time Linc started to excel in sports and develop his terrific body, other girls certainly did.

And that was the problem. Like any young boy who had girls throwing it at him left and right, Linc tried to juggle as many of them at one time as he could. Back then Roxanne wanted no part of that. She saw herself more as his conscience. The good friend who reminded him what was important and who refused to have a shallow relationship with him. Then as they got older, he calmed down. He actually started to be more honest with the women he dated. He let it be known that he wasn't looking for a serious relationship. Though that fact didn't seem to be much of a deterrent.

Except to someone like me, she silently added.

So why would he develop a romantic . . . sexual interest? In her? She didn't do anything to encourage it. At least she didn't think she had.

"Roxy, you've always treated me like one of the girls," he told her with a sigh. Just another one of the girls but with a male perspective.

One of the girls? Roxanne measured the width of his broad shoulders with her eyes. She had felt the toughness and strength of his body just minutes before. She shook her head. Cynthia, Gayle, and Monique had never touched her and got her body to humming. Linc was definitely all male. "What do you mean?"

"Do you remember what you said a little while ago about treatment room 16?"

She shook her head.

"You said and I quote, 'I just about had an orgasm right there in treatment room number 16.' That's the kind of thing a woman says to one of the girls or her man. And I'm not your man, am I?"

Of course not. She didn't have a man. Not anymore. And she felt disloyal to Jamal for even talking with Linc about this stuff.

"And I don't blame you for keeping me at arm's length. It was safer that way. I used to be a big dog. But in case you haven't noticed these past couple of years, this past year in particular, I've stayed away from anybody who wanted more than I was willing to give. I was tired of hurting people." He looked away from her then. Jamal had been right when he said Linc had overlooked the best thing that had ever happened to him. Things might have been so different if Linc had just opened his eyes sooner.

She wanted to comfort him. But her hands stayed balled at her sides, stayed where they'd been ever since he'd started touching her. Why was she suddenly afraid to touch him? And how could she be afraid to touch him, yet wonder what it would be like to kiss him?

"Linc, just because you've had a lot of a women doesn't mean that I thought you were a bad person. At first you were just young and horny like any teenage boy. You just had the good fortune of being a jock, so you got all the girls. Then, like you said, the older you got the more responsible you got. Think about it. It would have been a lot easier to just love 'em and leave 'em, but you took the high road."

Linc gave her a ghost of a smile. Roxy was giving him too much credit. He wasn't that noble. He did it as much for himself as for the women involved. "I did it because I wasn't getting anything out of it. I didn't realize it at the time. Maybe I wouldn't let myself realize it . . . because of Jamal . . . and because of what it might do to our friendship. I turned down other women because I didn't want them. I wanted you."

Roxanne stared at him. A host of emotions flashed across her face, each gone too quickly for him to label.

He, on the other hand, knew exactly what he was feeling. Regret. *I shouldn't have said anything. I've shocked the hell out of her.* Dimly he realized he still had her foot captured between his hands. He dropped it and backed away. Gave her some breathing room. What did he think he was doing putting the moves on her? That's just it. He hadn't been thinking.

"Roxy . . ." he began his apology.

The lights flickered and then came on, instantly dispelling what little intimacy was left.

"The lights are back on!" she said unnecessarily. She leapt off the couch. "The wine . . . the candle . . . must have gotten to us. We should go to bed. . . ." She didn't wait for Linc to respond. As she walked away, Roxanne hoped her stride looked normal. She wanted to run. But was too weak-kneed to attempt it.

The lights in Linc's room had gone out long before hers. She heard the shower running shortly after she closed the door to her room. Fifteen minutes later, Linc's lights went out. Roxanne threw down the book that she'd foolishly thought would take her mind off of everything Linc had said.

She got up from the bed and started to pace. What had sparked all these confessions from Linc? What had he been going to say to her before she cut him off? *You would have found out if you hadn't been a little coward and run away.* My God, he couldn't possibly be . . . interested? In me? After all these years? Maybe he was just lonely.

Is that why you wanted to kiss him? 'Cause you were lonely? She'd been lonely before, and the sight of Lincoln Weaver never made her breath catch.

"Linc is just a friend! A very, very good friend," she whispered to the voices in her head.

And a very, very good-looking friend, the voices quickly replied.

Roxanne walked over to the dresser and braced her hands on it. Linc was a friend who had wanted to lift her spirits. Things had been perfect. Maybe a little too perfect, and they just got caught up in the moment. They'd spent so much time together, and he knew her so well . . . something like this was bound to happen. It was a situation, she told herself. None of this was real. For him or for her.

Think about it, the trip *has* been magical. A break from real life. From Hope Springs. Her mama and the INS. The empty nursery. Linc just gave you a few days of what you needed. That's all. He knew she loved the water. So he'd seen to it that she'd been on or near it every day. The boats were so pretty and soothing, bobbing up and down in the harbor. They had cruised along the Mystic River on a steamboat the first day. She'd been on a replica of the *Amistad*. Then there was the dinner cruise aboard a nineteenth-century schooner last night. It was still a little nippy this time of year. She was wearing a sweater, but as they had stood on the deck, Linc had sheltered her from the cool wind with his body.

It had been a really romantic moment.

Romantic?

Is that how she had really felt at the time or is that her new take on it now that Linc had admitted that he found her attractive? Heck, she found him attractive, too . . . in an objective kind of way. Had never been shy about saying so. Anybody with two eyes could see he was a stud. That didn't mean she wanted him. Did it?

You did tonight . . . when he caressed your foot with those big rough hands of his. That sizzle that went up your leg wasn't objective. But what was one sizzle in twenty-nine years of friendship?

For the second time in less than six months, Roxanne felt her world had tilted.

A thought jumped into her head. The spa had an on-site astrologer. She wondered if she took emergency calls. Would she be willing to do a midnight tarot card reading? Roxanne was feeling in need of some guidance.

Chapter

24

Linc hadn't been asleep very long when there was a knock on his door. It was a short knock, but loud enough to rouse him from a shallow slumber.

Linc struggled to sit up in the bed.

"Linc?" Roxanne called to him, hesitating in the doorway.

"What's wrong?" he said.

"Nothing," she reassured him. She ventured farther into the room. "I was in bed reading . . . but I couldn't concentrate . . . and my mind kept wandering." She walked over to the edge of the bed. Linc saw that she was wearing one of her own robes tonight. A silk slip of nothing that stopped well below the curve of her behind. But he couldn't help noticing that curve all the same.

She looked down at him. The words caught in her throat. "I started thinking . . . about the past few days, about how special they have been to me. You knew exactly what I needed," she said. He always had. "Thank you."

He was silent for so long, she started to feel stupid. Her thank-yous could have waited until the morning. What was she doing in here? She was a big fat liar. It wasn't memories of the past few days that kept her up. It was the feelings that touching him and listening to him tonight had stirred up in her. Restless, curious feelings. "Well, I guess that's all. I'll see you in the morning." She turned to leave.

"Wait." Lightning fast, this hand snaked out and latched on to her arm. "Don't you know it's dangerous to come into a man's room in the middle of the night?"

"I'm not in any danger from you," she said, her breathing oddly ragged. Her skin burned where he held her arm. The sizzle was there again.

"I wouldn't be too sure about that," Linc said. He gave her arm a tug. She fell forward and landed on his chest. Roxanne braced herself with her other arm, then looked at Linc in surprise.

He waited, watching her reaction. She looked surprised but didn't rush to get away from him. "What did you really come in here for?" he asked. His eyes gleamed; she couldn't fail to see the lust in them. And he was way past caring. Not with the rise and fall of her full breasts moving against him, separated by only the thinnest of material.

Roxanne didn't know how to answer his question. She didn't know what she wanted. Except she had this urgent need to see him. To talk to him about anything. Everything. To be with him.

"You smell like tangerines," he said, bringing his nose in contact with the soft skin of her neck.

Roxanne gulped. "Um . . . it's the citrus soap . . . Northwoods brand." She couldn't stop herself from babbling. "You should try it."

He did. He flicked his tongue along the indentation in the hollow of her neck. He pressed a brief kiss there and felt her pulse speed up.

When she didn't run away, Linc became even bolder. He slowly moved his head even closer to her mouth. Their lips met, and it was like he had fantasized—only better. Much better. Roxy gave as good as she got. Splayed across him, she pressed him back against the mattress, her lips plundered his. He did not resist. He was hers for the taking. Had been for a long time.

Her lips left his. "Linc," she sighed, her face pressed against his. This was insane. But like any crazy person, Roxanne was incapable of controlling herself.

He was breathless and rock hard. His hand shakily moved up and down the length of her arm. He wasn't sure if he was trying to calm her or himself.

After a moment she lifted her head up.

His heart stopped beating. She had come to her senses. She was leaving.

Heavy locks brushed against his chest and face. She had only taken off her glasses and laid them on the nightstand. She stared down into his face. The expression on her face was unreadable. Her brown eyes were dark and luminous. Besides the moon and stars from the skylight above the bed, there was only a hint of light in the room.

"Linc," she said, before she dipped her head to kiss him again.

Roxanne didn't know what had possessed her. This was Linc! Her friend. Yet every instinct in her was screaming at her to forget all about that. Her heart was pounding in her eyes and sexual need was pooling, making her legs weak. She didn't see him as a friend but as a man. A man that she wanted to have. Right here and right now. She trailed wet kisses along his jaw, down his strong throat. The fur of his chest teased her face. She kissed one nipple then the other, circling it with her tongue. He smelled of soap and his breathing sounded harsh to her ears.

Linc groaned deep in his throat. "Roxy, you don't know how you're turning me on."

That bucked up her courage. She reached down to touch him then. She alternated between gently tugging on his hardened nipple with her teeth and stroking the length of him.

He groaned. If she kept that up, he'd come right here in her hand. And he was not going out like that. Linc covered her hand to keep it still.

"What's the matter?" she whispered. "Don't you like it?"

Did he like it? No, he didn't like it. He *loved* it. He'd waited too long for this moment. Hadn't really believed it would ever come to pass. He didn't know why now, but Roxy was presenting him with the gift of herself. And he intended to enjoy every minute of it for as long as he could. And he wanted her to enjoy it, too.

He stroked the back of her head, then pushed her hair to one side. "I like it just fine . . . but I want to take care of you, too."

That simple desire brought tears to Roxanne's eyes. She tried to blink them back. It had been a long time since anyone had taken care of her.

He undid the sash of her robe, threw it to the floor. Her nightgown soon followed. He held both breasts in the palms of his hands. "Roxy, I want us to love each other," he commanded in a low growl. "I want to taste you."

It was an indecent proposal. She should have been shocked. But she wasn't. This was Linc. He wanted to take care of her. She knew that. Believed it in her very soul.

Roxanne eased the pajama bottoms past his legs. He was so tall it took a long time, especially since she paused to leave him with lingering kisses along the way.

Once he was free of them, she lay across him facing downward. She gave a little jump when his hands cupped her rounded cheeks.

"Shush," he soothed as he parted her with gentle fingers.

As he stroked her, she lowered her head and touched the tip of him with her lips.

The contact of her warm, wet mouth against his hot flesh nearly killed him. Linc lifted his head and dipped his tongue into her very core. Roxanne stiffened, moaned, and then relaxed, gyrating her hips, urging him on.

Linc loved her with his fingers, his tongue, and his lips. He'd never felt this eager, this desperate to show a woman how desirable he found her. She ground against him. He held her in place and knew the exact moment when she came.

Her mouth was no longer stroking him. Her face was pressed against his pelvic bone. She moaned some variation of his name for a full minute. When she was done, she panted like she'd run a long race and started to shiver. She collapsed on top of him.

He grinned, proud of himself. "You OK, Rox?"

A little laugh bubbled up and burst forth. "What do you think?"

She eventually turned right side up. She brushed the hair out of her face. A teasing smile was in her eyes as she gazed down at him. She looked more relaxed then she had been in months.

"So, did you have to register that tongue as a deadly weapon?" she joked.

Linc chuckled. He didn't want to scare her, but she hadn't seen anything yet. He was just getting started.

He reached up to pull her down to him. She couldn't be close enough in his opinion. His hand landed on the gold chain around her neck. Jamal's wedding band. The metal, which was already warmed by Roxanne's skin, seemed to burn his fingers.

Linc felt a dip in his desire.

Jamal.

He would probably burn in hell for touching his best friend's wife like this. But was it any worse than the hell of not touching her, he wondered.

It couldn't be.

And Jamal would never expect Roxanne to cut men out of her life, he tried to rationalize. She wasn't that type of woman. She was too passionate and too sensual for that. And if it has to be someone, why not me?

He wanted to rip the chain from her throat, but he couldn't. That had to be her choice.

He lifted his hand away from the chain. He started to caress her bare shoulder instead. "Roxy, are you sure this is what you want?" he asked.

In response she leaned down to kiss him. He had to lift his head up to meet her. They kissed and Linc tasted him, her—them. She broke free of the kiss and began to lower herself onto him.

Linc prayed for some measure of control. His hands were at her waist. She was so much smaller than him. And it had been a long time . . . for both of them. She drew him in slowly, inch by inch. Linc closed his eyes and gave into the sensations. She was hot, tight, soft, slick, and oh, so sweet.

She was everything. And he was lost.

Chapter

25

Last night had been a mistake. Not for him but for Roxanne. For him, last night had been what he'd been hoping for, fantasizing about for months. No, if Linc was completely honest with himself, Roxy had been under his skin for years. And it wasn't about the sex—not that she hadn't rocked his world. But he saw the sex as a beginning, an expression of his desire to take their relationship in a different direction. But was that how Roxy saw it?

He took his eyes off the road. She was twisting her hair between her thumb and forefinger. Not at the ends like she usually did but at the root, the scalp. He wondered if it hurt. And more importantly what did it mean? She usually played with her hair when she was nervous or agitated about something. He hated the thought that she might be feeling that way because of him. And Roxy was much quieter on the ride back to the airport than she had been on the way to the spa. Too quiet. She'd told him earlier that she needed time to think. He knew it was selfish, but he didn't want her thinking. Not if she wouldn't share those thoughts with him.

He used to be able to read her. Now she wouldn't even look at him. Her hair hid her face like a theater curtain.

Roxanne kept her face turned toward the passenger side window, but she could sense the confused glances that Linc had been throwing her way. If he was confused, that made two of them. Not only had she gone to his room, she'd stayed all night. She made love to him like a woman having her first taste of water after wandering aimlessly through a dry desert. One sip and she couldn't get enough. Under the cover of darkness, being with Linc had felt so right. The morning had shed a whole new light on the situation.

It was the best night's sleep she'd had in months. Still, that hadn't prevented her from feeling embarrassed and guilty when she felt his warm breath at her ear, telling her that it was time to get up. The night was like a drug that made her forget a lot of important things. Like the fact that she was a widow, for God's sake! Jamal had meant the world to her. What kind of grieving widow knocked boots with her dead husband's best friend?

And what kind of best friend would let her? No! That wasn't being fair. She would not blame Linc. He didn't put a gun to her head. She had walked into this one. But had she confused lust for something else? Was she confusing friendship and caring for romantic love? If someone had asked her last week how she felt about Linc, her answer would have been so swift and unambiguous. She loved him like a brother, a close, close friend. She relied on him, was protective of him, and they understood each other—sometimes with only a look or by what was not said.

What was Linc to her? Today, she just didn't know. How could her feelings do a one-eighty in such a hiccup of time? What if they weren't real? What if last night was about days of intense togetherness, affection for Linc, and a need to express herself sexually again? She knew Linc was expecting more from her. But she couldn't be sure of anything. Not until she was back on familiar ground. She needed to get back to Baltimore and see how she felt then. In fact, she was eager to get home. She wanted to see how these new feelings for Linc would fare in familiar surroundings, where the memories of Jamal, her crazy family, his career, and just plain old day-to-day living would come into play.

Roxy turned to face him. She wasn't surprised to find his eyes on her. She gave him a hesitant smile. Suddenly realizing she was torturing her hair, she let her hands fall to her lap. She found she couldn't meet his gaze for very long. Her face went all hot. Flashbacks of how shamelessly they'd devoured each other haunted her. The images were by turns disturbing, embarrassing, thrilling . . . and precious. Roxanne switched her gaze from Linc to something safer, her hands. The same hands that had tried to explore every inch of him only a few hours ago. Roxanne couldn't believe that she was feeling shy with him.

Not after last night.

Encouraged by even the slightest of smiles, Linc's answering smile was broad. "Still thinking?" he asked in a tone that was much lighter than how he was feeling. Not knowing what was going on in her head was driving him crazy.

She looked up then. "Yes, Linc. I'm still thinking. All this hit me kind of suddenly. I can't believe your feelings changed a while ago, and I didn't notice. I'm just trying to catch my breath. I feel like I don't know which way is up."

He nodded his understanding. He'd felt the same way when all of a sudden he couldn't be in the same room with her without wanting her. He knew the timing was lousy. It was too soon after Jamal's death. Of course she hadn't been paying attention to him. She'd just lost her husband. And *before* she had sorted out her feelings, she'd slept with him. He hadn't asked her to think before acting. Now he'd have to suffer while she went through that process. But he couldn't help wanting to hurry it along. No one had ever praised him for his patience.

She must have sensed his worry. Roxanne reached over and touched his arm. "I'll try to think as hard and fast as I can," she told him. "This is all new to me. And I don't want to make any promises that I'll end up breaking later."

She didn't want to do that to Linc or herself.

Linc sighed, then she felt his arm relax. Relieved, Roxanne leaned back in her seat. She was sleepy and sore. She closed her eyes then smiled, remembering that she had missed her Flower Wrap massage. They had seriously overslept. There had been just enough time to shower, pack, grab a quick lunch, and head for the airport. It had been so long, she almost forgot that that's what happens when you stay up half the night making love.

Her smile deepened. But it was worth it.

Linc was worth at least a dozen missed massages.

By the time they dropped the car off, the earlier tension between the two of them had eased considerably. So much so that Linc and Roxanne were holding hands as they walked through the concourse. He happily shortened his stride to match hers. It made Linc realize that he'd never been in love before. When he was a teenager, there was no way something as innocent as holding hands would have made his heart swell to twice its normal size. It wouldn't have been enough. He would have been wondering when he got to the good stuff. Now he was realizing just being in the presence of someone you truly cared about was the good stuff.

"I hope we didn't forget anything," Roxanne said.

"I'm sure the inn will forward anything you left. Besides, where would you have put anything else? It was bad enough that you had to buy an extra duffle bag to carry all the stuff you bought. I'm sure the Mystic Chamber of Commerce cried when they heard you were leaving," he teased.

She bumped him with her hip. "You're gonna be crying, too. If you don't stop being such a smart ass."

Linc laughed and put his arm around her waist. He wanted her even closer to him. He led her to the airline's VIP lounge. It was conveniently located across from their gate, A-6. He looked at his watch, a gift from the team's owner. They had about a half hour before they started boarding. Linc rarely sat in the waiting area at the gate before boarding a plane. Not unless he wanted to be social. Someone was bound to recognize him, and before you knew it, there would be a small crowd. And even though he always flew first class—he needed the legroom as much as the privacy—Linc usually boarded last. Another way to avoid drawing attention to himself. That's the last thing he wanted right now. He wanted Roxy all to himself.

And he was in luck. No one else was in the small conference room. There was just a table with six chairs. A television. A few newspapers. It was not nearly as fancy as some of the lounges in the bigger hubs. There was no club representative, no complimentary food or beverages, no fax machines or paper shredders. Not that any of that mattered. They were still alone. It had been nice not to have cell phones and pagers interrupting them all weekend. He had even turned the ringer off the phone early this morning because he hadn't wanted to disturb her. After these past few months, it was nice to watch her looking so peaceful. He had resisted the urge to stroke her to wakefulness and love her until the sun came up. Eventually his own tiredness caught up with him, and he curled into her, falling asleep again himself.

Linc wondered when he'd be able to fall asleep in her arms

again. He hoped it was soon. Roxy wasn't the only one who had slept like a baby. Sighing, he took a seat in one of the chairs.

"Somebody is slacking on the job," Roxanne said. "These are old newspapers. Yesterday and the day before."

"There's a courtesy phone. I can call and ask someone to bring one over."

"Don't bother," Roxanne said. "I was thinking about going back to get one of those pretzels anyway. I don't know about you, but lunch went by in such a rush, it didn't even register in my stomach." More than likely, she burned off so many calories last night that she'd worked up an appetite, and missing breakfast hadn't helped. "I'm gonna grab something to read while I'm at it."

"I can come with you," Linc offered, leaping to his feet. It was crazy. He didn't want her to leave. Not even for five minutes.

She gently pushed him back down into the chair. "Not necessary. Put your feet up. You just drove for an hour, plus I know how cramped you get on planes. So stretch your legs while you can. Do you want anything?"

Trying to get a grip on his overwhelming need to be with her twenty-four-seven, Linc told her to bring him back a pretzel and Coke. After she left, he began sifting through the old newspapers. He picked up a sports page to see how the Cardinals were doing. It was early days yet, but at the start of every season, he was convinced that his hometown team had World Series potential—no matter what the so-called experts said. Linc laughed when he saw the standings. The Cards were in dead last place.

"Oh, well," he said, closing the paper and pushing it away from him. "There's nowhere to go but up." Just like him and Roxy.

Linc liked the analogy, so he went with it. This was the start of their season. The beginning. And it was a lot to live up to when your first game had been a perfect one. Last night had been nothing short of perfection. But he knew from Roxy's earlier reserve that they hadn't even been tested yet. This was one season he was determined to come out on top. He would not dwell in the cellar of Roxy's life. That's what "platonic friends" would feel like to him now. He was long past the buddy or pal stage.

Linc didn't want to consider the possibility that Roxanne would never come around to feeling about him the way he felt about her. Desperately in need of a distraction, he leaned forward to snag the television remote that was lying on the other side of the table.

He hadn't watched television in what? Four days? That had to be some kind of record. Linc used the TV the way some people used a radio or CD player, as background noise.

He flipped through the channels until he got to his favorite station, ESPN. It was the top of the hour. The sports news was coming on.

". . . And now more from the story that broke in Denver late last night . . ." A picture of Jamal flashed on the screen.

"Star football player Jamal Steele may have died but some secrets can't stay buried . . ." This was followed by a clip of Honey taking questions from a throng of reporters. A buzzing invaded his ears. He saw Honey's glossy lips move, but he couldn't decipher what she was saying. Whatever it was, it could only be bad. Linc felt his heart sink to the pit of his stomach.

"Oh, my God, Roxanne," he whispered. He had to find her.

Linc was reaching for the door handle when the door opened inward. Roxanne was holding several newspapers, local and national. A tabloid with a grainy black-and-white photo of Honey holding a fat, smiling baby caught his attention. The picture took up most of the page. A smaller photo of Jamal was tucked into the bottom right corner. Underneath, the headline read: WHO'S YOUR DADDY?

Roxanne thrust the papers in his direction. Her eyes were big and watery. Her chest was heaving as if she had run through the terminal to get back to him. "What is *this?*" she demanded. "Why would this woman make up a lie like this?"

He drew her into his arms. The newspapers were crushed between their bodies. He could feel a tremor moving through her whole body. He squeezed his eyes shut and rocked her back and forth. He was filled with regret.

How could he have forgotten the April deadline that Honey had given him? And it had been his brilliant idea to turn off his cell phone and not tell anyone but Dot where they were going. It was his fault Roxy had found out like this.

"Roxy, it's gonna be OK," he told her, rubbing her back.

She pulled away from him and looked up into his eyes. "How can you say that?" She scowled. "There's some crazy woman out there claiming that Jamal fathered her child. She even named her baby after him! Jamal Steele Brown.'"

That's when he realized that Roxy wasn't shaking because she was devastated. She was shaking with anger.

"Well, she's not gonna get away with this shit," Roxanne declared. "Why won't people just let Jamal rest in peace? First, they make him out to be a druggie, and now this. Jamal would never cheat on me. What reason would he have for doing that?" she cried.

Linc could have wept for what he was about to do to her. He gently led her over to the table. "Roxy, what did the papers say exactly?" he asked.

"I didn't read them all. But, basically, she's claiming that Jamal had a one-night stand with her the last time he was in Denver. She's a stripper. Jamal didn't go to strip clubs. Where would he have met her?"

"He met her at Cleopatra's Lair. That's where she works."

Roxanne stopped breathing. "Wh . . . what?" She felt like someone had kicked her in the stomach. Linc tried to cover her hands with his. She pulled back. Linc knew where the woman worked. What was he saying? "Are you telling me Jamal was cheating on me?" she demanded, all the while afraid that the answer would be yes.

Linc was afraid. Roxy didn't want him touching her, and he hadn't even told her the whole story yet. "Roxy, it's not what you're thinking."

"You don't know what I'm thinking," she shouted. In a quieter voice, she said, "Please, Linc, just tell me what you know."

So he did.

When he was done, Roxanne was silent for a full minute. The tears that had been falling down her cheeks had picked up speed the more he talked. "Are you telling me that you've known about this . . . since before Jamal died? And neither one of you said a word?" she said in a faraway voice.

He nodded.

"I can't believe it," she said. She couldn't believe any of it. That Jamal would get so drunk or whatever that he didn't know whether or not he had sex with someone. But worse, she couldn't believe that neither one of them, her husband or her best friend, had seen fit to clue her in on what had been happening. "Why?" she cried. She hurt all over, like she'd been in a fight.

"Roxy, you've got to understand," he pleaded but was afraid to try to touch her again. He couldn't bear the rejection. "You have to remember what frame of mind you were in last fall. I mean . . . you were really upset about not being able to get pregnant. Jamal only wanted to protect you. We both did. We weren't sure what the whole truth was. Honey was acting shady. Not showing up for the paternity test. Jamal didn't want to ruin your happiness for nothing."

She reared back and slapped him. Linc didn't flinch. He deserved it. "How could you think I would *want* happiness based on lies?" she cried. "What kind of happiness is that?" She swallowed, trying to clear her throat of the pain. "Linc, you don't know how much this hurts . . . I thought I could trust you and Jamal . . . to come to me with the truth about anything. Especially if it concerned me. I just can't believe this," she repeated.

Linc hated the way Roxy was looking at him. She stared at him like she'd never laid eyes on him before.

Linc touched his face. His cheek was stinging from the slap. To his surprise, his hand came away wet with tears. "Roxy, I'm so sorry," he said. "I don't know what else to say. At the time, I thought what we were doing was for the best. I never imagined it would explode in our faces like this."

She shook her head. "It hasn't exploded in your face, Linc. It's blown up in mine. I'm the one who looks and feels like a complete fool. At least you had an inkling that something like this might happen."

"Roxy, I know we . . . I . . . messed up. But I'll make it up to you," he promised.

"Thanks, but I'll handle it myself," she told him. "Your kind of help is why I'm sitting here now questioning if I ever really knew my husband . . . or you."

"Roxy . . ." he began.

"Linc, it's time for us to get on the plane. I have to go back and get my house in order," she said. She rose and walked away from him, leaving him there with nothing but his regrets.

Chapter

26

On the plane ride back to Baltimore, Roxanne read every last one of the newspaper articles about Jamal. The first-class cabin was full. As she scoured one article then the other, Linc had quietly pleaded with her to stop torturing herself. She had ignored him. She had to find the truth out from somewhere, and she apparently couldn't trust him any farther than she could throw him, which was not far at all.

When they collected their luggage at BWI, Linc had wanted to drive her home. So they could talk, he had said. Roxanne was not in the mood for talking. He grabbed her arm to keep her from walking off, and she asked him if he really wanted to create a fuss smack dab in the middle of the baggage claim area. He let her arm go and despite Linc's protests, she took a cab.

She was in pain. She just wanted to be alone to lick her wounds. She felt like a complete fool. How could Jamal have done something like this to her? How could he have put himself in such a vulnerable position and then kept it from her? She didn't want to believe he'd touch another woman. Not when they were so good together. And when he knew how important fidelity was to her. Roxanne's fingers sought out the golden band that hung around her neck. She clutched it and then brought it to her trembling lips. If Jamal hadn't done anything wrong, then why all the secrecy? And Linc? *He was my friend first. Shouldn't his loyalty have been to me?* Why did men always have to stick together no matter how foul the plan? No matter how rank the lie?

Huddled against one corner of the backseat, Roxanne wiped away the tears that streamed down her face. She saw the cabbie eyeing her in the rearview mirror. She probably looked like a crazy woman. But thankfully, he wasn't one of those nosy types. She wrapped her arms around herself. She was colder than she'd been in days. It wasn't fair. The spa had been a tease, a promise of a spring thaw that was not going to happen.

The cab slowed to a crawl after it turned onto her street. Roxanne's eyes widened in alarm. There were news crews all over the place. There were vans with little satellite dishes on top. Reporters were chatting with each other on the sidewalk. She wanted to tell the cabbie to keep going. But there was no place else to go. She couldn't go to Linc's. That was the last place she wanted to go.

When the cab turned into the driveway, the reporters rushed it. They started tapping on the car windows, firing questions at her through the rolled-up glass. Roxanne's stomach heaved. It was like the day of Jamal's funeral all over again. They were surrounding the car. Flash bulbs were going off in her face, and she felt like she couldn't breathe.

"You OK, miss?" the driver asked, sounding just as rattled as she felt. "You want me to take you someplace else? A hotel, maybe?"

"Huh?" Roxanne said, trying to clear her head.

"Get away from the frickin' door," Linc shouted. "Get back and let her get out."

What was Linc doing here? Hadn't she sent him on his merry way at the airport? Roxanne tried to locate him through the crowd of people blocking the windows. She didn't see him until a few seconds later when the door flew open.

Linc held out his hand. When she didn't take it, he leaned in and lifted her out. All around her the shouting continued. Roxanne put her hands over her face, not wanting to be tonight's news. Meanwhile, Linc hustled her over to the front door. He used his key to unlock it, ignoring the braying of the reporters at his back. What felt like an eternity later, he gently shoved her inside then closed the door behind her.

Through the tinted glass on both sides of the front door, Roxanne could see shadows. The reporters were still scurrying about like rats. She walked into the middle of the foyer. The house was absolutely silent. "Mama?" she called out several times. She stopped at the foot of the stairway leading to the second floor. Feeling alone and incredibly tired, she sat down on the bottom landing.

Linc came through the front door carrying her luggage. He took one look at her and dropped the bags where he stood. He walked over to her. "Roxy, are you OK?"

"What are you doing here, Linc?" she asked him.

"I couldn't let you leave the way you did. Did you really think I would just leave?" he asked. "We didn't even get a chance to talk." They hadn't had time. Not at the airport and certainly not in the midst of the three-ring circus that was going on outside.

Roxanne didn't say anything. Oh, they had had plenty of time to talk. From the minute Linc found out about Honey Brown, he'd had months to clue her in. Now he wanted to talk? Well, it was too late. The shit had already hit the fan. And it had splattered in her face. It was out there pacing back and forth in front of her house. "Linc, I don't want to talk. I don't want to do anything except wrap my mind around how the two men I cared about most could let me walk around like an idiot for months! Do you have any idea how betrayed and stupid I feel?" she cried. "I knew. I knew something was eating Jamal up inside right before he died. But he kept insisting that it was all about football. And silly me, I believed him. And you know why? Because I didn't think he would lie to me. I didn't think he was capable of it. I guess now I know better. I guess I'm just like every other woman who's been cheated on. I was the last to know."

Linc took in the dried tear tracks on her face. Her voice cracked like she was holding back even more. She sounded bitter and angry, but it was the hurt that leapt out at Linc. It was palpable. She'd made Jamal prove himself to her because she wanted to save herself from the kind of hurt she was feeling now. Her pain slashed Linc like a knife because he felt partly responsible. He and Jamal should have trusted her to be able to deal with the whole mess. But they hadn't and look where it had gotten them . . . him. "Roxy, I don't know how many ways I can tell you I'm sorry. I messed up," he said.

Roxanne regarded her old friend. Her new lover. He did truly look sorry but that didn't change anything. Most likely, Jamal had a child out in Denver. The one thing she could never give him. Both realities were equally depressing. She wanted to crawl into a ball and pretend that none of this was happening. Linc's regret didn't change a thing. "Linc, you should go home now."

He shook his head. "Where's Dot?"

She shrugged her shoulders. "Hell if I know. Maybe she got out while the going was good."

"C'mon Roxy. You know she wouldn't do that."

She passed a hand over her tired eyes. Her voice was flat when she told him, "Linc, I'm learning that people will do just about anything—if it means covering their own asses."

She was talking about him, of course, and Jamal. Linc tried not to get too upset about the digs she was making. She had just found out about Honey this afternoon. It was natural that she'd be pissed. Right? Roxy didn't hold grudges or her anger for very long. At least, she didn't used to, but from the way she was responding to him now he didn't know what to think. He forced himself to let go of the fear that threatened to eat him from the inside out. "Roxy, how can I help?" he asked.

"You can't," she told him. "I'm in shock right now, but I'll get over it."

He hoped to God that would be sooner rather than later. But she wasn't being realistic. "Roxy, you have reporters camped out at your door. You can't stay holed up in here forever. And I hate to bring this up, but if Honey Brown has gone public, a paternity test can't be far behind."

"Tell me something I don't know," she said. "And at any rate, it's none of your concern. I'll handle it."

"How?" he asked, stinging from her dismissal of him.

She glared at him. He was acting like he was the only game in town. She could handle her business without his help. Though he was leaning against a wall, he still towered over her. She stood up. She would not be intimidated by him. "I'll deal with it. The same way I have dealt with everything else life has thrown my way. You must really see me as some kind of helpless female. Well, I'm not, Lincoln Weaver. So stop playing the hero. I don't need you to res- cue me," she muttered, then stomped off upstairs.

Roxanne had to wade through dozens of messages before she found out where her mother was. She had spent the night over at Curtis's and hadn't heard about the news about Jamal until this morning. Roxanne dialed Curtis's number.

"Thank God, Roxy," Dot cried. "I've been worried crazy about you." Her mama had tried to reach her at Northwoods but couldn't get through. She and Curtis had planned to wait for her at the house, but kept right on driving when they spotted all the reporters. "Roxy, you know how flustered I get. I was scared I might say the wrong thing. I hope you're not mad at me?" Dot said in her little girl voice. Roxanne could tell she was crying.

"Mama, you did the right thing," Roxanne assured her. From the way her mother was crying and carrying on, you would think someone had cheated on *her*. She wouldn't be able to provide much comfort, so Roxy told her to stay put.

With a sigh, Roxanne hung up the phone. She knew Linc was still somewhere in the house. And short of kicking him out, he wasn't going to leave until he was sure she was OK. She debated for a minute about which of her friends to call. Then Roxanne punched in Cynthia's number.

Cynthia must have been sitting next to the phone. Roxanne didn't hear the first ring complete. "Cyn" was as far as she got.

"Roxanne, girl, what on earth is going on? What's this about some hoochie claiming that Jamal knocked her up? What kind of madness is this?"

"Cyn, the answer to all your questions is I don't know. Believe me, this is the first I'm hearing about it."

"Well, you know it's all B.S., right? Girlfriend is just trying to get a little attention. *Honey?* Now you know her mama didn't name her that. I saw her ghetto-fabulous behind on TV. Jamal wouldn't give somebody like her more than one glance . . ." And that was supposed to make her feel better, Roxanne wondered. ". . . I mean just about any man, even a gay one, would give her one glance. How could he not? When she got boobs and ass hanging out all over the place." Cyn's sympathetic cattiness brought a small smile to her lips. Not curious about Roxanne's lack of response, Cynthia said, "Never mind that, I hope you sicced your lawyers on her. They'll eat her alive."

Roxanne thought Southerners were supposed to drawl. Cyn

was spouting off like a volcano. But she'd raised a good point. Roxanne did need some legal expertise. Her first call would be to Mark Krautheim—since his name had come up more than once in the articles. "Cyn, I just walked in the door a few minutes ago. I was out of town . . . I took a little vacation." The serenity of Northwoods seemed like it happened in another lifetime. An alternate reality.

"Really? Where you been? How come you didn't invite me?" Cyn asked all in one breath.

Roxanne closed her eyes. Where she'd been was a whole other story. She needed to talk to somebody about that, too. But not right now. "Cyn, that's not important. But I have a pack of reporters camped out at my door. I don't know what to say to them."

Given a problem she was familiar with, Cynthia became a totally different person. She advised Roxanne to say nothing. And advised her to get her attorney to come over and request that they get off the property. They had no right to be there.

That sounded good to her. Then there was the problem of Linc. He wouldn't be so easy to get rid of. He wouldn't leave unless she had someone staying with her. She didn't have the energy to fight with him. As much as she hated to do it, she was going to have to ask her mother to come home. But her mother was not good under pressure. She would drive her crazy with all her dithering. Even if it was only for a few days. Roxanne hadn't forgotten the INS hearing was coming up. When it rained it poured. When Roxanne had left for Connecticut, she only had one problem. Now she came back to three. Her mama, Honey Brown, and Linc. Her head bowed with the weight of it all.

With a sigh she said, "Cyn, do you think you could prepare a statement for me. I'm not going to be able to say 'No comment' forever."

"Sweetie, I can do one better than that. It's Friday. I can hop on a plane and be there tonight, tomorrow morning at the latest. I put a hold on a couple of flights. I just need to make sure I still have a seat on one of them."

"Would you really do that?" Roxanne felt a lump forming in her throat. Despite the situation with Linc, she still had *some* great friends.

"Child, didn't I mention it? My bag is already packed."

After hanging up, Roxanne made another call. She was surprised at who answered the phone. "Tyson?"

"Yes," Monique's husband said. He gave a deep chuckle at her undisguised surprise. "And this would be the lovely Roxanne, I presume."

"Actually it is the stressed-out Roxanne," she replied. "But it's nice to hear a friendly voice. I was wondering if Monique was around."

"She certainly is. She's been wearing a hole in the carpet wondering when she was going to hear from you. Hold on a second. I'll get . . ."

Monique must have snatched the phone out of his hand. She repeated some of the same questions that Cynthia had. Roxanne gave her a little more detail about how long the secrets and lies had been going on.

"Well, I'll be damned," Monique declared when Roxanne finished the story. "And neither one of these geniuses thought to tell the other that things like babies don't just disappear if you ignore them? How men came to rule the world, I'll never know. But forget them," she said, "how are you holding up?"

"Horribly. I'm hurt, upset. Feeling hounded by the press. I'm pissed at Linc. I just want all of this to be over, and it hasn't even started yet. But Cyn's coming up for the weekend, so that should help."

"If you say so," Monique said.

Roxanne didn't invite her to elaborate. She already knew that Monique thought Cyn was a bit of an airhead. "Anyhow, I have a favor to ask of you. Feel free to say no, if you can't do it—"

"Stop qualifying and just tell me what it is."

Roxanne reminded Monique of her mother's upcoming INS hearing. "I don't think it's a good idea for me to go with her. I think it would only draw attention to it. I'm afraid any kind of publicity would just make it worse for my mother and Etienne. I also want to get this paternity situation cleared up as soon as possible. I need to be in Baltimore to do that. I'm, sure the immigration lawyer you recommended is top-notch, but I would feel better if someone I knew was there—"

"Don't say another word. I'll be there," Monique said.

"Are you sure?"

"One hundred percent sure. Two things are never far from my fingertips. My cigarettes and my Palm Pilot. And I already checked. I don't have to be in court at all this week. And the good thing about working for yourself is that I get to call all the shots." Knowing Monique's temperament that was probably for the best. She was much better at giving orders than taking them. "Did you say the hearing was on Tuesday?"

"Yes."

"I'm good to go then. I just need to cancel my counseling appointment."

Counseling?

Monique must have read her mind. "Yeah, you heard right. Counseling. Tyson and I are trying to work out our differences. Apparently I have some unresolved family issues that are spilling over into our marriage."

"That's wonderful . . ." Roxanne stammered. She couldn't quite absorb that Monique was seeing a marriage counselor. And that Monique was actually taking responsibility for some of the problems in the marriage. ". . . not the unresolved family issues . . . I mean, its good that you and Tyson are back together. You are back together? I mean he answered the phone." How long had they been seeing a counselor? she wondered. Roxanne felt a little guilty because the last time they had spoken, it had been to ask for advice about her mama's marriage. Now here she was again asking for more help.

"Umm . . ." Monique lowered her voice. "Let's just say, he's visiting."

"Still it's a start. I'm happy for you."

Never one to linger on "mushy stuff," Monique made plans for her trip to St. Louis. She opted for a hotel rather than inconvenience Roxanne's family even though Roxanne had told her it wouldn't be a problem. Roxanne insisted on paying all her expenses, including her legal fees. After a brief, heated skirmish Monique had agreed, but Roxanne had a feeling the subject would come up again later.

The one bright spot in what had been a dismal day was that Monique and Tyson were trying to keep it together. She wished Jamal had given her the same opportunity instead of keeping his troubles to himself. He hadn't turned to her. He'd gone to Linc. Roxanne closed her eyes. She didn't want to speculate on what that said about their relationship, since it hurt too much.

Roxanne made a few more phone calls. One to Gayle and then to her sisters and grandmother. Once everyone was semi-convinced that she was OK, Roxanne went back down to face Linc.

She found him in the den. He was listening to Al Jarreau. His eyes were closed, and there was an empty plate and half-empty glass of milk next to it on the coffee table. His hands were folded across his stomach, and she could see his chest moving in and out. He looked at home. And it pissed her off.

As if sensing her gaze upon him, he opened his eyes. They grew wary at the lack of welcome he saw reflected in hers. When she didn't speak, he nodded toward the plate, "I hope you don't mind," he said. "I made myself a couple of sandwiches. Tuna. I made one for you, too. It's in the fridge."

"I'm not hungry," she said.

"You were gone a long time," Linc said. Too long. He had thought once or twice about going upstairs to check on her, but something told him to let her be. A lot had been thrown at Roxy in a short amount of time.

"I had to return calls to some people. Folks were worried about me."

"I'm worried about you, too."

"Don't be, Linc; you don't have to guard me. You can go home. Cyn is coming."

He'd been given his walking papers. A smart man would have taken them. "So, you're not going to talk to me. Is that it?"

"We don't have anything left to talk about."

If that's what she was selling, he wasn't buying it. The very fact that she didn't want to talk showed him just how furious she was. And he couldn't stand the silence. Though they rarely argued, things always got back on track after she'd let him have it. Like when she'd been jealous—for no reason—of Desiree. She'd let it fly and it had cleared the air. He felt compelled to move her in that direction now. "You say we have nothing to talk about? Don't you want me to explain why Jamal didn't say anything and why I went along with it? Or how about what happened between us last night?" There; he'd finally seen something besides coldness flash in her eyes. And then whatever the emotion was, it vanished. He wanted to chase after it. Make her 'fess up.

"I especially don't want to talk about last night," Roxanne said evenly. "It's not high on my list of priorities at the moment."

What was he supposed to say to that? Make it a priority. He didn't think so. Roxanne was letting him know she was not in the mood to be pushed around. But he wasn't going to be pushed aside, either. "Fine. You're right, it's not the time." At least not for her. But no way was she gonna rock his world and then act like it never happened.

"Good," she said, taking a seat in a nearby armchair. She looked at the empty fireplace instead of him. "You can let yourself out."

"When does the blue-eyed man-eater get here," he asked, hoping to tease a smile out of her. He failed.

"Cyn should be here later on tonight or early tomorrow morning."

"Fine. That's when I'll be leaving, later on tonight or early tomorrow morning."

She glanced his way. His arms were now crossed over his chest, and his head cocked to one side. *Look at him, looking so, so Linc.* He'd been her self-appointed protector since age six, and he wasn't going to let her fire him just like that. He wasn't going to budge, and it would be pointless to argue with him. That would mean she'd have to talk to him, and she didn't want to do that, either. Besides, if she was honest with herself, as angry as she was with him it didn't mean she hated him. And it certainly was better than being alone. Linc would have to do. At least until Cyn could get here.

Chapter
27

Roxanne held the sleeping child in her arms. She stroked his dark, soft, curly hair with the back of her hand. He smelled of baby powder and milk and sweetness. Roxanne placed a light kiss on her godson's cheek. He sighed and snuggled more deeply against the cushion of her breast. She looked up and met Gayle's eyes. This was the first time she'd seen her friend since the days after Jamal's funeral. "He's absolutely beautiful," she told his mother.

"I know," Gayle said with all the shamelessness of a mother in love with her child. "I think he looks more like Reggie than me."

"Maybe," Roxanne agreed. "But he has his mother's disposition." MJ had hardly made a peep since she had arrived. He had easily accepted her arms around him, as if he knew she needed the comfort of his innocence. Like his mother, MJ was calm and watchful. Gayle hadn't batted an eyelash when Roxanne called up last night and asked if it was OK for her to come to Columbus for a few days.

They were sitting on the comfy overstuffed couch in Gayle and Reggie's family room. Both of them had curled their legs behind them. Knee to knee they faced each other. The taupe walls and creamy white woodwork reflected Gayle's easygoing nature. A large ceramic fruit bowl and a globe-shaped vase full of flowers sat on a square glass table.

"I've been worried about you, Roxanne. It's so good to see you in person," Gayle said. "I was starting to feel a little jealous. I've had to hear secondhand from Cyn or Monique how things were going."

"I'm sorry I haven't been to visit sooner," Roxanne apologized.

Gayle leaned over and gave her knee a gentle squeeze. "I understand, Roxanne. I'm just glad you're here now."

Gayle was the most levelheaded and compassionate of all her friends. But it was the baby sleeping in her arms, MJ, that had kept Roxanne away. She had been afraid of what she'd feel. She hadn't wanted her envy and loss to stain Gayle's happiness or strain their friendship. Then the paternity test results had come in, and after months of avoiding her, Roxanne was filled with this intense need to be with Gayle. Though a lot had happened in a week, it had an unreal air to it. Actually, her ability to have these out-of-body experiences, to be in a situation but not really present, was starting to worry her a little.

Maybe that's why she wanted to see Gayle. Her friend was about as genuine and down to earth as they came. Not that Cyn hadn't been great. She had been the calm, poised, put together spokesperson that Roxanne never could have been for herself. And Monique had flown to St. Louis as promised. When it was all said and done, Etienne had to go back to Haiti, but at least her mama was off the hook. With Monique's help, Roxanne would continue to try to help him get back in the country. But honestly, he wasn't at the top of her "to do list." And having Jamal's skeletons come tumbling out of the closet must have put the fear of God into her mama, because she'd told Curtis about Etienne *before* the hearing. Curtis was still in the picture and an annulment was in the works. *And* there was a zero percent possibility that Jamal could have fathered Honey Brown's baby.

That was the biggest news of all. The closest to home. So why didn't she feel relieved? There was not the jubilation that she had expected. Only a sense that she'd lost something. She just wasn't sure what. "I have to say that you're looking pretty good considering the circumstances," Gayle remarked. Much better than after Jamal's funeral. She tried not to show her uneasiness when Roxanne had called last night. Though she hadn't sounded too upset, there was an urgency in her voice, like she had to get away from Baltimore. Maybe that's why Gayle expected her to look like her world had come crashing down. There was a droop to her shoulders, and a sadness had replaced the optimism that was her trademark. But she didn't look defeated or overwhelmed.

Gayle felt her own body relax in response. She was confident the hopeful sparkle would return sooner or later. Roxanne was a survivor. The baby's daddy drama of the past few days had her down but not out. Gayle suspected that losing Jamal was the worst thing that could have happened. If Roxanne could weather that, she could handle anything. This paternity thing was just a blip on the screen.

Albeit, a pretty big blip.

Though the baby was not Jamal's, the sensationalized details had been splashed all over the tabloid papers and many so-called legitimate news programs. And there were pictures of Jamal with the woman. So there was no way to claim they had never met. Apparently somebody had taken them at the party back at the team's hotel. There was one in particular where Honey was touching his cheek, and Jamal was looking up at her. Gayle wasn't there that night, and she didn't care what the picture seemed to suggest. Roxanne was the only one that had ever captured Jamal's complete attention. Hadn't papers said he had a few drinks in addition to being on pain medication? Still, it looked bad and had to hurt. She and Reggie worked at the same bank. She cringed at the thought of her personal business being the topic around the watercooler at work, let alone being discussed and judged by thousands of faceless, nameless strangers.

"I can't imagine what you're going through," Gayle said in honesty. It was an invitation to talk. She knew that's why Roxanne was here even if Roxanne didn't know it herself.

"I'm glad the child isn't Jamal's," Roxanne admitted. "I mean . . . if he had been, I wouldn't have tried to deny him anything. But he would have been a living reminder of what Jamal had done." She lowered her eyes. "Doesn't that sound selfish?"

"No, it sounds human. What woman would be OK with a constant reminder of her husband's . . . unfaithfulness?"

Roxanne swallowed and focused on the top of MJ's head. She was a stranger to him, yet he'd come to her. He'd trusted her so easily, she realized. Children were all born innocent and pure of heart. "Still, it's not the baby's fault that his mother handled this in the way that she did," Roxanne argued. Though she had never met the woman, she despised Honey Brown for dragging Jamal's name through the mud the way she had. There had been other ways to handle it, and the woman hadn't even tried. "If only Honey, Jamal, or even Linc had come to me," she said, "instead of keeping me in the dark. Whatever happened between Jamal and that woman, it involved me, too. I should have been told."

Hearing the confusion and bitterness in her voice, Gayle asked, "How are things between you and Linc?" He was really the only one in this conspiracy of silence who continued to be a part of Roxanne's life. Jamal was dead. And Honey Brown was irrelevant now that the paternity test had turned out the way it did. But Roxanne was closer to Linc than she was to any of her girlfriends. They had met her in college, but Linc had known her since she was a girl. Since before she was a fully formed person. *Would their friendship be able to hold up under the strain of this lie?*

Gayle hoped so.

Roxanne shrugged. She hadn't talked to Linc all week. Not that he hadn't tried. She just wasn't taking his calls. She was pretty sure her mother had been feeding him information up until she had to go to St. Louis. The last three days had been the hardest. Honey had agreed to the paternity test—after Roxanne's lawyers paid her to take it. And Roxanne had waited. All alone.

"Linc lied to me, Gayle."

"He didn't mean to hurt you."

"But he did."

Seeing the jut of Roxanne's jaw and the grim line of her usually upturned lips, Gayle inquired, "Do you think it's possible that Linc is getting double the punishment because he's here and Jamal isn't?"

"What!" Roxanne cried, then she remembered the sleeping baby. She lowered her voice to a fierce, defensive whisper. "Why shouldn't I be mad at Linc? Nobody made him lie. He had a choice."

"Roxanne, you're absolutely right. Linc did lie to you, but he didn't start the lie. Jamal did. Are you going to punish him for his mistake *and* Jamal's, too?"

Roxanne didn't understand. Weren't they one and the same? Hadn't the two of them been in on it together? She shook her head.

"I know I have a reputation for being forgiving," Roxanne said, her lips twisting. She used to be proud of that image. "But I don't know if I can just let this slide . . ."

"Nobody's asking you to let it slide. Jamal made a bad choice. Linc made a bad choice. Are you going to cut off your nose to spite your face? Linc cares about you. Do you know how rare it is to have a friend who knows you inside and out? Someone who has been there from day one? Linc has been that kind of friend to you. Don't let your anger blind you," she urged her.

Roxanne stared at her friend. What was she supposed to do, forget that it ever happened? And then there was that night. Their night. She sighed as Gayle waited, searching her face for some sign of softening. "Gayle, you don't understand . . . me and Linc . . . It's complicated."

A flicker of surprise lit Gayle's eyes, and then she said, "Help me understand."

Roxanne hesitated. Her emotions had been a jumble. She had decided against telling Cyn anything because Cyn wouldn't have understood at all. A hunky, eligible man wanted you and you wanted him. It would have been one plus one equaling two for Cyn. But to Roxanne, it felt more like geometry. She'd struggled with geometry a lot in school, for you had to reason backward. You had to figure out how the equation was derived. Its source. Its origin. She hadn't had any time in the past few days to fathom how she and Linc wound up in bed together. She hadn't wanted to think about it. And being angry with him about keeping secrets from her made it easier.

Gayle could tell Roxanne was doing some deep thinking. But sometimes your thoughts were clearer when you spoke them out loud. "Roxanne, I know you and Linc went away for a few days. That's why you weren't at home when the story broke . . ." Gayle paused. She took a deep breath and hoped she wasn't stepping out of line. She then asked, "So what's the other story? What happened between you and Linc?"

If Roxanne hadn't been holding MJ, she would have covered her face. Her hair was pulled back with a thick ribbon, so she couldn't hide behind it, either. She raised her eyes to meet Gayle's. All she saw was concern, love, and a desire to help.

So she answered Gayle's question.

When she was done, Gayle smiled. It was a smile that drew attention to her high cheekbones and most of all her kind eyes. "Roxanne, why are you so upset about this? It's wonderful. Through all the pain of the past few months, you two managed to forge a new relationship. The friendship was already there. Stronger than a lot of people who started with the romance stuff."

"I don't know if I'd call it a romance . . ." Roxanne countered. "But it was definitely sex." If anyone had been looking at the rest of their trip together, they might have thought "romantic get-away," but neither one of them had been gentle with each other between the sheets. They'd gone at it like a couple of dogs in heat. Like they couldn't help themselves and couldn't stop until some primal urge was satisfied. "How do I know it wasn't just about being sexually frustrated?"

Gayle rolled her eyes to shoot down that theory. "You know you don't really believe that," she said. "Remember the drought and the pestilence?"

Roxanne couldn't hold back a smile. That's the expression she used to utter during those long, dry spells when she couldn't find a man. At least not a decent one.

"Didn't you used to say that you had to hoard sex the way a camel hoarded water?" Gayle teased her. "Something about savoring it while you could and holding on to the memories because who knows when you might be getting some again?"

This time Roxanne laughed. If she'd been having this conversation with Cynthia, it would have made sense, felt familiar. But sweet, shy Gayle? Being married and having a baby had changed her—for the better in Roxanne's opinion.

Gayle pointed a finger at her. "See. Even you have to laugh at the idea that you're such a sex fiend that you pounced on Linc because you couldn't control yourself." She sobered then. "We both know that's a lie, now, don't we?" It was a question that needed no answer.

"OK, so I admit it . . . Feelings were involved. But I haven't had time to figure them out."

"Because of that no good Honey Brown," Gayle said hotly. She deeply resented that woman's greed, and how it had intruded on her friend's budding happiness. "And it was all so unnecessary." Her expression softened when her eyes rested on her sleeping son.

"I can't imagine putting my child through something like that. And for what? Nothing."

Roxanne couldn't have agreed more. So the secret was out. And thankfully there was no "love child" to add insult to injury. So why didn't she feel finished? She didn't feel ready to let go of this thing yet. And until she did that, she couldn't think about Hope Springs, Linc, or anything else. She still had some questions. None that Linc could answer.

Though she had denied it, her anger at Jamal was mixed up with her disappointment in Linc. She needed to understand what had happened between her husband and Honey Brown. She wanted to know what this woman had meant to Jamal—if only for one night.

And the only living person who could tell her that was Honey.

She stood up and eased MJ in his mother's arms. He didn't stir. Why should he? He was home. At peace. Her smile was both grateful and apologetic as she announced, "Gayle, I'm sorry, but I won't be staying. I need to go to Denver."

From her seated position, Gayle held out for her free arm. When Roxanne leaned in for a hug, her friend whispered. "It's OK. I understand."

And Roxanne wondered why she'd ever doubted that Gayle would.

Chapter

28

The sign at the entrance of Honey's sprawling complex had bragged "luxury apartments." There was nothing luxurious about the place, but it wasn't a dump, either. Nicer than Roxanne had expected. The three-story buildings looked in a good shape, and the grounds were well maintained. Not a lot people were around. She spotted a group of kids playing on a swing set nearby. There was some kind of bike or walking path circling the property. Roxanne wondered if Honey ever took her little boy out for a walk over there. Then wondered why she even cared? The baby, thankfully, was no longer her concern. But his mother was another matter . . .

Roxanne knocked on Honey Brown's door. It was noon sharp. A giggle that was inconsistent with the seriousness of the situation bubbled up inside of her. High noon in the Old West. Somehow the timing was fitting. Roxanne was surprisingly calm considering that somewhere in the back of her mind, she had imagined this conversation ever since the news of the baby broke. When she'd gotten to Denver late last night, she'd thought about hunting Honey down at the strip club, then thought better of that idea. What kind of civil conversation could they have in a place like that? It was also the place where her husband had first laid eyes on Honey, and Roxanne didn't want to see it. She'd spent enough time picturing him there as it was.

She heard someone moving about in the second-floor apartment, and then moments later the door opened.

The first thing that caught her eye was the ocean of supple skin visible underneath the see-through material of the red teddy that Honey was wearing. She wasn't that tall but had legs for days. And curves. Roxanne's gaze finally met that of the woman who had changed her life. Honey looked a lot younger in person. Maybe because she'd just woken up and didn't have on a ton of makeup. Her hair was sleep-tousled. Shock and recognition registered in almond-shaped eyes. Though it wasn't supposed to be a competition, Roxanne couldn't help but compare. Some men might find *her* attractive—but she was pretty sure that had more to do with her personality than her looks. She looked OK, but Honey was flat-out sexy. And knew it. Only a sexually confident woman would open her door despite being practically naked.

Honey recovered first. "My, my, my, if it isn't the grieving widow herself," she said, with a mocking smile. "I've been dying to met you, Roxy—"

"Roxanne," she corrected. Only a few people got to call her Roxy, and Honey definitely wasn't one of them.

Honey flung the door open wider. "Well, come on in, *Roxanne. Mi casa es su casa.*"

"Thanks," Roxanne murmured as she crossed the threshold. Honey could say what she wanted, but she doubted she'd be here long enough to feel at home.

They were in the living room. The place was a mess. There were toys and boxes all over the place. Roxanne had to watch where she was walking to avoid knocking into or stepping on something. There was no sign of the baby. Jamal. Maybe he was still sleeping.

Honey noticed her checking out the place. Her eyes lingering on the toys. "Jamal is at the baby-sitter's. Sorry about the mess," Honey said without embarrassment. "But I'm in the process of moving." She may not have gotten the big payoff she'd been hoping for from Jamal, but the tabloids had paid her a pretty penny for her story. So she was outta here. She'd bought a condo across town. She only wished she could quit her job. But the money was too good to pass up. Right now, she was the hottest attraction in town. Honey scooped up an armful of clothes and dumped them in a nearby box. "Have a seat."

Roxanne shook her head. "I won't be here long. I just want to ask you a few questions."

Honey shrugged then sat on the couch in the space she had cleared. "Suit yourself," she said before reaching for a cigarette. "So shoot! Whatcha wanna ask me?" *This should be interesting. From the way Jamal and Linc had been shielding her, she never imagined little Roxanne would have the guts to show up at her place.*

"What happened between you and my husband?"

"Girl, you didn't have to come all the way to Denver to find that out," Honey said with a scratchy smoker's laugh. "Ain't you been reading the papers? Don't you watch the news?"

"Of course, I do," Roxanne said defensively. She really didn't appreciate being laughed at. "I just want to hear it from you . . . straight from the horse's mouth, so to speak."

"Watch it, *Roxy*, you're getting dangerously close to hurting my feelings," Honey warned. "I think you just called me a horse . . . a nag."

She's lucky I don't call her everything but a child of God! How can she sit there smiling, like this is all a big joke? Not when she's turned my life upside down. "Listen, I don't mean to insult you, but do you think you can help me understand how my husband wound up in bed with you? 'Cause I don't get it. Jamal would never cheat on me."

"*Never?* Girl, please! He was a man, wasn't he?" She didn't wait for answer. "All men are capable of cheating. All women, too." She quirked an eyebrow. "Are you telling me, you've never done something that was totally out of character? Something that you didn't plan to do, but it happened anyhow."

Linc. He was the first and only thing that came to mind.

Honey must have seen something in her eyes. "Uh-huh. Face it, sweetie. Shit happens. Even to your precious Jamal. By the way, I was really sorry to hear about his death. He was a good guy."

Something snapped inside her. "How the hell would you know?" Roxanne shouted. "You met my husband one time. One. So don't tell me what he's like. OK?" Her chest was heaving at the end of the outburst.

"Why don't you calm the hell down? I was just trying to offer condolences," Honey said from behind a cloud of smoke. "I'm being sincere when I say he was nice. He was. That's why I noticed him out of all the other guys in the club that night."

"Did you notice he was wearing a wedding band, too?" Roxanne asked.

"So were a lot of other people," Honey replied. "That didn't stop them from being there. Hootin' and hollerin' and generally acting like fools. Like they hadn't ever seen titties or snatch in their lives."

Roxanne closed her eyes at the image. When she opened them again, she asked, "Is that how Jamal was acting?"

"What do you think, since you know him so well?"

Roxanne couldn't think. She was too frustrated. She stared at Honey in all her undressed glory. How many men could resist a package like that? Like she said, Jamal was only a man. Right? She sighed.

Honey put out her cigarette then asked, "What do you want from me? Junior— I guess I should stop calling him that since Jamal ain't the daddy. Listen, I'm not a problem for you anymore. Jamal has no claim to your husband's fortune. If you hadn't come here today, you never would have heard from me again. So what is the problem?"

"The problem is that my husband promised to love and honor me until"—she paused, choking up—"until the day he died." Roxanne hated feeling the tears well in her eyes. She hated showing weakness in front of this woman who clearly wasn't the least bit sorry for all the havoc she had wreaked. "I believed him. I believed Jamal when he said those words, more than I've believed anything in life. I need to know if I was wrong to trust anybody that much."

Honey shook her head. Her expression pitying. "Now I see why Jamal couldn't bring himself to tell you anything. I feel sorry . . . *for him.* Who could live up to that kind of perfection day in and day out? You had him on a pedestal, and he had you on one. Baby, that's not love. That's a fairy tale."

Roxanne blinked and a tear escaped. Had she heard Honey right? She felt sorry for Jamal? "What are you talking about? I saw Jamal's flaws and Lord knows, I've got plenty myself. Don't try to twist everything. Cheating has no place in a marriage. Period. How is expecting my husband to be faithful the same as putting him on a pedestal?"

Honey laced her fingers and rested them under her chin. Roxanne felt like she was a specimen under a microscope. She suddenly felt open and vulnerable, under the unflinching scrutiny of this unapologetic, arrogant woman. Wasn't the shoe supposed to be on the other foot? Honey was the home wrecker, so why was she insinuating that it was her fault?

"I wonder what you see when you look at me," Honey said. "Scum? An unwelcome reminder of your perfect husband's lapse in judgment? The needle that burst the little bubble of happiness you'd been living in? I could pretend to care, but I really don't. We all got our rules that we live by. You got yours, I got mine. You think cheating is wrong. Fine. That's you. Yes, I threw myself at Jamal. I knew he was out of it. I knew he had a wife. But if he took me up on my offer, whose fault is that? If he was too afraid of disappointing his precious little wifey? If he was too scared that his marriage wasn't strong enough to get through this because his wife couldn't handle the truth? How is that my fault?"

The truth of what she had said rattled Roxanne to the core. She walked over to a wooden chair that was out of place in the living room. There was a box of dishes sitting on it, she dimly noted. Roxanne was glad it was there. It gave her something to hold on to. She needed some support while she mulled over the knowledge Honey had dropped on her. Jamal both loved and feared her. *And his fear was stronger?* She didn't want to believe it, but everything he'd done from the moment he'd awakened to find Honey in his bed pointed to that fact. She hadn't made any secret of her feelings about cheating. She would go to her grave believing that she had the right to expect that. But was it right to paint her husband as so perfect, so ideal that there was no room to own up to a mistake? Jamal wasn't even sure he'd done anything wrong, but he couldn't risk even sharing that with her because he was so certain that either the marriage would be over or she would be shattered.

"Roxanne, is this really coming as a surprise to you?" Honey asked, pulling her away from her troubling thoughts. "I mean, any man who gets caught doesn't want to fess up to it. That's human nature. I've known plenty of cheaters in my day. So trust me on this. Jamal was less concerned with covering his ass and more concerned with protecting you," Honey told her. "And Linc, believe it or not, was worse. I got the feeling that Jamal was worried about saying something that might set me off. But Linc? Linc had *me* worried about not pissing *him* off, and the sure way to do that was to hurt you. Either one of them would have done *anything* to protect you, even if it meant lying. So I didn't set this up, sweetie. You did. Your high expectations and easily wounded nature made it easy for someone like me to take advantage."

Roxanne opened her mouth. She wanted to deny it but couldn't. The circumstances were partially to blame. Not being able to get pregnant. Her budding depression about that. But mostly her idealistic image of Jamal as someone who could do no wrong had been at the root of his deception. He didn't think he could be imperfect and still have her love him. And he may have been right.

Back then.

Roxanne let go of the chair and used a finger to push the strap of her purse back onto her shoulder. "Honey, thanks for talking to me," Roxanne said. "It's been . . ." she faltered, looking for the right words. Sobering. Painful. ". . . illuminating. Don't get up. I can see myself out."

"Wait!" Honey called out. "Don't you want to know what happened that night?"

Roxanne turned around to face her. She felt depleted, but finally at peace. Honey had taken her to school. And she'd learned a lot. She was leaving a smarter woman than she had been when she had walked through the door fifteen minutes earlier. "No, I know all that I need to," she replied earnestly. "Thanks."

Honey stared after her in amazement as Roxanne, with head held high, walked over to and out the door. *The woman had come all this way and left without finding out that her husband hadn't laid a finger on me?* Not that Honey hadn't tried. After she arrived uninvited at Jamal's room, she had thrown her best game at him. Jamal had mumbled something about missing his anniversary, pushed her away, and passed out. He hadn't come to until the next morning.

"How many times do I have to tell you? Roxy is not here," Denise said, looking as aggravated as hell. In the five minutes he'd been here she alternated between putting her hands on her hips and folding them across her chest. Neither one was the friendliest of stances. Actually, when she saw him standing on her doorstep, Linc hadn't been sure she would even let him in. Roxanne's sister might look halfway decent if she didn't have such a surly attitude and put a smile on her face every once in a while. He didn't know what her deal was. Denise was angry every time he saw her.

Not that Linc was letting that faze him. He was worried sick about Roxy. She'd barely glanced his way when Cynthia, his much preferred replacement, had shown up. He'd kept away as long as he could. At first to give her time to cool down and then because he didn't want to draw even more media attention by being at her house twenty-four-seven. Which is exactly what he would have done—if she'd let him. On so many levels and for so many reasons, he'd been holding his breath for a week. He'd been scared that the press would somehow get wind of their trip to Northwoods. They would have had a field day with that info. "WIDOW FINDS COMFORT IN THE ARMS OF HUSBAND'S BEST FRIEND." And could either of them have denied it? He just hoped it was more than that. More than Roxanne needing comfort and any old arms would do. It had to be more than that.

Now he'd lost track of her. Her answering machine was so full, it wasn't accepting any new messages. No one had seen her at Hope Springs. Nor had they heard from her in several days. She loved that place, so Linc couldn't help but stress when he heard that. He finally stopped by the house. Now that Honey's paternity claims had been dismissed, the press had found someone else to harass. When Roxanne didn't answer the door, he let himself in. Linc figured she couldn't be any more pissed at him then she already was, so he was willing to take the risk. For all he knew, she might be sick or something. But she was nowhere to be found. He'd called Dot, who was still in St. Louis. She had decided to pay the rest of her family a long overdue visit now that she was no longer hiding from the husband that never was. Dot had sworn up and down that Roxanne wasn't there. But Linc hadn't believed her. It was not like Dot was a stranger to lying. She had already proven that. *So have you, buddy!* Linc had thought she might find it harder to do when he was asking her eyeball-to-eyeball. Even if Roxy wasn't there like Dot had said, it shouldn't be too difficult to pry her whereabouts out of Dot.

So he'd flown to St. Louis as soon as he could get a flight out. He'd rented a car and driven straight over to her family's house. He should have known that Denise would be the only person in the family not at church. She probably hadn't dragged in from club-hopping the night before until the early morning hours, which might partially explain her bleary-eyed hostility.

"So you're telling me, you have no idea where she is?" Linc repeated.

"Do you have a hearing problem?" Denise said as she reached up to retie the bandanna that was slipping from her head. "I said, I ain't seen her."

Though she was dressed in a long T-shirt and shorts, Linc suspected this was her sleeping outfit. He'd probably woken her up. Too bad.

"Look at you," she said. "Looking all frantic and distraught. You been sniffing around Roxy since you were kids." She gave him a considering look. "But I haven't ever seen you looking this desperate. What's the matter? Y'all have a lover's quarrel?"

"Wh . . . what?" Linc sputtered.

"Oh, don't be looking all surprised. You might have hid it from Roxy and Jamal. But I knew. I've known since junior prom," she crowed. "Roxy's date was Mr. Octopus. His hands were all over her, and you were drilling holes in him. If looks could kill, homeboy would have dropped on the spot. I felt sorry for your poor date. You weren't giving her the time of day. And then she had to put up with you dropping her off first *and then* bringing Roxy home because she didn't know her date had been spiking her punch all night long. Never mind that I was there with my date. You could have told us to bring her home. But did you?" she scoffed. "Of course not, it was Linc to the rescue. Lucky, lucky, Roxanne. She's had not one but two heroes in her life. Then again, if you can believe what you read in the papers, Jamal might not have been such a prize after all. You must have thought you'd won the lottery when you realized you wouldn't have to compete with Jamal for her attention anymore . . . or . . ."—she drawled and raised an eyebrow.—". . . maybe it hasn't made any difference. Roxanne has never been interested in you in that way. Never has been. Never will be."

A nerve jumped in Linc's jaw. She was deliberately provoking him. And it was working. The second he realized he'd balled his fist, he knew it was time to leave. He spun around without a word. If she'd been a man—or maybe even a woman who was not related to Roxy—he would have decked her where she stood and watched with satisfaction as she crumpled to the floor.

He leaned against the hood of the rented car and took in big gulps of air. He was so angry and frustrated, he couldn't see straight. Denise was the most jealous . . . petty . . . ungrateful person—if you could call her a person—that he'd ever met. She hadn't seemed the least concerned that her sister—the one who put a roof over her head and made her life easier—was missing. *Or maybe you're just angry because there was a kernel of truth in what she said. Maybe Roxanne will never have the kind of feelings for you that you want her to.*

He didn't want to think that. Either way, even as a friend, he wouldn't be able to rest until he knew that she was OK. Linc took a few more breaths and began to massage the knot that had developed between his neck and left shoulder blade. He tried to put Denise out of his mind. He would come back after church was over and talk to either Dot or LaToya. Or maybe he should join them at church and say a prayer or two himself.

His cell phone rang. Linc fumbled in his pocket for it. He caught it before voice mail kicked in. "Linc here."

"It's me."

A wave of relief washed over him. Thank God. "Rox, are you OK? I've been trying to reach you for days. No one knew where you were."

"I went away for a few days. I'm sorry if I worried you," she said in a voice that felt subdued to his ears. Quiet and more hesitant than was normal for her. Apparently, Dot hadn't been lying. She wasn't with family. Maybe she'd been with friends.

"I am glad you're safe. I'm actually in St. Louis right now. I was looking for you."

"I went to visit Gayle. I hadn't seen the baby yet," she paused. "Then I went to Denver."

The dismayed groan was out before he could swallow it down. "Roxy. Why did you do that? Please don't tell me you had a run-in with Honey Brown."

"Don't worry," she attempted to joke. "No punches were thrown. That's not my style. Plus, she probably would have kicked my ass."

He didn't know about that. Roxy wasn't one to start a fight, but he'd seen her defend herself on plenty of occasions. She knew the art of war in their neighborhood. Never show fear. Stand up for yourself or be prepared to be picked on and bullied until adulthood. But she seemed OK. She didn't sound too upset by her talk with Honey.

"So how did it go?" he asked.

"Differently from what I had expected," she answered truthfully. "But it was good."

Good? He couldn't imagine how. It had to hurt coming face-to-face with the woman her husband had *allegedly* slept with. He would never believe anything had happened, especially after the paternity test. He only wished Jamal had lived long enough to find out the truth as well. It was a shame that he had died with unnecessary guilt on his conscience.

"Actually, the talk with Honey made me think about a lot of things," she said.

"Such as?" he prompted. Linc was feeling frustrated. Roxy was speaking in such vague general terms. She wasn't telling him anything.

"It made me think about my expectations and my high standards."

"What would Honey Brown know about high standards? I hope you didn't put too much stock in anything she had to say."

"Oh, but I did," Roxanne said. "And it was good. It made me realize that I'd been expecting too much of Jamal, you, even myself."

"Roxy, no." She was blaming herself. He closed his eyes, oblivious to any curious stares he might be getting from neighbors who had seen him lurking around the car for several minutes now. "We should have told you," he said.

"Maybe so. But now I wonder if I set up conditions that made you feel like you couldn't. I wasn't shy about letting you and Jamal know that I couldn't take *any* stress and strife from men. I might as well have written it across my forehead, blazoned across my chest. I'm the one who said, I can't deal with anything less than perfection. Can I blame you if you took me at my word?"

Linc couldn't believe he was hearing this. He didn't know what to make of it. She was taking partial responsibility but not sounding guilty or down on herself.

"True love has to include forgiveness. It has to acknowledge that people aren't perfect," she said. "Does that mean I would have gotten over Jamal cheating on me? Who knows? But he wouldn't have been held hostage by his fear of destroying me, either. Because you know what? I've realized I'm a lot stronger than I thought I was. And I wish Jamal had been given an opportunity to see that."

Linc didn't know what to say. He'd never heard Roxanne be so . . . grounded. So completely rooted in what is, rather than in what should or could be. Curious, he asked, "What did Honey say to you?"

She sighed softly. "She told me what I needed to hear. The truth. Not about what happened between her and Jamal. But the truth about me. Jamal and me. Me and you."

"Me and you?" he parroted.

"Yes. We've never talked about what happened at Northwoods. Linc, the entire trip was like a dream. And what happened between us that last night, scared, confused, but most of all touched me. To protect myself, I focused on the first two feelings and not the last one. I realize now that things happen for a reason, and I'm ready to explore that reason."

Linc could have cried. In fact, his eyes did mist. He silently apologized for all the times he had teased Jamal about being whipped. Hearing Roxy offer what looked like a chance, an opportunity to see how far their feelings could take them, he didn't feel possessed or controlled by her. Just happy, hopeful, and eager to start the journey. "Roxy, you don't know how I've been praying you'd at least give me . . . us a chance. I'm more than ready," he said. "Are you still in Denver? Maybe we can meet up at Northwoods." They had been happy there. They could recapture some of the magic.

"Linc, Northwoods was beautiful and romantic and all that good stuff, but this time, let's be real. In Baltimore. Let's see what happens when we try this in the real world."

The phone still pressed to his ear and his heart pounding in his chest, Linc got into the car and started it up. Roxanne didn't know it yet, but whenever and wherever they were together, it was real. And he couldn't wait to get back to her so that she could find that out for herself.